## PRAISE FOR *IS SHE REALLY GOING OUT WITH HIM?*

**One of *The Nerd Daily*'s Most Anticipated Books of 2024**

"Cousens has a well-earned reputation for writing delightful love stories, and this one more than delivers. The enemies-to-lovers chemistry between Anna and Will is both believable and steamy, and Cousens deftly plays with rom-com tropes while crafting a journey of self-discovery in the wake of divorce. A supremely satisfying love story with all the charm readers have come to expect from Cousens."

**—*Kirkus Reviews* (starred review)**

"Original and witty, this novel is a true delight, one that had me reading nonstop to find out what happened and making me miss the characters once it ended. Who says parents can't have fun?!"

**—Zibby Owens, bestselling author of *Blank* and host of *Moms Don't Have Time to Read Books***

"Cousens is a master at writing enchanting, laugh-out-loud stories that tug at your heartstrings. You will be charmed!"

**—Mia Sosa, *USA Today* bestselling author of *The Worst Best Man***

"Zippy dialogue, a great cast, and a delicious enemies-to-lovers plot made me want to turn my phone off and read it in one sitting. . . . Charming, with so much heart and Cousens's trademark wit—a fab read."

**—Cesca Major, author of *Maybe Next Time***

"Sophie Cousens has been one of my favorite writers for years now, and *Is She Really Going Out with Him?* proves that she is only getting better and better with each book. This book has it all: heart, humor, and buckets of charm. Cousens has done it again!"

**—Falon Ballard, author of *Right on Cue***

"Brimming with Cousens's trademark wit, charm, and richly drawn characters, *Is She Really Going Out with Him?* is a page-turning romance that spotlights parenthood, community, and knowing your worth."

**—Ellie Palmer, author of *Four Weekends and a Funeral***

"Sophie Cousens masterfully slips another gorgeous life lesson between page after page of pitch-perfect jokes and a romance that builds just right. This one might be her most touching yet—that the path back to ourselves is always through the eyes of the people that love us most."

**—Jessie Rosen, author of *The Heirloom***

## PRAISE FOR *THE GOOD PART*

"Bestselling Cousens . . . knocks it out of the park with this whimsical story that is reminiscent of the movie *13 Going on 30*. . . . This heartfelt and unique rom-com will have readers on the edges of their seats up to the emotional conclusion." **—*Booklist* (starred review)**

"A moving and funny reminder that life is meant to be lived one day at a time." **—*Kirkus Reviews* (starred review)**

"*The Good Part* left me buried under an avalanche of emotions and with a new appreciation for life's small, beautiful moments. This is a book to read twice—once to feverishly tear through the pages and a second time to savor." **—Annabel Monaghan, author of *Nora Goes Off Script* and *Same Time Next Summer***

"Warm, funny, joyful, and wise . . . If you want to giggle and feel *all* the swoony feels do pick up a copy of Cousens's latest." **—Cesca Major, author of *Maybe Next Time***

"A tender and delightful exploration of that age-old question: *What if?*" **—Allison Winn Scotch, bestselling author of *The Rewind***

"Delightfully zany and full of heart, the perfect read for anyone who has ever felt a little lost in their own life (and who among us hasn't?) . . . New favorite Sophie Cousens book." **—Becca Freeman, author of *The Christmas Orphans Club***

"Sophie Cousens is one of a select few authors I will happily allow to break my heart again and again, because it's just such a pleasure to find out how she'll mend it." **—Sarah Adler, author of *Mrs. Nash's Ashes***

"A delightful and thought-provoking new novel . . . [Cousens] sprinkles some magic throughout the pages." **—*Country Living***

"Funny and heartfelt . . . Perfect for fans of romantic comedies with a touch of whimsy, like *13 Going on 30* and *Freaky Friday*, and authors like Josie Silver and Rebecca Serle." **—*The Nerd Daily***

"Relatable . . . [and] also a good reminder to be present and appreciate life as it is in the moment." **—*The Michigan Daily***

"Sophie Cousens's most hilarious, entertaining, and heartwarming work yet. It will remind you of Sophie Kinsella's *Remember Me?*"

**—*Woman's World***

"Cousens is a master at building emotional impact without becoming maudlin or sentimental. . . . Fresh and relevant." **—Bookreporter.com**

"A modern day *13 Going on 30,* Sophie Cousens's latest will make you laugh, it will make you cry, and most of all, it will make you want to live."

**—The Everygirl**

## PRAISE FOR *BEFORE I DO*

"A thoughtful and romantic story about the moments and choices that change our lives in unexpected ways . . . Cousens has created something special with this lovely tale." **—Washington Independent Review of Books**

"Witty and heartfelt, *Before I Do* takes a familiar trope and turns it on its head, and readers will find themselves tearing through this book to find out how it ends." **—*Booklist***

"A charming and surprising take on a classic love-triangle formula."

**—*Kirkus Reviews***

"Witty and emotionally rich . . . Readers will be especially drawn to Audrey, a woman unafraid to chase her own happiness and face challenges head-on. This is sure to charm." **—*Publishers Weekly***

"The perfect feel-good book." **—*Reader's Digest***

"I am the biggest fan of Sophie Cousens! She always delivers a true, laugh-out-loud rom-com with a ton of depth."

**—Lizzy Dent, author of *The Setup***

"I adored this novel! Funny, clever, poignant, with characters that just leap off the page . . . Thoroughly recommend!" **—Emily Stone, author of *Always, in December***

## PRAISE FOR *JUST HAVEN'T MET YOU YET*

"A perfectly charming escape. I laughed, I teared up, and I smiled my way through."
—**Helen Hoang, author of *The Kiss Quotient***

"A delightfully romantic tale of one woman's search for her happily ever after in the form of the owner of a swapped suitcase."
—**PopSugar**

"Fiction slowly becomes truth in this highly enjoyable, delectable tale."
—**GoodMorningAmerica.com**

"Sweet [and] funny . . . It's just the story to offer a little romantic escapism during the holiday season."
—**CNN**

"Cousens imbues the entire story with an uplifting sense of hope. . . . The Jersey setting creates a cozy, windswept background to the deliciously slow-burn romance. A warm, witty, and absolutely charming seaside holiday that's perfect for fans of Sophie Kinsella."
—***Kirkus Reviews* (starred review)**

"Humor and poignancy keep the pages turning. Fans of Sophie Kinsella and Josie Silver will find plenty to enjoy."
—***Publishers Weekly***

"At times heartbreaking and incredibly hopeful . . . Readers of Jill Mansell or Mhairi McFarlane will definitely enjoy."
—***Library Journal***

"For the friend who loves curling up at home, pick up *Just Haven't Met You Yet,* a fun meld of drama and romance."
—***Parents***

"Reading Sophie Cousens is like meeting a new best friend. She makes you laugh, she makes you cry, you feel like you've loved her forever, and you don't want to let her go."
—**Clare Pooley, author of *The Authenticity Project***

"This book is pure, unbridled joy."
—**Rachel Lynn Solomon, author of *The Ex Talk***

## PRAISE FOR *THIS TIME NEXT YEAR*

"A funny, pull-at-your-heartstrings read . . . it's a hug in book form."
—**Josie Silver, author of *One Day in December***

"[A] second-chance romance that makes you feel unabashedly hopeful."
—**Refinery29**

"The characters in this page-turning novel are richly drawn and transform substantially, especially Minnie, and all suggest that maybe happy ever after is up to us."
—**NPR Books**

"If you make time for just one holiday read this year, make it Sophie Cousens's *This Time Next Year.*"
—**PopSugar**

"With its distinctive British charm and New Year's Eve midnight magic, this swoony debut holiday love story is about two people whose paths have crossed numerous times."
—***Parade***

"Cousens's debut is ripe with both emotional vulnerability and zaniness."
—***Publishers Weekly***

"A brilliantly written story about love, redemption, friendship, and self-empowerment . . . This book is an absolute delight. . . . A feel-good tale to cozy up with."
—***San Francisco Book Review***

"Rom-com readers will revel in Cousens's wry, lively story, which probes themes of self-discovery, acceptance, and forgiveness, and the abiding nature of friendship."
—**Shelf Awareness**

"Sparkling and uplifting."
—**Mhairi McFarlane, author of *If I Never Met You***

ALSO BY SOPHIE COUSENS

*The Good Part*

*Before I Do*

*Just Haven't Met You Yet*

*This Time Next Year*

# IS SHE *Really* GOING OUT WITH *Him?*

A NOVEL

SOPHIE COUSENS

G. P. PUTNAM'S SONS
NEW YORK

PUTNAM
—EST. 1838—

G. P. PUTNAM'S SONS
*Publishers Since 1838*
An imprint of Penguin Random House LLC
penguinrandomhouse.com

Library of Congress Cataloging-in-Publication Data has been applied for.

Trade paperback ISBN: 9780593718902
Ebook ISBN: 9780593718919

Printed in the United States of America
2nd Printing

*Book design by Angie Boutin*

*For Ridhima. There aren't many greater joys than a long lunch with you. One day I will write sci-fi for you.*

---

*"The more I know of the world, the more I am convinced that I shall never see a man whom I can really love. I require so much!"*

**—Marianne Dashwood, in Jane Austen, *Sense and Sensibility***

*"Above all, be the heroine of your life, not the victim."*

**—Nora Ephron**

IS SHE
*Really*
GOING
OUT WITH
*Him?*

# PROLOGUE

"'ONCE UPON A TIME THERE WAS A BEAUTIFUL MAIDEN WHO WAS trapped in an enchanted castle. The castle was surrounded by a forest of thorns and guarded by a fearsome dragon—'"

A girl with long brown pigtails starts frantically waving both arms in the air, so I pause from my reading.

"Yes, Isla? Do you need the toilet?" the teacher, Mrs. Hollybush, asks the girl.

"What's the dragon's name?" Isla asks. More small hands shoot up.

"Are dragons nocturnal?" asks a boy wearing purple glasses.

"Is it home time?" comes the muffled cry of a girl who's pulled her school jumper up over her face.

Mrs. Hollybush sighs. "We've talked about this, 1H, please just let Ethan's mummy read the story. There'll be time for questions at the end, okay?" She gives me an encouraging smile, then nods for me to continue.

Every Friday afternoon my son Ethan's primary school invites a parent to come and read a book to their child's class. Ethan has been asking me to sign up for months. It's been a disruptive year, with Dan and I separating, so I've been trying to assuage my mum guilt in other small ways: pretending I enjoy board games, cooking waffles at weekends, and now ducking out of work early to read a fairy tale to thirty noisy six-year-olds. As I sit perched on a tiny chair, looking out at the children sitting cross-legged on the carpet in front of me, my gaze falls on Ethan. He beams, thrilled to have me here. I return his smile, then turn back to the book.

"'The dragon scared everyone away, but a few brave princes tried to rescue the fair maiden. They would need to fight their way through the thorns and defeat the beast to win her hand in marriage.'"

"Does she have Lego?" shouts out a little boy with wild blond curls.

"No, Kenny, she doesn't have Lego. That's not part of the story," Mrs. Hollybush interjects with a tight smile. I notice she has a slight eye twitch.

"What does she play with?" Kenny asks. "Does she have a brother?"

"Does she have Pokémon cards?" asks a girl with a distractingly runny nose.

"Does she have *really* long hair?" asks a boy lying on the floor with his eyes closed.

Mrs. Hollybush claps her hands three times, which prompts the children to sit up straight, then zip their mouths closed. I pause for a moment, but they are quiet, so I continue.

"'One day a handsome prince was riding by. He spied the fair maiden at the window of the tallest turret and immediately fell in love with her.'" I clear my throat. I did not choose this book, and I'm not sure I approve of the messaging. How could the prince possibly fall in love with her from that far away? Even if you believe in love at first sight, which I don't, from the ground, with a giant, fire-breathing dragon in the way, how much of this maiden could this man possibly see? "'The prince managed to fight his way through the thorns, reach the castle gates, defeat the dragon, leap the drawbridge, and—'"

"Did the dragon die?" cries a little girl with red felt-tip pen around her mouth, her eyes wide with concern.

"I don't think so. It probably just got tired and ran out of fire," I say, hiding the graphic illustration of the prince stabbing the dragon in the heart.

"Dragons don't run out of fire," Kenny scoffs. Then there's a hurling sound as a child sitting right by my feet throws up all over the carpet, spattering my black suede boots.

"Oh, Jason, oh no, not again," Mrs. Hollybush says with a groan. She jumps up to deal with the situation, grabbing a pale Jason by the elbow, then pointing me in the direction of the hallway. "I'm so sorry, Mrs. Humphries, the guest toilet is along the corridor."

In the bathroom, I use a green paper towel to wipe off my shoes, feeling grateful that I chose a career in journalism rather than teaching. After washing my hands, I pull out my phone and take a moment to check my e-mail. At the top of my inbox, there is something from the government. Why is the government e-mailing me?

From: HMCTS Divorce Services
Subject: Your divorce is now complete

Dear Ms. Anna Humphries,

Your decree absolute has been granted and you are now divorced. You can find your certificate of decree absolute attached. This is the final document proving you are now divorced. You will need to show this certificate if you get married again, or should you wish to change your name.

Divorce Services, UK Government

A sudden wave of nausea hits me, and I hold on to the washbasin to steady myself. My legs feel as though they might buckle. Twelve years of marriage dissolved in an e-mail. *An e-mail?* What did I expect, a scroll delivered on horseback, a town crier? A reverse wedding ceremony where we solemnly retract our vows? I know we live in a digital age, but an e-mail just feels so callous, so cold, so . . . so woefully inadequate. Did Dan get this e-mail too? How did he feel when he opened it? Relieved? Upset? A confusing combination of the two?

My chin begins to tremble and my eyes start to water. *Oh no, please, not now.* I've held it together this far, I can't fall apart now, at my son's school. I knew this was coming, of course I did, but I didn't expect it to happen like this. *I'll need to change my name, apply for a new passport, I'll have to tick a different box on forms now . . . No, no, don't let your mind spiral, Anna. Just go back to the classroom, finish reading the stupid book, then you can go home and digest this in private.*

Below the e-mail from the government is a new message from Dan. Maybe he got the same communication and feels strange about it too. Clicking it open, I see it's just one line: Can you show these to the kids so they can see what I'm up to? D. He's currently on holiday in South America, climbing Machu Picchu, the "trip of a lifetime." He's attached photos of himself looking tanned and happy, standing beneath bright blue skies with the Incan citadel in the background. So no, he's not feeling sick about the divorce e-mail, he's having a lovely time enjoying his newfound freedom. *I always wanted to see Machu Picchu. It's number three on my bucket list, it wasn't even in Dan's top ten.*

Looking at the photo of my ex, I am hit with a sudden pang of nostalgia for the Dan I used to know. The Dan I fell in love with at university, who held my hand beneath the table at a pub quiz, who liked me wearing his rugby shirts so they'd smell of me, who first kissed me in the rain outside a lecture theater at nine in the morning, then as I walked away up the steps called after me, "Anna Appleby, I'm going to marry you one day." Pushing my phone to the bottom of my bag, I splash my face with cold water and head back to the clamor of the classroom.

The vomit has been cleaned up, Jason sent to the school nurse, and Mrs. Hollybush is full of apologies. But I can't hear what she's saying, because a ringing has started in my ears. My head is pounding, my skin feels clammy and hot. A child thrusts the storybook back into my hands, the teacher claps the children into zipped-up silence, I let out a long, slow exhale through pursed lips. But as I look down, the words swim in front of my eyes. "'The prince carried the fair maiden out of the enchanted castle, and they rode off into the sunset. They were married in a beautiful wedding and lived happily' . . . happily . . ." I pause; my throat feels parched. I can't finish the sentence.

"Happily ever after?" little Isla suggests as the room begins to sway.

"Maybe," I mutter beneath my breath. Looking down at the illustration of the fairy-tale wedding, a mental corset pings open. "Or maybe there's no such thing as happily ever after. Maybe they had a good few years of being happy, then they slowly drifted apart, argued about who left crisp packets in the carriage and dirty washing all over the turret floor. Maybe the prince got really into triathlon training and left the princess at home with the kids every weekend. Then one day they realized they were lonely in each other's company and that they didn't love each other anymore." The children look up at me in confusion, and Mrs. Hollybush—eye twitching faster—lets out a burst of nervous laughter. I stand up from my tiny chair and hold the book aloft. "Maybe these kinds of stories are perpetuating a damaging narrative of a woman needing to be rescued by a man, telling little girls that getting married is the goal, that life will make sense once they're in love. But it's a lie, because everything ends, even the greatest love stories." Then I start ripping the pages out of the book, throwing them like confetti around the classroom. "Maybe the maiden was happy with her dragon, maybe she didn't want to leave her nice, safe turret. Maybe the prince was a jerk!" The children squeal with delight and shock, and Mrs. Hollybush claps her hands, attempting to restore order, but this time it doesn't work. They leap around the room trying to catch the torn pages.

"Smash the patriarchy!" I cry.

"Smash the patriarchy!" the children repeat, wild with glee.

MY SISTER, LOTTIE, picks me up from the headmaster's office. The school was understanding when I feigned not feeling well. Mrs. Hollybush kindly suggested that "maybe something is going around," but she also said she would have to remove me from the "reading parents" list, and that I would need to pay for a replacement book.

"What happened?" Lottie asks me as we sit in her car, waiting for Ethan to be let out of school. "The headmaster said you'd had 'an episode'? What kind of episode?"

I silently pass her my phone, with the e-mail open, and watch her as she reads it. To look at us, you wouldn't think Lottie and I were sisters. I have long, dark hair and skin that tans easily, while she is a pale English rose, with blond, wavy hair curling into a halo around her face. If this were a fairy tale, she would be the good witch, and I would be the bad. "I didn't expect to get an e-mail," I tell her. "I don't know what happened. I lost it reading a fairy tale about happily ever afters."

"Oh, Anna," Lottie says, reaching across the car to tuck a strand of hair back behind my ear. The gesture unsettles me. For as long as I can remember, it's my little sister who has been the emotional one. At thirty-three, she's four years younger than me. I've had two decades of her crying to me about boyfriends and breakups, swearing she could never love anyone as much as *insert name here.* I was always the stable, sensible one, ready with a box of tissues and an appropriately uplifting movie. Now she's happily married, and I'm ripping up schoolbooks. She pats my hand, and I close my eyes to try to stop myself from bursting into tears. "I think the problem is, you bottle everything up and then occasionally it all bursts out," Lottie says.

"I don't know why, but seeing it written down, it all seems so final. I feel like such a failure," I tell her, letting my shoulders slump as I hear how pathetic that sounds. "Dan's in South America living his best life, and I'm here, getting divorced in a primary school toilet. The wording of the e-mail too—'if you get married again'—I genuinely can't imagine ever wanting to meet someone else."

"I know it feels awful right now, it's too soon to think about anything like that. But it will get easier, I promise you." Lottie strokes my hair, circling her fingers around my crown just like our mother used to do when we were children.

"I'm thirty-seven and I'm done with love," I tell her.

"No, you're not, but you're still grieving. Trust me, this time next year, or maybe eighteen months from now, everything is going to look so different. You'll have moved on. I know you can't imagine it now, but you'll be dating; you might even have met someone. There is a whole new chapter waiting for you, all you need to do is keep turning the pages."

I give her a grateful smile, but I want to scream that these trite generalizations do not apply to me. My thoughts are interrupted by a clunk as Ethan opens the car door and jumps into the backseat.

"Hi, Aunt Lottie! Did Mum tell you what happened?" he says, bouncing up and down with excitement. "Mum ripped up a schoolbook, then blamed it on Patrick E."

"Who's Patrick E.?" Lottie asks.

Ethan shrugs. "I don't know. Mum wanted to smash him."

"The patriarchy," I explain, covering my face with my hands.

"Oh yes, I know him," Lottie says, biting back a smile, as she thrusts her car into gear. "That guy's got a lot to answer for."

# ONE YEAR LATER

GOOGLE SEARCHES:

*Does face yoga work?*

*Do pain aux raisins count as one of your five a day?*

*Will there ever be a Modern Family reunion?*

# CHAPTER 1

"ONLY ME," LOTTIE CALLS AS SHE BUSTLES THROUGH THE FRONT door, then presents me with an armful of sunflowers.

"Thank you, but you really don't need to keep bringing me flowers," I say, lifting them out of her arms.

"They're only from my garden," she says, waving me away with a hand. "Sunflowers are so cheering, don't you think?"

While I live in a three-bedroom semidetached in the suburbs of Bath, my sister and her husband, Seb, have moved into a country house with sprawling gardens and an apple orchard. Lottie makes her own jam, which she gifts people for Christmas. I'm embarrassed to admit what I gave most people for Christmas last year, but it starts with "Amazon" and ends with "vouchers."

"Are Jess and Ethan still awake?" she asks, following me through to the kitchen.

"In bed, but not asleep. Don't go up there or they'll want to come down and play cards with you."

"So, I met this new client yesterday," she tells me, climbing onto one of the barstools beside the kitchen island. "Fergus. He's South African, owns a pecan farm. Recently divorced." She opens her eyes wide.

"Right," I say, refusing to fall for the bait. Lottie runs her own business designing high-end treehouses, so she's always meeting interesting clients. I wouldn't have believed there was a market for forty-grand treehouses, but apparently, there is.

"I think you should meet him," she says.

"But I don't even like pecans," I say, being purposely obtuse. "If he were a walnut farmer, or even almonds, then maybe, but pecans? Not for me."

"Anna, seriously. You're just his type; I showed him a photo of you, and he wolf whistled."

"Yuck."

"Well, it wasn't a wolf whistle exactly, more of a whistling exhale, like 'Phewough!'"

"You are not selling this guy," I say, laughing now.

"It doesn't need to be a big deal, just a casual drink." She pauses, watching my face. "Any night you want, I will come over and babysit. I'm only twenty minutes away."

As I transfer the sunflowers to a vase, Lottie takes them from me and starts rearranging them herself. Watching her, I can't help smiling.

"I appreciate the thought, Lots, but honestly, I don't want to date. I am very happy on my own."

"You're *very* happy, are you?" Lottie asks, narrowing her eyes at me, then blowing a blond wisp of hair away from her face.

"I am perfectly content. Work is going well, the kids need me more than ever. I don't see a hole in my life that needs filling." Lottie raises an eyebrow at me, and I reach across the kitchen island to slap her shoulder. "Filthy woman."

"Even if it's not dating, I think you should get out more, take an art class, join a book club, something just for you. Your life can't be all about work and the children, then sitting on your sofa scrolling Instagram while watching Netflix."

"But there's so much TV I haven't seen yet," I say, pulling a goofy face as I open the fridge and take out a bottle of wine. "And I know no one will believe I've moved on until I'm seeing someone, but that is society's expectation, it has nothing to do with what I need. I am in my hibernation era."

I know there are plenty of women on Instagram who got divorced and took up running or weight lifting or started their own aromatherapy candle business. They look and feel better than ever, phoenixes risen from the ashes, embracing their "new chapter." I am not a phoenix. I am a dazed pigeon, looking for crumbs. But I am fine with that; being a phoenix looks exhausting.

Dan has moved on. Everyone knows Dan has moved on. Bath is a small place, and friends have seen him out on the town with various women. My colleague Kelly swiped past him online two weeks after he moved out, which was awkward. He's now dating some twenty-five-year-old called Sylvie, though I doubt it will last. I imagine he's having too much fun playing the field, after sitting on the bench with me for so long.

"Surely you miss"—Lottie smacks her lips—"you know . . ."

"What, sex?" I ask, pouring us both a glass of white wine, then I remember Lottie isn't drinking because she's four months pregnant, so I tip the contents of her glass into mine and start making her an elderflower spritzer with crushed ice and a wedge of lime, just the way she likes it.

"Yes. You don't need to be looking for a boyfriend or a husband. You could just join the apps, have some fun."

"Having sex with some random man I met on the internet is not my idea of fun," I tell her. "And weirdly, no, I don't miss it as much as you might think."

"My friend Tasha didn't have sex for five years and she got vaginal atrophy. Use it or lose it, sister."

"'Use it or lose it'? Who are you?" I say, laughing at her as we carry our drinks and a bowl of crisps through to the living room.

I take the too-low armchair and offer Lottie the couch.

Looking around the room, I feel a tinge of embarrassment. Lottie is family, she wouldn't judge or care, but she must notice how differently we live these days. It's not that her house is bigger or more expensive than mine (though it is both those things), but Lottie's home feels loved, cared for, full of complementary color schemes, while mine feels a little like my bikini line: neglected.

When Dan left, he took some lamps and two side tables that I haven't replaced. The furniture I do have is inoffensive and neutral, mainly chosen for its durability or price tag rather than any coordinated vision. The bookshelves are overloaded with jigsaws and board games that the children have outgrown, and the foot of this L-shaped room still holds Jess's old play kitchen and a dresser full of long-forgotten toys. Everything is tidy enough, but also cluttered and chaotic.

"Sorry about the mess," I say to Lottie, pushing a box of Lego beneath the sofa with my foot.

"Don't be silly, I love your house, it feels so lived-in," she says, but then, looking around, adds, "Though if you did ever want to redecorate, I could help you do a spring clean. We could make a weekend of it."

"Thanks, but it's not really a priority right now," I say, wondering, somewhat meanly, how long Lottie's beautifully curated aesthetic will last when she has a toddler roaming the house. Lottie only shrugs, undeterred by my rejection of every one of her suggestions.

"This is the client I told you about, Fergus," she says, opening her phone and leaning over to show me a picture of a man with gray hair and designer stubble. "He's fifty-four but looks younger. What do you think?"

"I think he looks fifty-four and like he would tell me a lot of information about pecans," I say as my cat, Katniss, jumps onto my lap and starts purring appreciatively as I stroke her head.

"Fifty-four isn't that old. What's your cutoff?" Lottie asks.

"I don't have a cutoff, because I'm not looking to meet someone. What is it with married people and their assumption that all single people must be just yearning to get back into a coupled state? People are not chopsticks; they do work alone."

"Okay, I know, but humor me. Who else is there? What about your hot neighbor? He's your age, that would be *so* convenient," Lottie says, tucking her legs beneath her like a dainty doll. "I know it's tragic and everything, but there is something so romantic about a young widower."

"Noah? Ha! Noah has the social skills of a spoon."

"Okay, what about at work?" Lottie asks. "Who's that tall, sexy guy with the glasses? The one I met when I took you for lunch that time?"

"Will Havers? Um, no," I say, pulling my lips into a grimace.

"Yes, him! What's wrong with him?"

"Where do I start? He's arrogant and entitled, way too young—"

"What is he? Late twenties? People wouldn't think twice about a thirty-eight-year-old man dating a twenty-eight-year-old woman," Lottie says, sloshing her drink into her lap as she gesticulates.

"I know, but regardless of age, he's not my type."

"You don't have a type, you had a Dan."

She might be right, but my patience with this conversation has expired.

"Will Havers is a serial dater who objectifies women. I know for a fact he only dates girls under thirty-three and over five foot eight. He wears shirts monogrammed with his initials, thinks he's God's gift to journalism, can't pass a mirror without checking himself out, *and* he mansplains in meetings." I finish my rant, exhale loudly, then take a large swig of wine. Lottie grins. "What?"

"For someone you have zero interest in, you seem to know

quite a lot about this man," she says, raising an eyebrow at me. "At least we're narrowing down your age bracket: younger than fifty-four, older than twenty-eight." Lottie taps her nose and gives me a sly grin. "I'm just happy to hear you sound so passionate."

"I am not passionate about Will Havers," I say, throwing a cushion at her. She bites back a smile as she hands me the bowl of crisps. Just as I think the Spanish Inquisition might be over and I might be allowed to enjoy a peaceful evening, we hear the sound of two baby elephants thundering down the stairs.

"Auntie Lottie! I told you I heard her," Ethan yells as he dives onto the sofa beside her. "Can we play poker?" Ethan is only seven, but Lottie has been teaching him all the card games she knows. She is one of those fun aunts who loves board games and knows how to make papier-mâché.

"Not poker. Maybe a quick game of Uno, then straight back to bed. It is a school night," I tell him.

"I'm brilliant at Uno," Ethan tells us.

"Mum always cheats at Uno," says Jess, who, at twelve, has taken up a new hobby—criticizing everything I do.

"I do not," I say, giving up my chair and moving to sit on the floor.

"Uno, Uno, Uno!" Lottie chants, and I see I am outnumbered.

"Ooh, crisps," says Ethan, taking the bowl from my lap.

GOOGLE SEARCHES:

*Health benefits of pecans*

*In Uno can you stack Draw 2 cards on top of one another?*

*What is vaginal atrophy?*

# CHAPTER 2

THE NEXT MORNING, AFTER WALKING ETHAN TO SCHOOL, I GET THE bus into town, then I need to speed-walk up the high street if I'm going to get to my desk by nine o'clock. *Bath Living* has offices in the historic center, on the ground floor of a Georgian town house. I've been at the magazine for five years, and my job has provided much-needed stability while the rest of my life was falling apart. Jonathan, the managing director, is a sweetheart. He lets me work flexible hours, and while I started out as freelance, I'm now a staff writer with my own column. I know lots of people hate their job, so I count myself lucky that I have nothing to complain about on that front.

As I'm hurrying up Monmouth Street toward the office, someone falls into step beside me. "Morning." I turn to see the looming figure of Will Havers smiling down at me. Scrap that, I do have *one* complaint. While I've thrown on whatever clothes I could find in my rush to leave the house, Will is always perfectly styled. Today he is modeling "spring work wear" from his catalog of looks: blue suit trousers, a crisp white shirt, and a perfectly tailored beige trench coat. He's also sporting his trademark dark-rimmed glasses, which I suspect he wears more for fashion than for vision.

"Morning, Will," I reply. It's a five-minute walk to the office. *I can be civil for five minutes.* Though I'm power walking as fast as I can, Will has such long legs, he need only saunter to keep pace with me.

"Good weekend?" he asks.

"Yes. You?"

"Wonderful.

"I saw the layout for your piece on the art exhibition at the Pump Room," he says.

"Right," I say, unable to hide my suspicion. Will has only been at the magazine for six months. He's the same level as I am but acts as though he's more senior and has a habit of giving unsolicited feedback.

"I liked your interview with the graphic artist, it's smart, funny," Will tells me.

"Thank you," I say, turning to look at him. I can't believe he brought it up just to give me a compliment.

"If it were me, I would include a few more photos of guests at the opening," he says, swinging his leather document wallet, which has *WH* embossed in gold on the side. "People like seeing the fashionable faces invited to these events as much as they like seeing the art." *And there it is, the feedback I didn't ask for.*

"It's about the exhibition though, the artist, it's not a who's who," I say tightly, trying to increase my pace.

"Sure," he says, nodding just once. "I don't mean to criticize." *Except he does.* "Jonathan has asked me to look at how we can skew toward a younger demographic. With events like this, the social angle always helps. We need people to tag us on their socials, make the exhibition look like it was the place to be. The art is secondary."

"Secondary?" I say while exhaling a burst of angry air. "This isn't *Hello* magazine. It was a serious piece about a serious artist."

"Which is why it was seriously dull," Will says, and I can

hear him smiling before I stop on the street and turn to glower at him, one hand planted on my hip. "Sorry," he says, with a smile that says he's not sorry at all. "I'm only winding you up, it wasn't dull. I just think you should review the photos before it goes to print, make it look like people were actually there."

"Will, I have been working as a journalist for longer than you've had facial hair, so I don't think I need your input, but thank you," I say through gritted teeth.

"Five typos says otherwise, but sure," Will says under his breath.

"There were not five typos in that article." I feel my rage building now, while Will remains infuriatingly cheerful.

"If we're counting grammatical errors, yes, there were five."

Glaring up at him, I take in the strong jaw, the green brooding eyes, the mouth that looks as though it's permanently trying to conceal some private amusement. He reminds me of a cartoon villain or the man on the cover of a romance novel. His good looks are so boringly predictable, it's all 2D perfection, there's no nuance to his face at all.

"It hasn't been proofread yet. It's allowed to have typos," I explain through clenched teeth. "And I'm thrilled you have time to pore over other people's work looking for their mistakes, but some of us have lives." I pause. "People that do that are not team players, they're pedants."

"People *who* do that are not team players," Will says, biting his lip. We finally reach the office, and Will opens the door for me. "I'm just trying to raise everyone's game, Anna, make the magazine as good as it can be. I would be open to feedback from you."

I claw back the urge to say, "My feedback is to go fuck yourself," and instead opt for, "You're a typo, Will." Which might be the worst comeback I've ever delivered and causes Will to scrunch up his face in confusion.

"Mature," he says, hanging his coat on a peg in the hall, then reaching to take mine, but I snatch it back, childishly. I don't need his help.

Inside, the open-plan office is abuzz with undefinable energy. Colleagues are gathered around each other's desks talking in hushed whispers. No one is doing any work.

"What's happening?" I ask Karl, who sits opposite me. He is vaping furiously, though we're not supposed to vape inside. Karl wears his hair in a man-bun and has veneers so white they sometimes distract me from my work.

"Jonathan's called a company meeting," Karl says. "Val heard from some guy she met at Yogalates, who knows someone who works in accounts, that the magazine's gone bust." Karl makes a show of biting his fingernails. "I can't lose my job. I just bought a Shih Tzu."

A vortex of fear starts swirling in my stomach. I can't lose my job either. There aren't many publications in Bath, and I would struggle to find anything this flexible.

"Oh, and I need a small business owner to give me a quote on rising tourism numbers, any ideas? You always know who will be good," Karl says.

"Sure, I'll send you a list," I say. Then the girls at the sales desk beckon Karl over, and he hurries off to talk to them. The magazine is a social workplace. With twenty-two staff, there are often people going for drinks after work or gossiping in the communal kitchen. I am not part of all that. I'm friendly to everyone, but when I'm here, I need to get my head down and my work done so I can leave on time to pick up Ethan from school. Making small talk with twenty-three-year-olds about their nail extensions or with Karl about his hierarchy of dog breeds is not an efficient use of my time.

"Everyone!" Jonathan calls, sticking his head out of his office. "Living room, five minutes."

Jonathan Courtauld is a gay, graying Don Draper type with extravagant yet impeccable taste. He inherited the magazine from his father, who ran it the way his father had run it in the 1960s. Everything about the place is an anachronism, including the office itself, which feels more like an elegant private home than a workplace. Jonathan's art collection adorns the walls, and bookshelves full of first editions line the halls. All the "necessary but ugly stuff," like photocopiers and printers, is discreetly hidden away behind closed doors.

The living room, which doubles as our meeting room, is decked out with velvet sofas, antique Persian rugs, and a large ottoman stacked with books on art and design. In the corner there's an ornate, old-fashioned drinks trolley for "cocktails at five" on Friday afternoons. I'm told Jonathan makes a mean gin sling, though I wouldn't know.

Jonathan looks pensive as we all file in and search for somewhere to sit. Will takes the armchair next to Jonathan. Casey, Jonathan's twenty-two-year-old assistant, walks across the room and runs a hand along the back of Will's chair, brushing his neck as she goes. Will turns to grab her hand, then smiles at her, and she gives him a lovelorn look. I can't believe how unprofessional they're being, flirting at work. Last week, it was Emily in accounts, permanently hovering by Will's desk. I honestly don't know how the man gets any work done.

Unlike the rest of us, Will doesn't look worried about this unscheduled meeting. In fact, I don't think I've ever seen him look worried. I heard one of the younger girls, Kelly, say that he comes from money. His family owns a house on the Circus, one of the most prestigious addresses in Bath, so maybe this is all just a hobby for him.

"In my father's day, every coffee table in the county would have a copy of our magazine," Jonathan says wistfully. "Vendors wouldn't dream of advertising their property anywhere but in our pages." He starts pouring tea into china teacups, then places each one into a delicate saucer before handing them around. "Unfortunately, my dears, that is no longer the case. While we are still the premiere lifestyle and culture publication in the Southwest, print orders are down and our weekly online edition isn't getting the numbers we need to secure sufficient advertising revenue."

Murmurs circle around the room as people absorb what he's telling us. I feel a surge of panic. My divorce was expensive, I have to cover the mortgage on my own now, and I have hardly any savings left. What will I do if I don't have a job?

"But I have good news," Jonathan continues. "We have found an investor, a company with just the right online expertise. Crispin Hardman from Arch Media is going to bring us into the twenty-first century, ha ha." He laughs nervously as he sets down the teapot. "It won't be plain sailing, we'll all need to adapt. As you know, I'm the biggest luddite of all, but he's seen something special in our little publication. He's confident in our ability to evolve."

Jonathan looks across at Will. "We have Will here to thank." Jonathan reaches out to squeeze Will's shoulder. "I didn't want to alarm anyone until we had a solution, but over the last few months, Will has been helping me put together a pitch for investors. He's gone above and beyond to get it right." *Will knew about this and didn't tell anyone?* "Well done, Will." Jonathan leads a round of applause while Will at least has the grace to look awkward. "Now, I'll be talking to you all individually about what this means," Jonathan says once the clapping has subsided, "but I think we should all see this as a wonderful opportunity."

*A wonderful opportunity?* It sounds like a big change, and one thing my life does not need is more change.

I'm first to be called into Jonathan's office for a one-to-one.

"Exciting news," I say, with false cheer, as Jonathan closes the door behind me.

"I'm afraid I was putting a rather brave face on it out there, Anna. The reality is jobs are going to be on the line."

"Oh." My stomach lurches.

"I didn't think it was good for morale to speak too plainly, but investors like to clear out any perceived dead wood." Jonathan smiles and rolls his eyes as though this is some minor inconvenience. *Am I dead wood?* "And I'm going to be honest with you, Anna. Crispin is not the biggest fan of your column." Jonathan sits back in his chair, then hunches his shoulders around his neck, raising his hands in mock surrender.

"Oh?" I say quietly.

"Afraid not. He thinks According to Anna is—hang on, I'll pull up his e-mail." Jonathan moves a stack of papers from his desk and logs on to his computer. "Here we are: 'the humdrum ramblings of a mundane middle-aged existence.'" Jonathan pulls an apologetic grimace. I feel myself bristle. "Don't shoot the messenger. I just wanted you to know what you're up against."

"But readers love my column. I get e-mails about my column."

"Our current demographic might, yes, but Crispin wants us to appeal to a younger, more 'aspirational' readership. He wants a column about nightlife and dating, full of drama and vulnerability. Someone who people will get invested in personally, who they'll log in week after week to read about."

"I write about dating and nightlife, I write about everything," I say, crossing my arms defensively. Then I notice my smudged, messy manicure, applied by Jess, and fold my hands into fists. When I look up, Jonathan is holding up last month's publication.

"'My Date Night with the Bridgertons,'" he says, looking back at me. Jonathan picks up another issue from his desk. "The month before, you led with 'Why Slipper Socks Are My New Wardrobe Essential.'" Jonathan shoots me another kindly grimace.

"I can be more aspirational if that's the steer. I can go out more," I plead, though even the thought of having to put on real clothes and leave the house after dark makes me feel ill.

"I'm sorry, Anna, but I'm giving the back page to Will. He's pitched me a 'man about town' dating column."

"Will?" I exclaim, rising out of my chair, so I'm now standing in front of Jonathan's desk. "But he already has the food column."

"The way Will pitched it, he takes the whole back page, readers have the chance to really get to know him, build a personal connection." *Will pitched to steal my column? That is a new low, even for him.* Jonathan gives me a sympathetic frown. "This isn't personal, Anna. Arch Media commissioned opinion polls. Will is popular among the elusive eighteen-to-thirty age bracket."

"And what was I?" I ask nervously.

"You get a high approval rating with the over-sixty-fives." Jonathan bites his lip, and I groan in frustration.

"You can't just take my column without giving me a chance," I say, trying to sound stern.

Jonathan sighs. "The new leadership team want a dating column, and you don't date."

"I could date, if dating were required," I offer rashly.

"Really?" Jonathan looks skeptical, then checks his watch. This gives me an uneasy feeling that we're nearing the end of our allotted meeting time. "You're a good journalist, Anna. You have a talent for finding stories no one else sees, your interviews are always well researched, beautifully written"—he pauses—"but writing a column is a more personal undertaking, it's a different kind of journalism. Maybe your time would be better allocated elsewhere."

I shake my head. If I lose my column, I'll be first out the door when they start making redundancies. "Jonathan, please, give me a chance."

Jonathan looks down, and I realize I'm now leaning across

the desk and tugging on his sleeve like a pleading child. As I let go, he closes his eyes, resigned. "One week—write a fresh and original column about dating, or I'm giving it to Will," Jonathan says, rubbing one eye with the heel of his hand. He looks exhausted.

"Yes, I will, I promise. Thank you, thank you!" I turn to go before he can change his mind.

"Anna," Jonathan calls after me, and when I turn back, I see compassion in his eyes. "I know it's tough, getting out there again. But if you can be honest, vulnerable, I think our readers will relate to the challenge of looking for love again after heartbreak, to being on the wrong side of thirty-five and leaping back into the dating pool without the life preservers of youth and optimism."

"'The wrong side of thirty-five'? Who decided there was a right side and a wrong side?" I ask with a frown.

"That's the spirit," he says, clapping his hands. "Write that."

Back at my desk, I pull up the draft layout for my article about the art exhibition. I see immediately that Will is right. The pictures are too static, too empty; I've prioritized the art over the event and the space looks dead. I'm going to have to change it. *Damn.* As I'm clicking through the photos of the event, a subtle blend of sandalwood, pine cones, and freshly ironed linen puts my senses on high alert.

"I'm sorry about the column, Appleby," Will's voice comes from behind me.

"Your sources are inaccurate, Havers," I say without turning around. "Jonathan's excited about the new direction I pitched for my column."

I swivel my chair around now, unable to resist. There it is. So fleeting, anyone else might miss it, but I see the pulsing muscle in his jaw, the fractional slip in that cocksure grin. He's disappointed.

"New direction?" he asks.

"Yup," I say breezily. "I'm going to write a dating column, something fun and aspirational."

Will raises an eyebrow at me, with a hint of a grin. *Why is he grinning?* "You have some real dates lined up to write about? Not Roman Roy from *Succession*? Though I do so enjoy reading about your TV crushes."

Leaning on the edge, Will picks up a pen from my desk and starts clicking and unclicking it. He flashes what I imagine he thinks is a charming smile, but it makes me want to stab him in the hand with that pen. All the younger women in the office may fawn and giggle over Will, but his charms don't work on me.

"Don't you have work to do?" I ask with a sigh. "Menus to peruse, calories to count, cutlery to critique?" I say, flapping a hand at him as though he's a giant fly.

"Just know that if dating's too much pressure for you, I'm more than ready to turn my ten-inch column into twenty," Will says, running a hand through his thick brown hair.

"I don't think anyone needs more inches from you, Havers."

We lock eyes. If I blush now, he'll know that innuendo wasn't intentional. *Do not blush, do not even blink.* In my head, I count slowly to ten, holding his gaze, channeling my inner iceberg. He looks away before I get to five. *Ha. I win.* I know, I know, I am a grown woman behaving like a child, but this is what he reduces me to.

"My approval rating says otherwise," Will says, putting the pen back down.

"I'm sure you were popular when you were writing for *Teen Girl* magazine, but *Bath Living* is for grown-ups. I don't think fifteen-year-old girls are buying it."

His face falls, and I savor the moment. I've been saving that one for just the right opportunity. I did some digging into Will's CV. He claims to have worked at Publishing Global from 2019 to

2021, but a little detective work revealed he was actually employed by a subsidiary magazine, *Teen Girl*. I pulled a few old editions and found an excellent advice page he authored entitled "How to Talk to Boys."

Will clears his throat. *I got to him. I finally got to him.*

"Well, if you're ever stuck for dating venues, I get twenty percent off at the Townhouse. Just mention my name to the maître d'," Will says, standing up and turning to walk back to his desk. *What, no comeback?* I start to doubt myself. *Was that too mean?* But I don't have time to worry about Will's feelings. I need to come up with a real date to write about and I need to do it fast. Taking a deep breath, I open my phone and search "dating apps."

GOOGLE SEARCHES:

*Fresh and original dating ideas*

*Least scary dating apps*

*Is it worth watching the American version of The Office if I've seen the British one?*

# CHAPTER 3

I SOON REALIZE I CAN'T DO THIS ALONE. SOMETHING AS SIMPLE AS filling in an online dating profile is beyond me; I don't know where to start or even which app to choose. With a pang of alarm, I realize I am thirty-eight and have never dated. I had a boyfriend at secondary school, Tim, then there was Andrew in my first year at Bristol uni, then I met Dan. All three were friends first, so I've never been on a date with someone I didn't already know. The idea of trying to "sell myself" in an online profile makes me cringe. Reluctantly, I cross the office to talk to Steph and Kelly, two colleagues in their twenties who work in sales. If anyone knows about dating apps, they will.

"Hi," I say, interrupting their conversation about the TV show *Traitors*.

"Hi," Kelly says, turning to look at me. "Did you want to talk about ad layouts for the gallery piece?"

"Um, no, this isn't about work—well, it is, kind of." I clear my throat, embarrassed to ask. "I need to join a dating app and don't know where to start. If I took you both for a drink after work, could you help me?"

Their eyes light up and they clap their hands. "Oh yes!" cries Steph. "I knew this day would come. My calling!"

"Makeover!" Kelly squeals.

"No, no, I don't need a makeover, just a dating profile. It's for work."

Steph and Kelly are both what I'd call "next-generation beautiful." They're hot, but a lot of work goes into it. *A lot.* There's contouring makeup, eyelash extensions, and fake nails, which must preclude them from doing any washing up. Steph's balayaged hair is neatly pressed into waves, while Kelly has blond extensions down to her waist. I can't imagine anyone with children having this level of commitment to looking good.

"You came to the right place," says Kelly, reaching out to squeeze my arm. "Of course we'll help you."

THEY'RE BOTH FREE after work, and Dan's mum is taking the kids out for her birthday this evening, so I don't need to rush home. Kelly suggests the Botanist, a trendy cocktail bar on Milsom Street.

"Okay, first things first, profile pic," says Steph, scrolling through photos on my phone. "Found one." Steph holds up my screen to show Kelly a picture of me in a bikini.

"That's from my honeymoon! That's not what I look like now."

"Have you got any more bikini shots? You might as well show a full-body shot, you've the figure," Steph says.

Kelly nods. "You need to identify your selling points. You're hot, that's all anyone cares about."

"Thanks, but no, I haven't worn a bikini since I had children, and I don't think I'm comfortable putting a half-naked photo of myself online."

"This one?" Kelly asks, showing me a photo of myself and Dan at a concert. "You look young and up for it here. We could crop him out."

"That's because I *was* young. I was twenty-eight. No, please don't look at any photos more than two years old," I tell her.

"You literally have no recent photos of yourself. Look, your selfies file is all just pictures of your kids," Kelly says, showing me a picture of Ethan grinning with a mouth full of Cheerios.

"I can take one now," Steph offers, tilting her head in sympathy. "The lighting is good in here. Do you have any makeup you could put on?"

"I am wearing makeup," I tell her, and she leans forward to inspect my face, as though she doesn't believe me.

"Where?"

"Let's come back to the photo," Kelly suggests, patting my hand. "We'll do that at the end."

"Fine," says Steph, taking a sip of her white wine spritzer. "Right, so are you looking for love, friends, coffee dates, or hookups?"

"None of the above," I say.

"You have to put something," Steph says. "If it's for a dating column you should say you're looking for love. I don't think the hookup scene here is *Bath Living* material."

"Fine, put that. Though is it disingenuous if that's a lie?"

"Don't worry, everyone lies online," says Kelly. As she scrolls to the next screen, I lean over Steph's shoulder to see what she's doing. "Right, interests. What are you into? Music, nature, gaming, self-care?"

"Are those the only options?" I ask.

"No," Steph says. "It can be anything."

"What am I into? Being a mum, my work. I have a cat, though I wouldn't say I'm a 'cat person.' I don't treat her like a fur baby or have a T-shirt with her face on it or anything." I laugh, then say seriously, "Don't put that."

"Like, do you go to the gym, are you into yoga, macramé?" Kelly asks, her voice rising an octave with every suggestion. I shake my head. "Okay," says Kelly slowly, and I can see it dawning on her, why I need their help with this. She turns to Steph. "She doesn't need to be defined by her interests." They go on to ask me about my star sign; my love language; my position on Covid vaccines; what my sleeping habits are; what I eat, drink, and dream; my Myers-Briggs personality type. Kelly lists a catalog of potential interests: aquariums, jujitsu, road trips, paddleboarding, activism, craft beer, TikTok, gospel singing, Marvel movies. It feels like the most invasive and bizarre job interview I've ever had.

"That is the weirdest list, I'm not interested in any of those things," I say, exasperated. "Okay, just put theater, travel, and 'trying new things.'"

"Travel is good, that's an easy talking point. Have you been anywhere interesting recently?" Kelly asks, looking thrilled to have found something.

"Nowhere recently, but I'd like to travel more in the future." I pause. "If people are going to ask me where I've been, maybe don't put travel." I look at the list again. "Gin and tonic?"

Steph shakes her head. "Might put people off. Take pets off too. Divorced cat lady who likes G&Ts—it's not a winning vibe."

I sigh. "I don't have time for 'hobbies.'" I wave the waiter over to order us a third round of drinks. "Can I put TV? Doing household admin? Being a parent?"

"People really just go on the photo," Kelly says, patting my arm sympathetically, then stopping when she remembers we don't have a photo either.

"You need to give people *something* to go on," says Steph. "I met my boyfriend because on our profiles we both love Roblox and we both want world peace. He DMed me suggesting Roblox might be the answer to world peace." She makes a lovesick grin. "It was *so* funny."

"See, there's someone out there for everyone," says Kelly,

"even Steph. Now, the fun part. What are you looking for in a man?" Kelly asks, swiping to the next screen. "I assume man? You'd widen the net if you put both."

"Just a normal, nonpsycho, ordinary man," I tell her.

"You need to be more specific," says Steph.

"Okay, then I guess someone kind, funny, smart."

Steph pretends to yawn. "Boring. Everyone wants that. I'm thinking height, hair color, age, build. Do you want them to work out? Do you care about their politics or if they eat meat? Do you have a thing for facial hair? Are there any sexual proclivities they need to be on board with?"

I raise my hands in surrender. "Ideally taller than me, average height, I guess over five ten. Around my age, I don't know, older than thirty-five, younger than fifty." Kelly and Steph simultaneously scrunch their noses up at the idea of fifty. "Okay, forty-seven. Forty-five?" They both nod, deeming forty-five to be acceptable for someone my age.

"Kids, no kids? Wants kids? Are you done with kids? Can you even have more kids?" Steph asks, swiping to the next set of questions.

"Those don't feel like first-date questions."

"People want to know these things, but fine, put 'not sure,'" Kelly instructs Steph. Then Steph lifts the phone, cries, "Smile!" and snaps a photo.

"We'll use this one for now. Don't worry, I'll add a subtle filter to even out your skin tone."

"Don't add a filter," I say. "I want to look like me."

"You need a filter. Everyone uses a filter." She hands me back my phone. "One profile, good to go." As she says it, the phone pings with a notification from the app. "Ooh, someone likes you already!" says Steph, clapping her hands in delight.

"Don't look so terrified, I love this for you," says Kelly, putting an arm around me. "Dating is like riding a bike. You just need to get back in the saddle and then the muscle memory kicks in." She winks. It's unnerving.

I thank them both for their help, then settle the bar bill. On the bus home, my phone pings with notifications and I scroll in wonder at this portal to potential dates. Could I fancy Hamish, forty-three, with his bulging biceps and interest in falconry? What about Paul, thirty-eight, who has a photo of himself at the top of a mountain, his arm around some poor cropped-out girlfriend? What went wrong between Paul and this girl? Is she on the apps too? Does she know Paul is using a photo with her shoulder in it to try to get laid? Then I remember Dan was on these apps. He signed up just weeks after he moved out. He will have answered all the same questions. Did he use a photo of us and crop out me? Is that how he met Sylvie? What if his profile is still active? What if I'm scrolling and I find a photo of cropped-out me?

My mood shifts. I don't want to be thinking these thoughts. So, I flick over to Instagram and open my favorite account, @paul hollywoodkneadsdough, which features videos of, you guessed it, Paul Hollywood kneading dough. It's comforting, hypnotic, sexy for reasons I can't explain. Then I get so absorbed in Paul pounding a focaccia dough that I miss my stop.

GOOGLE SEARCHES:

- *Statistical likelihood of getting murdered by someone you meet online*
- *Hobbies that don't take too much time or effort*
- *Dan Humphries, Bath, dating profile*
- *Paul Hollywood focaccia fan fiction*

# CHAPTER 4

WHEN I WAS EIGHT YEARS OLD, I RODE MY BIKE INTO A WALL. I WAS going down a steep hill and I couldn't brake fast enough. I flew over the handlebars straight into the side of a house and banged up my face, chipped a tooth, and dislocated my collarbone. So, when people tell me something is "just like riding a bike," I get wary. All I can think about is the potential for injury and that however cautious you are, you can't account for all the other idiots on the road. Yet despite my misgivings, here I am, back on my metaphorical bike, having a drink in a bar on a Saturday night with a stranger I met online. Richard, thirty-seven, whose profile picture is him holding a giant wheel of cheese.

"So even if it tastes like Parma ham and it looks like Parma ham, if it's not from Parma, then it's not Parma ham, and you can't label it as such," Richard says, putting his pint down with a bang to punctuate his point. I scramble to pick up the threads of this conversation as I realize my mind has drifted to memories of cycling into a brick wall.

"So, you're the ham police," I say, trying to look enthusiastic.

"Technically, my title is 'management and safeguarding of product regulation,'" he says proudly. "I work across the whole EU."

"Have you ever busted into a warehouse waving a gun, shouting, 'Come out with your hams up!' Ha ha," I laugh, pleased with my own joke, but Richard remains stony-faced.

"We're not armed. It's a desk job. We enforce the rules through legal channels. Correction: I did once do a warehouse certification course, but we were there to learn, not to arrest anyone."

"Right, no, I was joking," I say, attempting a self-deprecating eye roll. Then I worry the eye roll might be interpreted as petulance, so I tack on a maniacal grin. *Why are facial expressions so hard to get right?* Subtly checking my watch, I calculate that I've been on this date for seventeen minutes. *Is that all?* Kelly tells me that an hour and a half is the absolute minimum you need to stay if you don't want to appear rude. But I've already been on two other dates this week and I'm physically and mentally exhausted. On Wednesday I met Phil, thirty-four. He smelled of changing rooms and lectured me on nuclear fuel, though I couldn't work out whether he was for or against. After an hour he said he had to go because he had a dog waiting for him at home. He didn't suggest meeting again.

On Friday, I met David, forty-three, who "plays the saxophone, is a Gemini, likes monogamy and solo camping." He told me I looked like "Mila Kunis on a bad day," explained he was divorced—"no kids, thank God"—then started an inappropriate line of questioning about childbirth and how it had affected me "down there." I left, telling him I had a dog waiting for me at home. I didn't suggest we meet again.

Online dating is exactly what I feared it would be, and it's made me feel a thousand times worse about being single. At home, alone on my sofa, I can delude myself into thinking that if I *wanted* to meet someone, I could. Now I see that might not be the case. Everyone normal is taken, online dating is horrible. I will die alone. I need to start contributing more to my pension. I should start weight training, so I can stay mobile well into my eighties.

Looking across at Richard, I try to evaluate whether this is a bad date, like the others, or whether I'm simply out of practice. Objectively, Richard is a good-looking human. He has a sharp blond hairstyle, tanned skin, and the kind of arms you only get from either being a professional woodsman or spending an unhealthy amount of time at the gym. But while he looks good, there's something unnervingly cold about him. He's like the villain's henchman in a Bond movie, the guy who skis cross-country shooting at 007. He gets killed in the first five minutes, but no one really cares. He probably doesn't even get credited with a name at the end, he's just Henchman One, Richard from Bumble.

"So, remind me what you do, Anna?" Richard asks while signaling to the waiter for another round of drinks. *Should I order a coffee to stop myself from yawning?*

"I sell counterfeit Parma ham on the dark web," I tell him, and Richard's brow furrows. "No. Um, no. I am a journalist." I pause. "Remember? We had a long conversation about it over text?"

Richard flushes. "Oh, right, yes, I'm online with a few people so it's hard to keep track of people's particulars."

"Of course. Me too," I say, reaching for my wine, even though I've just put it down.

In my urgent quest for a column, I replied to a handful of men who lived within a two-mile radius and were able to meet ASAP. David and Phil's messages were fine, perfunctory, but I had higher hopes for Richard. His messages were excellent, his response time perfect. He asked me questions and gave thoughtful answers. We had a long back-and-forth about journalistic integrity. Honestly, given how good he was at messaging, I am surprised, even a little disappointed, to find how awkward this evening has been. In person, there is none of the warmth and intelligence he conveyed online.

"We had that conversation about the role of the BBC, remember?" I say, hoping to prompt his memory.

"Oh, right, yeah." Richard scratches his neck, avoiding my gaze. "The thing is—and I'm going to be honest now, Annie, because it's good to start things on the right note, isn't it?"

Is it worth telling him that I hate being called Annie? Probably not. There's a window of opportunity where you can correct someone who calls you the wrong name; after that, you have to either never see them again or just be that new name forever. "Because I'm so busy, it's hard for me to engage with online dating in the way I'd like to," Richard explains. "My day starts at six a.m. and often doesn't end until past eleven."

"Oh, do you have kids too?" I ask.

"No, I have a training regime." Richard flexes his arm muscle to illustrate. The prospect of talking to Richard about bench presses and dead lifts makes me hanker for the heady excitement of the Parma ham conversation. "And I don't know if it's the same for you, but as a man, you need to engage in a lot of back-and-forth before anything materializes into a real-life meetup. Of those, only a few will turn out to be viable candidates." *Viable candidates? Is he conducting a lab experiment?*

"Right," I say, nodding slowly.

"It's a numbers game. You need to put the time in, and there's never enough time."

"Never." I finish my wine with a wince. It tastes like mulled sawdust.

"Hence, I outsource some of the initial back-and-forth. You probably won't believe this, but I used to have trouble securing that first meeting in the flesh."

The way he says "flesh" makes me flinch. "What do you mean? A friend helps you?" I ask nervously.

"Kind of," Richard mutters, eyes glued to his pint. "There's this app that can field messages for you." He pauses, a flash of embarrassment crossing his henchmanly face.

"What, like AI?" I ask, and he nods.

"I'm only telling you this because we're getting on so well. Obviously, I won't use the app to text you now that we've met in person."

"Obviously."

Right. So, the nice, inquisitive guy I've been chatting with for the last few days was a computer. Well, it's a column. Even if it makes me feel so depressed I want to throw my phone in a blender, it's a column.

WHEN I GET home thirty minutes later, I find Lottie sitting on my sofa knitting a baby blanket, with *Love Island* on in the background and Katniss stretched out on the armchair.

"You're back early. That's not a good sign," Lottie says, muting the TV.

"No, and I'm not sure I'm going to be able to write an 'aspirational' column if it's all this hellish." I let out a sigh as I kick my shoes off. "Maybe I should meet your pecan man."

"You might have missed your window with that one. Last I heard, he met some hazelnut heiress at a nut convention."

"Wow. I just don't know how to play this game anymore. In the seventeen years I was with Dan, all the rules have changed." I crawl onto the sofa and flop my head into my sister's lap. "I wish you could just meet people the old-fashioned way, in real life."

"Yes, but that would still involve leaving the house. Eligible men aren't just going to come and knock on your door."

"Hi," Jess says, sleepy-eyed, standing in the doorway dressed in black-and-white-checked pajamas, her fine blond hair ruffled into bedhead tufts.

"You're still up?" I ask, getting up to give her a hug. At twelve, Jess has reached the age where she's embarrassed by public displays of affection from me, so I take every opportunity to get my hugs in when we're at home.

"It's only nine thirty." She pauses, then asks, "Was your date that bad?" I turn to frown at Lottie.

"She asked," Lottie says, then tilts her head toward Jess. "Are you feeling any better about the Penny situ?"

"What's she done now?" I ask, and Jess groans. Penny is Jess's frenemy at school, the queen of Year Eight, arbiter of taste, and instigator of many tears.

"It's not a big deal," she says, then sighs as though loath to repeat it. "She said I was like the default character in a computer game. And she said it in front of the whole class, so now everyone's calling me Default."

"That is so mean," I say, outraged, though also secretly impressed with the sophistication of children's insults. When I was at school, you'd just get called "loser" or "specky git." "Do you want me to call her mum?" I offer, then immediately sense I've said the wrong thing.

"No, Mum!" Jess throws her head back. "Do not call her mum."

"She probably comes from an unhappy home," says Lottie. "We should be feeling sorry for her."

"MUM!" comes a wail from upstairs.

"Ethan is still awake too?"

"He was asleep," Lottie says, her cheeks flushing pink.

"Can we have hot chocolate?" Jess asks, reaching down to stroke Katniss, who is winding a feline figure of eight around her legs. "I'll make some with the Velvetiser."

"Sure."

As I leave the room, I hear Jess telling Lottie that Penny was annoyed with her because Jake Tenby sat next to her in assembly, but she doesn't even like Jake anyway, so she doesn't know what Penny's problem is. *Why didn't she tell me any of this?*

Upstairs, I find Ethan's nightlight on. He's sitting on the floor beside his bed.

"I had an accident," he says with a sniff, pulling his head into his knees.

"It's okay," I say gently. At seven, Ethan is a little old to be bedwetting, but since Dan moved out, he's had the occasional setback. "Why don't you choose some clean pajamas, then come down for a hot chocolate. I'll change your bedclothes."

"I didn't mean to do it," he says quietly.

"Of course not. These things happen, honey," I say, kissing his head.

"Dad gets mad when it happens at his house," Ethan mutters.

I bite back the urge to storm out of the house, beat on Dan's door, and yell at him. It is an urge that overtakes me more frequently than is probably healthy.

"Well, he shouldn't," I say, stroking Ethan's arm. "It's not something you can control, and it's easily fixed."

Downstairs, I find Lottie pulling all my plain white mugs out of the kitchen cupboard, looking for the hand-painted colorful ones at the back. Jess is scrolling through my phone.

"Um, excuse me," I say, holding out my hand.

"Mum, these guys in your favorites file are all totally beige."

"That is private, thank you," I say, swiping the mobile from her.

Jess shrugs. "So you're dating now?" she asks, trying to sound casual, but I can see she wants to know.

"Are you looking for a boyfriend?" Ethan asks, pulling his Ninjago dressing gown around him, then clambering up onto the barstool next to Jess. Lottie hands him a hot chocolate with far too much cream for this time of night, and I lean over to scoop some off with my finger.

"No. I have everything I need right here," I tell them, wrapping an arm around them both. "It's just something I'm doing for work, research."

"She just wants a new friend," Lottie says, "to do things with."

I glare at Lottie, nervous about where she's going with this.

"How do you want your hot chocolate, Mum?" Jess asks me.

"Oh, just however it comes."

"Kieran's mum and dad are getting divorced. You could be friends with his mum?" Ethan offers.

"Or his dad," Lottie says, hiding a smile behind her mug.

"Kieran's dad loves BMX, though, and Mum hates bikes," Ethan tells Lottie.

"I don't *hate* bikes," I say, irritated at this narrative of Dan's.

When people ask why your marriage failed, they often want a simple explanation. Was there someone else? Did you have financial problems? But the truth is usually a million little things. One of our million little things was Dan's sudden, all-consuming interest in road bikes.

The year before we separated, he became obsessed. Every evening, he would scroll biking websites, looking at kit he might need, spending money we didn't have. He became evangelical about a "high-protein diet" and critical of me for choosing cornflakes for breakfast. Every weekend he would be off doing events with his triathlon club, and every evening he would disappear into the garage to train or tinker with parts. I know you shouldn't argue in front of your children, and we tried not to, but they must have overheard a few clashes about the time and money he was spending on his new hobby. At the ages of five and ten, they concluded that we were separating because Mum hated bikes. I do hate bikes, but I don't want them thinking that's the reason our family fell apart.

"Tilly's dad is divorced, and he hates bikes too!" Ethan says, bouncing up and down on the barstool.

"I am not looking for someone who hates bikes," I say, rolling my eyes.

"You should let these two pick your dates for you," Lottie suggests. "They probably know you better than the algorithm."

This makes me laugh out loud. "Right."

"I can find you someone to date if you need me to," Jess offers. "Someone way cooler than Sylvie."

"I don't need someone 'cooler than Sylvie,' it's not a competition."

"Her legs are longer than my whole body," Ethan tells Lottie.

"No, they're not. That would be impossible," Jess says, pulling Ethan onto her lap to cuddle him like a little-brother hot-water bottle.

"They are," he says, "I saw her in her underwear. They were up to my neck."

And there it is, the cherry on my cake of a day: hearing about the length of Dan's twenty-five-year-old girlfriend's legs—from my children.

"Why are you seeing this woman half-naked?" Lottie asks.

"She moved in with Dad. She's there all the time now," Jess says with a shrug.

"What?" I say, unable to hide my surprise. Jess shifts uncomfortably, perhaps worried she's said something wrong.

"He said he was going to tell you," she says cautiously, and I try to regain my composure.

"Right, sure. No, he did, I forgot," I bluff, then turn to Ethan and ask, "How do you feel about her living there?"

He shrugs. "She was there most of the time anyway."

*I can't believe Dan moved someone in without telling me.* The thought of him "moving on" so completely, of him cohabiting with someone, makes me feel nauseous. It shouldn't be worse than him sleeping with half of Bath, but somehow it is.

"On that note, I think it's bedtime," Lottie says, reaching out to squeeze my hand beneath the kitchen island. I force a smile as I hug Jess and Ethan good night, then Lottie herds them both upstairs. Alone, I close my eyes and chastise myself for being so sensitive. It's been eighteen months since he moved out, a year since the divorce was finalized. I should be over it. When Lottie comes back downstairs, she gives me a sympathetic look.

"It's natural to be upset, you know," she says, watching me closely.

I shake my head, not sure I can cope with more sympathy. "I'm fine, honestly."

After saying good-bye to Lottie, I tidy up the kitchen, then head up to bed. Katniss follows me. She's not supposed to come upstairs, but tonight I let her curl up on the end of my duvet, her low purr a welcome sound in the too-quiet room. Lying in bed, I look across at my cluttered bedside table, all the creams I keep forgetting to use. The table on the other side sits empty, wiped clean, a reminder that no one sleeps there anymore. I've always loved this bedroom, with its vaulted ceiling and large dormer window, but Dan's presence, or rather his absence, still feels so evident. There are clothes drawers he emptied that I have not filled, his coffee stain on the carpet that never completely came out. The bed is king-sized, but I still sleep right over on the left. Does anyone sleep in the middle of a bed this big?

Lying in bed, scrolling Instagram, I click onto Dan's account. There's a new photo of him lifting weights at the gym. He would never have posted something like that when we were together. He looks so different now; his whole body has changed shape. He used to be an oblong and now he's a triangle. Next, I look up @sylvielovenfitness. I've looked at her account before, so I know what she looks like—a young, Swedish Gwyneth Paltrow with a white-blond bob. She is more active on social media than Dan and has tagged him in a bunch of photos. There's one of them out running together, ugh. One of her doing a headstand at the foot of her bed. Double ugh. Then one of her holding a door key, kissing a half-obscured Dan on the cheek. So naff. So cheesy. *So unacceptable he didn't think to tell me this.*

*This isn't healthy, I need to unfollow him.* Closing the app, I open Ethan's class WhatsApp group and try to enlarge the photo of Tilly Bradshaw's dad. He's not unattractive, though the photo is too grainy to see his features clearly. I've never noticed him at drop-off, so he can't be that hot.

*What am I doing?*

I'm not going on a date with Tilly Bradshaw's dad just because he's single and he hates bikes. *Why* does he hate bikes, though? Did his ex-wife become obsessed with cycling too? Does he have bike-related childhood trauma like me? Why does this small nugget of information immediately make him more interesting to me? Before putting my phone away, I mindlessly click onto Will Havers's WhatsApp photo, curious to see what he's chosen. It's of a distant figure, presumably him, on a steep ski slope. It's black and white. Of course it is. What a knob. "Look at me, I'm really good at skiing, as well as everything else." Then I quickly delete my own WhatsApp picture, the one of me cuddling Katniss, in case anyone should make such mean judgments about my choice of photo.

GOOGLE SEARCHES:

*Sylvie Nilsson*

*Sylvie Nilsson boobs fake?*

*Teach yourself how to do a headstand*

*How many series of Outlander are there?*

# CHAPTER 5

THE NEXT MORNING, ON MY WALK TO WORK, I CALL DAN.

"Hey," he says. "Everything okay? I'm getting on a train in five minutos."

"I'll be quick," I say, bristling at his use of the word "minutos." "Please don't get angry with Ethan if he wets the bed. That will only make things worse."

Dan sighs with a familiar combination of irritation and impatience. "He's nearly eight, Anna. You baby him."

"Getting frustrated with him won't help. I'll send you an article about it."

Dan goes quiet on the line. It's a new technique he's developed when we disagree; he just stops talking and hopes I'll move on. In this instance, it works.

"Also . . ." I pause, bracing myself. "I hear from the kids that you have a new living arrangement."

"Oh, right. Did I not mention that? I'm sure I did," Dan says, clearing his throat.

"No, I definitely would have remembered. That's a big step, Dan. I haven't even met this woman, and now she's living with my kids?" I clear my throat. "They don't need any more disruption. It's not fair on them if she'll be gone in a few months—"

"She's not going anywhere, Anna," he says irritably. "I'm in love with her."

"Right, good. Well, a heads-up would have been nice," I say, feeling the words dry in my mouth and a rush of blood heat my cheeks. *Why do I feel embarrassed? What have I got to be embarrassed about?*

"Like you gave me a heads-up before cutting up my credit cards?"

Classic Dan, countering a reasonable request with an entirely separate grievance from two years ago.

"I'd like to know a bit more about the woman living with my children," I say, feeling hot, panicky anger pressing against my chest.

"What do you want to know?" Dan asks. I use his pausing technique, waiting for him to speak. It works. "We met at Tri Club." *Of course they did.* "She was born in Sweden, she works in public relations. Do you want me to send you her CV?" He sighs. "Anna, it's been two years, you can't begrudge me for moving on. You should too."

This rankles. It's only been eighteen months since he moved out and only a year since the official divorce came through. I still have cans of food in my cupboard purchased by Dan. I have dry shampoo in the bathroom that I had when we were together. Okay, so I don't use the dry shampoo often, and the onion marmalade is probably out of date, but the point stands.

"I'm not begrudging you anything, and I have 'moved on,' thank you. Please just do me the courtesy of keeping me in the loop with any other major life changes. If you're having another baby or something, I'd rather not hear about it from Ethan."

"Sure. You want me to ask my girlfriend if she can sync you into her ovulation app?"

"Oh fuck off, Dan."

I hang up, aggressively stabbing the screen with my finger. How many calls have ended with those four words? I hate the angry, sweary person he brings out in me. I don't want to be that person. *Is she really using an ovulation app, or was that just a joke?*

Walking through the front door of the office, I come face-to-face with Will Havers standing in the hall. He is singing "Build Me Up Buttercup" to himself, which feels incongruous.

"Morning, Appleby," he says, smiling at me with that infuriating, well-rested face. I take a moment to imagine Will's morning. He probably got up early to go for a run, had a nice leisurely shower, had time to shave and then brush *and* floss his teeth, caught up on the news over a quiet cup of coffee while listening to birdsong and Radio 4. I shouldn't resent someone for having a morning that doesn't involve throwing together packed lunches, prompting forgotten homework, and searching for lost sports kit—I know I chose to have children—but for some reason, I do, I really do. I'm sure we'd all have time to correct every single typo if we got to start our day in such a delightful way.

"Morning," I say curtly.

"You look stressed," he tells me.

"What makes you think I'm stressed?" I snap.

"You're tugging your hair." *Am I?* "You do that when you're anxious."

I clasp my hands together, embarrassed. When things were at their worst with Dan, I developed an unconscious habit of hair pulling. I only realized I was doing it when I noticed a small bald spot appearing behind one ear. It's grown back now, but there's a telltale tuft of regrowth that I need to comb down with hairspray every morning to stop it from sticking out. I am mortified that anyone, least of all Will, might have noticed this about me.

"Do you count how many times I use the bathroom too?" I ask.

"Usually three. Five when you've been drinking the night before," he says, following me into the office. I turn to shake my head at him, and he laughs. "I'm joking, I am not keeping track of your bathroom usage."

When I get to my desk, Will is still next to me, and I look up, my eyes questioning.

"How's the dating column going?" he asks.

"Great. I'm excited." *Two lies in just three words, impressive.* "I love this, by the way," I say, pointing at his monogrammed document wallet. "Is it from WHSmith?"

"Funny," he says, a smile playing at the corner of his mouth. "Listen, I've got a table at Henry's on Thursday night. Amazing seafood, impossible to get a reservation. Do you want to come?"

This question throws me even more than the ovulation-app quip of Dan's.

"What? Me? Why?" I ask, feeling my forehead crease into a deep frown.

"Why?" he laughs. "Because the food is supposed to be incredible, and I thought it might be nice."

"Is this some ploy to steal my column?" I ask, swiveling my chair to face him, then crossing my arms. Whatever game he's playing, I don't have the bandwidth today.

"No. I need to review the place for my food column, and I prefer not to eat alone." He pauses, looking at me with an intensity that suddenly makes the air between us feel charged.

"What, so like a date?" I say, more in shock than horror, but it comes out as horror.

Will crosses his arms. *Is he blushing?* "No, never mind, just trying to be friendly."

Now I'm thoroughly confused. Will doesn't do friendly. This must be part of some diabolical plan. "Well, thanks for the invitation, but I'm afraid I can't this week," I say, then shoot him an unsteady smile. *What if he really is just trying to be friendly?*

Maybe I'm still in fight-or-flight mode from my conversation with Dan. My hackles sometimes feel permanently raised.

"Sure, maybe another time," says Will. He looks as though he wants to say something else, but now Malik, one of the junior copywriters, is hovering by my desk, waiting for me to review something, so Will walks away.

*What was that all about?* I don't have time to dwell. I quickly scan Malik's copy and mark up some changes, then I need to prepare for my ten a.m. with Jonathan. I sent him my column last night, "Love in the Time of AI." I have to say I'm pleased with it. Not only is it the story of a terrible date, but it's also a deeper examination of AI communication, how it might affect the world of online dating.

"So?" I ask Jonathan as I walk into his office at one minute to ten. "What did you think?"

"It's clever," he says, with less enthusiasm than I'd been hoping for.

"And funny?" I suggest. I *know* it's funny. Lottie proofread it for me. She said it was hilarious.

"Yes, it's funny," Jonathan acknowledges. I sense a "but" coming. "But . . ."

"But?"

"It's a little bleak, Anna."

"Bleak?"

"Here, where you detail a future of virtual boyfriends who fulfill all your emotional needs and a drawer full of sex toys to fulfill your physical ones—that's bleak."

"I was being facetious."

Jonathan takes his glasses off and pinches the skin between his brows. "Our readers don't want facetious; they want hope. They want to feel empathy, a connection. They want to feel optimistic, not depressed."

"Depressed? Jonathan, come on. It's wry!"

"Crispin didn't like it," Jonathan says, his face somber. "This isn't a judgment about you as a journalist, Anna. I just don't think you're in the headspace to come at this from the angle he's looking for."

Panic floods through me. I genuinely thought he was going to love it.

"You're a great writer, but being a columnist is a more personal undertaking. You need to be willing to show a little of who you are, to be vulnerable on the page. This piece tells me nothing about you, your divorce, how you feel about it. It all feels rather . . . well, snide."

*Vulnerable? Vulnerable!* If he only knew just how vulnerable I feel *all the time*. Having to be strong for Jess and Ethan, to not go to pieces when I learn Dan has moved in with Sylvie, to hide how much it hurts when he says he's in love. To have the financial strain of running a household entirely on my shoulders. To question whether I am even lovable now, since the fun-loving, carefree girl I was no longer exists. Then I picture Ethan's little face, his excitement at telling me about Tilly's dad, and I think about this job that's kept me sane through everything. I will not be labeled dead wood.

"I do have another angle," I say before giving myself time to fully think it through. "I'm not sure online dating is for me. What if I set out to meet someone the old-fashioned way, only dated people I met in real life?" I pause; Jonathan looks intrigued. "My son suggested setting me up with his classmate's dad because we're both divorced and we both hate bikes."

Jonathan bursts out laughing, a genuine laugh. "How to find a man in ten dates . . . chosen by your children," he says, moving his hand through the air as though it's a headline on a billboard.

"Um, well, they wouldn't all need to be chosen by my kids, that was just one example."

"No, it needs to be your kids, that's the unique selling point.

It's brilliant. Just the kind of thing Crispin is after. It's a fresh take, no one else has done it." *Did I pitch this? I don't think I did.* "And you have to go out with whoever they suggest." Jonathan is still talking. "Be open-minded and vulnerable. Take it seriously. No cynicism."

"No cynicism," I say, crossing my fingers behind my back. *Why am I agreeing to this? This is the worst idea I've ever had.*

As I'm wrestling with what I've just signed up for there's a knock on the door and Will's head appears around it.

"Ah, Will, perfect timing. Anna here has just bought herself ten more weeks on the dating column. Ten dates, found from real life, all chosen by her children. An anti-online-dating column," Jonathan says, rubbing his palms together.

"Maybe not ten," I mutter. "I could start with five, see how I go."

"I like it," Will says with a smile that doesn't reach his eyes. *He does not like it. I can tell by the pulse in his jaw.* He's annoyed he's lost his chance to steal my column.

As I'm savoring the sweetness of victory, Will walks into the room and takes a seat in the chair next to me. Why is he sitting down? This is *my* meeting.

"Though people do like to hear both perspectives when it comes to dating. Maybe I could do an online column as a contrast. We could pick a theme to write about each week, do a his-and-hers, online/offline, cover all bases," Will suggests, his face animated.

"Cover all bases?" I repeat, looking back and forth between Will and Jonathan.

"Oh yes," Jonathan enthuses. "The working mum looking for love in real life, versus the man about town who only has time for the apps." Jonathan grins. "You're onto something there, Will, and with both of you on the back page, we'd be appealing to the broadest possible range of readers."

*What? You've got to be kidding me.* "Why does there need to be a second column at all? Isn't my idea enough to stand on its own?" I ask, sounding like a petulant child. I don't know why I'm so annoyed about this, but it feels like I had my eye on something good and Will just can't let me have it.

"A rising tide lifts all ships, Anna. I'll let you guys hammer out the details. I have lunch with Bonhams, toodle pip." Jonathan stands up, grabs his Burberry trench coat and trilby, then pauses in the door. "'Philosopher,' nine letters, fifth letter T?"

"Aristotle," I say, and Jonathan claps one hand against the doorframe, then pulls a pencil and his newspaper out of his satchel before he leaves.

Alone with Will, I let my fake smile drop. "You just had to muscle in on my idea, didn't you?"

"I'm not muscling in on anything," he says, slowly stretching his arms above his head and shifting to sit with one ankle resting on his thigh. "This way we both get a column, and our readers get two different perspectives. Everybody wins."

"Because you care so much about the readers," I say, rolling my eyes as I stand up.

"I get it, you don't like to collaborate, but I want this column, and the MD likes it, so it looks like it's happening," Will says, his voice uncharacteristically sharp. Then he stands too, so he's towering over me.

"Why would you want this?" I ask. "You don't need extra credit. You're already the golden boy who won over the investors with your winning pitch. They're hardly going to make *you* redundant."

"I'm not worried about that," Will says, taking off his glasses, then stowing them in his pocket.

"Right, so you just have a burning desire to become the next Carrie Bradshaw, do you?" I scoff.

"I need it for my portfolio. I want to show I can author a column about something other than food. Dating has broad appeal. I don't want to be pigeonholed as the food guy."

"You could add *Teen Girl* to your portfolio."

His mouth creases into a smile. "Anyone would think you were scared of a little competition, Appleby."

"What would I be scared of, exactly?" I ask, taking a step toward him, refusing to be intimidated by the foot of height he has on me.

"Scared that my column will be better than yours. That my dates will be more fun," he says, closing the space between us by another inch.

I jut my chin forward. "I don't think the magazine needs an X-rated column, so you might be limited on how much 'fun' you can write about, Havers."

"Right, because that's all a date with me would be," he says, shaking his head, a flash of something new in his eyes and a lift to his eyebrow. "You don't know me. You reject any attempt I make to get to know you. I really don't get what your problem is, Anna." His piercing green eyes stare directly into mine, and the narrow space between us crackles with some furious energy. My palms start to heat, and I struggle to think straight.

"You really want to know what my problem is?" I ask, and he nods. "I've been here six years, I work hard every day, late into the night sometimes, I never take a lunch break, I know this magazine better than anyone. Then you swan in with all this swagger and confidence and start critiquing other people's work when no one asked for your feedback. You ingratiate yourself with Jonathan, volunteering to write up secret pitches none of us were even told about." I take a beat. *It feels so good to be saying all this.* "I heard you asked for a raise before you'd even finished your probation, so I'm guessing you already earn more than me, even though I have years more experience, but you probably think you deserve it. You asked for a brand-new ergonomic office chair, even though the rest of us are making do with the crappy old ones, and HR ordered you one, just like that." I snap my fingers. "You think you can charm everyone into doing exactly what you want, but it won't work on me. Okay?" I take a breath; the air in the room pulses with emotion.

Will reaches for his glasses and puts them back on. "So, you dislike me for wanting a comfortable chair, for being ambitious and good at my job?" he says, his voice calm and even. He raises a hand to his chin in a faux pose of contemplation. "I won't apologize for trying to make the magazine better, and if you think you've earned a pay rise, you should ask for one. Your lack of confidence and unwillingness to take a lunch break are not on me." His eyes are steely now, a cool detachment in his tone. "Now, we're working together on this column whether you like it or not, so let me know when you're ready to have a constructive, professional, grown-up conversation." He walks past me toward the door, reaching for the handle, then pauses, turning to give me a final withering look. "And, Anna, if I needed to charm you, trust me, I would have."

Then he leaves and I pick up the paperweight from Jonathan's desk and make to hurl it at the door but groan in fury instead, placing the paperweight back down carefully. What a narcissistic sociopath. I am riled and infuriated and ready to punch something, but my skin tingles also with a new exhilaration. Because now, this is war.

GOOGLE SEARCHES:

Journalism jobs in Bath

Signs someone might be a narcissistic sociopath

Who is the actor in Outlander?

How old is Sam Heughan?

Sam Heughan, wife

# CHAPTER 6

I DON'T KNOW WHO CAME UP WITH TEN AS AN ARBITRARY NUMBER for everything. *How to Lose a Guy in 10 Days, 10 Things I Hate About You, 10 Years Younger*—why does it always have to be ten? Six feels more than adequate. I e-mail Jonathan to suggest I start with five dates.

"I need to talk to you two about something," I tell Jess and Ethan as we sit down for chicken fajitas at the kitchen table.

"Is it about the vase in the bathroom?" Jess asks, fiddling with her phone.

"No, why? What's happened to the vase in the bathroom?" I ask.

"Nothing," Jess says, her eyes darting back to her phone. She scrolls, then frowns at the screen. I look to Ethan, who shrugs.

"Phone away, please," I say, nodding toward Jess's hand. Dan and I agreed she could have a phone for secondary school. We thought she needed one if she was going to be walking home from the bus, but sometimes I worry she's too young to be so constantly connected. We don't allow her on social media, but she's still always messaging people. Since she's struggling to make friends at her new school, I don't want to cut her off from her old ones.

"I wanted to talk to you both about my work," I say, pouring myself a glass of wine. Lately my policy of not drinking alone or on weeknights has become less a policy and more a general guideline, which nobody, least of all me, adheres to. "So, as you know, I am very happy being on my own, I'm not looking to meet anyone."

"Sure, Mum," Jess says, shooting her eyes toward the ceiling.

"Well, I am, but work wants me to go on some dates for my column. I was thinking, rather than let the internet choose people, it might be fun if you two came up with a few ideas."

"What?" Jess frowns. "Why?"

Just as Ethan cries, "Great idea!"

"It would be like a science experiment. It could be fun." *There is no part of me that thinks this could be fun. I imagine a seminar on the history of tax codes would be more entertaining.* "It's just an idea. Online dating has been written about so much already, I was trying to think of something new." As I sit down, Katniss jumps up and curls into my lap and I start stroking her head with my free hand.

"You can go out with Tilly's dad!" Ethan says, gesticulating wildly.

"Yes, you have mentioned Tilly's dad. Though we might have to widen the net beyond your school friends' divorced parents."

"What would the rules be?" Jess asks.

"I guess you could take it in turns to pick someone. It would need to be someone who's single, who lives locally, someone I could feasibly ask out."

"And we get to pick where you go," Ethan suggests, kneeling up on his chair.

"Um . . ."

"Yes, otherwise you'll just go for a drink at a pub and it will be mega boring," Jess says.

"Fine, you pick where we go, within reason. I'm not going on a date to Rome or Legoland."

"Yes! Legoland!" Ethan cries. *I should not have mentioned Legoland.* The children look at each other, silently conferring.

"Okay, we'll do it," says Jess, and Ethan nods eagerly.

"But I don't want you feeling responsible if people say no, or if they don't amount to anything. They wouldn't be *real* dates, it would just be for the column. You know I'm very—"

"Happy on your own," Jess says, finishing my sentence. "Yes, you've said that like fifty thousand times."

As I'm clearing the plates, Ethan tips a small bag of plastic dragons onto the table in front of Jess. "Dragon school?" he asks hopefully. Jess used to spend hours creating stories for Ethan with his toys. She does it less now, but if he catches her in the right mood, she might just oblige. He's in luck tonight. She picks up a red dragon and taps it on the table.

"This one's a Stitch Dragon and a Fire Walker, she has the power to transform."

Ethan is soon caught up in Jess's story, and I watch them affectionately from across the room. Like any siblings, they sometimes squabble, but they can also be so kind to each other that it makes my heart swell.

The moment is interrupted by a sharp knock on the door, which is strange. No one knocks on your door after eight o'clock, except maybe knife-wielding maniacs. Cautiously, I check the video doorbell and see that it's Noah from next door. Great. I might prefer a knife-wielding maniac; at least then I could call the police. Noah is a more benign menace.

"Hi, Noah," I say as I open the door.

"You trimmed my hedge," he says, pointing a fierce finger at me.

"I trimmed *my* side of the hedge," I say calmly. "It was getting out of control."

Noah and I are engaged in an ongoing dispute about the height and bushiness of our shared garden hedge. I want it trimmed to a normal height, so it doesn't block out all the light in my garden, while he wants it wild and untamed, towering over us like the Wall in *Game of Thrones*. He's got a thing for birdwatching and thinks he's "creating a habitat." Last week, knowing he was away, I took it upon myself to trim a few inches from the top. Just enough to keep the sun on our patio in the evenings. I didn't think he would notice.

"It is my hedge, you can't trim the top, only the bit that overhangs your side," he says, mouth tight, dark eyes swirling with rage. Noah is a reclusive widower in his early forties. I suppose he's attractive, if you can ignore the Crocs worn with socks, the grubby grandpa shirts, and the unbrushed hair. Lottie is convinced he's just a wounded pup, in need of rehoming, but I see him as one of life's petty aggravations that needs to be endured, like noisy building work or getting your IUD replaced. Ironically, it was Dan who started the hedge dispute with Noah, but in the spoils of war, Dan got the car and most of our savings, and I got the house and the ongoing feud over the hedge. Lucky me.

"Noah, I don't get any sun in my garden after five o'clock because of that ridiculously tall hedge, and I am not usually home until after five, so you are condemning me to live in perpetual darkness."

"You can't cut it in the spring, birds are nesting in it. You probably scared them all away, hacking away like that."

"I didn't hack away. It was a small trim, perfectly within—"

"Touch it again, and I will escalate this to the council," Noah says, his index finger waggling wildly now. Then he turns to stomp down my steps, shoulders hunched around his ears.

Back in the kitchen, Jess and Ethan eye me warily.

"It's fine. It was only Noah," I explain with a dismissive wave.

"Maybe you shouldn't have cut it, Mum," says Jess. "He really loves that hedge."

"And I love sunlight and vitamin D. Whose side are you on?"

As I load the dishwasher with enough plate clanking to convey my irritation at Jess's lack of loyalty, my phone pings with a message.

Neil Bradshaw

Hi Anna, Neil Bradshaw here. I believe Tilly and Ethan have been talking and they think we should hang out. Do you want to do a playdate one weekend? Take the kids to the park or something? I know what solo parenting can be like, so strength in numbers C etc. Neil.

*A playdate? He's asked me out on a playdate.*

"Who's that from?" Jess asks, noticing me pause to read the message again.

"Tilly Bradshaw's dad, he's suggesting a playdate." I narrow my eyes at Ethan. "What *exactly* did you say to Tilly?"

"I said you were looking for men to make friends," Ethan says, looking thrilled to see his words cause some effect.

Jess reaches for my phone, and I let her read the message.

"He's just making it sound like a playdate in case you say no. Reply, 'Cool, let's hang out, but not with the kids.'"

"I'm not going to say that. I might have to see this guy at the school gate."

"He loves fishing!" Ethan cries. "Say you want to go fishing."

"Don't be ridiculous," I say, laughing, but then I look up and see they both look serious.

"You asked for our help," Jess says, folding her arms across her chest.

"Fine," I say with a sigh as I compose a response to Neil.

Anna Appleby

Sounds good. Keen to hang out sans kids, if you are? Ethan says you like fishing. Never been, but I'm always up for trying something new.

Which must be the lamest message I've ever sent in my entire life.

My phone dings immediately.

Neil Bradshaw

It's a date! Don't have the kids on Sunday. Let me know where you live. I'll pick you up and we'll head to the river.

*Looks like I'm going fishing.*

GOOGLE SEARCHES:

- *Neil Bradshaw, Bath. Serial killer?*
- *Hedge trimming, rights and rules, Avon and Somerset*
- *How many series of The Marvelous Mrs. Maisel are there?*
- *Who is Mrs. Maisel actress married to in real life?*

# CHAPTER 7

NEIL'S DENTED GRAY ŠKODA PULLS UP OUTSIDE MY HOUSE. AS HE GETS out of the car, he immediately trips over a paving stone, then laughs at his own clumsiness. Neil looks exactly how I imagine a tired, middle-aged divorced dad to look. If they were making an advert for KFC where the father is taking his kids out for a family bucket, they'd cast an actor who looked just like Neil. He's average height, with thinning hair, a short beard, and a slightly round gut, but his face is attractive and he has kind eyes.

"Ready to catch some fish?" Neil asks jovially. Then he opens the passenger door for me and gives a flourish of his hand, as though he's a footman showing me into a royal carriage. A few dozen brightly colored loom bands lie strewn on the floor of the car like confetti.

"What's your story then?" Neil asks, once we're driving.

"My story?" I ask.

"Yeah, how come you're divorced? Don't say if it's too personal. I find it's easier to blurt these things out, get it out of the way." He tightens his hands around the steering wheel. "People assume I cheated on Sheila, and that's why she left, but it was the other way around. I know there isn't always someone else"—he glances across at me—"but there usually is."

"Right," I say. The question makes my chest tighten.

What was our story? That we were happy for fourteen years, busy and tired, but always a team. Then somewhere along the way, something changed. Dan got passed over for a promotion at work. He said he thought he would have achieved more by thirty-five, that he felt like he was on a treadmill, every day the same. He started losing his hair and when he looked in the mirror, he saw a middle-aged man. He told me he didn't want to die having done nothing with his life, which hurt because our life, our family, didn't feel like nothing to me. He became harder to live with, started drinking more, laughing less.

I found myself doing everything around the house and for the children. He was struggling to function, so I picked up the slack. Small things I hadn't noticed before began to inexplicably annoy me: the way he dried himself after a shower, his inability to iron his work shirts, how he ran his tongue around his teeth after a meal. Sometimes I felt disgusted by him. I felt as though I were walking on eggshells, especially when he'd had too many beers. He was clearly depressed but couldn't talk about it, and we were all drowning in his misery. I didn't let myself question whether I had fallen out of love with him, didn't admit to myself how lonely I was. I certainly didn't confide in anyone how bad it had gotten.

Then one day, it was as though Dan woke up and decided to be the master of his own destiny. He quit his job, found a new one, stopped drinking, and started taking antidepressants. He shaved his head, bought books on nutrition, and took up cycling. Things looked hopeful for a while, but then I realized that among all the things he wanted to change about his life—his hair, his job, his waistline—I was on the list too. When he asked for a divorce, I felt relieved, and then ashamed, and then heartbroken.

But I don't tell Neil any of this, I just say, "Dan left me. There wasn't anyone else, though there is now."

"Sorry to hear that," he says, offering me a wine gum from the glove box by way of consolation.

"I'm fine, life goes on." I hear myself repeating the line I say to everyone who asks how I'm doing.

"Well, clearly he's a wanker," Neil says, pulling a face, crossing his eyes, and sticking out his tongue. It's unexpected and childish and makes me exhale a short, sharp dart of laughter. We move on to lighter subjects. Neil tells me about his job in IT and asks about my career in journalism. We talk about the children's school and he does a funny impression of their new headmistress, her nasal, clipped voice. Slowly I feel myself start to relax.

When we arrive at the lake, Neil collects a cool box, rod, and canvas bag from the back of his car. I offer to carry something, but he says he's "got a system." We head through a wooden gate, which leads onto a footpath that hugs the bank of the lake. It's an idyllic spring day. Wildflowers sprout along the side of the footpath, and there's a bosky smell of new growth after a long winter. A couple with young children on bikes run past us, the man yelling at his son to keep away from the water. Neil and I share a look, gratitude that today, that is not us. As we stroll around the lake to find the fishing spot, Neil's gait relaxes, like he's an amphibian returning to his natural habitat.

Once we find the spot, Neil opens his case full of fishing tackle and shows me how to bait a line. He hums to himself, and I can see in his face that this is his happy place. "My grandad used to say fishing is like life," he tells me, looking wistfully across the water. "You don't know when you're going to hook something good or when your line is going to break, but if it were easy, where would the satisfaction be? Fishing's the thing that's kept me sane this year."

"I like that," I say, returning his smile. Looking across at him, I wonder whether Neil is the kind of man who could grow on you. Perhaps beneath the scruffy cargo trousers and slightly tragic air, there's a hidden sexiness just waiting to be discovered. Whether I could fancy him or not, he seems far more normal than any of those men I met online. Maybe this "dates picked by the kids" idea isn't so crazy after all.

Our peaceful moment of reflection is fractured when a man on a mountain bike sweeps past, causing two ducks to launch themselves off the footpath and into the water, disturbing Neil's line. He scowls at the cyclist, and I realize this might be a good opportunity to bond with him about our mutual dislike of the sport.

"Bloody cyclists," I mutter with a pantomimed eye roll.

"Right, cycling is such a cult these days," Neil says, taking the bait. "When people invented bikes in China or whatever, they were just a method of getting from A to B; no one shaved their legs to improve their 'aerodynamic performance.' This cult of fitness, selling all this unnecessary kit to people—it's maddening."

"I completely agree," I say.

"Sheila's new bloke is a cyclist," Neil tells me as he winds in the fishing line. "He's this middle-aged guy with a bigger gut than mine, but he shaves his legs, as though that extra mil of wind resistance is going to make all the difference. Wanker." Neil's friendly face is now blighted by an ugly sneer. *Is that how I sound when I talk about cycling? Is that how I look?* The thought stops me in my tracks.

"I did nothing wrong, and now this guy gets to put my kids to bed at night," Neil goes on. "I'm relegated to Weekend Dad because Sheila wanted to fuck some guy she met at a marketing conference. How is that fair?"

"I know, it sucks," I say. Now I feel bad for bringing up bikes.

"Sorry for swearing." Neil shakes his head, then lets out a slow exhale. "You want to have a go at a casting?" he asks, holding the rod toward me.

"Sure."

Now that we're back to fishing, Neil's happy demeanor returns. He launches into a lengthy explanation about lead drops, spigots, and cast trajectories, but he might as well be speaking Greek. From his demonstration it looks like you just give the rod a bit of a flick, then lob the end into the water.

"You want me to hold on behind you, do one together?" Neil asks, and I suspect this might be one of those moves men pull, like standing behind you to guide your pool cue.

"I think I'll manage on my own," I tell him.

"Okay, wait there a sec," he says, then leaves me holding the rod while he goes to get something from the cool box. Just as I start to think I might almost be enjoying myself, my phone pings, distracting me, then the name on the screen makes me scowl.

Will Havers

**Can I get a heads-up on a theme for your first column? I need to write mine.**

No "please," no "thank you," no "sorry for bothering you on a Sunday." Typical. Holding out my phone with one hand, I decide to take a selfie with the lake in the background. Maybe I could get a shot midcast; that would give him a clue. Lifting the rod with one hand, I give it a quick backward flick, and then I'm about to launch it forward toward the lake, when there's a guttural scream from behind me.

"AGGGGGHHH!" Neil yells.

I spin around to see him crouching on the ground, the fishing line attached to his face, the hook embedded in his cheek, with a streak of blood dripping down into his stubble.

"Oh God, oh no, what happened? Was that me?" I cry, quickly pocketing my phone.

"Never cast when someone is standing behind you," Neil says with an agonized groan.

I feel like that's something he probably should have mentioned in the initial briefing, because this is definitely not the kind of hookup anyone is looking for on a first date.

AS WE WALK briskly back toward the car, I offer to drive Neil straight to the hospital, but he insists he's fine. He says he's done this before, it's only a small hook, he just needs his wire cutters so he can cut the end of the barb before removing it.

"Are you sure you should be doing that yourself?" I ask, feeling slightly faint whenever I look at the bloody hook attached to his cheek.

"I'm fine, it just hurts to talk," he says, clutching his jaw. I can't think of anything appropriate to say, so we walk the rest of the way in awkward silence.

As he bends down to climb into the driver's seat, Neil lets out a deep groan.

"Are you sure you don't want me to drive?" I ask, but he slowly shakes his head. As Neil fiddles with the sat nav, I take the opportunity to scroll through the photos on my phone. The selfie I took by the lake came out surprisingly well, so I send it to Will with a fishing rod emoji. Even if we are now secretly at war, I need to present a veneer of professional cooperation, lull him into a false sense of security. He replies with a thumbs-up, which I can't help feeling underwhelmed by as a response. Then a few minutes later another message from him, a screenshot of one of his old *Teen Girl* columns, "How to Talk to Boys."

Will Havers

In case you need a refresher.

"What's so funny?" Neil asks, and I realize I must have laughed out loud.

"Nothing, sorry," I say, guiltily stowing my phone in my bag.

As Neil turns the car onto an A road, we approach a group of cyclists riding two abreast on the road in front of us. Neil slows the car.

"Look at these wankers, taking up the whole road. Shall we have some fun?" he says with a smirk, dried blood at the corner of his mouth. Then he revs the engine and accelerates right up behind the cyclists before dropping back just in time.

"What are you doing?" I ask, panic seizing my insides. He might be joking, trying to scare them, but it's dangerous and not at all funny.

"We'll show 'em who owns the road, eh?" he says, revving again. One of the cyclists swerves into the hedge, another turns around to shout at us, but Neil only edges closer, the bumper almost tapping one of the cyclists' wheels. I cover my face; I want to scream. *He's trying to kill them. This will be attempted murder, and I'll be an accomplice.*

Neil opens his window. "Get off the road, wankers!"

"Oh God!" I yell, bracing myself for a crash. All the cyclists now swerve into the bush, in genuine fear for their lives, and Neil gives them the finger, cackling with glee as he accelerates away.

"Jesus, Neil, you could have killed someone!" I say, heart racing as I struggle to catch my breath.

"I wasn't going to hit them," Neil says. "Just make 'em think twice about taking up the whole road."

I'M STILL SHAKING when Neil drops me home.

"Well, we'll have to do this again properly," Neil says, pulling up to the curb.

"You're sure you'll be able to deal with the . . . face issue?" I ask while wondering if I should be calling the police

"Yeah, it's a scratch." He shifts his body toward the passenger seat, then looks bemused to find me already on my front step, giving him a brisk wave.

"Good luck then, must dash, desperate for the loo. Thank you for today! So, so sorry again about the hook-in-the-face situation." I call down the steps as I fumble with my bag, looking for my house keys.

Shutting the front door behind me, I take a long deep breath, then google "How to anonymously report a crime in the UK." Of all the information I'd hoped to be researching after a first date, this is not it. I find a number for Crimestoppers. Should I pretend to be one of the cyclists, report the incident along with his registration plate? He might get a warning. Only I don't know his registration plate because I'm not Nancy sodding Drew. Plus, if he gets a call from the police, he might know it was me. He might lose his license, it might jeopardize his custody agreement, so that he'd get to see Tilly and his son even less than he does now. He might kidnap Ethan in revenge. The whole plot of *Taken* flashes through my mind. I would not be as skilled as Liam Neeson in getting my child back. I take another deep breath. Was he *really* going to hurt those cyclists, or was he just trying to impress me? Maybe the hook injury skewed his judgment. Perhaps it's best I give him the benefit of the doubt.

The children aren't back from Dan's yet. Still feeling rattled, I pace the hallway then find myself opening the door to the garage. I've hardly been in here since Dan left; it holds too many negative associations, reminding me of all the evenings he chose to spend in here rather than with me. Surveying the dusty floor, I try to envisage this as something other than Dan's workout space.

I am seized by a sudden need to be busy, to distract myself from thinking about Neil and those cyclists. On a whim, I pull down a huge turquoise all-weather rug from the rafters. I bought it years ago to cover our chipped patio, but Dan deemed it "too girly." Unfurling it, coughing at the dust, I lay it out on the garage floor. It instantly softens the room. In the far corner, beneath a tarpaulin, I see a wooden chair leg that I recognize. *My chair.* I found it in a junkyard. It had these beautiful carved wooden legs and a high round back, though the material was stained and threadbare. After watching some online tutorials, I reupholstered it in bright blue Liberty-print fabric. It's shoddily done, the fabric too baggy around the seat, but seeing it makes me smile. I remember being so proud of this chair. When we repainted the living room, Dan moved it out here "for safekeeping," then never got round to putting it back.

With a burst of energy, I clean the dust off, then heave the chair through to the living room. I pack up the play kitchen and all the long-forgotten toys, then move them out to the garage. Pushing my Liberty-print chair into the empty space, I add my TBR pile onto the empty shelf beside it, then stand back to admire my new reading nook. I feel a disproportionate sense of achievement. *Why have I not done this before?* I make a promise to myself—I will only use the nook for reading, no scrolling.

An empty picture hook hangs on the wall above the chair. There used to be a photo of Dan and the kids here, but he took it with him, and I haven't replaced it. Suddenly inspired, I go to the downstairs cupboard and find what I'm looking for. It's a framed photo of Lottie and me on our bikes as children. She had it enlarged and framed for me when she found the print in an old album. We're probably eight and four, both freewheeling with our feet off the pedals. It's a great snapshot of childish joy, but I never hung it because I don't like how I look in the photo. You can still see the fading bruises on my face from the cycling accident I'd had a few weeks before. But now I look at it with fresh eyes, and I see a girl who got back on that bike, even though she'd been hurt. I hang the photo above my chair, to remind myself that bruises heal, and I do not hate bikes.

GOOGLE SEARCHES:

*Home decor inspiration on a budget*

*How to make your own secret-door bookcase*

*Can you safely remove a fishhook from your own face?*

# CHAPTER 8

THE CHILDREN COME BACK FROM DAN'S HOUSE WITH A BIN BAG FULL of dirty clothes. I bite my tongue as he ushers them through the front door. He never does their washing. They return as though from holiday, clothes ready to be laundered by yours truly.

Dan doesn't usually linger when he drops the kids off on a Sunday night. But tonight, as Jess and Ethan race inside, vying to be first to the TV remote, he pauses on the doorstep.

"Can I have a quick word?" he asks, scuffing his trainers against the step. I still can't get used to how different Dan looks. His muscles now bulge from beneath his Aertex shirt, and he must have had his teeth whitened because they look brighter than they were before. "Why isn't Ethan doing football this term?" he asks.

"He doesn't like it."

"So, you just let him quit, without telling me?"

"He doesn't like football, he likes field hockey," I say tightly. This is the first time Dan has expressed any interest in the children's extracurricular activities.

"So, we're raising a quitter?"

"We're raising someone who has the right to choose what they're interested in."

Dan rolls his eyes, then takes a step backward. "Just consult me in future." He bounces down the steps, then pauses on the street. "Did you see there's a new series of *Port, Starboard, Murder* starting tonight?"

"Is there?" *Port, Starboard, Murder* is a crime drama we watched religiously for four series. It's one of the few TV shows we both enjoyed.

"It's on Apple TV," he says. "Use my log-in, if you like. I'll text it to you."

And then he's gone. And this is what an ex-husband is: one minute exasperating and petty, the next, reminding you why you loved him in the first place.

"Hey, where are all my toys?" Ethan yells from inside, and I walk back through to the living room.

"I moved them to the garage. They're all toys you don't play with anymore."

"What! I play with them all the time!" Ethan cries as I pull him into a hug.

"I haven't thrown anything away, just had a sort-out. You have all that room in your cupboard if you want to move any of them upstairs."

"I think it looks good," Jess says. "Maybe there'll be room for a fish tank now?"

"Oh yeah, great idea," Ethan says, instantly forgetting about the toys. He goes over to assess the new space, measuring it with footsteps just like Dan would do. "Can I get a pet axolotl?"

Jess pulls a face at me, like she doesn't know if she just helped or made things worse. "What's for dinner?" she asks, striding toward the kitchen.

"Can I, Mum?" Ethan asks.

"I don't know what an axolotl is," I call back, following Jess into the kitchen. "I have a casserole in the freezer. Are you hungry now?" Watching her standing by the open fridge door, I swear she's grown an inch in the forty-eight hours she's been away.

"It's an amphibian salamander. Kenny has one," Ethan says, walking in behind me. "They eat bloodworms."

"I don't want to eat meat anymore," Jess says, closing the fridge door. She looks down at her phone, and her eyebrows dip into a tense frown. "Sylvie says eating meat is causing climate change. She says if we're not part of the solution then we're part of the problem."

"Why don't we go out for dinner?" I suggest, suddenly feeling disinclined to cook. "Sunday-night treat."

AS WE WALK up the street to the vegan café Jess has suggested, Ethan asks, "How was fishing?" as though he's only just remembered that I went.

"Fine. Good," I say, reluctant to tell them much more about it. "We didn't catch anything."

"Give it a score out of six," Ethan suggests.

"Six? It needs to be out of five or ten," says Jess.

"Why?" he asks.

"Three out of six," I tell him, opting not to factor in the journey home.

Once we're seated in the café, Jess opens the menu, her eyes wide with delight. "Sylvie says this place is great."

I feel as though I'm playing that children's game Simon Says, where you only follow the instruction if Simon says it. With Sylvie Says it's more of an internal game I'm playing with myself, where I must resist the urge to shout, "I don't give a flying fuck what Sylvie thinks," but instead smile and nod agreeably. It's not a good game, it takes a great deal of concentration, and it is not at all fun. As I'm concentrating on playing Sylvie Says, a waiter with peroxide-blond hair approaches the table.

"Hi, I'm Caleb. Have you dined with us before?" he asks. Caleb is in his twenties and has luminous skin, jutting cheekbones, and a tattoo on his neck that looks like a smudged chessboard.

"No," says Jess, beaming up at him. "It's our first time."

"This food looks weird," says Ethan, staring across at another table's meal.

"Well, just try it and you see if you like it, what's the worst that can happen?" I tell him.

"So, you can choose to eat tapas style with a few small plates from here," Caleb says, handing me an open menu, then indicating the left-hand column, "or each pick a larger dish from the right. It's all delicious, so you can't go wrong." His upbeat energy is contagious, and I start to feel more enthusiastic about this Sylvie Says food. "Would you like to know the specials?"

"Sure," I say with a shrug, watching Ethan turn the menu over twice, looking for something he recognizes.

"Would you like me to tell you the specials or rap them?" Caleb asks.

Jess giggles, and Ethan perks up. "Rap!" he shouts.

What follows has all of us laughing as our waiter tries to rap a list of dishes, which in no way rhymes or works as a rap. But he delivers it with such bravado, moving his whole body to an imaginary beat, that he has the whole café applauding.

"Do you always rap the specials?" I ask once he's finished.

"Only for my prettiest customers." He grins at me, then turns on his heel and dances back toward the kitchen.

Once he's out of earshot, Jess leans forward and hisses, "He's got serious rizz. You should ask him out."

"Jess, he's about fourteen," I whisper back.

"Fourteen-year-olds can't work in cafés. He said you were pretty," Jess says, eyes wide with conviction.

"Waiters say that kind of thing to everyone. They're just trying to get a good tip." Caleb is undeniably attractive; twenty-five-year-old me would have clocked him immediately. But I've never asked a stranger out in real life, and someone this young and good-looking feels like an ambitious place to start.

When he brings our food over, Jess nudges me beneath the table. "My mum wants to ask you something."

My throat starts to constrict and I'm filled with a sudden urge to run from the restaurant. "No, I don't, it's fine," I say, shaking my head at Jess, then giving Caleb an embarrassed look.

"Are you single by any chance?" Jess asks him, bold as brass.

"Yes," Caleb says, looking at me. "Don't look so nervous. Whatever the question—the answer is yes," he says, and when he grins, he looks like a rock star. Jess laughs and taps the table with her hands.

"You shouldn't say yes when you don't know what the question is," Ethan points out. "What if the question was 'Will you poke your own eye out with this spoon?'" He holds up his spoon in a threatening manner, and I reach across the table to press it back down onto the table.

"True," says Caleb. "Let's hope that's not the question."

He looks at me and winks. *Is he flirting with me?* Jumping to my feet, I beckon Caleb across to the service area. If this conversation is really happening, I don't want to have it in front of my children.

"Sorry about that," I say, feeling flustered. "I'm a journalist, I'm writing a column where my kids choose people for me to ask out and, well, do you maybe want to have a coffee sometime?" I feel my cheeks flush, but then a rush of adrenaline at the fact that I managed to get the words out.

"Sure," he says, running a hand back through his hair. He looks delighted.

"How old are you?" I ask, smiling now.

"How old are you?" he counters.

"Probably too old for you."

Caleb pulls clean knives and forks from a tray on the counter. "What's your cutoff, age-wise?"

"Well, I'm thirty-three," I fib. "So, I don't know, twenty-six?" I don't know why I just lied. Maybe I want to see if he'll believe I could be thirty-three?

"Lucky for you, I'm twenty-seven," he says.

He's twenty-seven? He doesn't look twenty-seven. But then, stones, glass houses, and all that. Maybe I shouldn't dwell on the age question.

"I'm Anna. You don't have to call me, but here's my number if you're ever bored and fancy a vegan beer. Sorry." I scribble my phone number on a napkin, and Caleb reaches for my hand.

"Stop apologizing. I would love to go out with you."

Now I am the one who feels young and inexperienced, a clueless child who doesn't know how this works, while he is gloriously mature and straightforward.

"Did you give him your number?" Jess asks, once I'm back at the table.

"I did."

She nods, something resembling respect in her eyes. "Way to go, Mum."

GOOGLE SEARCHES:

*Is it bad to lie about your age?*

*Age difference, George Clooney and Amal Clooney*

*What shampoo does Amal Clooney use?*

*Orders shampoo*

# CHAPTER 9

I GET TO THE OFFICE BEFORE WILL. HIS LOVELY NEW ERGONOMIC desk chair is just sitting there, unoccupied. Smiling to myself, I wheel it over to my desk, then swap it with mine. *Am I deserving of a comfy new chair with superior back support? Yes, I am.* Tapping my pen against my lip, I pretend to work, but really, I am strategizing. I've never waged war on a colleague before. What do I even want? An apology? For him to leave? Or do I just want to wipe that smug look off his face?

When Will arrives, I watch him notice his lack of a chair. He glances across the office at me. I stretch my arms out on the armrests, doing a little shimmy to show how comfortable I am. While I can't quite make out his expression, I suspect a hint of a smile. Then he sits down in my old chair, adjusts the height, and pulls out his laptop. A few minutes later I get an e-mail from him.

From: Will@BathLiving.com
To: Anna@BathLiving.com

Anna,

How was fishing? I'm sorry things got heated last time we spoke. It wasn't professional. Please can we discuss the column and how it's going to work? Can I buy you a coffee at Colonna & Small's?

Will

Hmmm. An apology. Not what I was expecting. He hasn't even mentioned the chair. Maybe this is a tactic: invite me out for coffee, then snatch it back as soon as I get up. Either way, I need caffeine. I reply, Come on then, and stand up to put on my coat.

As we walk toward the café, I hand Will a printout of my column about the date with Neil. "If we're going to have a common theme, it makes sense for you to follow my lead," I tell him. "I can't pick and choose who I date. It's up to my children, and honestly, they don't have a huge network."

"Makes sense," he says, reading my column as we walk, making my shoulders tense. *Why is he suddenly being so reasonable?* I know it shouldn't matter what he thinks, I don't need his validation, but I'll concede he does—occasionally—have useful editorial notes. When he laughs, a sparkler of delight flares inside me, and I have to stop myself from asking him which bit he's laughing at.

When we reach Colonna & Small's, Will finds us seats at a narrow wooden table.

"Do you think it's too gruesome?" I ask him.

"No, it's funny, poor guy." He winces in sympathy. "You have four typos."

"Will! It's a first draft," I say, stamping on his foot beneath the table. He laughs and flashes me an amused look.

"Ow. Do you want to read mine?" he asks, pulling up a document on his phone and handing it to me. As I read, I try to maintain a neutral expression. His column is about choosing someone on an app, but there's a running metaphor about fishing. It's about patience, and "using the right line," and the temptation to put the catch of the day back in the hope of finding something better. It's clever, well written, has zero typos, and is the perfect complement to mine. *Damn it.*

"It's good," I say, handing back his phone.

"No feedback? No areas for improvement? I value your editorial judgment."

"Honestly?" I pause, and he nods. "I think the last line is a little crass."

"What?"

"Well, you make it abundantly clear you 'hook, line, and sinker'–ed this woman. Do you really need to spell it out?"

Will sets his elbows on the table and taps a fist against his mouth, his jaw tensed. He's annoyed. *Why can't I just give him a compliment?* It's well written, it's witty, so why do I find it so hard to just say that? I think it's because he *knows* it's good. I suspect he's not looking for notes, he's looking for praise.

"Thanks for your honesty," he says, taking his glasses off, resting one tip against his mouth. I can't help but notice how smooth his lips are. They look perfectly soft, surprisingly full. I briefly imagine running my thumb across his bottom lip, then force myself to look down at my coffee cup, confused by where that thought came from.

"I just don't think it needs those final lines. We get it, you're a stud," I say quickly.

"Why do you have this impression of me?" he says. "That I'm some serial shagger?"

"You're telling me you're not? Will, come on. You wear your date suit at least once a week."

"What's my 'date suit'?" he asks, grinning now.

"The slim-fit vibrant blue one. You always wear it for a first date." I pause, worried he's going to ask why I take so much notice of what he's wearing. "Plus, you crow about it so loudly in the office, everyone within a four-mile radius knows when you're going on a date."

"I'm not necessarily sleeping with everyone I go for a drink with. That line was just a play on words." He drums his fingers against the table, his brows knit together. "And even if I had slept with her, why should that be a bad thing between two consenting adults?" He pauses, leaning back in his chair. "Are you slut-shaming me, Appleby?"

His tone wrong-foots me. "No, not at all. You do you. I'm just thinking of our average reader, how they might perceive things. I think the 'looking for love' narrative you spun Jonathan would play better here."

All at once, his face falls, and he leans his head into his hand.

"What? What's wrong?" I ask in a hushed voice, leaning across the table toward him. I have never seen Will look upset before.

"The truth is, I had my heart broken a few years ago," he says quietly, his face dipped into his hand. "I've found it hard to be open to anything serious since then. I find myself going from meaningless fling to meaningless fling because the risk of anything else feels like more than my heart can handle."

"Oh, Will." I quickly get up and cross over to the other side of the table, sitting on the bench beside him, so I can put an arm around his shoulder. I have never seen this side to Will; I can't believe that beneath all that cocksure confidence, he is willing to cry in a crowded café. Now I feel awful that I've upset him, but also distractingly aware of how firm and broad his shoulders are. "I'm so sorry, I had no idea. I shouldn't have made such a personal comment. You're right, I don't know anything about you, it was wrong of me to assume."

"When I meet someone that I like, after a few dates I just

freeze, shut down. I'll probably be alone forever." Will wipes his eye, and I start gently rubbing his back.

"You're a great guy, Will. You're smart, you're attractive. You're still really young. I know heartbreak can be hard, but I'm sure eventually someone will come along who makes the risk—" I stop talking. Will has tilted his head toward me. He is not crying. He is smiling, a sly grin plastered across his face. "What?"

"You're too easy, Appleby," he says, eyes glinting.

"What? Was that a joke?" I push him away from me, so I can see his expression more clearly.

"I knew it. Beneath that rottweiler exterior you're just a soft little puppy," he says, beaming at me.

"You made all that up?" I ask, feeling my cheeks heat as I gently punch him on the arm.

"Just testing a theory. Seems like you're fine with me sleeping around, as long as it's because of some emotional trauma." He tilts his head, challenging me to deny it.

"You're despicable. I really thought you were upset," I say, narrowing my eyes at him as I sit back down on the other side of the table.

"Sorry to disappoint you." Will holds my gaze, his eyes the color of a forest you could get lost in. "But I think you're right," he says, "it might read better without those lines. I'll edit it before sending it to Jonathan."

I roll my eyes at him, pick up my coat, and stride out of the café. All my instincts about Will were correct, and working with him on this column is going to be a real endurance test.

Back at the office, I nip to the loo, and when I return to my desk, the chair is gone. In its place sits an overturned wastepaper basket. Resisting the urge to laugh, I look across at Will, but he's sitting in the chair, studiously ignoring me.

I think today I might have lost the battle, but the war is not over.

---

THAT AFTERNOON, THE whole editorial team has a meeting in the living room. Jonathan gushes about the columns Will and I have submitted. They're "just what the magazine needs," and he "can't wait to see what we come up with next." Will swells with pride. I can see him physically expanding, like a silverback gorilla puffing out its chest. I want to reach over and pop him with a pin.

"I'm glad I'll have something fresh to show Crispin. He's coming to the office next week." Jonathan pulls a cartoon grimace. "He's going to reinterview everyone, give people a chance to prove how indispensable they are." Jonathan chuckles, though I don't see how this is funny. "You'll all be fine." He holds out a hand toward us. "He needs local journalists, it will be accounts and marketing who bear the brunt of it." He pauses, and a few of the more junior writers exchange worried looks. "If it's any consolation, he's cut my Friday afternoon cocktail budget to the nub. Bleak times, bleak times."

Jonathan's reassurances are anything but reassuring. A newly framed "Keep Calm and Carry On" poster has appeared on the wall in the main office, and I suspect it's having the opposite effect on morale. I've also noticed Jonathan's postprandial sherry, which he usually indulges in at around three o'clock, is now being consumed at eleven a.m. He's a stickler for convention and has told me it's "unseemly" to have a drink before "the sun is over the yardarm." I don't know what this translates to in normal language, but I doubt it's eleven a.m.

"In any case, back to today's business. What's on everyone's agenda next week?" Jonathan asks, sitting up straighter in his chair and fiddling with his tie. "Anna, are you still covering Hay this weekend?"

"Yes, of course," I say, surprised he needs to ask. I attend the Hay literary festival every year. It's only a two-hour drive from

Bath, and it's a highlight of the events calendar for me. Two whole days of book talks and panel discussions. It is heaven. I had to swap two weekends around with Dan to make it work, and now I owe him one in the favor bank, but it will be worth it.

"Excellent. I loved how you covered it last year," Jonathan says. "Are you imagining a double-page spread, or could you stretch to four? You had an embarrassment of riches last time."

I blush and take a breath to answer.

"I'm going too," says Will, casually raising his pen in the air.

"What?" I ask, a little too sharply.

"I've been asked to host a panel, stepping in for someone who dropped out," he says, knitting his fingers, then reaching both hands behind his head, as though he's having a nice relaxing time at the beach.

"What? What panel? Why?" I ask, possibly too aggressively. People in the room look back and forth between us.

"One of the organizers called," Will explains. "They were looking for a local journalist who knows about books; I said I'd do it. Come along if you like?" His face is a picture of innocence.

Verbal darts ping inside my mouth, but I swallow them down. Who called, and why didn't Will put them through to me? He knows I cover arts and culture. He's purposely muscling in on my turf *again*.

"Will, that's excellent news—you're a credit to us, you really are," Jonathan says, standing up and walking across the room to pull out his drinks trolley. "Anna, let's stick with two pages for your coverage of the festival. Will, could you pen a couple of pages about this panel? Maybe get Anna to take a few pictures of you in action?"

"Absolutely," says Will, then he turns to me. "We could drive up together if you like, save on petrol." His mouth is all friendly smiles, but his eyes are a gloating green.

"I'll have to check my schedule," I say evasively, feeling my neck prickle with heat. There's a snapping sound and I look down to see it was the nib of my pencil, pressing too hard into my notepad.

AFTER THE MEETING, Steph finds me in the loos washing my hands in cold water, trying to dampen my inner rage.

"It wasn't a cold call, you know, this person who offered Will the gig in Hay," she says, handing me a paper towel.

"Oh? What was it then?" I ask. If there's gossip to know, Steph will know it.

"Some woman who fancies him. A friend of a friend introduced them in London. He wasn't interested, until he found out she worked for the literary festival. The panel is being livestreamed; he probably sees himself as the next host of BBC's *Beneath the Covers*." Steph shakes her head, then sighs. "I bet he'll get it too."

"He's unbearable," I mutter.

"Hot though, right?" she says, winking at me, and I flick my wet hands at her until she starts laughing. "By the way, Kelly, Karl, and I are going out tonight. You want to come?"

"I can't. But thank you."

"Anna, you never come out," she says, then puts her hands together, pleading with me. "Next time?"

I pause, realizing I just said no as a reflex. "Maybe," I say, then give her a genuine smile.

AS I'M LEAVING the office, Will intercepts me at the door.

"Shall I pick you up from yours tomorrow morning?" he asks sweetly, as though he's suggested taking me on a picnic to Cotton Candy Land.

"I'd rather drive separately, but thanks."

"That's interesting," he says, looking like someone who's

about to make a winning move in a game of chess. "Only because I seem to remember a column you wrote that highlighted people's reluctance to car-share as one of the main reasons we have a traffic problem in Bath."

*Checkmate. Damn him.* "Fine, we'll go together, in my car. I will drive," I say.

"There's more space in mine," he says.

"I have a Volvo estate, so I doubt it."

"Okay, my car is nicer," he says, his mouth curling into a boyish grin.

"I don't want to be stranded if you decide to leave early."

"We'll come back whenever it suits you. And we can brainstorm next week's column in the car."

I rack my brain for another excuse, but nothing is forthcoming. "Fine," I say, relenting. "I'll text you my address." He saunters away, and my gaze is drawn down to the curve of his firm physique in the perfectly tailored trousers he's wearing. Snapping my eyes away, I chastise myself for such an inappropriate eye line. *Why is it always the biggest arses who have the most incredible arses?* Someone's probably written a thesis on it, where gluteal firmness is inversely proportional to agreeableness of personality. Either way, I'm not relishing the prospect of spending a two-hour car journey with such a perfect arse.

GOOGLE SEARCHES:

*What time does "the sun pass over the yardarm"?*

*What's a yardarm?*

*Do Paul Hollywood or Sam Heughan narrate any audiobooks?*

# CHAPTER 10

THAT EVENING, AS I'M PUTTING DOWN FOOD FOR KATNISS, I GET A message from Neil.

Neil Bradshaw

**Sorry our date got cut short on Sunday. Can I take you out for dinner next week? Nx.**

Oh no, now I'll have to think of an excuse. I could say work's too busy, invent some long-term ailment or fish allergy? In the end I go with:

Anna Appleby

**Hi Neil, thanks again for Sunday, I think on reflection I am not quite ready to date. So sorry again about the accident. Has your cheek recovered?**

The only good thing about divorce is you can use it as a get-out-of-jail-free card.

He replies immediately.

Neil Bradshaw

**The wound got slightly infected. I'm on antibiotics, no biggie. Let me know if you ever change your mind. N. 👍🙏**

Right, new rule: no dating any parents from school, it's just too awkward. My phone pings again; this time it's a message from an unknown number.

Unknown Number

**Hey Anna. Want to go to a house party tonight? Caleb.**

*Tonight, as in now?* It's already eight o'clock. My first thought is, obviously, no. I'm in my pajamas, I don't have childcare. But as I'm about to politely decline, Lottie calls and I end up telling her about the charismatic young waiter I gave my number to.

"You have to go! You'll only stay up late watching TV and googling who celebrities are married to." She pauses. I can't deny it. I have a problem. "I'll come and sleep at yours, you can stay out as late as you like," she offers, and now I've run out of excuses.

Half an hour later, my sister is sitting on my bed helping me find a "house party"–appropriate outfit. I settle on a short silver skirt that I bought at a vintage market and have never had the opportunity to wear, paired with a fitted, black cashmere jumper and flat black boots. Caleb sends me the address for the house party and suggests we meet there at ten. *Ten!?*

"All the young people go out late," Lottie reassures me. "Ten is early."

"Not for me," I say with a groan.

Lottie looks at me in the mirror, a fond expression on her face. "I love this, but maybe not these boots."

"What's wrong with the boots?" I ask, offended.

"They're a bit . . . sensible," Lottie says, kneeling down to riffle through my shoe rack.

"Well, I'm going to have to walk, so it makes sense to be comfortable. I'm hardly going to wear—" Lottie is holding up a pair of gold high heels I don't remember buying. "No, absolutely not."

"Fine," Lottie says, relenting, "wear the sensible shoes tonight, but one day, you have to wear these, they're fabulous." Then she gets to her feet and rubs my back. "I love this. How many times have you helped me get ready for a date? I don't think I've ever helped you. Do you remember when I was fifteen, I had a cinema date with Fergus Gibson from the year above? You let me wear your brand-new designer jeans." She lets out a happy sigh. "I've never loved you more."

"Something tells me you're more excited about this date than I am," I say, giving her a teasing look.

"Getting ready is the best part! All that anticipation of what might happen. I miss that," she says wistfully.

As I watch Lottie riffle through my wardrobe, I feel a tightening knot in my stomach.

*Is there something wrong with me? Why can't I feel excited?* The main emotions this dating column has elicited in me are fear and anxiety.

"You've dated so much more than I have," I tell Lottie. "When relationships ended, you were so good at picking yourself up and getting back out there; I always admired that about you. You always seemed so certain that true love was just around the corner."

"And it was," she says with a lovesick grin. "It just took me a little longer to find it." She pauses. "You're going to find it again. I know you will." She reaches out to stroke my cheek. "Now, have you shaved your legs?"

"Lottie, please. What do you think is going to happen here?"

"Isn't it best to be prepared for all eventualities?" she asks, watching me in the reflection of the mirror.

"I think the best preparation here is for me to have a strong cup of coffee."

In the kitchen, the coffee machine is overflowing with used pods, so I empty it into the bin. The bin is full, so I push the contents down, and my hand lands on a shopping bag that I don't recognize. Curious, I open the bag and find all of Jess's Sylvanian Families, small woodland animals dressed in clothes. I let out a gasp, as though I've stumbled upon a severed foot. These are Jess's most treasured toys. I show the bag to Lottie.

Lottie frowns, understanding the significance. "Surely, she can't have meant to throw those away?"

I shake my head in disbelief. "We donated a load of old toys recently, but she loves these, she makes those little stop-motion videos with them," I say, rescuing the bag, then wiping off the outside with a cloth. "Is this it, the end of her childhood?" I ask, pulling out a small hedgehog wearing dungarees, feeling a heavy tug of nostalgia.

"Oh no, do you think she's going to get a boyfriend and start vaping?" Lottie asks.

"I hope not." We transfer the little figures into a new bag, then I stuff the old bag in the bin and the toys in a cupboard above the fridge. I'll have to deal with this later.

THE HOUSE PARTY is in a flat near Oldfield Park, and since I don't want to risk arriving before Caleb, I don't get there until ten thirty. I ring the bell, my heart racing, and someone buzzes me in without even asking who I am. The flat is scruffy, with a studenty vibe. The sparse furniture looks like it was salvaged from a yard sale, there are bikes crammed into the hall, and the carpet looks older than anyone at the party.

"Hi, I'm looking for Caleb?" I ask a girl with green sparkly eye shadow, but she just shrugs and then glances down at my boots.

"Nice boots," she says, and I have no idea if she's being sarcastic or not.

"Thanks," I say doubtfully. The flat isn't big and there aren't many people here, so I quickly locate Caleb opening a beer in the kitchen.

"Hey," he says, his face creasing into an enormous smile.

"Hey."

"You look great, I'm so glad you could come," Caleb says, fishing a beer from a bucket full of ice and handing it to me. I clutch it, hoping the cold might still my nerves. I don't know why I'm so on edge, you'd think I'd never been to a house party before.

Caleb introduces me to the people who live here: Zeek, with the skin pallor of someone who doesn't get enough sunlight, dressed in jeans and a tie-dye T-shirt. Jasmine, braless in a halter top with impossibly pert boobs and plump, youthful cheeks. Coco, of ambiguous gender, who sports a buzz cut and bright blue lipstick, then Chai, with a mane of curly black hair skimming her bare midriff and navel piercing. I have to stop myself from staring at this willowy flame of youthful perfection, but I am an aging moth, transfixed.

"You okay?" Caleb asks, touching a hand to my arm. I nod, anxious that he's noticed my anxiety. "We're early. Most people won't come until midnight."

*Midnight? I hope he's not expecting me to stay until midnight.* Caleb takes my hand and leads me through to the living room, grabbing three Ping-Pong balls from a fruit bowl on the sideboard, then setting out a row of plastic cups on the windowsill.

"How many do you think you can land?" he asks, handing me a ball. Gingerly, I aim and take my best shot. Out of three, I'm delighted when the last one goes in; several people cheer, then it's Caleb's turn, and he lands all three. Caleb spins me around in a victory dance, genuinely delighted. There's something so assured in the way he takes my hand; he is entirely unselfconscious. I start to relax. *Maybe this will be fine.* Neil and those men from the apps all had a world-weariness about them—as though they had seen what life had to offer and were disappointed. Caleb, by contrast, is like a child with a treasure map, everything an opportunity for adventure. *Am I world-weary? Is that why I focus on the risk of humiliation and disappointment rather than delight in the joy of possibility?*

"I want to show you something," Caleb says, finally tiring of our game and leading me up a stairwell, through a fire escape, and out onto the roof. Here, we find the most amazing view out over the city, Bath Abbey lit up in the distance.

"Oh wow, what a view."

He takes off his jumper, lays it on the roof, then beckons for me to sit down. "So, Anna, tell me your dreams. What do you want out of this life? What does life want out of you?" he asks, running a hand through his bright blond hair.

"What does life want out of me?" I repeat in bemusement. *I am definitely world-weary.*

"Yeah. What's your thing?"

"My thing? Well, I work as a journalist," I tell him. "I've got two kids, who you met. Last night I had a dream about climbing a ladder covered in pigeons. I have a lot of dreams about pigeons for some reason."

Caleb laughs. "You're funny. So, journalism, is that your calling?" he asks, and I shrug. He raises both arms toward the stars, exposing a slim, taut navel as his T-shirt rises up. "I'm studying ecology management—I think that's what the world wants out of me, to help on a practical level, to till the soil like our ancestors, but like, in a macro way."

"I see," I say, though I don't see at all.

"What's your big want?" he asks, shaking his hands at the sky.

I pause, looking out over the city, at all the lights in all the windows. Each one a person with their own hopes and fears, dreams and disappointments.

"I think I just want to get through the day without anything bad happening," I tell him. "Is that enough? I want my kids to be happy, I want them to do well at school, I want to keep my job so I can provide for them."

"That's a lot of wants for your kids," Caleb says, pressing his hands together and then twisting his body. For a moment I think he's praying, but then I realize he's stretching. "What about *you*?" He taps his joined fingers against my shoulder. His eyes are sincere, as though he really does want to know.

"I suppose I want to laugh again, I want some of the lightness back. I want my life not to be over when I'm barely halfway through. I want to not feel like I'm a failure because I got divorced." I pause to look at him, and he shifts his body around to face me rather than the skyline. "Do you remember those books where you could choose your own destiny by skipping to various pages?"

"Like select your own story on a video game?" he asks.

"Yes, something like that. I feel like I must have chosen the wrong path at some point, that I should go back and read the book again, make different choices."

"What would you change?" he asks, fiddling with a pendant around his neck.

"I don't know. Probably nothing. I wouldn't not have met my ex, I wouldn't not have had my children. There were plenty of good times." I pause. "I guess I always hoped I'd get to be one of those old couples you see laughing and holding hands in their eighties. Isn't that the ending most people want for themselves? I wish I'd gotten to fall further into love rather than out of it."

"That doesn't sound like something you had any agency over," Caleb says. "You can't regret things that are out of your control."

"True." I nod, surprised by his considered response. He reaches out to hold my hand, then leans in to kiss my cheek, and it doesn't feel like a move, it feels like a kindness.

"What does this mean?" I ask, pointing to the tattoo on his forearm. "Is it an ampersand?"

He nods. "It symbolizes how nothing lasts. Unlike the infinity symbol, this says there will be an end, a new beginning, a next chapter, good or bad." His eyes flit across to my face. He pauses, rubbing his forearm. "You think it's cheesy?"

"No, I like it," I say, shaking my head, all cynicism uncharacteristically dormant. Though I'm not really into tattoos, I realize that on Caleb, I genuinely like it. It suits him and I appreciate the sentiment.

"Do you have tatts?" he asks, then grins. "Let me guess." He closes his eyes, then says, "A small rose on your right shoulder blade."

"No, never got any," I tell him with a smile.

"Jasmine does tattoos, she's amazing at stick and poke. I'm sure she'd do you one if you wanted."

"Maybe," I say, though what I mean is, "No way, not in a million years."

When we get back downstairs, the party is heaving. Every surface has someone occupying it. Even though it's late, I'm now wide awake. When Zeek offers me a brownie from a golden biscuit tin, I gladly take one because dinner with the kids feels like a distant memory. The brownie is claggy with a soily aftertaste, but now I've drunk enough beer not to care.

As the music shifts to something more up-tempo, Caleb pulls me up to dance. Looking me in the eye, he says, "You're great," with a beaming smile. I can't think of the last time anyone said something that nice to me. My head spins as Caleb pulls me close in a dance. I let him, shutting off the self-conscious part of my brain that's telling me I haven't been this close to a man who isn't Dan in seventeen years. It feels nice, but also strange. *You're overthinking everything,* I tell myself. *Just relax.*

Over the next few hours, Caleb and his friends sweep me up

in their music, their energy, and their optimism. Having lost all desire to go home to bed, I find myself laughing at everything, though it's not clear what's so funny. My heart is pounding.

"I feel a bit strange," I confide to Caleb as we tire of dancing and sit down on a scruffy, torn sofa.

"That will be the brownies kicking in," he tells me. "Zeek makes them strong."

"Brownies? Why, what was in them?" I ask, feeling my forehead bead with sweat.

"Pot. Chill, it's all good." Caleb squeezes my shoulder.

Well, I've taken it now, there's nothing to do but go with it. "I'm having the best time," I tell Caleb.

"Me too," he says. Then he leans in to kiss my cheek again. It's chaste, and sweet, and makes me smile. I rest my head on his shoulder as he wraps an arm around me. I feel like a teenager, sitting on this shabby couch, flirting with a hot boy. *This is great. This is what I've been missing. My twenties weren't that long ago, I am still that person inside, I can be that person again.*

Soon we're dancing, sweaty and wild and unselfconscious. Time becomes stretchy. I'm talking to Jasmine about her tattoo business; I'm on the balcony calling Dan. I feel confident and strong, like this is the best possible time to tell him I want him to wash the children's clothes, that I am not a laundry service. I'm in the kitchen, Caleb is making me a cheesy toastie, there are bottles and cans strewn everywhere, but we just push them out of the way, giggling as hot cheese runs out of the sandwich and onto our hands. Jasmine is here. A great idea. An ampersand on my inner arm. Yes, yes. Just the same as Caleb's. I'm sure, *I'm sure.* A pain that's not unpleasant. More music, more dancing, someone hands me a tequila shot. My stomach tells me to stop, but this is the most fun I've had in years.

Caleb squeezes my hand and pulls me up from the living room sofa. *How did I get back here?*

"Let's get you some air," he says, his pupils huge.

"Sure," I say, leaning into him, gripping his hand in mine, feeling glad I have something to hold on to while I try to put one foot in front of the other. How did I get so wasted? Caleb leads me back to the roof, the cold night air hitting me with a sobering slap. We find a group of people all vaping or passing around rollies. Caleb asks them to make room so we can join the circle.

"You okay?" Caleb asks, leaning his chin against my shoulder, and I nod. "If you're going to puke, just let me know, I'll grab you a bucket." He reaches out to rub my back and in the dim recesses of my mind I make a note: if I ever fall in love again, I hope it's with someone who will find me a bucket to be sick in.

"If there's a God, do you think he knows he's God?" someone in the circle asks, a girl wearing a velvet headband and a T-shirt that reads *No Problemo*. "Or do you think God is more of an insentient power?"

People contemplate this for a while, nodding, as though this girl has asked something deeply profound.

"If there's a God, I don't think they're gendered," says Jasmine, pressing her hands together.

"I don't know how anyone can believe in a God when innocent children are dying in war every single day," says the girl next to Jasmine. She looks young enough to be my daughter, with a mouth full of braces and a smattering of acne on her forehead. "Like, who can see that kind of suffering and still believe in a higher power who would allow that?"

"Religion is an elaborate thought conspiracy, designed to oppress the masses," says Zeek, and several people make noises of agreement.

"The two arms of oppression, religion and the patriarchy," says someone else.

"I don't agree. How can you look at a shell with the Fibonacci spiral, or a dragonfly mating in midair, and believe that came into being by accident?" Coco says, voice light and ethereal. They hold up their hands as though holding an imaginary orb. "God is beauty. God is love."

"Intelligent design," Caleb says. "I get that."

It has been many, *many* years since I last sat around and debated the existence of God. On the one hand I admire their ambition—it beats talking about the school run or house renovations—but there's also something painfully naïve about it. Do they really think they're going to solve the mysteries of the universe, wasted, at three in the morning? *Shit, is it three in the morning?*

"What do you think, Anna?" Caleb asks, turning to me. Everyone in the circle looks in my direction. They want to know what I think. *What do I think?* There are many things in life I haven't made up my mind about yet: whether Apple products are *really* worth the money, who the best Batman is (Ethan swears it's Robert Pattinson), and whether I believe in God. I keep thinking I will get around to deciding these things, that I will trial a different smartphone, that I will take a weekend and watch all the Batman movies back-to-back, but somehow it never feels like a good use of time. So, for now, I will maintain my brand loyalty to Apple, I'll take an uneducated guess at Christian Bale, and as for God—I remain undecided.

"I think it's late. I think I'm drunk. I should go home," I say, not wanting to rain on anyone's parade by telling them what I really think—that they're recycling well-worn ideas debated for as long as humans have existed. How everyone's time would be better spent studying, trying to get a decent job, saving for a house deposit, and contributing to a decent pension scheme. I must be sobering up if I'm thinking about pension schemes.

As I stand, Caleb jumps up to follow me and I wave goodbye to everyone in the philosophy circle. Downstairs I feel wobbly on my feet, the hallway spinning.

"You can crash here if you like," Caleb offers. He reaches out to hold my hand, and I lean into him.

"I should get back," I say, but my legs are having a hard time holding me.

"Grab a few hours' kip, there's loads of room." Caleb pushes open a door with his foot. On the other side is a bedroom; the walls are covered in Moroccan-style throws and posters of Frank Ocean and Harry Styles. A girl is passed out on one side of the bed in her clothes. I don't know when I last "crashed" anywhere, but the decision is now out of my hands, because my legs are taking me to the bed in a desperate bid to be horizontal. *Just a quick nap, then I'll call a cab.*

WHEN I WAKE up, my head is pounding and I have no idea where I am. When I find limbs draped across my body, like a complex human seat belt, my first thought is that my children are in bed with me. But once my eyes focus, I see that this is not my bed, these are not my children. What might have felt warm and cozy a minute ago now feels like an intolerable invasion of my personal space. I am not comfortable sharing a bed with—I pause to count—four people I don't know. Slowly extracting myself from the Jenga game of body parts, I slide out at the bottom of the bed.

The house is quiet, the party over. I find a bathroom, and my stomach clenches as I see the state of the place. Cigarette butts in the sink, vomit on the floor, a blocked toilet. *Who lives like this?* But I know the answer—students, students live like this. I decide to wait for my bathroom at home. Back in the corridor, I check my phone and see several missed calls from Lottie, then two messages asking if I'm okay. Shit. I quickly text her back, telling her I'm fine and on my way home.

Pulling up a taxi app, I see Caleb leaning against a wall, vaping. He smiles when he sees me, and I feel reassured after the horror of the bathroom. My eyes fall on his long eyelashes. He really is very pretty. Perhaps too pretty.

"Hey."

"Hey. You're still awake," I say, stating the obvious.

"Took some uppers, couldn't sleep," he says, his eyes firing with tired energy. "You leaving? Can I call you?"

"Thank you for inviting me, I had fun. But I'm not thirty-three, I'm thirty-eight. I'm sorry, I don't know why I lied," I say, biting my lip.

"I'm not twenty-seven either," he says, stretching his arms in a full-body yawn.

"Right."

"Closer to twenty-two."

*Twenty-two. Shit.* "I see." I swallow hard, relieved nothing happened between us.

"You don't look that old, you're hot," he says. He's sweet, but right now I feel every one of my thirty-eight years. But I'm also fine with it. I am not twenty-two anymore, and I don't want to be. I want to sleep in my own bed, in clean sheets, and use my own bathroom. I want to get to bed at a reasonable hour and be able to function in the morning.

"I think this was more of a one-off," I say, reaching for his hand.

"Fair enough," he says, putting his vape into a pocket and squeezing my hand back. "I enjoyed buzzin' with you, Anna."

"Thank you for being so lovely to me," I tell him.

"You won't forget it." He nods down at my arm, where I see an inky smudge. Lifting my arm toward my face, I see the black lines of a tattoo, pink and raw around the edges. An ampersand, etched onto my forearm. *What? You've got to be kidding me.* "Jasmine usually charges two hundred quid for those," Caleb says. The sight of it makes me feel nauseous. *How the hell am I going to explain this to my children?*

WHEN I GET home, it's five in the morning. I find Lottie asleep on the pullout on Ethan's floor. He must have had a bad dream. I can't believe I left my pregnant sister to deal with my children while I was out taking drugs and getting tattoos. Finding a blanket, I lay it over Lottie, watching her for a moment. She has all this ahead of her, becoming a mother, the recalibration of her identity, her marriage. She has always been such an idealist when it comes to love, and as I tuck the blanket over her, I make a silent prayer: *I hope you never lose that.*

Walking back across the landing to my bedroom, I stand in the doorway and stare at the king-sized bed I shared with Dan for over a decade. His side of the bed is empty, but with Lottie having slept in it, it looks as though he just left. Will this house always be haunted by him? All I want to do is fall into bed, but now I'm seized by an urge to rearrange the furniture. I move Dan's bedside table, making way to shift the bed out of the middle of the room and up against the window, covering the ghost of the coffee stain on the carpet. It's a small change, but when I lie in the middle of the bed, looking up through the dormer window from a different angle, it feels significant.

GOOGLE SEARCHES:

Tattoo removal

Cheap and painless tattoo removal

How long do effects of marijuana last?

# CHAPTER 11

"ANNA, I NEED TO GO. JESUS, YOU SMELL TERRIBLE. HAVE A SHOWER before Dan gets here, won't you?" Lottie's voice wakes me up.

"Dan's here?" I come to asking, wondering why everything in the room is in the wrong place.

"Not yet. He's coming to walk the kids to school. You said you had a work trip?"

"Work trip?" *Shit. Will Havers is coming here, and so is Dan. No, no, no.*

"Good night, was it?" Lottie says, grinning at me.

"Sorry I got in so late. What happened with Ethan?"

"He had a bad dream, so I suggested a sleepover. Don't apologize. I'm glad you went out, tell me all about it later, now I have to run, I have a client meeting." Lottie kisses me on the head just as Ethan comes in to tell me he can't find his PE kit, quickly followed by Jess, who says she's lost her violin music and then blames Ethan for moving it. I have a thumping headache, an acrid taste in my mouth, an urgent thirst, and a looming sense of remorse.

No time to shower or drink water. I look for violin music, throw PE kit in the dryer, start to make a packed lunch for Ethan, realize there's no bread, try to make a lunch out of crackers and an apple, remember Ethan has gone off apples, adjudicate a fight over who has control of the music system, find a plaster to hide my tattoo—I can't have that conversation right now—and answer a flurry of questions from Jess about where I was last night. I mumble, "Caleb called, he was lovely but too young. Um, four out of six."

"There's no milk," Jess groans, picking up her phone from the sideboard.

"Jess, do you need to be on your phone over breakfast?" I ask.

"Everyone shares homework over WhatsApp, I'm checking what I need to hand in today!" she says, staring at me with unblinking eyes, as though this was the stupidest question imaginable.

"Why are you wearing that plaster?" Ethan asks.

"Just a graze," I tell him, pulling down my sleeve. The doorbell rings; saved by the bell. This is why I shouldn't drink. The prospect of talking to Dan about logistics with a brain that feels like spaghetti, especially now that he's all smug and teetotal, is too much. But when I open the front door, it isn't Dan, it's Will. He's standing on my doorstep, hands in his pockets, a huge smile on his fresh, well-rested, irritatingly perfect face.

"Morning!" he says, his voice chiming like the opening bars of a Christmas tune.

"I'm not ready," I say with a frown. His eyes dart down, then he blinks rapidly before averting his gaze. It's only then that I realize what I'm wearing; short gym shorts and an oversized tee that has been washed so many times it's almost see-through.

"Don't worry, I'm early," he says, no apology. I can hardly leave him waiting on the doorstep, but the last thing I want to do is invite him into my home, to witness firsthand the chaos of my existence.

"I just need to get my kids to school . . ." I pause, then add with a heavy sigh, "Do you want to come in?" I hope he will take the sigh as a hint and offer to wait in the car, but he doesn't. He takes off his long camel coat, hangs it on a hall peg, then strides past me into the kitchen.

"Jess, Ethan, this is my colleague Will," I explain, grabbing a cardigan and pulling it on over my skimpy outfit. The children both stare at Will as though they've never seen an adult human male before.

"Hi?" Will says, raising his hand in a wave. "Sorry to intrude on breakfast."

Jess looks back and forth between Will and me. I know what she's thinking, she's thinking, *Why didn't you tell us about this hot Ken doll you work with?*, and I try to communicate with my eyes, "He might look pretty but he's a pain in the arse." It's a lot of nuance for a look.

"Mum's hungover," Jess tells Will.

"Jess, I am not hungover," I say sharply. "I am just insufficiently rested."

"She had a date last night," Ethan adds. "She woke me up moving furniture. The whole house was shaking."

"The whole house was shaking?" says Will, raising an eyebrow at me, his eyes twinkling with delight.

My face burns with embarrassment, and I hide in the fridge, looking for milk that I know isn't there. "Here, oat milk, vegan friendly," I say, handing it to Jess for her cereal. There's a pause as she considers the oat milk. I worry she's going to launch into a rant about how I never buy enough milk for the week, but the vegan card works, and she happily pours it over her Shreddies. Then I suddenly remember the Sylvanian Families I found in the bin and feel like bursting into tears. I take a moment to pause, to stop what I'm doing and look at my daughter.

"Are you okay?" I ask softly, putting my arm around Jess and kissing her hair, but she just turns to gives me a strange look.

"Yes. Are you?" she asks, shaking her head, pausing her spoon in midair before lifting it to her mouth. Clearly, this isn't the time to discuss it.

"Coffee?" I ask Will, filling the Nespresso machine with water.

"I'm good," he says, half-raising a palm. It doesn't feel like an "I'm good, I don't want coffee," it feels like an "I'm good, you've got your hands full and don't look capable of doing an extra task." As he raises his hand, I glimpse a monogrammed *WH* on the *inside* of his shirtsleeve. *Is everything he owns monogrammed?* It feels so tacky and at odds with his otherwise impeccable fashion sense.

"Do you write for the magazine too?" Ethan asks Will.

"Yes. I started out penning the food column, but recently I've been diversifying, taking on a more varied role to strengthen my portfolio." I can't help smiling because Will is talking to my seven-year-old as though he's at a job interview.

"Do you get to eat loads? How come you're not fat?" Ethan asks, and Will laughs.

"Ethan!" I cry, giving him a warning look.

"It's a constant challenge," Will says with a smile.

"Are you an expert on every food then?" Ethan asks. "Like, could you do a blind taste test with potatoes? I could do crisps, I'm brilliant at crisps."

I hand Ethan a plate of toast, spread messily with peanut butter. "That's not really what restaurant reviewers do," I explain.

"I'd back myself in a blind potato test," Will says, pushing out his chest to stand even taller.

"Will backs himself in most things," I can't help adding as I load the dishwasher with breakfast bowls, then set it running.

"Which is the best, Burger King or McDonald's?" Ethan asks, and Will laughs again. It's a warm, rich laugh that makes me think of hearty Irishmen drinking Guinness around a stone fireplace.

"Those are not the kind of restaurants Will writes about," I explain. Ethan looks disappointed.

"I'd go to Burger King for the Whopper, then head over to McDonald's for the fries and a Filet-O-Fish," Will says, clapping his hands together once. Ethan looks delighted with this answer.

"Ethan, breakfast." I nudge him as I rush around the kitchen throwing water bottles, homework, and snacks into book bags. Jess can sort herself out now, in terms of what she needs for school, but Ethan would go to school barefoot if I didn't remind him to put his shoes on. I brush my hair back into a ponytail, painfully aware that Will is witnessing me in "frazzled mum mode."

"This isn't a normal morning," I explain, rolling my eyes around the room before landing them on Will. "It's not usually this crazy."

"Yes, it is," says Ethan.

"Mum can't handle late nights," Jess tells Will, as though she's an adult confiding about her errant child. I have a fleeting image of Zeek, Coco, and Jasmine waking up this morning in their sprightly twenty-something-year-old bodies, having no one to sort out but themselves. I feel a brief pang of jealousy. Then I remember the state of their bathroom and the jealousy evaporates.

"I'm sorry about this," I apologize again to Will, but he only looks amused. He's bought a ticket for "Anna's shit show life" and is enjoying his role as ghoulish voyeur.

"What's your favorite color?" Ethan asks Will.

"Blue."

"Favorite animal?" Ethan asks.

"Ethan," I say, shaking my head, "stop interrogating him."

"Bears."

"Good one!" Ethan says, nodding.

"What's yours?" Will asks him.

"Duck, then lemur, then armadillo. It was armadillos first, but then I changed it."

"What's your mum's favorite?" Will asks.

"Cats," Ethan says, turning up his nose as though this is boring.

"What are her favorite flowers?" Will asks.

"Peonies," Jess tells him, and I look back and forth between them in bemusement.

The doorbell rings and I'm glad that for once, Dan isn't running late.

"Morning," Dan says as I open the door. He's wearing a too-tight Aertex, tucked into chinos, and his face is unusually somber.

"Kids, Dad's here!" I call back into the kitchen.

"You okay?" Dan asks, narrowing his eyes at me.

"Sure, why?" I run a hand over my face, worried there might be a stray blob of peanut butter hanging from one nostril. But before he can answer, the kids are in the hall throwing on their coats and shoes and I'm caught up in the cyclone of "leaving the house."

"See you Sunday, Mum," yells Jess.

"Love you," says Ethan, enveloping my waist in a bear hug, as I cover his head with kisses. "Feel better."

"Can you wait on the street for a second?" Dan asks Jess and Ethan once they're out of the front door. "I need to have a word with your mother."

This does not sound good. "This isn't a great time," I say, nodding toward the door, hoping my subtle head movement will convey that I have a colleague waiting in the kitchen who really does not need to hear whatever grievance Dan has this morning.

"Two a.m. is also not a good time, Anna." Dan's hard stare shifts to something resembling pity. "I know you're struggling with this, but you can't call me at all hours of the night. It's not fair on me and it's certainly not fair on Sylvie."

"I called you?" I ask weakly. I don't remember calling him,

but since I don't remember getting a tattoo, it stands to reason I could have made some phone calls too.

"Three voicemails, most of them unintelligible." He pauses, sighs, then gives me his "disappointed" face. "If you're finding things hard, maybe you shouldn't drink so much. It's not good for the children to see you so"—he pauses, weighing his words—"unhinged."

"Unhinged?" I parrot.

"I can see how this might be challenging for you. But I don't want to have to put a time window on when it's appropriate for you to call me and when it's not. I'm proud of how unboundaried we are. We put the work in and it's better for everyone if we can all get along."

What are these words coming out of Dan's mouth? "Put the work in," "unboundaried"? These are not words I have ever heard Dan say. *Has he been having therapy?* Before I can muster a response, Dan puts a hand on my shoulder, then leans in to say, "And I say this in the spirit of friendship, but you shouldn't give up on your appearance. You need to show up for yourself." He taps his heart, gives me another pitying, intense gaze, then bounds off down the steps in his too-snug chinos.

My body starts to tremble. I don't know whether I'm shaking with rage, or hangover, or an infection from my unsterilized tattoo, but for a minute I'm unable to move because every part of me thrums. Putting a hand over my chest, I take five deep breaths to try to steady myself. Back in the kitchen, Will looks at the floor; I take that to mean he heard the whole conversation.

"Sorry about that. You weren't meant to be here this early, so . . ." I trail off. "You'll have to give me a minute." I run upstairs, clamping my teeth to stop the tears. Running a brush through my hair, I wipe away last night's mascara from beneath my eyes, have a quick shower, then throw on my favorite jeans and green silk blouse. Glancing in the mirror, I don't think I look too bad, considering. There's a flush to my cheeks from the hot shower, and my eyes look brighter than I feel. Grabbing the weekend bag I packed after dinner, I hurry back downstairs, aware I'm now keeping Will waiting.

"Ready?" I ask. Will is standing in the hall and opens the front door for me. He's only being courteous, but even this irritates me. This is *my* house; I don't need anyone opening *my* door for me. And I don't need people coming into *my* house and telling me I look like shit. Will nods his head toward a sports car, an MG parked on the road. "It's my dad's, I borrowed it," he explains. "I thought we could travel in style."

"Cozy," I say diplomatically. I've never understood people's interest in vintage cars. They're more likely to break, and they have none of the right sockets for charging your phone, but as I climb into the passenger seat, I'll admit something about this car—the shape of it, the smell of old leather—conjures a spirit of adventure.

We travel in silence until we're on the main road out of Bath. Will must sense my need for quiet as he doesn't try to make small talk. Scrolling through my phone, I view my call history and sent e-mails, checking whether there is anything else I did last night that I need to apologize for. There's an e-mail from Amazon confirming an online order for a toastie machine. Wow, drunk me cannot be trusted.

"Do you want to talk about it?" Will asks, his fingers tapping the steering wheel.

"About what?" I ask, putting my phone away.

"Whatever you like, your date last night, your patronizing ex-husband, the delightful spring weather we're having. We have two hours of driving ahead, so possibly all three."

"I'm good with the radio," I say, twisting the old-fashioned dial, feeling a burn of irritation that he's mentioned Dan. When it comes to family, even ex-family, it's not anyone else's place to criticize.

"Suit yourself," Will says with the smallest shake of his head. The chatter of the radio feels too much for my throbbing skull, so I reach to turn it off.

"Sorry, I'm not good company this morning."

Will points toward a backpack behind his seat. "Can you reach my bag?" he asks, and I stretch backward, then pull it onto my lap. "Open it," he instructs me. Inside, I find a large thermos and two tin mugs. "Coffee," he says. "It's good."

"Do you take your own coffee everywhere?" I ask, remembering he usually has a thermos on his desk at work.

"Life's too short to drink bad coffee," he says as I unscrew the cap and the most wonderful aroma fills the car.

"Oh, wow, that smells amazing," I say, inhaling deeply.

"Do you want milk? I have hot milk in there too. I wasn't sure how you took it."

"I'll just have it how it comes, thanks. Can I pour you one?"

"Black for me, thanks," he says.

As I carefully pour two cups of the dark black liquid, I feel myself soften. I am not angry at Will, not today. It's myself I'm angry with. "Thank you for the coffee, and for driving. I probably wouldn't be safe on the roads this morning."

"You're welcome," he says, and I turn to watch his face in profile as he drives. He really does have the most stupidly perfect features: a nose that's delicate but masculine, a well-defined jaw, an expressive mouth, and a full, lustrous head of dark brown hair. It's so neatly trimmed around his collar—I wonder how often he gets it cut. He starts humming "Build Me Up Buttercup" to himself but then stops, sensing my eyes on him. "What?" he asks, rubbing a palm self-consciously along his jawline.

"I've never seen you with a hair out of place. You're always so put together."

"'Put together'?" he asks, turning to narrow his eyes at me. "Are you trying to give me a compliment, Appleby?"

"No. I find it disconcerting. You look exactly the same, every day. I've never seen you look tired, or like you didn't have time to shave, or like you slept through your alarm. It makes me think you might not be a real person."

"I'm not, I'm a simulation," he says, and I lift my hand to cover a smile. "You only get to see me wild and unshaven when you reach the next level of the game." I don't know quite what he means by this, but I feel myself blushing. "Are you going to tell me what you got up to last night, then?"

I decide I might as well tell him about my date, since he'll need to write a column to complement it. "I went on a date with a waiter I met. He told me he was twenty-seven, but he turned out to be twenty-two."

"Appleby, I'm shocked," Will says, his voice soft and low. "How old did he think you were?"

"Thirty-three," I admit, curling my body in on itself.

"You could be thirty-three," he says, glancing across at me. "It must have gone well if you ended up 'moving furniture' with him."

"I was not 'moving furniture' with him. I was genuinely moving furniture. By myself."

"Likewise intriguing. Tell me the highlights," Will suggests. "We can outline your column now."

So, I sip Will's delicious coffee and tell him all about last night, about the hash brownies—he feigns shock and disapproval—the bed full of bodies, and the forgotten phone calls to Dan; he bites his lip in sympathy. Finally I mention the accidental tattoo, which sets him off laughing, to the point where we have to pull the car into a lay-by.

"Show me this tattoo," Will says, holding out his hand. I pull off the plaster and hand him my forearm. His fingers close around my wrist and he gently tugs my arm toward him so he can inspect it more closely. The sensation of his fingers around my wrist sends a tingle up my arm. I must still be fragile, overly sensitive to touch, because now I feel a wave of giddiness.

Will tuts, then says, "What will your mother say?"

I frown, pulling back my arm, cradling it protectively. *I think I wanted him to like it, but I don't know why when I'm not sure I even like it myself.*

"So should I find an older woman online? Do we make this week's column about age difference?"

"What's your definition of 'older'? Thirty-five?" I ask, and Will doesn't respond. "What's your usual cutoff? Twenty-three?"

"Thirty-three," he tells me with a slight shake of his head, but I know this already. Kelly once showed me his Tinder profile. His search criteria are someone between twenty-three and thirty-three who's over five foot eight and lives within a four-mile radius of Bath.

"What happens on the night of a woman's thirty-fourth birthday that suddenly makes her so undatable?" I ask him as he pulls the car back out onto the road.

"Are you telling me you don't have an age range? Didn't you reject this guy last night for being too young?"

"Being a student is a totally different life stage, plus that's a fifteen-year age gap. How old are you?"

"Thirty," he says.

"Right, so you're willing to consider women seven years younger than you but only three years older? Let me guess, they have to be six foot tall and a size eight too?"

"No, but I do prefer dating tall women. I'm six foot three, I don't want to strain my neck constantly looking down at someone," he says, which makes me laugh out loud.

"Ooh, diddums. Do you strain your liddle widdle neck when you talk to me?" I say in a baby voice.

"Talking while we're sitting down is fine. If I was trying to kiss you while standing up, then I might," he says. Despite the mischievous glint in his eye, the mention of kissing makes me look away. "How do you know seven years younger is my cutoff, anyway?"

*Oops*. "I might have seen your dating profile," I admit. Will grins at this confession, and I chastise myself for making such a rookie mistake.

"Look, everyone has a set of criteria when it comes to dating," Will tells me. "Whether it's subconscious or explicit. Online, we're forced to be specific, but we all have an idea of what we're looking for." He shakes his head. "You didn't put a height range?"

"I put a normal range! Five foot eight is not within normal range for a woman."

He turns to look at me, briefly pursing his lips, eyes heavy with a cool smugness. "You know, anyone would think you were upset about being outside my search criteria, Appleby."

"Oh please, I am thrilled to be outside of your search criteria," I say, shifting toward the passenger window, annoyed that his teasing makes me sink down in the chair and hide behind my coffee cup.

"I'd make an exception for you. You seem worth the neck strain," Will says. I know he's joking, but now I feel slightly giddy and curse my body for reacting this way.

"Well, sorry to disappoint you, but you aren't my type either. I would not date a giraffe man-child," I say primly. Then he catches my eye and we both start to laugh, though I'm not sure what's so funny.

"The main flaw with online dating is you can't convey sexiness. Maybe we could do a column on this," Will says, his eyes back on the road. "Sexiness is indefinable. It has nothing to do with age or build or hair color. I saw this interview with Catherine Deneuve; she oozed sex appeal even in her seventies."

"Plus it can't measure where people are in their lives, how ready they are for a relationship."

"Right, there's no drop-down menu where you rate the state of your heart."

I shift forward in my seat, warming to our discussion, drumming my fingers on my seat belt. "So, let's say you meet the perfect Amazonian, twenty-six-year-old version of Catherine Deneuve. Then what? Are you looking for Mrs. Right or Miss Right Now?" I pose it playfully, but I am curious to hear what he says.

"That's a big question," Will says, the corners of his eyes creasing in contemplation as he taps his hand against the wheel. I notice how strong his hands look, as though he could rip a pineapple in half if he wanted to. *Why am I thinking about ripping pineapples in half? That's not a thing people do.* "Why do you want to know?" Will asks, and I try to stop thinking about pineapples.

"We have a long car journey, and we're cowriting a column about dating," I say with a shrug. "I'm interested, as a journalist."

"'As a journalist,'" he says, his voice mockingly serious. "It would depend on the person. Ideally, I'd want to live a little more before I settled down. I don't want a girlfriend just for the sake of it." He pauses, the jokey tone absent now. "But if you meet your perfect woman, even if it's not the perfect time, then you readjust your plans, don't you?"

"There's no such thing as a 'perfect woman,' Will," I say, lifting my eyes to the sky.

"I said *your* perfect woman, not *a* perfect woman, like if I met 'the one.'"

"You seriously believe in 'the one'?" I ask him.

"Yes, I do," he says, turning to look at me, his eyes wide with uncharacteristic innocence. "Don't you?"

I make a "pfff" sound and shake my head.

"Did you believe in 'the one' when you were married?" he asks, his voice gentle now.

"How long does it take you to decide whether or not someone is 'the one'?" I ask, ignoring his question to me.

He pauses, glancing into the rearview mirror. "I think you know quite quickly whether something's going to be mind-blowing. I am happy on my own, I don't need to be with someone. So, I don't tend to go on more than a couple of dates with anyone unless I can see it's going to be something serious. Why is that so terrible?" he asks.

"It's not," I say, shifting in my chair, struck by the fact he used the same phrase I often use. "You epitomize men of your generation. You swipe and you swipe, looking for something better. There's always someone hotter, younger, taller, smarter, thinner. All these apps are designed to create an itch you can never truly scratch. No one is 'mind-blowing.' It's ridiculous to set your bar that high."

"That's not what I do," he says, his jaw clenched as he rubs a palm up his neck, his eyes unwavering from the road ahead. "And whatever your judgy ex-husband did to make you so cynical, don't project that onto me." His words burn like oil spattering from a hot pan, making me physically flinch. "You shouldn't let him talk to you like he did back there." Will's voice is softer now, and the pity is so much worse than the anger or the teasing.

"You know, I'm getting a second wave of hangover. I don't think I want to talk anymore," I say, pulling my earphones out of my bag, plugging them in, and then turning to face the window.

"Anna—" Will tries to say something, but I hold up a hand to stop him.

"Let's just get there, shall we? Honestly, I really have got a headache."

A hot arc of tears rises behind my eyes, and I focus all my energy on stopping them from spilling over. I have always tried to keep the drama of my home life away from work, and I hate that Will witnessed Dan talking to me like that, that he saw me as the victim I so desperately don't want to be. I also don't know why I'm airing such a strong opinion about Will's dating policy. It's not unreasonable, what he's saying. Why shouldn't he hold out for his perfect woman? It has nothing to do with me.

GOOGLE SEARCHES:

*What percentage of people believe in "the one" / soulmates?*

*Can you have more than one soulmate?*

*Quiz: what percentage cynical are you?*

# CHAPTER 12

WHEN WE FINALLY ARRIVE IN HAY, WILL DRIVES STRAIGHT TO HIS HOtel. He hasn't even asked me where I'm staying.

"We're here," he says, turning off the engine.

"I'll just walk to my B and B then, shall I?" I ask, incapable of shaking my irritation.

"What's the name of your place?" Will asks.

"Rose Hill something," I say, getting out my phone to look it up, but when I look back at Will, he's pointing across the road.

"Can you walk across the road, or you need me to valet you to the door?"

I stick my tongue out at him, and he sticks his tongue right back, which makes my mouth twitch with the urge to smile.

"Good luck with your talk," I say, getting out of the car to grab my bag from the boot. "Try to remember to let the panelists get a word in."

Will gets out of the driver's side and opens the boot for me. "I will write a memo on my hand." He pauses, leaning against the roof of the car. "Will you come? It's tonight at eight. I'm kind of nervous and it would be good to see a friendly face in the crowd." He gives me a mock grimace. "Okay, a face in the crowd."

"I have a pretty full agenda, but I'll see," I say airily.

ONCE I'VE CHECKED in to my sweet little B and B, I lie back on the chintzy bedspread and cast my eye around the room. It is full of eccentric British details: lace doilies on every surface, a mahogany cupboard designed to conceal the television, and a collection of ornamental ducks waddling their way along the skirting board. It is the kind of room you would laugh about if you were with someone, but on your own it feels mildly tragic. Pulling a pillow over my face, I let out an audible groan. Why do I care about Will's dating policy? Am I jealous that it's easy for him? Maybe I *am* offended to be outside his search criteria. Not because I have any interest in him myself, but because Will's tastes reflect what most men are looking for—young, fertile, baggage-free. Most men are not looking for someone like me. Dan can easily date a woman in her twenties; he could have five more kids if he wanted to. It's only women who seem to have a sell-by date.

This must be the hangover speaking. I don't even *want* to meet someone, so why am I obsessing over this? I'll go to some talks, enjoy the festival, forget all about last night. I look down at the tattoo on my arm and groan again. From my research—Google—tattoo removal is painful and expensive. How can I have been so stupid? I guess it could have been worse, I could have gotten Caleb's name inked onto my skin.

Getting up from the bed, I glance out of the window and realize I can see right into the window of the hotel opposite. Will is on the second floor, unpacking his bag. *Shit*. Before he sees me, I leap back onto the bed like a panicked frog. Then, getting onto my hands and knees, I slowly slide off the bed and crawl toward the window so I can draw the curtains without his seeing me. Risking one more peek, just to check he didn't notice me looking, I see him sitting on the bed with his head in his hands. He looks upset. Was that me? Did I upset him? No. No one upsets Will. He's probably just tired from driving. Maybe he really is nervous about hosting this panel. I quickly close the curtains. I shouldn't be looking into anyone's hotel room window, least of all a colleague's.

After a power nap, a brisk walk in the fresh air, and a bowl of hearty chicken soup, my lingering brain fog finally starts to ease and I open my meticulously planned agenda of talks and interviews. *Bath Living* readers always appreciate a local angle, celebrating homegrown talent, so I've scheduled coffees with several West Country writers who are involved in the festival. Just being here, around so many people celebrating books and reading, feels so restorative. The day flies by, and I barely think about Dan or Will or my ampersand tattoo.

When I get to Will's panel that evening, I look for a seat as I deal with a flurry of text messages from Dan. Jess says she won't wear any of the clothes he has at his house, and he's going to nip back to mine to pick up what she wants. He knows where the spare key is hidden but wants to check I haven't changed the code for the alarm. Jess has become particular about the style of T-shirt she'll wear, baggy, in a color palette of black and white. She doesn't feel comfortable in anything else. While I want Jess to have her clothes, I don't like the idea of Dan being in my house without me. Will he look in the bedroom and see I've moved the bed? I can't imagine a similar scenario where I would ask to let myself into his house. But I put Jess's comfort over my own and text him the new alarm code.

The audience chatter subsides as Will walks onto the stage. He's dressed as "Intellectual Ken" in a crisp white shirt, his favorite blue suit, and those trademark dark-rimmed glasses. I can't help smiling when I see him, his familiar gait. He introduces the panelist and the topic they'll be discussing, contemporary adaptations of Shakespeare in literature. Will is articulate and confident, clearly well-read on the topic. But he also deflects questions to other panelists and makes sure the quieter author gets a chance to speak. When the panel veers too far off topic, he skillfully pulls the dialogue back to the books, posing questions that keep everyone engaged. In short, he was born to do this.

I'm so caught up in the panelists' conversation that the end comes too soon. I planned on sneaking out early so Will wouldn't see me during audience questions, but now I've missed my opportunity. Someone in front of me raises their hand, and I try to sink down in my chair, but I can see from the delight in his eyes that Will has clocked my presence. Once the questions are over, I try to hurry out of the marquee but there's a crowd of people to navigate. When I finally emerge, I run straight into Will, who is waiting at the exit.

"You came," he says, eyes alive with some private victory. "Couldn't resist seeing me take the literary world by storm?"

"I booked before I knew you were chairing," I explain, my body tense with irritation. "It was good, well done."

"'Good'? That's all I get? Where's the insult hidden inside the compliment?" he asks with a grin, shifting his weight from side to side. He's full of energy, high on the adrenaline.

"By 'good' I mean you held your own alongside four heavyweights of literature. You didn't embarrass yourself." Will narrows his eyes. "Though you were touching your crotch a little too much. You need to find something to do with your hands."

"I was not," he says, lowering his voice, and I grin because even though he knows I'm joking, I've successfully planted the *tiniest* seed of doubt.

"Will, darling, that was gorgeous!" I turn to see a woman about my age in a sleek dress and heels lean in to air-kiss him.

"Hi," Will says, brushing a hand through his hair. The woman glances toward me and Will holds out a hand to introduce us. "Hen, this is a colleague of mine at *Bath Living*, Anna Appleby. Anna, Henrietta Stone, editor of the *City Book Review*."

"Hi." I raise my hand in a little wave.

She looks me up and down, then says, "Anna Appleby, well, isn't that a name for journalism."

"Yes, or porn," I say with a laugh, but as soon as it's out of my mouth I see I've misjudged the tone of the conversation. *Why did I say that?* Of all the words not to be saying in the first thirty seconds of meeting someone, "porn" would be up there.

"Indeed," Henrietta says, giving me a thin smile, while Will covers his mouth and feigns a cough. "You're not the pretty little reason we couldn't get Will to leave Bath, are you?"

Will shakes his head, his cheeks flushed. "Um, no. This isn't her."

"We offered him an editorial position, but he wouldn't move to London. Said matters of the heart were keeping him in Bath. Such a waste of talent. Look at him!" She reaches out to squeeze his cheek. "You rarely get a brain like his in a package like that."

"It wasn't the right time," Will says, removing her hand from his face, then tugging at the collar of his shirt. I've never seen him look so flustered.

"These openings only come up once in a blue moon, you have to make your career a priority." She's still looking at me, and I nod reflexively. "I'm sure you'll be snapped up if you're really back on the market," Hen tells him, reaching out to straighten his shirt lapel. "Do a few more events like this. Pull yourself out of that backwater before you drown." Then she kisses him on the cheek while simultaneously seeing someone she knows behind him, calling, "Stanley!" as she hurries away without saying good-bye.

"Backwater?" I mouth. Will avoids my gaze and tugs at an earlobe. I suddenly have so many questions, but before I can ask any, we're interrupted by two teenage girls who want Will to sign their program. He does so graciously, and I tingle with delight at the amount of ammunition that has just been handed to me.

"Do you want to get some food?" he asks, turning back to me.

"Only if you sign my napkin afterward," I say, unable to resist. He glares at me, but his mouth twitches. As we walk away from the marquee, I ask him, "So are you going to tell me why you turned down a job at the *City Book Review*?"

"If you tell me why you're so annoyed that I did this panel," he says. His strides are so long, I need to power walk just to keep up with him, but then he notices and slows his pace.

"I'm not annoyed," I sigh. "It's just, if someone called the office looking for a local journalist, I usually cover arts and culture—"

"They wanted me. It's my contact," he says matter-of-factly.

"In the meeting, you said someone cold-called the office. That wasn't true?"

"No, I put myself forward for it. I just didn't want Jonathan to think I was looking around for other work. I'd like to do more stuff like this in the future—interviews, on-screen reporting. I didn't know you were looking to do that too."

"I don't. I'm not." I blush, feeling stupid and petty. "I could never do what you just did. It's just with the column and then this, it feels like we're covering a lot of the same ground. If anyone is going to be made redundant—"

"You're feeling threatened. I understand," Will says. He stops walking and turns to face me. I pause too and look up at him. His eyes flicker across my face, lingering on my lips, and now my gaze settles on his. In my belly, a tiny roller coaster freewheels down a bend and spins into a loop-the-loop. It unbalances me, like an intrusive thought, a sensation I don't want to be feeling. I break eye contact and turn to keep walking.

After a few steps I say, "When they were little, I took my kids to the playground. There was this boy on our street who was always there, James Bailey. Every time Ethan wanted to go on the swings, James would jump on the swings, then Ethan would head to the slide, and this kid would start walking up it, to stop him from going down. So then Ethan goes to the monkey bars, and there's James, lying on top of them. You're that kid. You're James Bailey."

Will laughs out loud, a warm burst of sound. "What ride is it you want to go on, Anna?" he asks, all smooth flirtation.

"Oh please, don't try and flirt your way out of this. You know you're doing it. You're trying to prove you can do my job better than me."

"That's not what I'm doing," he says, his voice silken. I'm carrying a heavy tote bag full of books, which Will wordlessly takes from me, slinging it onto his shoulder as though it weighs nothing.

"I can carry my own books," I protest.

"Well, I can't walk at this pace. Come on, I'm hungry." Even in an act of chivalry, he manages to be rude. I don't even know why I've agreed to go to dinner with him, when I could be ordering takeout and watching *Emily in Paris* in my hotel room. But now my curiosity has been piqued. I want to know who he was so in love with that he couldn't bear to leave Bath.

WILL CHOOSES A Thai restaurant with dark wooden walls and dim lighting. There are red paper lanterns strung from the ceiling and a mosaic of the Buddha along the back wall. A handful of other diners are already eating, but it's quiet and the waiter quickly finds us a table. Once we're settled, Will looks across at me, his eyes glinting with mischief. "I finally get you to have dinner with me. Shall we count this as a date? Write it up for the column—two sides of the same evening?"

"This is not a date. This is two colleagues consuming food in the vicinity of each other," I say. He pretends to look disappointed and taps his fist against the table. "Besides, my kids didn't pick you and you didn't find me online, so it wouldn't count for either of our columns."

"Your kids have met me now. I'm sure they'll suggest me once they run out of waiters." He fixes his gaze on me, then raises both eyebrows. I shake my head and drop my eyes to the menu. I hate this about Will. While I know he couldn't be less interested in me, he still turns on this flirtatious charm, he can't help himself, and I'm nauseated with myself for responding to it. It's like when the musical score in a movie makes you cry, and you know you're being manipulated by the sound edit, but you still can't stop the swell of emotion.

"Is that why you made a point of coming to my house early?" I ask.

"Sure, let's go with that," he says, eyes back on his menu.

"Are you going to tell me why you turned down Henrietta's job offer?"

"I couldn't move to London at the time," he says. "Do you like red or white?"

"She said matters of the heart were keeping you in Bath."

"You are nosy, aren't you, Appleby?" he says, shooting me a rakish frown.

"Just making conversation," I say with an innocent shrug.

"If I tell you, then by Monday the whole office will know."

"They won't. What's said in Hay stays in Hay, I promise."

The waiter comes over with a basket of prawn crackers and then asks if he can take our drinks order. Will opts for a bottle of red. Once the waiter's gone I say, "You didn't wait to hear if I even wanted wine."

"I ordered your favorite."

"How do you know my favorite wine?"

"You told me at the work Christmas party, a light pinot noir."

I don't even remember talking to Will at the Christmas party. Now we're getting off topic. "Well remembered. Come on, tell me about the great love of your life, the reason you gave up the job of a lifetime," I say, leaning forward, resting my elbows on the table.

"This is your interview style, is it?" he asks, holding my gaze with unabashed directness. "No foreplay, just beat it out of me."

My cheeks heat. "Intense eye contact and innuendo doesn't work on me, Havers. It's pretty unsophisticated, actually."

"It's working a bit though, isn't it?" he says, biting his bottom lip. He takes his glasses off, lays them on the table by his plate, then fixes me with overblown, smoldering "come to bed" eyes. I laugh out loud.

"I can assure you, it is not. I am immune to your charms and you're prevaricating on answering me." A frown line appears between his eyebrows, and I sense I've won a minor victory, because now he blinks and leans back in his chair.

"Fine. If you must know, her name was Maeve. I met her in Mr. B's bookshop," Will says, fiddling with his napkin. "We both reached for the last copy of *The Remains of the Day*."

"Nice," I say.

"I let her have it," he tells me.

"How chivalrous. So Maeve is why you turned down the London job?"

"Yes." He takes a breath, then runs a hand through his hair. "It was complicated."

The waiter returns and Will pauses his story while the man pours the wine and takes our food order. Will orders a prawn pad Thai and I ask for the same. "How spicy would you like it?" the waiter asks.

"However it comes," I tell him.

"Medium, but with chilis on the side for mine, thanks," says Will, handing back the menus. I take a sip of the wine; it's delicious.

"How do you like it?" he asks.

"I've had better." I pause, and he grins, knowing I'm lying. "You were saying?"

"Why do you want to know this?" he asks with a sigh.

"I'm innately nosy."

"Fine. Admit you like the wine, and I'll tell you everything."

"It's exquisite. It's the best wine I've had in years, my tongue is dancing in delight."

Now when he smiles it's a real smile, not a curated attempt to charm. He looks like a boy who just bowled his first wicket, and his joy makes me ache with an unexpected pleasure.

"I'll need to tell you some backstory first, about my family."

"I love a bit of backstory," I say, knitting my hands beneath my chin.

"I have three brothers. There's George, Harry, me, then Simon, the youngest. When Simon was seventeen, he was involved in a bad car accident. His friend was driving, a guy who'd passed his test two days before." Will's jaw tenses, and he grips his bottom lip between his teeth. "This was ten years ago. My brother is paraplegic now; mentally, he's not who he was before."

"Oh, I'm so sorry," I say, my heart in my mouth. I don't know what I was expecting him to tell me, but it wasn't this.

"My mother died when I was eight, so it's just me, Dad, and my brothers."

"That must have been so difficult," I say, leaning further across the table, feeling terrible for ever having teased Will, for making assumptions about his life, his background.

"We grew up in this incredible house on the Circus. It's worth a bit now, but it wasn't when my great-grandfather bought it. We all love that house, it's full of memories of our mother, her taste, her things, but it's a historical building, not the easiest to adapt for a wheelchair." He takes a breath, fiddling with the stem of his wineglass. "When we realized Simon wasn't going to get any better, that this was how his life was going to be, we knew

Dad wasn't up to looking after him alone, not on top of keeping up that house. He has some help, but my brothers and I agreed, if we wanted to keep the family home, one of us would always need to be in Bath to support them."

Will rubs his eyes. Then he puts his glasses back on. "I was studying at Bath uni at the time, so I was there anyway. We agreed I'd stay until I was twenty-four, then Harry would have finished his MA in Oxford and could come back. Four-year rotations, that was the idea." Will takes a prawn cracker and snaps it in half. "Only Harry got selected to play rugby professionally. It's all he ever wanted. I wasn't going to ask him to give that up."

"So you stayed?" I ask.

"I stayed. George was living in Switzerland. He said, 'Give me six months, I'll look for a job in the West Country.' But then I met Maeve." He pauses, gives me a look, as though I must know the rest. "She'd just started a postgrad at the university. I knew George wasn't ready to leave Switzerland; he was about to get promoted. And now I only wanted to be where Maeve was. I had a decent job at *Teen Girl*." He pulls a face. "I wasn't in a rush to go anywhere. Dad agreed to convert the top floor into a flat for me and Maeve. It was great, for a while."

"What happened?" I ask, leaning further toward him.

"Things didn't work out," he says, rubbing a hand across his lips, and I can see I'm not going to get the whole story. "I was naïve to plan my life around her. It was the first time I'd been in love. Well, the kind of love that makes you want to change all your plans." Will frowns, as though he thinks himself a fool. I feel an urge to reach across the table and squeeze his hand, to tell him he isn't the first person to do that and he certainly won't be the last, but then our food arrives, so we pause to thank the waiter. Then I squeeze a piece of lime over my noodles as I wait for him to go on.

"By this point, George is married to his Swiss girlfriend, Lena. She's pregnant, but there are complications, they're consulting with a specialist. It's not a good time for them to move. Harry says he'll quit rugby but . . ." He shakes his head. "I couldn't ask him to do that just because I had itchy feet and a broken heart."

"That sounds tough," I say, picking up my fork. Our food smells delicious and we pause our conversation to start eating.

After finishing his mouthful, Will says, "I had all these ambitions, jobs I wanted to apply for, places I wanted to live. All the exciting stuff seemed to be happening somewhere else, to somebody else."

"Did you tell your dad you felt that way?" I ask.

"No. I always told him I was happy in Bath, loved living with him and Simon, which I do, *I do.* Simon and I, we're incredibly close. But . . . Bath is a city that feels like a town that acts like a village, you know?"

"I know," I say, and I do.

"I can't feel sorry for myself." He twists the stem of his wineglass on the table. "Bath is my home. I'll probably end up back here eventually, but right now I feel like a bird who's had its wings clipped. I never got to fly the nest." He looks up from his wineglass, perhaps weighing how much to tell me. "Now things have changed again. George and Lena are moving here with their family. Harry's coming back too. He's got a job coaching Bath under-fifteens." Will pauses, lifting his gaze to mine. "I'm finally free to go wherever I want."

"So you're leaving?" I ask, feeling a tug of disappointment that makes no sense. Professionally, it would be better for me if Will left; I'm less likely to be made redundant.

"I don't know." He runs a hand through his hair. "I feel guilty even thinking about it. Simon is my best friend, he relies on me. He would be devastated if I moved away."

"That can't be the only reason you stay," I tell him.

"I've started asking around, so we'll see." Will looks up at me beneath lowered lashes. "That's why I'm trying to diversify my portfolio. My experience is too narrow, my network too small." He pauses, looking worried. "I'm telling you this in confidence, Appleby."

"What's said in Hay stays in Hay," I say, zipping an imaginary zipper across my lips.

"You'll be happy, you'll have all the rides in the playground to yourself again," he says, raising his glass in the air as though making a toast.

"But who will I turn to for unsolicited feedback on my grammar and spelling?"

"You can e-mail me."

Our eyes meet and we smile at each other. I suddenly understand him so much better, just from this one conversation. I realize where his drive comes from, why he's reluctant to get into a relationship. I see a boy without a mother who has put everyone else first for years, and my antagonism toward him melts away. Watching Will pick up his chopsticks again, I notice what exceptional table manners he has. He is an engaging dinner companion; I haven't looked at my watch once. Perhaps I have been too reticent about spending time with new people. There is pleasure to be had in the right kind of adult company. This evening I've felt a long-held tension inside me start to loosen its grip.

"You're a good brother and son. I hope your family appreciates you," I say, finally reaching across the table to squeeze his hand. He looks pensive, all that smirking confidence gone, his piercing green eyes half-hidden beneath dark, heavy lashes.

"Let's talk about something else," he says, pulling his hand away, then taking his glasses off again. "I don't think I've ever talked about myself this much to anyone." He gives me a playful, pained look. It's adorable.

"So, what you told me in the café *was* true," I say, clapping my hands down on the table, as though I've just found a missing puzzle piece.

"Can we just go back to ribbing each other, to you glowering at me like you can't stand me? I can't handle you looking at me with those pitying eyes, Appleby."

"Fine," I say, reaching out to pick up his glasses from the table, then putting them on myself. He lunges for them, but I push my chair back so that he can't reach. Looking around the room, I don't see anything distorted. The lenses are clear. "I knew it! They're fashion lenses."

Will flushes bright red. He's totally thrown, all composure gone.

"I have never seen anyone blush so hard," I say, finally handing them back.

He shakes his head, face still red, but now there's a smile playing at the corner of his lips. He bites it back. "You're going to delight in telling everyone that, aren't you?"

"No. Your secret's safe with me, that your vanity knows no end," I say, thrilled.

"It's not vanity," he says, putting them back on. "Not entirely. I used to need glasses, then I got laser eye surgery, and—it's ridiculous, I know, but part of me missed wearing them, having something between me and the world. I also look too young without them. It was harder to be taken seriously—"

"Poor Will, it's so tough being so fresh-faced and gorgeous," I say in a babying voice, reaching across to squidge his cheeks.

He juts out his chin and narrows his eyes at me, then reaches across to put the glasses back on me. "They look cute on you." As his fingers brush my cheek, I feel an unwelcome flutter inside me. He flexes his fingers as though he felt it too.

When he leans back, he says, "Your turn. Tell me, are you going to see this twenty-two-year-old again?" Now it's my turn to blush, and I'm glad I have his glasses to hide behind. "Maybe getting back in the saddle will make you less of a sourpuss, Appleby." He gives me an overblown wink. I don't know if it's the drinkable wine or the fact he's shared so much, but I find myself wanting to be honest with him too.

"I'm certainly not getting 'back in the saddle.'" I pause. "Caleb was attractive, fun, I think he liked me, there was a moment I could have . . ." I trail off.

"Kissed him?"

I nod. "Maybe I should have. Maybe I should be more spontaneous. But I didn't feel that—" I stop, suddenly self-conscious again.

"What?" he asks. "What didn't you feel?"

I shrug.

"Tell me," he says, nudging my foot beneath the table. *Why does this feel like we're flirting? And who is flirting with whom?*

"That draw, like gravity, like the kiss is inevitable," I say. Will's eyes meet mine and now I have to look away, because my stomach drops. "That sounds silly."

"It doesn't. I know exactly what you mean," he says, and there's a crackle in the atmosphere, a shift, like an oyster slowly opening to the air. Will clears his throat. "So how did you end up doing this job? Did you always dream of being a *Bath Living* journalist?"

"No, but then I hadn't planned on having a baby at twenty-five. I barely had time to work out who I was, or what I wanted, before becoming a mother. I'd done an MA in news journalism, which I loved. I'd learned to use a camera, edit footage, put story packages together. Then I applied for this graduate training program at Al Jazeera. It was highly competitive, would involve a lot of travel. If I got it, Dan said he'd give up his job and come with me."

"You didn't get it?" Will asks.

"No, I did. But then I found out I was pregnant." I pause. "Suddenly it didn't feel so sensible for Dan to quit his job and follow me to Doha."

"Ah, I see."

"While the children were young, it made sense for Dan's career to be the priority. When I was ready to go back to work, I'd had such a long break, I was out of touch, technology had moved on. It was easier for me to get a job in print journalism."

"Well, you're an excellent writer. Clearly you have a talent for it," Will tells me.

"Except for all the typos," I say, and his mouth twitches into a smile while he rubs an earlobe.

"Your writing was actually one of the reasons I applied for a job at *Bath Living*."

"What?" I ask in surprise, and he drops his gaze and starts fiddling with his fork.

"I had the impression it was all property and interiors, then I read this interview you did with Lucy Prebble, the playwright. It was so engaging and well researched. It made me think there was scope for the kind of writing I'd like to do."

I'm so surprised, I just look at him, dumbfounded.

"You're not good with compliments, are you, Appleby?" he says. "What do you get up to outside of work? What are you into?"

*The hobbies question again. Is it possible to exist in the world without hobbies? Unless I can say, "Hi, I'm Anna, I like crochet and paddleboarding," am I akin to the default character in a computer game—a soulless avatar?*

"You saw my life this morning, that's basically it," I say with a tight smile.

"You must do something that's just for you?" he presses.

I try to think. There must be something. "I did a sculpting course when I was pregnant with Ethan. I wasn't particularly good at it, but I loved getting lost in the process."

"Why did you stop?" he asks.

"Money was tight. Dan didn't think we could afford to spend money on my 'indulgent hobby.'"

"And now?" Will asks.

"Maybe now it's me who sees it as indulgent."

"Maybe you are worth a little indulgence."

The full beam of Will's attention is intoxicating. We talk and talk, until I look around and realize we are the last ones in the restaurant.

"We should get the bill," I say, signaling the waiter.

"Don't go back yet. Come for another drink with me," he says. "There's this delightful pub across the road, all low wooden beams and mismatched furniture."

"I don't know," I say, shaking my head. Something about this new friendliness with Will feels more dangerous than being antagonistic toward him ever did.

"Excellent, I'm glad you agree," he says with a grin, standing up to go.

It doesn't take much to persuade me. Maybe it's just the lubrication of half a bottle of wine, or the fact that I'm having such a nice time, but he is the Pied Piper and I am his enchanted little rat.

Once we're settled in a cozy corner with more red wine, I take his glasses from his face.

"You don't need these to appear smart. As soon as you open your mouth it's obvious how intelligent you are."

"Anna Appleby, was that a compliment?" he asks, leaning toward me.

"You'd better write it down, because you won't be getting another one."

He inches closer, our hands touching on the table now. The air feels thick with anticipation. He smells incredible, like Christmas morning and clean sheets. *Is he going to kiss me?* I tilt my chin toward him. This is a terrible idea, it would change *everything.*

"Are you messing with me?" I ask quietly, our faces still inches apart.

"No. Are you messing with me?" he asks in a whisper. He strokes the side of my hand with his little finger, and it sends a bolt of electricity through me. His eyes scan my face, and I'm sure he can see everything I'm feeling.

"We should probably call it a night," I say, pulling back my hand.

"Probably wise," he says, leaning back in his chair, but there's a definite flicker of disappointment. Why? Was he genuinely feeling the same connection, or is this just one long game of chicken that he doesn't want to lose?

SAFELY BACK IN my hotel room, I boil the kettle, hoping a cup of tea might right this shift in reality. I have stepped into an alternate universe where now, rather than hating Will Havers, I want to kiss him. Of all the people to suddenly be attracted to, Will would not be my first choice. I'd be joining the ranks of all the other doe-eyed women in the office who fawn over him; it's unconscionable. Hopefully in the sober light of day I will see sense, and we can go back to how things were before. *Thank God* I left when I did.

A full moon shines bright through a gap in the curtains. Walking over to the window to admire its clarity, my eye drifts across the street. Will's light is on. He's walking around in his boxer shorts, his physique unexpectedly broad, the curve of his arm muscles visible from here. It's only a second, a glimpse, before I look away, but in that exact moment, he looks up at my window. *Shit.* My light is on too. Did he see me?

Backing away from the window, I duck down to the floor and draw the curtain as best I can from the bottom. Of all the hotel rooms in all of Hay, I had to have a view right into his. My phone pings with a text message.

Will Havers

What are you looking at?

Oh God. Oh God. No. I can't ignore it. I have to reply. What do I say?

Anna Appleby

Full moon tonight. It's impressive.

Will is typing. My heart is pounding, simultaneously wanting this to be happening as much as I really do not want this to be happening, whatever this is.

Will Havers

Come back to the window and point it out, I can't see it.

Slowly, I open the curtain and make a cartoon jab at the moon. He's standing by the window now, still in only his boxers, looking straight up at me. My God, he has an incredible body. I gulp. He looks down at his phone.

Will Havers

I feel underdressed for this moon meeting.

Anna Appleby

I'm sure the moon doesn't mind.

Will Havers

Either I'm going to have to put some clothes on or you're going to need to take some off.

He looks back up, lifts his chin, challenging me. I could shut it down, scold him for crossing the line we've been dancing around all night. But the fizz inside me springs back into life with a vengeance, the playing-with-fire fizz, which is like fizz coupled with the danger of unexploded fireworks. Without letting myself think, I use my free hand to unbutton my shirt, letting it slide open to reveal my bra, then shrug it off my shoulders so it falls to the floor. He puts one hand up to lean on the window frame, typing with the other.

My breath is loud in my own ears.

Will Havers

I have no interest in looking at the moon anymore.

I just want to look at you.

When I read the message, I stumble slightly, my feet losing their grip on the ground. I steady myself, leaning on the windowsill, then look back outside. He's waiting for me to answer. What's going to happen now? There is no scenario that I'm prepared for here. The street looks empty, but if someone walked by and glanced up, they'd be able to see me, standing here at the window in my bra. For what seems like an eternity we just stare at each other, neither moving, neither reaching for their phone. It's another game of chicken.

Will Havers

Something is ruining the view.

Anna Appleby

Oh yes?

Will Havers

Your skirt.

I shake my head at him. I'm not getting any more naked, but I can see him smiling from across the street, and something about the distance between us makes me feel brave and also incredibly hot. Again, before I can overthink it, I unzip my skirt and let it drop to the floor. Standing there in my underwear by the window, I have no idea where this confidence has come from. My eyes dart right and left, checking the empty street. Will places a palm against the window.

Will Havers

That's much better.

Anna Appleby

I think I probably need to go to bed now.

Will Havers

Don't you dare.

I shake my head, then give him a little wave as though this interaction has been a normal, everyday occurrence. I start to close the curtain but then whip it back open. He starts to close his, then does the same, like some adult version of peekaboo. I see him laugh. Pulling the curtain around me like a toga, I slip off my bra, hold it briefly up to the window before dropping it to the floor. Where has this brazenness come from? My phone pings again.

Will Havers

Come over here, you minx.

I step briefly into view, one arm covering my chest, and blow him a kiss, then I jump back onto the bed, my heart pounding, body buzzing, laughing at the thrill of it. This delicious feeling envelops me, like a witch picking up a long-lost wand. I am still capable of this—of flirting, of wanting someone, of being wanted, of being someone other than an ex-wife and a mother.

Anna Appleby

Show's over. Sorry.

Will Havers

Any hope of an encore?

Anna Appleby

Night, Will.

Will Havers

You're killing me, Appleby.

Lying back on the bed, my body hums with this new feeling. A long-forgotten part of me is waking up, and it feels wonderful, like emerging from hibernation into a spring full of possibilities.

GOOGLE SEARCHES:

- *Are there CCTV cameras on streets in Hay?*
- *Specifically, CCTV outside the Rose Hill B&B?*
- *Is it illegal to strip by a window or just frowned upon?*

# CHAPTER 13

THE NEXT MORNING, THE EVENTS OF LAST NIGHT DON'T FEEL REAL. I roll over in bed and kick my feet up and down as I check my phone to prove to myself that the messages between Will and me exist. They do. We had a surreal, moon-themed seminude flirtation. My gut is a heady mix of remorse and residual excitement. Flipping over onto my back, I rapidly pound my fists up and down on the mattress and let out a small squeal. What will happen now? Will he mention it? Will it be weird when I see him? Is this going to escalate into something? Maybe tonight . . . *Surely it can't.* I can't think about it now, it's too distracting. I feel like a teenager with a crush on someone inappropriate, like their friend's dad or the school gardener. It's too shameful to shine a light on.

To distract myself, I indulge in some long-neglected self-care. I shower, shave, and pluck my body hair back into some semblance of order. Then I moisturize from top to toe and take the time to blow-dry my hair. I know I shouldn't need to do this to feel sexy, and that by conforming to gendered expectations about body hair I am no doubt supporting the patriarchy, but as I slip smooth legs into skinny black jeans and my feet into the sparkling gold heels I just happened to pack, I feel more myself than I have in years. When I look in the mirror, I swish my long dark hair back and forth, pleased with what I see.

Heading out of my B and B and toward the festival hub, I pass a boutique that sells lingerie. *I don't need lingerie, don't be ridiculous. You don't play one round of crazy golf, then go buy a whole new set of clubs.* But now I'm in the shop picking out three sets of lacy knickers and bras. In the changing room mirror I'm embarrassed by how gray my current bra is, how frumpy my knickers. *I'm not doing this for anyone else,* I tell myself. *This is just for me. I need new underwear anyway. This has absolutely nothing to do with Will.*

His lack of communication is torture, but as I'm standing at the till about to pay, I get a message.

Will Havers

Morning, Appleby.

I grin like a teenager when I see his name appear on my screen; there's a hot pulse between my legs as I remember him seminaked in the moonlight. What if he invites me to his hotel room now? Would I go?

Anna Appleby

Morning . . .

Will Havers

Something's come up. I need to get back tonight, sorry. Can I leave you my car to drive yourself home? I can leave keys at your B&B.

The disappointment is intense, as though someone has let the air out of the balloons I've been carrying around all morning. The disappointment is followed swiftly by anger—anger at myself for feeling disappointed, for dolling myself up, for shopping for new underwear. *I'm such an idiot.* Of course last night wasn't a big deal for Will. He probably does things like that all the time, while I've only ever been naked with two different men.

Anna Appleby

**Sure. All okay?**

Will Havers

**Fine. Just need to be somewhere and a friend offered me a lift. I didn't want to leave you stranded.**

I'm surprised he isn't telling me more. Does it have something to do with his brother, a job opportunity? After our conversation last night, this feels like he's pulling the veil on his private life firmly back down.

"Are you buying these?" the shop assistant prompts me, reaching for the lingerie in my hand.

"Yes, yes, I am," I say as brightly as possible. Just because no one's going to see them, it doesn't mean I don't deserve nice underwear. I felt good wearing them; that's worth something. Out of the shop, I decide to nip back to the B and B, so I don't have to take a shopping bag to all my talks. As I turn onto my road, I see Will on the pavement. He must have just left the car keys at my reception. Something stops me from calling out to him, paralysis over what to say. That's when I see her: a beautiful, tall blond woman standing by an Audi, car door open, waiting for him.

As he walks around to the passenger side, they share a joke, laughing before she gets into the driver's side. So, this is the "friend" who's offered him a lift. Someone who just happens to be his exact type. My stomach tightens, an unpleasant wrench, like my gut is being twisted. *I've made a complete fool of myself.* It's been such a long time since I've felt attracted to someone. I forgot that when you have a crush, you're opening yourself up to a world of disappointment.

Backing away down the street, I duck behind a pillar box to wait until they drive away. As I stand there, crouching out of sight, a shameful memory forces its way into my mind, a last-ditch attempt to revive my waning sex life with Dan. Lighting candles in the living room, sending the children to Lottie's, opening the door in a red silk negligee. He looked right through me, muttered that I was going to "burn the house down with all these candles."

I peer around the pillar box and see the car is gone, so I can walk across the road to the B and B. Right, new rule: No more flirting with Will. No getting sucked in by the eye contact and the stories about his broken heart and his tragic family. Thank God I stopped things when I did.

Once I've dropped my shopping back, I try to enjoy the rest of the festival. But as I wander between events, now I can't help feeling that I'm miles away from where I need to be. Jess sends me a few selfies, suggesting she's bored, while Ethan texts me from Dan's phone asking what I'm up to. I've been looking forward to this weekend for months, and now that I'm here, I just want to be somewhere else—at home with my children.

DRIVING BACK ON Sunday, I discover the appeal of vintage cars. I can almost taste the engine as I drive, feeling the thrust of the gearbox in my palm, and I have to stop myself from speeding when I hit a stretch of open road. When I get home, I only have half an hour to spare before Dan arrives with the kids. Unpacking my bag, I shove my new underwear to the bottom of a drawer, not wanting Lottie or Jess to notice what I've been buying. Then I text Will.

Anna Appleby

What do you want me to do with your car?

He replies a few minutes later.

Will Havers

Can you park it outside yours? I'll pick it up tomorrow. Thanks.

It's so perfunctory and formal. Has something happened? Does he regret drunkenly flirting with me? In the sober light of day, is he revolted by the idea?

When the children get home, Ethan gives me a huge hug as soon as he gets through the door. Jess walks straight past me and up to her room. I take both these things to mean they've missed me. Dan rolls his eyes at Jess. "She's such a teenager already, glued to her phone," he says under his breath. "Sylvie says we should give her valerian and passionflower to help with her moods."

"Is that something prescribed by a doctor or by *Game of Thrones*?"

Dan glares at me. "Sylvie knows about this stuff. She's done a course in herbal medicine. We've got to try something, Anna, she's not exactly a barrel of laughs to have around these days."

"It's not Jess's job to entertain us. She's not a clown."

Dan rubs a hand over his face; he looks tired. "I need to swap weekends with you in a few weeks. Sylvie's parents are over from Sweden, I'll text you details. Also, Ethan hasn't done his homework." Then Dan turns to start rifling through my post. "Have you seen a letter from NatWest? I'm expecting a new card reader."

"You need to redirect your post," I say tightly, annoyed about the homework. Dan has the log-in details for Ethan's homework app; he can easily access everything from his phone.

"I know, I know. Jesus," Dan says with a groan. Four minutes in his company and already my cortisol levels feel spiked. He doesn't find what he's searching for, gives me a strange look, as though he wants to say something, but then thinks better of it.

"What?" I ask irritably.

"I was just going to say, you look nice. Did you change your hair?"

Oh great, now Dan thinks I took his feedback to heart. I shrug and Dan rolls his eyes. He's at the bottom of the stairs before he turns around and takes two steps back toward me. "Sylvie wants to meet you. She wants you to come for dinner."

"Oh," I say, blindsided.

"She feels weird that we speak on the phone. She doesn't get that this"—he pushes a finger back and forth in the air between us—"is just logistic." *Ouch.* "Those late-night phone calls didn't help, Anna." Dan lets out a tired sigh. "I think she'll feel better once she's met you. Will you come?"

*She'll feel better once she's met me? Why? Because she'll see what a haggard old crow I am and realize Dan couldn't possibly have any residual feelings?*

"Sure, text me a date," I call down the steps.

He gives me a curt nod, then turns to go. Why did I say yes? Why didn't I say I'd think about it? I don't want to sit and watch Sylvie play house with my ex-husband. Now I'll have to try to get out of it.

When Ethan and Jess get back from Dan's, there's always a period of adjustment. I've learned it's best not to ask them too many questions or try to force them to recalibrate too quickly. I just put some music on, prepare food, then let them come to me. Ethan is first to be lured in by the smell of homemade hummus and toasted pita bread.

"Mum, I've thought of someone for your next date," he tells me.

"Oh, right," I say, having briefly forgotten about the stupid column.

"The man from the show with the dog in the snow!"

"Right," I say slowly while handing him the hummus, "I might need a *bit* more to go on." It sometimes takes a while to decode what Ethan is talking about. Once he told us about "the island that looks like an angry parrot with no feet," which turned out to be Ireland, and that for tea he wanted "the round bread with the footprints in"—crumpets.

"You know, the show about the policeman in the snow with the dog," Ethan explains, "the show you watch all the time. His face is on all the posters."

Now I know who he's talking about. Ryan Stirling, the star of *Port, Starboard, Murder,* is currently performing in *Richard III* at the Bath theater.

"Ryan Stirling?" I ask, laughing. Ethan nods. "I can't go on a date with Ryan Stirling."

"Why not?" he asks, his face a picture of innocence. "He might not know anyone in Bath. He might want to make new friends."

Ethan is right about one thing: I do have a huge crush on this particular actor. He's probably the main reason I enjoy *Port, Starboard, Murder.* Well, him and his cute little doggy sidekick. In the show Ryan plays a British detective, Brandon Farley, who's called in to help with a crime that took place in international waters. He's a good cop, but he wouldn't hesitate to bend the law if it meant taking down the bad guy. There are thousands of memes dedicated to Brandon Farley saying his catchphrase: "You want to play by the letter of the law? Then don't play with me."

"What have you got to lose?" Ethan asks, parroting a question I'm always asking him.

This is technically true. I have been meaning to book a ticket to see him in *Richard III.* I could e-mail Ryan's agent, tell him about the column, see if he might meet me one night after his show. The mere thought of meeting Ryan Stirling for a drink sends a buzz of excitement through me.

Jess comes downstairs, having changed into tracksuit bottoms and a black hoodie.

"Did you get the clothes you wanted this weekend?" I ask, and she nods. I sense she's upset about something, but I know she won't tell me if I ask the wrong questions. "Did you have fun at your dad's?" She shrugs and I reach out a hand to rub her back.

"Penny is having a roller-skating party next weekend. Practically everyone else is invited," Jess says, pulling her hands up into her hoodie sleeves.

"I'm sorry, honey, that's not kind of her."

"Whatever. I don't want to go anyway," she says, but I can see that she does and my heart aches for her. Jess walks across to the fridge and takes out some juice.

"I saw you threw some of your toys away. Did you really want to do that, hon?" I ask gently, and she looks thrown. "It's okay if you don't want them anymore, I'd just rather we gave them to Lottie for her baby or took them to Goodwill." She turns her head to look out of the window. "I rescued them from the bin. Are you happy for me to give them away?"

"Whatever," she says, and my heart sinks as I see the drawbridge being raised. I decide not to push it, and by the time we sit down to eat a broccoli-and-pasta bake, her mood has thawed.

"Sylvie said she is going to invite you for dinner. You won't believe Dad's place, she's totally redecorated," Jess tells me.

"We can't put our stuff anywhere," Ethan adds with a sigh.

"It's minimalist. I like it, it smells nice, like a White Company store," Jess says.

"I don't," says Ethan. I look around at our kitchen, crammed full of schoolbooks, the children's artwork, and half-finished crafts. The vibe is anything but minimalist.

"Well, everyone is different, the world would be a boring place if we weren't."

"I think you'll like her, Mum," says Jess. *I will not like her. I already know from her Instagram page that I will not like her.* "Oh, and I've thought of who your next date should be."

"I already chose one," Ethan says. "Ryan Stirling."

"Ryan Stirling is a long shot, honey," I say, patting him on the shoulder, then turning to Jess. "Who were you thinking of?"

"Michael," Jess says, her face settling into a satisfied smile as though I'm going to think this is genius. Ethan and I exchange a look. Neither of us know who Michael is. "Michael!" she repeats. "Our parcel delivery guy."

"Oh," I say, handing Jess a plate of pasta bake.

"And I can't believe you don't know Michael. I talk to him *all* the time."

If it's the man I'm thinking of, then Michael is a slightly rotund man in his thirties. He does always give me a cheery hello whenever he's dropping off parcels, but I'm surprised to hear Jess is on first-name terms with the man.

"Brown hair, tight trousers?" I ask Jess.

"Yes," she says, staring at me unblinkingly, waiting to see what my objections might be.

"Well, he's a little, um . . ."

"What?" She raises one eyebrow at me. "You're above dating a delivery driver?"

"No, not at all," I say, affronted. "I'd just assumed he was, um, well, that he might prefer men."

Jess opens her mouth wide in cartoon shock. "How would you know that? You don't even know his name! Just because he sings songs from musical theater doesn't mean he's gay." She's right, and now I feel guilty for making assumptions. "Last week, he told me he'd broken up with his partner, Gail," Jess says.

"First of all, since when have you been having heart-to-hearts with the postman about his love life? And secondly, Gale could be a man's name."

"There's a Gail in my class, she picks her nose the whole time," says Ethan. "Her desk is covered in boogers."

"He said 'she,' is that enough evidence for you, Detective Mum?" Jess says, taking a bite of pasta. "You need someone to write about. Why not him?"

"Why not indeed. Fine, I will ask him."

Since my sexy texting with Will has turned into perfunctory "car picking up" admin, no doubt because he's off having fun with the tall blonde, there's all the more reason to keep myself busy. Secretly I have more faith in my celebrity crush Ryan Stirling agreeing to go out with me than Michael the singing postman, but as my new mantra goes—what have I got to lose?

GOOGLE SEARCHES:

*Ryan Stirling, wife?*

*Ryan Stirling fan fiction*

*Ryan Stirling naked*

*How to erase your search history*

# CHAPTER 14

WE DON'T HAVE TO WAIT LONG BEFORE AN OPPORTUNITY ARISES with the singing postman. The doorbell rings as we're having breakfast.

"Hi!" I say, opening the door and giving the deliveryman my best Julia Roberts smile. "Michael, is it?" This man has seen me in my pajamas, with greasy hair and Cheerios stuck to my dressing gown. If he is straight, there is no way in hell he finds me attractive.

Michael looks back and forth between Jess and me. "Yes. Here you go," he says, scanning the barcode, then handing me a parcel addressed to Jess. She is hovering on the stairs.

"I ordered new highlighters," she tells me.

Michael holsters his scanner, and I realize if I'm going to do this, I don't have much time.

"This is going to sound crazy," I say, pausing to laugh, but then the laugh only makes me appear crazier. I stop and clear my throat. "I'm a journalist and I write a dating column where I try to date someone new each week but without the use of the internet, so people I meet in real life." I clear my throat again. He looks confused and slightly afraid. "My daughter suggested you." I laugh again, then let it fade into a sigh.

"You want to go on a date, with me?" Michael clarifies, looking bemused.

"Yes," I say, trying to radiate sincerity.

"She likes books," Jess calls from the stairs. "She writes about them too." For a moment, I wonder what she's doing, then realize Jess is trying to sell me to him. *Hello, new low.*

"Won't your husband have something to say about that?" Michael asks warily, holding up a parcel addressed to Dan Humphries.

"Oh, right, sorry, no. We're divorced." I pause. "He hasn't changed his address yet." I take the parcel, and we all hover by the open door. Now it's awkward because he hasn't said yes or no and I just want to shut the door and pretend this never happened.

"My dad is crap at that kind of thing," says Jess. "They're one hundred percent divorced. Dad lives with someone else now. She's Swedish."

Michael's eyes flicker with sympathy.

"Let's forget I said anything," I say, waving a hand in front of me as though I can erase the words from the air.

"I'll go out with you," says Michael, and now I'm even more confused. Turning around to look at Jess, I see she is shooting me "See, I told you so" eyes.

"You will?" I ask, doing a double take.

"Sure. It's good to have something to look forward to." He gives me a kindly nod, then hands me a notepad and pen. "Write down your number. I'll juggle my shifts, see what I can sort out."

He will juggle his shifts. This is too humiliating; the sexually ambiguous postman is agreeing to take me on a sympathy date.

---

ONCE I'M IN the office, I rush off an e-mail to Ryan Stirling's agent, hoping to get all my humiliation for the day over early. I know it's highly unlikely the agent will even relay the message, but it's worth a shot.

"Hi." A voice comes from behind me, and I spin around in my chair to find Will standing right there. I say "my chair"; technically it's his chair. I took it back because I got to the office first and, well, I like this game.

"Hi," I say, trying to keep my voice flat and professional, but it comes out squeaky and girlish. An image of Will in his boxers staring up at me in the moonlight forces its way into my mind.

"How was the rest of the festival? Sorry I had to leave early. Did you manage the car okay?"

"Yes, I 'managed the car okay,'" I say, crossing my arms in front of my chest, tilting my head to one side as I look up at him. "It has a scratch on the passenger door, one hubcap is missing, and I picked up four speeding tickets, but apart from that, I managed."

He narrows his eyes, a hint of a smile on his lips. "You'd better be joking, Appleby. My dad will—"

"What? Dock your pocket money?" I cut in, arching an eyebrow.

Will bends down, closer to my ear, then says, "I'll come by and pick it up later."

His words feel loaded, and my cheeks heat as though he's said something highly suggestive.

"Take the keys now, I might not be in," I say, handing him the car keys from my drawer. He reaches to take them, and I become hyperaware of every point where his hand makes contact with mine.

"Out on a hot date?" he asks, his tone teasing.

"Possibly," I reply, flicking my hair back over one shoulder. I don't have a hot date, I'll be in, doing what I do most evenings—laundry, dishes, and helping with homework—but I don't want him to imagine me sitting around waiting for him to pop by.

"Well let me know once you have something firmed up," Will says.

"Why? So you can keep tabs on me?" I ask archly.

"No." He frowns, confused. "So I can work out what my column needs to be about."

*Oh, right, the column. Oops.* "Sure. Will do," I say briskly, swiveling my chair back around to face my desk. Will doesn't walk away immediately, I can feel him standing behind me for a moment, but then he leaves, and my heart starts pounding unnaturally fast in my chest. Great, now I have a full-blown crush on stupid Will. This is a disaster. It's distracting and pointless. He already has every girl in sales fluttering their eyelashes at him, he doesn't need me to further inflate his enormous ego.

Putting my earphones in, I try to focus on work. It takes me most of the day to write up my feature on the literary festival and make some follow-up calls to two local authors. As I hang up from a call, my WhatsApp pings.

Will Havers

So when's the next full moon?

Reading the message, I look over at his desk and see he's watching me. He tilts his chin, raises both eyebrows, and bites his lip. My insides swirl into hot jelly, and I swivel back to my computer so he can't see me redden. What unbelievable gall. Does he really think he can blow me off, go home with some other woman, and then continue this low-level flirtation with me?

Anna Appleby

What happened in Hay stays in Hay.

Will Havers

Shame.

Anna Appleby

Wouldn't want you cricking your neck.

Will Havers

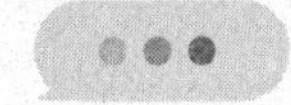

And then nothing. When I turn to sneak a look across the office, I see he's left his desk. Turning back to my screen, I have a reply from the agent.

Dear Ms. Appleby,

Thank you for your e-mail. I must admit in fifteen years as an agent I've never received a request quite like this one. I passed your message on to Mr. Stirling, and he said he would be delighted to meet you for a drink and is flattered that your son chose him as a potential suitor. If you are free on Thursday night, could you meet him at the stage door after his show? I'll leave a comp ticket for you at the box office if you'd like to watch the play. I suggest you do; Mr. Stirling is wonderful in the role.

Best wishes,
Evan Greenswab

*What? He said yes?* I do a little excited dance in my chair. Who else could I ask out under the pretext of research? Brad

Pitt? Bradley Cooper? They probably live too far away. Colin Farrell? Now I'm just being ridiculous. My mind jumps from Colin Farrell to Dan. Dan loves Ryan Stirling. Imagine if this date went well, imagine if I started *seeing* Ryan Stirling. I know divorce isn't a competition you can win, but if it were, this would be the mother of all trump cards.

"Everyone," Jonathan says with a clap, walking out into the open-plan office. "Crispin from Arch Media is coming down on Thursday. He wants to meet the team, sit in on some meetings. Can everyone make sure they have something intelligent to say?" He looks flustered. "Especially you two." Jonathan points to Will, who's standing by the water cooler, and then to me at my desk. "Crispin loves the new dating column. Let's make sure we've got copy for him to read, fresh ideas to get him excited."

Jonathan scurries around straightening pictures and fluffing cushions, as though Crispin is going to be judging *Bath Living* on its soft furnishings rather than its bottom line. As Will walks back past my desk, I call over to him, "I've just sorted a date for next week's column."

"That was quick. Who?" he asks, coming over to perch on a corner of my desk. He smells like pine needles, soap, and the clean, good kind of sweat. I can't help looking at his glasses. Now that I know, it's so obvious that the glass in them is clear.

"Ryan Stirling," I say, shifting self-consciously in my chair. "I asked him out via his agent. He said yes."

"Your kids chose Ryan Stirling?" Will asks with a frown, then he pushes up his shirtsleeves, revealing a tanned, firm forearm. *Is he doing this on purpose?*

"My son saw a poster for his play," I explain, trying not to look at the taut flex of muscle in front of me. I imagine Will has no problem opening jars, even ones that are really stuck. He'd probably just pop those lids off, one after another. *Pop, pop, pop.*

That's certainly one of the downsides of being divorced; I have no one to help me with stuck jars. I mean, sure, I'm not miserable anymore, but the jar help was always appreciated.

"Anna?" Will says. I look up and realize he must have said something, but I missed it because I was daydreaming about watching him open pickle jars. I don't even *like* pickles.

"Sorry," I say, shaking my head.

"I've heard Ryan Stirling is an arsehole," Will says with a frown.

"Lucky I'm not looking to marry the guy then," I say airily, peeved he isn't more impressed by my celebrity date. "What's the online equivalent of dating an A-lister?"

Will taps his fingers on my desk, his eyes serious, no hint of a smile. This is so strange; a few minutes ago we were flirting via text, now he's all business.

"There's this exclusive dating site supposedly used by celebrities and millionaires. If I could get access to that, it might mirror your angle."

"That could work," I say, impressed he came up with that on the spot.

"Membership is all through personal recommendations, so it's a long shot," Will explains. He glances down at my desk, and I realize my latest pay slip is sitting open right there. He frowns. "You need to ask for a pay rise, Appleby."

I snatch it up and shove it into my drawer. *Rude.* Will looks at me now, and it might be the first time we've made real eye contact since the window in Hay. I can't read him at all. He looks somber and sincere, but also like he's trying to stop himself from undressing me with his eyes. Then, as if he knows what I think he's thinking, his eyes dart away. "And tonight, I have a date with a forty-five-year-old marine engineer."

"Ah, the 'older woman,'" I say. "Poor you, how will you cope being in the vicinity of such decrepitude?"

"I'll try to be strong. If you could send me some talking points for people of your generation, that would help."

"Sure, I'll e-mail you, is it still douchebag@fullofmyself.com?"

He grins as though he enjoys it when I'm mean to him. It definitely feels like we're flirting again. But I need to knock this silly crush on the head. It's taking up brain space I don't have, and it can't lead anywhere good. On the drive to Hay he basically admitted that's he's playing the field until he meets "the one." I don't think I could handle being toyed with, then discarded, especially by someone I have to work with.

I turn back to my computer and wave a hand in his direction, batting him away. As he leaves, he presses the lever on my chair so that my seat drops right down, and I find my chin level with the desk. Mature.

GOOGLE SEARCHES:

*How to stop yourself from having a crush on someone*

*Men opening jars*

*Ryan Stirling opening jars*

*Paul Hollywood opening jars*

*Erases search history*

# CHAPTER 15

WHEN I GET HOME FROM WORK, I OPEN THE FRONT DOOR AND SEE Katniss, curled into a strange position on the stairs. She doesn't look normal, her body too rigid, too straight, too . . . I run forward to touch her, find her cold, and jump back. Oh God, she's dead. A shiver goes through me. Poor Katniss. Sitting on the floor in the hall, I just stare at her familiar black-and-white fur. How many times has she curled onto my lap, the sound of her soft purr the backing track to my evening? I'm only grateful I didn't walk through the door with Ethan. He will be devastated, as will Jess.

What am I supposed to do now? Do I take her to the vet? How do I get her there? Am I supposed to pick her up and carry her? The idea turns my stomach. Should I bury her in the garden? With my hand shaking, I google "What do I do with a dead cat?" just as my phone rings. It's the office, probably Jonathan with notes on my Hay piece.

"Hello," I say, my voice quiet.

"Where did you go? I wanted to talk to you." It's not Jonathan, it's Will. Without meaning to, I let out a small sob. "What's wrong?" he asks, his voice immediately shifting to concern.

"My cat died. I just walked in the door and found her dead. I don't know what to do."

"I'll be right there."

I'm too upset to think about how weird it is that Will Havers is coming to my house to help me with my dead cat. All I can think about is how upset the children are going to be, how I don't want them to see her. What if this was my fault? What if I left too much food out? Maybe Noah poisoned her in revenge for the hedge. No, that's ridiculous, Noah loves animals. Katniss was quite old, maybe it was simply her time.

When Will arrives twenty minutes later I haven't moved from the hall floor. I let him in and nod toward the rigid furry mass on the stairs. Wordlessly, Will ushers me through to the kitchen, makes me a cup of tea, starts opening cupboards until he finds an empty cardboard box, then disappears back into the hall.

"I'm sorry," he says gently. "Shall I drive you to the vet? Or I can deal with it if you'd rather not go."

With a nod, I stand up to get a coat. "Thank you, I'll come."

THE VET IS sympathetic. He asks how old she is, but I don't know because we got her as a rescue. The vet guesses she was about twelve and says that's a good age for a cat. He says he can try to determine the cause of death if that's what I want, and I say that I do. As the vet is talking to me, Will reaches out to hold my hand and this makes me want to burst into tears. Will being kind and supportive is even more confusing than Will being irritating or flirtatious.

"I'm sorry, Mrs. Humphries," says the vet, handing me Katniss's collar.

"It's Ms. Appleby now," I say quietly.

"Sorry, I'll be sure to update our files," says the vet with a nod.

Back in the car, Will and I sit in silence.

"I need to pick up Ethan from school in twenty minutes," I say eventually.

"I'll drive you," Will offers, and I look up at him in surprise.

"You don't need to do that."

"I want to."

"Why are you being so nice to me?" I ask. "I'm not giving you your chair back."

Will shrugs, a dimple forming on his cheek. He reaches across the car, takes my hand, and squeezes it. The firm warmth of his skin is so comforting, but beneath that, there is another feeling refusing to be dampened.

"I like you. Is that enough of a reason?" he says, and I feel myself smiling.

While Will drives me to Ethan's school, he starts singing "Build Me Up Buttercup" quietly to himself.

"You're always singing that song," I tell him.

"Am I? Sorry."

"Don't apologize. I like it." As I look out of the window I see a ginger cat walking along a wall and it conjures a fresh wave of grief over Katniss. "Do you have pets?" I ask Will, hoping conversation might distract me.

"My brother has a tortoise, but he's pretty antisocial. He hides in the garden for weeks." He pauses, then goes on.

"We had a dog when I was a child. Well, he was Mum's dog, really, but she let Simon name him, so he got called Big Dog." This makes me smile.

"So you shouted 'Big Dog' when you took him for walks?"

"We called him BD. He was a Bernese mountain dog, so he really was big. Simon must have been four or five; he wanted to train him to be a real mountain rescue dog. He'd get me to play dead somewhere in the house, then BD would have to find me." Will smiles at the memory. "He was the worst rescue dog, he'd just lick my face until I stopped pretending."

"Sounds like a good technique to me," I say.

Watching Will, I see his face pass through a spectrum of emotions—fond recollection morphing into something more painful.

"When Mum died, BD stood sentry in the hall for weeks," he tells me. "He didn't understand that she wasn't coming home. One day, Simon pulled a beanbag into the hall and joined the dog's vigil. Dad didn't think it was healthy, tried to get them to do something else, but they wouldn't. One night, after a particularly miserable dinner, none of us knew what to do with ourselves, least of all Dad. Simon had laid out cushions in the hall. He wanted us to sit with him. So, we did. We all sat on the floor with the dog and we talked about Mum. It was the first time we'd seen Dad smile in months." Will pauses, lost in thought for a moment. "Maybe BD wasn't such a bad rescue dog after all."

"That's a lovely story," I say, touched. We share a look, a smile of understanding. Then his phone rings and I see a face flash on the screen, a photo of the beautiful blonde he rode home from Hay with. He rejects the call, then shifts uncomfortably, checking and rechecking the rearview mirror as though this woman might be behind us. She calls again, I see her name on the screen—Deedee. Will answers the call, flicking it onto speakerphone and laying the phone in his lap. He rubs his neck, and I get the feeling he doesn't want to talk to this woman in front of me.

"Hey you," comes the woman's voice.

"Hey, Deedee, I can't talk right now, I'm in the car with a colleague. Can I call you back in a bit?"

"Sure, hon, speak later." Her voice is perky, and she has an accent I can't pinpoint.

Will looks across the car at me, his face apologetic, his eyes guilty.

"Who was that?" I ask, unable to help myself.

"No one. Nothing that can't wait," he says with a tight smile. "Listen, I'm sorry if I confused things in Hay, I have a habit of doing that." His eyes are now trained on the rearview mirror. *What does he mean, that he has a habit of getting women to strip for him or a habit of confusing things?*

"It's fine, I'm not confused," I say, because now it all makes sense. He's started seeing this woman. Now he's trying to let me down gently to avoid any awkwardness at work.

"I really like you, Anna. Our dinner on Friday was—"

"It's fine," I say, cutting him off, not needing him to spell it out. "We both had too much to drink, let's leave it at that." He shifts in his chair, frowning at my response. He should be pleased I just made this conversation a whole lot easier for him. I shoot him a broad smile so that he knows I really am fine about it. "I appreciated having a friend today, Will. Thank you."

ETHAN AND JESS take the news about Katniss better than I thought they would.

"She was old, Mum. It was her time," says Jess in a gentle, comforting voice.

"She wasn't that old," I tell them.

"She was blind," says Jess.

"Only in one eye."

"Now she's with Katsu in cat heaven," Ethan says, nodding, his little brow furrowed into a pensive frown. I was braced for their misery, but they appear to be the ones comforting me.

"It's okay, Mum," says Jess, rubbing my back with the same circular motion I use on them when they're sick. "She was a great cat."

"Shall we watch *The Aristocats*?" Ethan suggests. "It's what Katniss would have wanted."

"Good idea," I tell him. Then, after throwing a pizza in the oven, I take the cat litter, the cat bed, and Katniss's scratch pole out to the garage. The children snuggle up beside me on the sofa, and we have dinner in front of the TV, watching *The Aristocats*. For once, I let myself cry in front of Jess and Ethan. The tears are 98 percent about the cat, maybe 2 percent about Deedee.

GOOGLE SEARCHES:

*Average lifespan for a cat*

*Cat caskets*

*Where does the name Deedee come from?*

*Dee Dee Warwick, Suspicious Minds music video*

# CHAPTER 16

ON WEDNESDAY, I HAVE DINNER AT DAN'S TO LOOK FORWARD TO. I'D rather stick toothpicks in my eyes, but I've left it too late to cancel and I suppose I should meet Sylvie if she's going to be part of the children's lives. I also need to appear normal and "non-stalkery" after the late-night phone call incident. The last thing I need is for Sylvie to think I'm still in love with her boyfriend. Jess and Ethan seem inexplicably excited as the three of us walk the four blocks to Dan's house.

"Sylvie's a great cook," Jess tells me. *Stab to the heart.*

"Dad's place smells funny now," says Ethan.

"Funny how?" I ask hopefully. "Funny bad?"

"Sylvie uses scent diffusers. I like the smell," says Jess. *Second stab to the heart.* Our house probably smells of residual cat litter and damp washing. "You'll like her, Mum, she's smart, she reads loads." We haven't even arrived yet and I'm already at nine out of ten on the "Sylvie is unbearable" scale.

"Hiiiiii!" Sylvie cries, opening the front door. Though I've seen pictures of her on Instagram, nothing can prepare me for how beautiful she is in real life. She's willowy and long limbed, with taut, tan skin, white-blond hair, and impossibly straight teeth. She's wearing a camel cashmere sweater, gray leggings, and Ugg boots, as though she's modeling quiet luxury at an alpine resort. I knew she was going to be pretty, but she's absolutely fucking luminous. How did Dan wangle someone like her? But then perhaps I'm thinking of the old Dan, depressed and withdrawn. Sylvie's with shiny, new, highly motivated Dan, who is triangle shaped rather than oblong.

"So great to meet you," Sylvie simpers, putting a hand on each of my shoulders. "Obviously I've seen photos, heard your voice on messages." She leaves a loaded pause. "But it's so *special* to finally meet you in real life. Goodness, aren't you tiny!" Already low-level barbs about the drunken voice note and my small stature, and I'm not even through the door. *Man, she's good.*

"Hey," says Dan, coming up behind Sylvie and putting a hand on her waist. He's wearing a jumper that looks identical to hers. *They're wearing his-and-hers jumpers.* "Come in, come in."

I've been to this house before. I've picked the kids up from outside or from the hallway, but I've never been all the way in. When he left us, Dan rented a flat, then took out a "huge mortgage" to afford this three-bedroom home. The first thing I'm struck by is how neat everything is. There is no mess or clutter or washing racks full of laundry. *Where is all their stuff?* The walls are white, and the furniture is gray and beige. It reminds me of a White Company store running low on stock. The only color comes from the huge, framed photographs of Dan and Sylvie adorning the walls. In each one they are posing while doing wholesome outdoor activities like hiking up a mountain, riding their bikes, or holding surfboards on a beach.

"Wow, so many photos," I can't help observing.

"Daniel hung them all himself," Sylvie says, wrinkling her nose at me in an expression I think is meant to be a shared acknowledgment of how cute Dan is, but if it's that, then she's misjudged her audience. Looking at all the photos of the places they've been, I wonder how they've fitted so much in. They can't have been together more than three or four months, yet they've been on all these trips and had time to mount them on the wall like relationship hunting trophies.

Sylvie puts a throw over the white sofa before indicating I can sit down. When I turn around, I discover the kids have abandoned me and disappeared up to their rooms. *Traitors.* On the glass coffee table, Sylvie places a bowl of pistachios and an empty bowl beside it.

"For the shells," she mouths, as though I am a heathen who might be planning to simply slip the shells down the back of their sofa. I set myself a secret challenge to see how many nut shells I can slip down the back of their sofa.

"It's so nice we can do this, isn't it?" Sylvie says, perching on the arm of the beige armchair opposite, then fixing me with a huge smile of dental perfection. "Daniel and I were just saying last night, there's so much toxicity around divorce, with terms like 'broken home.' So unnecessary, so damaging." I'm seized by an inexplicable urge to throw the bowl of pistachio nuts all over the rug and start crunching them into the luxuriously deep pile. "Words are important. People need to use the right terminology; it's about creating a loving coparenting dynamic."

"Sure," I say, forcing my mouth into a smile as Dan hands me a gin and tonic. He's made it just how I like it, with plenty of ice and lime. This annoys me too. Maybe I've changed. Maybe I don't like my gin and tonic this way anymore. Maybe I've gone off limes entirely. He's reinvented himself as "Daniel," he's become a totally different person, living in a different house with a different woman, and here I am, just the same, drinking the same predictable drink.

"My grandparents were divorced. They modeled what a healthy separation looks like. I've seen it done right." Sylvie is still talking at me. "I think it can be amazing for kids to have exposure to two different mothering figures. Variety can never be a bad thing, can it?"

*Two mothering figures?* They do not have two mothering figures, they have one mother and one Sylvie. My skin starts to itch. I don't know if I have the strength to endure this.

Looking across to the kitchen, I watch Dan dressed in his preppy-style outfit rinsing dishes before putting them in the dishwasher. How many times did I ask him to do that? Did he ever do it? No, he did not. Now Sylvie's got him doing it in a matter of months. *Don't say anything. It will just make you look bitter and petty.*

"Did you hear that Katniss died?" I ask him.

"Oh yes, the kids said. I'm sorry." Dan briefly bows his head. "I know you loved that cat." *Did he* not *love that cat? She lived with us for seven years.*

"So much sadness," says Sylvie, giving me a pained look. "My friend Vespa had her dog's ashes made into a paw-shaped pendant. Just precious."

"Mum, look at this!" Ethan shrieks, running down the stairs and charging across the living room with something in his hands.

"Ethan, let's remember to use our indoor voice," Sylvie says in a gentle, singsong way, but Ethan doesn't take any notice, he's too excited to show me a Lego car he's been building. I am thrilled by his return. "Isn't this awesome?" he says, showing me. "I did it all by myself, no help. It goes and everything."

"That's brilliant, well done, you," I say, watching as he demonstrates all the movable parts.

"We're trying to encourage non-screen-based activities when the children are here," Sylvie explains. "All the Silicon Valley guys who invented this technology, they don't let their own children near screens. What does that tell you? Our house rule is no screens upstairs or after dinner, isn't that right, Daniel?"

Dan is constantly on his phone, so I'm expecting him to give me a look that says, "Yeah right." But he doesn't; he just nods, then walks across the room to hand Sylvie a soda water, kissing her lightly on the head as he does so. "There you go, honey."

"Sorry to be a party pooper, I'm not drinking right now," Sylvie says, giving me a strange, unblinking look.

"You'll never wrestle Anna's nightly G&T away from her," Dan says with a smirk, sitting down beside me on the sofa, "or her phone out of her hand."

"It's not nightly," I correct him. "Maybe Thursdays and Fridays." Then I realize it's Wednesday.

"Every day is Friday, right?" Dan says with a laugh, then reaches out as though to pat my thigh but stops himself. He used to do that at dinner parties, when I'd told a story that he didn't think was funny or appropriate, this gentle thigh pat, code for "stop talking now."

*Keep it friendly,* I tell myself. *It's better for the children if we all get along.*

"Will you lay the table please, Ethan?" Sylvie asks gently, and my son obediently puts down his Lego and goes to do as he's been asked. "Uh-uh-uh," says Sylvie, nodding her head toward the Lego. "Back where it came from, please."

With only the smallest head droop, Ethan does as he's asked, trotting off to take the Lego car back upstairs. *Who is this boy? And what has Sylvie done with my son?*

"I like your decor," I say, looking around the room. "Very white. It's like being in a cloud."

"Sylvie's got an eye for interior design," says Dan. "We like the minimalist look."

"It's easy to be minimalist when you don't have any of the kids' stuff here, though, isn't it." *Oops, it just slipped out.* I quickly cover with a laugh.

"We have their stuff here," Dan says, his eyebrows sinking into a frown.

"I mean their washing, their homework, their sports kit, toys. That stuff takes up space." I grin like a maniac, as though my smile might help gloss over the implied criticism.

"We don't think it's fair to ask Sylvie to do the kids' washing," Dan tells me. "It's not her job."

"No, it's yours," I say, rictus grin still in place. "You're their father. When they're with you, you need to do their washing. It's not fair on me otherwise."

Dan clenches his fists as though he's squaring up for a fight, then he glances at Sylvie, takes a deep breath, and lets out a long, slow exhale.

"Can we have one evening where you're not having a go at me about post or washing or homework or whatever, Anna?" he says quietly. "Just give it a rest, please." He makes a face at Sylvie as though to say, "See what I mean?" just as Jess and Ethan reappear from upstairs.

I swallow down the volcano of rage threatening to erupt out of me. *Am I really in the wrong here?* Downing the rest of my gin and tonic, I excuse myself to go to the toilet. In the downstairs loo there are more photos of Sylvie. Sylvie wearing a bikini on a yoga mat, Sylvie kayaking down a wild river. Sylvie sitting on a fucking elephant. Just looking at these photos makes me feel like a failure. She's thirteen years younger than me, and I haven't done half these things, been to half these places.

Nosing around their medical cabinet, I see Dan's prescription rifaximin. I'm glad to see that he's still got digestive issues, despite Sylvie's wholesome cooking. He can no longer blame his irritable bowel on me. Sitting on the closed toilet seat, I try to get a grip on what I'm feeling. *Am I jealous?* No, I don't think so. I'm irritated and confused. Irritated because Sylvie is irritating, confused because I don't know how to navigate this. For the children's sake I know I need to be civil, that it will make everything easier, but something about this new house, this new life, this new "Daniel," makes me feel more like a widow than an ex-wife. What happened to the Dan I used to know? Where did he go?

"You have to try," I say, giving myself a pep talk in the mirror, before heading back out into the beige lands.

For dinner, Sylvie serves up a selection of vegetarian tapas. Annoyingly it's all delicious. Ethan rejects most of it and asks for baked beans instead, which feels like a small win for me, though I hate myself for even thinking it.

"This must have taken you ages," I tell Sylvie. "It's yummy."

"I know it's not fashionable to say so, but now that we're living together, I'm happy to abide by more traditional gender roles," she says. "Daniel works hard all day, his new job is incredibly demanding. The least I can do is put a wholesome meal on the table when he comes home. My friends think I'm crazy because I get up at five, but I just love to have my workout done and my face on before the day begins," Sylvie says cheerfully.

"Well, you're a better person than me," I say dryly.

"You're lucky, you have such beautiful skin," Sylvie says. "I'm sure you don't need to wear makeup every day. I still get breakouts, so skin care is a big part of my self-care routine."

Jess saves us from more tiresome details about Sylvie's skincare routine by telling us about a school trip she's going on to the Cheddar Gorge. Then Ethan interrupts, asking who invented baked beans and why there aren't any other vegetables canned in sweet sauce. For a moment it feels just like old times: me, Dan, Ethan, and Jess all sitting around a table, talking over each other. Only now there's a Sylvie sitting here too.

"So, Anna, are you dating yet?" Sylvie asks as she brings out a dessert of cinnamon stuffed apples. What they're stuffed with, I'm not sure, but it looks like more pieces of apple.

"Sylvie," Dan says, shaking his head at her, then nodding toward the kids. It's the first glimpse of tension I've seen.

"What?" Sylvie looks at him beneath lowered lashes. "They're old enough to understand these things."

"Mum's going out with Ryan Stirling," Ethan says, and Sylvie and Dan both burst out laughing.

"Another date with the TV, hey, Anna?" says Dan, fixing me with a condescending gaze, then wrapping his arm around the back of my chair. I seethe, shifting away from him.

"The *Port, Starboard, Murder* guy?" Sylvie asks. "Oh, he'd be my fantasy boyfriend too, he's so sexy. But then we already know we have the same taste in men, right, Anna?" *Eugh, eugh, Sylvie, eugh.*

"It's not a fantasy. Mum's really going out with him," Jess says, and there's a defensive note in her voice. She hears what they're doing. Dan pushes out his bottom lip in confusion.

"Yes, I'm seeing him tomorrow night," I explain with as much nonchalance as possible. "These apples are wonderful, Sylvie. You must give me the recipe."

"Sorry, what?" Dan laughs, pushing up the sleeves of his jumper as though he's suddenly too warm.

"He's in Bath, playing Richard the Third at the theater. I asked him out and he said yes."

The story sounds much more impressive if I leave out the agent/column part.

"Really? Ryan Stirling? You asked out *the* Ryan Stirling and he agreed?" Dan sounds jealous—jealous that I get to spend an evening with his man crush. "I introduced you to that show," he mutters, as though this should give him first dibs on Ryan.

"Well, I'll be sure to credit you in the wedding speech," I say, which causes Jess to spit out her apple as she chokes on a laugh.

"Messy, messy," mutters Sylvie as Jess jumps up to get a napkin.

"I'm joking, I'm not marrying anyone. I'm very happy, just the three of us," I say, while looking at Ethan.

"I think you mean the five of us," says Sylvie, putting an arm around Ethan. Now I think it's best we go before I say something I might regret.

WHEN WE GET home there's a letter for me on the doormat. It's been hand delivered and the lettering is written in ornate calligraphy. Inside is a cream-colored card with more beautifully inked writing.

*Ms. Anna,*

*Michael Giner requests the pleasure of your company.*
*This Saturday, at 4 p.m., for tea. The Jane Austen Centre. RSVP.*

Then his phone number is written below. I show the card to Jess in amazement.

"He's really run with the low-tech, old-fashioned brief," I say.

"I told you he'd be good," Jess says with a satisfied grin. There is something delightful about being sent a handwritten invitation. It certainly feels more special than a Tinder DM saying, "Wanna hang?" As I'm turning the card over in my hand, Jess's phone pings. She gets it out of her pocket, but her face falls when she reads the message.

"What's wrong?" I ask her, and she looks up as though she's surprised to see me there.

"Nothing, some homework I forgot about. I'll do it now."

I watch her drag her feet slowly up the stairs, her shoulders drooped. I feel sorry for her. When I was at school, if you forgot your homework, you didn't know about it until you got to class. Maybe it was better that way.

Once the children are in bed, I lie awake thinking about "Daniel" and Sylvie's decor. Is that beige, gray palette his taste or hers? What was "our taste"? This house ended up being a series of compromises. We couldn't agree whether to paint the kitchen cabinets dark green (my preference) or white (his), so we compromised on a wishy-washy light blue. He wanted a white leather sofa, I wanted a blue velvet one, so we ended up getting something that neither of us loved but that both of us could live with. How many nights did we sit scrolling through Netflix, unable to find something we both wanted to watch? My preference would be for a period drama or reality TV, while he'd always opt for a sports documentary. We'd compromise with a crime drama. Hours of my life wasted watching TV I never really wanted to watch. I don't have to compromise like that now, and the thought makes me feel better about this evening.

It's good that Dan is settled and happy; it's better for the children. Though I'm not quite ready to feel it, I also know that deep down, I am glad he is happier. He has obviously found whatever it was he was looking for. On autopilot, I pick up my phone and open Instagram. It's what I reach for when I'm feeling anxious or upset. But today, peering through these windows into other people's lives doesn't bring me the satisfaction it usually does.

Closing the app, I open my e-mail and send a message to Johnny the handyman, asking when he might be available to come and repaint my kitchen cabinets. No more compromise. Then I pull up a paint website and search for the exact shade of dark green paint I have always coveted. This Cinderella might not have a prince, but she shall go to the Farrow & Ball.

GOOGLE SEARCHES:

*Books to get you out of a reading slump*

*Kitchen inspiration, dark green cabinets*

*Farrow & Ball, but cheaper*

*Where can I watch Poldark, season one?*

# CHAPTER 17

"I HAVE A PACKAGE FOR YOU," NOAH CALLS OVER THE FENCE AS I'M leaving home the next morning. "It was left on your doorstep, but you were out. I took it in for safekeeping."

"Oh, thank you," I call back. "You didn't need to do that." Our street isn't exactly rife with package-stealing criminals.

"Wait there," Noah tells me, then disappears into his shed and comes back with a box the size of a barbecue. "It's heavy, you want me to carry it in?"

"That would be great," I say, opening the garage door in the hall. "Thank you." Once he's put the package down on the floor, Noah stands up and pulls a leaflet from his back pocket.

"I got you this," he says. As he hands me the piece of paper, his eyes shift to the floor.

It's a printed form. Across the top it says, "Bath and North East Somerset, Complaint Form—High Hedge."

"What is this?" I ask him.

"If you want to take issue with the hedge height you should do it through the proper channels. It's two hundred pounds for the council to mediate our dispute. I'm willing to split the cost of it with you."

"I'm not paying the council a hundred pounds, Noah. I haven't touched your hedge since we last spoke about it." I let out a sigh. If purgatory exists, I imagine it's paved with council complaint forms.

"I want to be assured that you're not going to destroy my property when my back is turned. Please just fill out the form," Noah says, pulling his beanie hat down over his ears, then marching back toward the door. Is this why he took my package in, so he could harass me about the hedge?

Once Noah's gone, I rip up the form he gave me, then pull my jumper over my face, screaming into the wool to try to expel the rage. It helps. Then, kneeling on the floor, I rip open the huge package. Inside, I find a giant block of sculpting clay and a small case of sculpting instruments. There's a note printed on the delivery receipt.

It isn't indulgent. Will.

As soon as I read it, I feel an overwhelming surge of emotion. I cover my mouth with a hand, to stop a sob that isn't there. What a thoughtful gift. But then my gratitude is replaced by suspicion. What does this mean? Is this apology clay, pity clay? Sorry Your Cat Died clay? Whatever the motive, it is a lovely gesture. And as I press my hands against the sides of the box, I feel my fingers tingle with anticipation.

WHEN I GET to the office on Thursday morning, everyone is in a fluster over the prospect of Crispin's arrival. Jonathan is wearing his best tweed suit, Karl is dusting artwork on the walls, and

Steph is putting posh soaps in all the toilets. Everyone looks busy with something other than work. Everyone except Will. He is at his desk, head down, ignoring the chaos going on around him. I want to go and thank him for the clay, but he is wearing noise-canceling headphones—universal code for "Do not disturb."

When Crispin arrives at eleven a.m., I'm surprised to find he is not much older than me. He wears a perfectly tailored gray suit, and his dark Afro is cut short and forms a sharp line around his forehead.

After introductions have been made, Jonathan claps for quiet, and Crispin addresses the staff on the office floor.

"Every acquisition is a journey," he tells us, his voice firm and commanding, like a politician at a press conference. "There are going to be bumps in the road, but I hope the destination is going to make it worthwhile. I'm here to listen. I want to learn who you are and what you do. I'm not the guy who buys a publication, then guts it like a fish. I want to get in the water and swim around with you first."

Jonathan laughs, and I notice the awestruck look on his face as he watches Crispin talk.

"We're looking to future-proof *Bath Living,*" Crispin continues. "So I hope you'll be collaborative in the weeks and months to come as we work out what that future might look like."

Everyone gives Crispin a round of applause, but I'm not sure why we're clapping. His speech sounded like a eulogy to me. When Jonathan ushers Crispin through to the living room, the rest of us let out a collective exhale.

I feel the slightest touch on my arm and turn to see Will standing behind me.

"How did Jess take the news about Katniss?" he asks.

"Better than I thought she would. Thanks again for your help," I say, tucking a strand of hair behind my ear. "And thank you for the clay, you really didn't need to do that."

"I thought it might get you started," Will says, then fidgets, as though he doesn't know where to put his hands, and finally settles on crossing his arms.

"How was your date with the marine engineer?" I ask.

"Good. She gave me some excellent career advice," he says, eyes glinting. "Maybe older women are the way forward. Are you meeting Ryan tonight?" he asks, and I nod. "Will you text me when you get home?"

"Will, I'm a big girl."

"I know, but I still want you to text me."

He reaches for my arm and briefly runs a finger over the new plaster covering my tattoo. His touch sends a throb of delight up my arm, the giddiness back with a vengeance. "Don't get his name tattooed on you or anything, will you, Appleby?" he says, eyes boring into me as he runs his thumb down to my wrist before letting go. It feels territorial, and I want to feel indignant, but I'm too focused on trying to quell the giddiness. The moment is punctured by someone calling my name. It's time for my one-on-one with Crispin.

"Look, Anna, let's cut to the chase," Crispin says before I've even sat down. "I've read your work. You're a good writer, professional, proficient. Your interviews are top-notch." He knocks a fist gently against his other palm. "But the direction I want to take this magazine in, it's going to be more personal, more authored, less Bath, more Living, if you see what I'm saying?" He studies my face, looking for understanding, so I nod slowly. "You know why the youth love TikTok, Anna?" He doesn't wait for me to answer. "Because people bare their soul on there. People talk about their depression, their love life, their weight issues, their divorces." He pauses, letting that last word linger in the air. "People our age don't get it. Stiff upper lip and crack on, right?" He chuckles, wanting to share the joke, but all I can offer him is a confused smile.

"I thought you liked the new dating column," I say, feeling defensive. "It has a personal angle, just like you asked for."

"It does, and the concept is great, really, it's great. It has so much potential." He pauses, letting his legs splay open as he lifts one foot to rest on his other thigh. "I don't want you to think you have to change your entire writing style to keep your job here. We need nuts-and-bolts writers too." *Nuts-and-bolts writers? Is that what I am?* "Arch Media is a global network. We're micro, local, but with a macro mindset. I'm just pushing buttons here. That's what I do, I'm a button pusher. I want to push you." He taps a fist against his chest. "You need to crack this open and bleed words—feed the vampires."

"Feed the vampires?" I repeat.

"Readers don't just want words anymore, they want blood, sweat, tears—raw humanity served up as emotional sushi."

"I don't know what that means," I say tightly.

"I think you do," Crispin says, holding my gaze for a moment. "I think you know you do." Then he stands up from his desk and claps his hands together. "All that talk of sushi has made me hungry. Good chat. Percolate upon it." He shakes my hand, hard.

Before this meeting I wasn't too worried about losing my job. I know I'm well respected at the magazine, I'm a good journalist. But now my confidence falters. What if that isn't enough? What if Crispin is right, the world wants sushi and I only know how to cook fish fingers?

GOOGLE SEARCHES:

*TikTok*

*If I download TikTok will it start tracking me?*

*Journalist jobs, Bath*

*Who is Aiden Turner from Poldark married to?*

# CHAPTER 18

AT HOME LATER THAT EVENING, I RUSH ABOUT TRYING TO FIND SOMEthing to wear to the theater. Why don't I have any "theater clothes"? Lottie has plans, so my colleague Kelly has offered to babysit, but she's running late. I'll need to be out of the door the minute she arrives if I'm going to make opening curtain. When I finally find something appropriate to wear, a denim dress with tights and gold heels, I notice Ethan itching his head as he sorts through his Pokémon cards on the floor.

"Mum, when I get an axolotl I'm going to call it Ninja Kid."

"Why are you itching?" I ask him.

"I'm itchy."

Walking across to him, I squat down and gently tilt his head so that I can inspect the back of his neck. There is a cluster of telltale red spots. Shining my phone torch into his hairline, I see something crawling. *Nits. Shit.* I let out a groan.

"What? Is it nits?" Ethan's voice is high-pitched and panicked as he swivels around to look at me. I grimace. We haven't had a lice infestation in years. When Jess started school, it felt as though we were constantly delousing her. She has long, thick hair, and I would spend hours in front of the Disney Channel combing conditioner through it with that dreaded narrow comb. It makes me feel itchy just thinking about it.

"Don't worry, your hair is short, we'll get rid of them in no time. I'll pick up a treatment from the chemist in town," I say, giving him a reassuring pat on the shoulder while also keeping him at arm's length. Ethan starts itching again, and now I reach a hand up to my own hair. Am I itchy, or is it psychological? Oh God, what if I have nits and I give them to Ryan Stirling? No, no. I'm being paranoid. I might wear my hair up, just in case.

When Kelly finally arrives, the first thing Ethan says to her is "I've got nits," and she recoils back toward the door. Not the best opener for a new babysitter.

"It's fine, they can't jump across the room," I tell her. If Kelly bails on me, I won't be able to go and I can't easily get in touch with Ryan to reschedule. Besides, this is one date I really don't want to cancel. Then Jess walks down the stairs scratching, and Kelly looks at me like I've asked her to babysit Medusa and Medusa's little brother. "Don't panic. We can fix this," I say, while having no idea how I'm going to fix this in the two minutes I've got before I need to leave.

Four minutes later, the children are both wearing swimming caps in front of the TV and Jess looks like she wants to murder me.

"I can't believe you've given me nits, fleabag," Jess groans, elbowing her brother.

"How do you know you didn't give *me* nits?" Ethan says, punching her on the arm.

"Let's not play the blame game, okay? These things happen, it isn't anyone's fault," I say, itching my own neck. "I will get you both treatments, and we'll sort it before school tomorrow. Okay?" Kelly perches on the edge of the sofa, as though it too might be infested with lice. "I'll, um, I'll pay you danger money," I tell her with a half smile, half grimace, "on top of what we discussed."

By the time I get near the theater I've convinced myself I have nits too. My head feels alive with tiny crawling insects, and whether it's paranoia or not, I'm not going to feel comfortable sitting so close to other people in the theater for two and a half hours. I'd hoped to project myself as a confident, sexy, together woman, and I'm not sure that's going to happen if I'm scratching like a feral cat. Nipping into a late-night chemist on the high street, I grab three boxes of lice treatment. At the till, I notice a display of silk head wraps. They're designed to wear at night to protect your curls, but they could pass for fashion. *Could they pass for fashion?*

When I arrive at the theater, the last bell has rung and I'm the only person left in the foyer. Picking up my comp ticket from the box office, I slip on my new green silk cap before being ushered to my seat in the stalls. Sitting to one side of me is a woman in her fifties who, bizarrely, is wearing a similar silk cap in light blue. She gives me a nod as I sit down. I assume she's sympathizing with my lateness, but then as the lights go down, she leans over and says, "God bless you."

It's only ten minutes later, when I notice her frail hands, that I realize she might have cancer, or be recovering from cancer, and she must have assumed I have cancer too. Now my guilt about abandoning my nit-ridden children is surpassed by the guilt I feel for receiving unearned cancer sympathy. Sinking down into my seat, I try to focus on the play. Ryan Stirling is incredibly hot, with such a natural stage presence that I'm soon lost in the production. The whole audience is so enthralled, you could hear a nit cough.

During the interval, the lady beside me clasps my arm. "Can I get you a drink, dear?"

"Oh no, let me get *you* one?" I say overeagerly.

"I insist. We girls must stick together," she says, nodding toward my head. I don't want to embarrass her by explaining that I don't have cancer, if that's what she thinks. It's too awkward and might involve my bringing up the nits situation. I'll probably never see this woman again, it's politer to say nothing.

When we stand up, I notice her outfit is a cascade of color. She's wearing a rainbow-colored skirt, a bright green shirt, and a white sequined waistcoat. She looks amazing, like a fashionista you might see strutting the streets of Manhattan. She heads to the bar and comes back with two proseccos.

"Thank you, that's very kind," I mumble.

"Loretta," she tells me.

"Anna," I say, shaking the thin hand she proffers.

"Three months in remission," she says, raising her glass to mine in a toast. "After four years of treatment. Hair's still refusing to grow." She taps her cap with a flourish of her hand. "How about you?"

"Oh, nothing like that," I say ambiguously. *What am I doing? Why don't I just tell her she made a mistake? Because it's rational to assume that no one would be wearing a silk bed cap as a fashion statement.*

"You're young, you're strong," she says, clasping my hand again. "Nothing puts your life into perspective like the big C." Loretta goes on to tell me her life story as we sip our drinks. I'm happy to listen to her talk, she's had a fascinating life. I learn she's a scientist who's helped develop a pioneering type of gene therapy that will save thousands of lives once it's been properly trialed. She's traveled the world, been married twice, and has the perfect voice for audiobooks.

"Are you married?" she asks eventually.

"Divorced," I tell her. "Though I don't love the term 'divorcée.' It makes me think of Zsa Zsa Gabor."

Loretta laughs. "I had a friend who referred to herself as PM, 'post-married,' which I liked. You're not doing it all alone, are you?" Her voice is full of concern. I'm going to assume she means divorce, though I suspect she means cancer.

"I'm close with my sister, I have two great kids," I tell her.

"Good," she says, "then embrace being PM. This is your rock era."

"Excuse me?"

"Fleetwood Mac." She smiles as though this should be enough for me to know what she means. "They thought they were a blues band, then they lost Peter Green and were forced to reinvent themselves. When Lindsey Buckingham and Stevie Nicks joined, they found their rock era and became one of the greatest bands in history. That could be you, you just need to find your Stevie Nicks."

"I don't really know their music," I admit.

"Oh, you'll know it when you hear it. There's no funk I couldn't pull myself out of, belting out 'Go Your Own Way' while dancing around the house in my knickknacks." I can't help smiling at this, and as the lights go down, Loretta squeezes my arm on our shared rest and whispers, "Your rock era."

The second half of the play drags, and I struggle to keep my eyes open. As a rule, Shakespeare is best enjoyed before seven p.m., or after a double espresso. Ryan Stirling taking his shirt off before a battle scene briefly perks me up, but when the crowd starts applauding, I realize I must have nodded off and my head is lolling gracelessly on Loretta's shoulder.

"Oh, I'm so sorry," I say, jerking upright, flustered, as everyone around us rises from their seat for a standing ovation.

"Don't apologize. You must listen to your body; when it needs rest, you rest." Loretta pats my hand. As the applause finally recedes, she turns to face me. "Now, I know I'm just a strange woman you happened to sit next to at the theater, but I see in you a kindred spirit, Anna."

I'm flattered to hear this, and apart from the awkward misunderstanding, I have loved talking to her too.

"Can I give you my digits, if you ever need the ear of someone who's been there?" she asks, and I nod.

"That's incredibly sweet of you," I say, taking the business card she's extracted from her handbag.

"It's a landline number. I'm rarely in but do leave a message. I can't abide mobile phones. Who wants the world in their pocket? Not I."

This makes me laugh. Loretta has a wonderful energy and I want to bask in it a little longer. "Did you enjoy the play?"

"Went on a bit, didn't it?" she says, giving me a sly grin. "Though he's rather easy on the eye."

As I bid Loretta good-bye, I sorely regret not clearing up the misunderstanding between us. She probably would have laughed about it. I might have liked to go for a coffee with her, but I didn't put her straight when I had the chance.

In the theater bathroom, I pull off the silk cap and try to fluff up my flat hair. I can't have Ryan Stirling questioning whether our date was arranged by the Make-A-Wish foundation. Leaning toward the mirror to inspect my hairline, I see nothing moving. I'll just assume I don't have nits while simultaneously not putting my head anywhere near him.

At the stage door, a crowd of female fans are waiting for Ryan to emerge. My heart sinks when I see them. It's already ten o'clock. If he signs all these people's programs, he won't be free until eleven; I'll struggle to keep my eyes open. Just as I'm contemplating grabbing a coffee from the theater bar, the stage door opens, and a voice calls, "Anna Appleby?" The crowd parts like the Red Sea as I put up my hand and cry, "That's me!"

A man dressed in a black polo shirt, wearing an earpiece, beckons me forward and the crowd eyes me enviously, perhaps wondering why I have been singled out. I mutter, "Journalist," under my breath as I hurry forward.

The man in black leads me down a corridor.

"Do not ask Mr. Stirling for a selfie," he instructs. "He doesn't do photos after the show." I'm led into a brightly lit dressing room, and there he is, Ryan Stirling, *the* Ryan Stirling. He's dressed in jeans and a white shirt, and a young woman is wiping makeup from his face.

"Anna?" he asks, his voice loud, as though he's still projecting from the stage. I nod, suddenly starstruck. "Don't worry, we'll head out the side door, avoid the baying mob. I'll be there all night otherwise." He gives me an overblown eye roll. "Did you enjoy the play?"

"Yes. You were great, wow, amazing," I blurt out before I can rein in my fangirling. He grins, as though I've answered correctly. Then he bats away the makeup lady, holds out a hand for his coat, and leaps out of the chair.

"Shall we depart?" He puts a hand on the small of my back, steering me out of the dressing room, then through another door, out onto a dark side street. He's much smaller than I expected him to be—he can't be more than five foot eight—but up close, his face is even more perfect than it looks on TV. He has a square jaw, hooded eyes, and a slight Roman nose. He looks like a man from another era, a gladiator or a Viking warrior. He's so beautiful, I need to make a concerted effort not to stare at him.

In the street outside the back of the theater, there's a car with blacked-out windows waiting for us. Ryan opens the car door for me, then climbs in beside me.

"Where are we going?" I ask.

"Somewhere we won't be disturbed. Nothing worse than being in a bar and having napkins thrust in your face to sign." He leans forward, shakes out his arms, then trills air through his lips.

"Forgive me, this is how I de-Richard. There's a lot that goes into the performance. I have disturbed sleep if don't get him out."

"Oh, I can imagine," I say, though as someone who has never acted, I don't think I can.

The car drives to a discreet private members' club called Pleets. Ryan trills his lips for the duration of the journey. The doorman must know the car because as soon as we arrive, he opens a small, hidden side door. Inside the club, we're shown along a dark corridor, then into a cozy, dimly lit room. Adrenaline coursing through my veins, I'm now wide awake. This doesn't feel real. I'm on a secret night out with Ryan Stirling, *the* Ryan Stirling. *I wish Will could see me now. I mean Dan. I wish Dan could see me now. Do I mean Dan or Will?* The thought confuses me for a moment. Why am I thinking about either of them?

"Here we go," Ryan says, walking into the room and indicating a low, curved black leather sofa. To the left is a bar with a red strip of light emanating from beneath it, and a backlit display of bottles. It feels like a miniature nightclub, or, more worryingly, the kind of room where you might get a private lap dance.

"We'll be able to hear ourselves think in here," Ryan says, his hand on my lower back again. I assumed we'd grab a drink at the theater. I don't think I appreciated how different "going for a drink" might be when you're so recognizable.

"So, tell me again how amazing you thought the play was," Ryan says, sitting right next to me on the sofa, then splaying his legs out wide so that our thighs are touching. His eyes glint, as though he's joking, but he waits for me to answer, so I'm not sure he is.

"Oh, you were wonderful. So many words to remember." *So many words? Is that really the best I can come up with?*

"You're sweet," Ryan says, briefly dropping his eyes to my chest. "It does take a lot of practice. It's not like TV where they can feed you lines a scene at a time. The Bard's language makes it easier. The poetry of it feels right on your tongue; it's not like trying to memorize the phone book." When he says the word "tongue," he sticks his out and wiggles it in my direction. I find the gesture off-putting but I'm not sure why. It's Ryan Stirling's tongue, it can't be off-putting.

A shy-looking waiter comes over to take our order, and I use the opportunity to shift my body and put a few inches of space between us. Regardless of the nit situation, I'd rather get to know him from a slightly less intimate distance. Ryan orders a fruity cocktail for me and a whiskey for himself, then he dismisses the waiter with a wave of his hand.

"So, Anna Appleby, I have to tell you, I've never agreed to date a fan before," he says with a smirk, then slowly passes his tongue across his lower lip. "When my agent showed me your e-mail, it tickled me. I was in a ticklish sort of mood." He runs a hand up my arm to tickle me, and his touch makes me flinch.

"Ha, well," I say, clasping my hands in my lap. "I wouldn't say I was a fan, per se." Ryan's face falls. "Well, no, I am a fan. I've watched every series of *Port, Starboard, Murder*—I love that show."

"Of course you do," he says, running his tongue over his bottom lip again, then shifting closer to me and putting an arm around the back of the sofa behind me. *What's with the tongue? Is it too big for his mouth?*

"But, um, it's really this column I'm writing that inspired me to get in touch." I'm so distracted by his proximity that I'm talking faster than I normally would, blurting out words like an audiobook on double speed. "I'm writing a series of columns for *Bath Living*, on whether it's possible to date offline—"

"Yes, yes, I remember," he cuts me off. "Your 'son' suggested me." He lifts his fingers into inverted commas, then moves his hand onto my shoulder, where he starts twirling a piece of my hair. Oh God, Ryan Stirling is twirling my hair, *my hair*, what if he sees something moving in it? All the blood in my body would rush to my face and there'd be none left in the rest of me. I'd just collapse in a heap on the floor, anemically white except for my beetroot-colored head. Every muscle in my body feels tense. I don't think it's just the nit paranoia making me uncomfortable here; the hair twirling feels inappropriate. We've only just sat down, and I'm yet to finish a sentence. I reach up to tuck the piece of hair behind one ear, gently nudging away his hand, but some instinct in my gut is telling me to get up and leave.

"Which is your favorite series then?" he asks, moving his hand back to his lap as the waiter reappears with our drinks.

"Series two, I love Faye Carraway," I tell him. Faye is the actress who plays his sidekick. This feels like a safe topic for conversation; I could talk about *Port, Starboard, Murder* all night.

"Well, she's a bitch," Ryan says, his face shifting into an unpleasant sneer. "I'm too much of a gentleman to say more, but trust me, the 'chemistry' everyone said we had—I deserved a fucking BAFTA for that performance."

"Oh wow, you'd never know that you didn't get on," I say, clutching my drink and taking a large swig of what tastes like pure vodka.

"I didn't say we didn't get on. I said she was a bitch." Ryan shifts away from me now, slouching back on the sofa, both arms spread along the top of it. "Now you've ruined my post-show buzz by mentioning Faye." He stares at me, and his mouth moves into a smile, as though he's joking, but the smile doesn't reach his eyes. They lock on to me, like lasers finding their target, cold and unblinking.

"Sorry," I say, laughing nervously.

"How are you going to give me my buzz back?" he asks, his voice quiet.

"I could tell you all the great things there are to do here in

Bath?" I say lightly, glancing down at my drink, not wanting to look him in the eye. "I'm a great tour guide. Have you seen the Roman Baths yet?"

"I don't think the Roman Baths are going to give me what I'm looking for," he says. When I lift my gaze, his eyes are still on me. They seem darker, pupils bleeding into his irises so they appear almost black. He throws back the whiskey he's holding, then licks his lip. There's the tongue again.

"Why don't you tell me about the first time you got off thinking about me?" he says. "In as much detail as possible."

"Excuse me?" My body tenses, my hands clasping my drink so hard that I can see the pads of my fingers, white through the glass.

"Tell me your fantasy, I'll do what I can. You want me to arrest you in character? You want to call me Detective?" Now he lunges across the sofa toward me, clasping one hand around the back of my neck, while the other grabs hold of my thigh. "Don't be shy. You can tell me all the bad, bad things you've done, naughty girl." He smells of whiskey and stale stage makeup. His movement is so sudden, his hands so forceful, that my body freezes, my eyes searching desperately for the waiter, but I see he's made a discreet exit, and we are entirely alone in this small, dark, windowless room.

"No, no, thank you." The words come out as a whisper, though in my mind I am shouting. *Why am I not jumping up? Why do my limbs feel paralyzed?*

"Playing coy? You want to play by the letter of the law, then don't play with me," he whispers into my ear in his Brandon Farley voice. "Shall we just get out of here?" he asks, seemingly unaware of how repulsed I am by his clammy hand running up my thigh. "My hotel's just around the corner."

My body is still frozen in shock; I can't move. I open my

mouth, but my brain can't formulate words. His hand inches further up my skirt, and finally I manage to speak. "I have nits!" I blurt out, my voice a hoarse whisper.

"What?" He moves back a few inches, relaxes the hand on my neck. "What did you say?"

"I have nits. I wouldn't get so close," I say, louder now, and this time it has the desired effect. He jumps back as though I've slapped him.

"What the fuck?" He scowls at me, brushing himself down. "Why would you come here with . . . with that?"

"It wasn't planned. This was a mistake." I stand up, backing away. The more space I manage to put between us, the more my panic subsides and my voice returns. "And for future reference, just because someone likes the show you've been in, it doesn't mean they want to be pawed within minutes of meeting you."

Ryan glares at me, his short legs still splayed wide on the couch. I feel so foolish, all I want to do is run. I don't want those cold eyes on me a moment longer. As I turn to leave, Ryan says, "You look a lot older than your byline photo. I'd call that false advertising."

In the corridor, the doorman opens the outside door for me. "Get home safe, ma'am," he says, and there's a note of sympathy in his voice. Does Ryan Stirling come here after every performance, picking out a different fan from the stage door? I think I have been dangerously naïve.

Walking down the cobbled street, I burst into tears. That was so awful. *He* was so awful. They say never meet your heroes; you probably shouldn't date them either. The man just finished a three-hour play; obviously he had no interest in getting to know me. He just liked a photo he found of me online and assumed I'd be willing. I made the mistake of thinking I knew him because his face was so familiar.

At home, when Kelly asks how the evening went, I brush her off with a broad "Disappointing" and an exaggerated yawn. I pay her an extra thirty quid for the nitconvenience, then go upstairs to put one of the treatments on my head. Soaking in a too-hot bath, I try to scald away the memory of Ryan's hands.

Replaying the conversation in my head, I wonder, if I'd acted differently, could the evening have gone another way? If I hadn't mentioned Faye Carraway, if I'd been less uptight. Could there have been a scenario where I'd have *wanted* to go back to his hotel room? No, I don't think so. From the second we met, I felt something off about him, a darkness.

Rigorously combing through my hair with a nit comb, I find nothing. I do not have nits, though my scalding bath can't wash away the skin-crawling feeling. As I dry myself in silence, my phone pings with a message. Will. He's sent me a screenshot of an online dating profile: "Tiffany." She's twenty-five and has poker-straight dark hair, eyebrows that are artfully drawn, and a face that looks familiar.

Will Havers

She's hardly Ryan Stirling but still technically a celebrity . . .

Now I recognize her; she's the daughter of a famous footballer who starred in *Celebrity Love Island*. He must have gotten access to the exclusive dating app he was telling me about.

Will Havers

I told her my rival columnist was on a date with an A-lister, and she was my best chance to compete. The things I do to keep up with you, Appleby.

I want to reply, but then he might ask me how things went with Ryan.

Will Havers

You're probably still out with RS. I'll stop distracting you.

I leave it for a few minutes, then I remember I did promise to text him after my date. I'll need to say something.

Anna Appleby

I'd rather have spent the evening with Tiffany. Ryan Stirling = sleaze bag ☹

I've hardly pressed send before Will is calling me. *Why is he calling me?*

"What happened?" he asks as soon as I answer, his voice full of concern.

"It's fine, he's just a tool. I left after twenty minutes."

"I'd heard he was." Will's voice is so warm and familiar, now I'm glad that he called. "I'm sorry, I should have warned you. What did he do?"

"He thought I was a fan who was just there to . . . well, you know," I sigh.

"Are you sure you're okay?" He sounds so sincere, so full of concern, that my voice breaks as I say, "No, it's fine."

"Do you want me to come over?" Will asks.

"No, honestly, I'm okay."

"I could go heckle his play? Write up a bad review?"

This makes me laugh. "No, I'm just nursing a bruised ego." I pause. "He said I looked older than my byline photo." I let out a dramatic sigh.

"Then he doesn't know what he's talking about. You're the most beautiful woman I know." The compliment takes me by surprise. I don't know what to say, but I feel my face break into an enormous smile and a warm feeling settling in my chest.

"That's definitely not true but thank you for being nice."

There's a pause on the line.

"I'm not being nice," he says, and it sends a dart of pleasure through me.

"Night, Will."

"Night, Anna," he says. We both linger on the line for a moment, until finally, he hangs up.

When he's gone, the room feels too quiet. My whole body feels flushed, and now I won't be able to sleep. Picking up my headphones from my bedside table, I search a music app for Fleetwood Mac. The joyful, upbeat sound of "Go Your Own Way" fills my ears. I *do* know this song. I smile at the thought of Loretta dancing around the house in her underwear. Turning up the volume, I get out of bed and dance downstairs in my pajamas, imagining the soundtrack to a jubilant scene, not the scene where the heroine gets groped and humiliated by her celebrity crush.

I guess some things in life you don't get to choose; you can't choose the plot, but you can choose the soundtrack. As "Everywhere" comes on, I turn up the volume and shimmy around the living room, lip-synching to the words, not caring who might be looking in. Soon my blood is pumping, my skin is sweating, and my soul starts to sing.

GOOGLE SEARCHES:

*Fleetwood Mac, greatest hits*

*Anna Appleby byline photo*

*Ryan Stirling, creep, Reddit thread*

# CHAPTER 19

THE NEXT TIME I SEE WILL, HE'S SITTING IN A COFFEE SHOP LAUGHING with someone. I'm walking past and he's in the window, impossible to miss. I'm surprised to see him in this part of town. He doesn't live anywhere near here. Then I recognize his coffee companion—Deedee. They're laughing together; she has her hand on his arm as Will shows her something on his phone.

My body tenses, in anger or jealousy, I'm not sure. Logically, I know I have no right to feel aggrieved. Nothing really happened between us, I don't have a claim on him. He's writing a column about dating other women. But this feels different. He told me he doesn't go on more than two dates unless he thinks it could be serious, so is this something serious? Why would he be meeting her all the way out here and why was he so cagey when she called him in the car? Tucking myself around the next street corner, I can't help testing a theory. I pull out my phone and call him. He picks up after two rings.

"Hi, Anna," he says, his voice warm, almost affectionate.

"Hey. I'm on my way to the office, I'm passing Colonna & Small's. Do you want me to pick you up a coffee?"

"Oh no, thanks, I'm going to be in late today. Thank you, though."

"Hot lead for a story?" I ask, peering around the corner, watching him talk to me on his phone. Deedee flicks her long blond hair, then pouts her pillowy lips.

"No, a dentist's appointment," he says, then clears his throat. He's not a good liar. "They're calling me in now. I'll see you later?"

"Sure," I say, then hang up.

Why is he lying to me? Why doesn't he want me to know he's seeing Deedee? Because this is Will, and I should have known. The flirty behavior in Hay, the thoughtful gift, and the cozy late-night phone calls—is this all part of some strategy to manipulate me? What did he say that day in the office? "If I needed to charm you, trust me, I would have." My chest contracts. No, no one could be that diabolical. *Could they?*

AN HOUR LATER, when he arrives in the office, Will comes straight over to my desk and presents me with a cinnamon bun from the bakery that he knows I like.

"For you," he says, all sweetness and light. I swing around in the ergonomic chair that I've re-stolen.

"Let's see them then," I say.

"See what?" he asks.

"Your lovely clean teeth?"

He blushes, then rubs his neck, which I notice he does when he's uncomfortable. "It wasn't a clean. Just a checkup."

I fix him with a skeptical look.

"What?" he asks.

"Nothing. You've just got a little . . ." And I reach my finger to scratch between my teeth, then leave him desperately trying to find a crumb that isn't there.

---

AT MIDDAY WE both have a catch-up meeting with Jonathan. Our latest column went online last night and must have garnered more than average views, because Jonathan is in an exuberant mood. He's wearing a checked three-piece suit and a yellow cravat, which he twirls around his finger as he talks.

"I have been getting so many e-mails about your column, not just complaints either, compliments too," Jonathan says. "It's just what we need to shift people's perception of *Bath Living* as a fusty old property paper. NitGate was hilarious, Anna."

For the article I focused on my nit predicament rather than the anonymous actor's wandering hands. "And yours, Will," Jonathan says, clapping a hand against his thigh. "I love this competitive tone you've added, your hunt for a celebrity online to rival Anna's A-lister. You two pitted against each other, it's quite charming." As Jonathan is speaking, Will takes his glasses off and nods, acknowledging his praise. I can't feel so happy about it. The evening with Ryan has made me feel icky about the column, about involving my children in this and putting myself in situations where I am vulnerable. Jonathan is prone to being effusive, and he's being too generous about my column. It might have been funny, but I left out all my real feelings, sanitizing it. It's not the emotional sushi that Crispin wants.

"Didn't I tell you we'd be able to collaborate?" Will says, tilting his head toward me.

"You did, you did," Jonathan says. A look passes between the two men, and I have that uncomfortable feeling again. *Has Will been flirting with me just to get me onside?*

"I have some news," says Will, leaning forward in his armchair, resting an elbow on either knee. "A national newspaper got in touch. They want us to write a version of our column for their Sunday supplement. It could be great exposure for *Bath Living*."

"You didn't me tell this," I say, narrowing my eyes at him.

"I haven't had a chance. I only just received the e-mail," he explains, picking up his glasses from the desk and putting them back on.

"A national newspaper!" Crispin cries. "My goodness. Will, what an asset you are."

"They want us both to write it, they just happened to contact me," says Will, his eyes shifting to his hands, clasped in his lap. "It's Anna's idea of dating offline that they were drawn to."

"Yes, well, write whatever they want you to write. Opportunities like this don't come along every day of the week. Celebratory macaroon?" Jonathan asks, thrusting a delicate cream-colored box toward Will.

"I haven't even seen this e-mail, I don't know what I'd be agreeing to," I say, feeling a stab of petulance.

"You'd best get Will to *fill you in* then," says Jonathan, with an uncharacteristic hint of snark as he bites down on a pink macaron. *Does he know something?* I narrow my eyes at Jonathan, but he just pouts in response.

As we leave Jonathan's office, Will pulls me into the photocopier room, then shuts the door behind us. "What are you doing?" I ask, my heart racing.

"Sorry to drop that on you in there," he says. "I sent an editor at the *Times* my CV and attached a link to our column. That's why we're on his radar for this feature," Will tells me, his voice lowered. "I couldn't exactly tell Jonathan that."

"That's the problem with lying. It gets hard to keep track of who you've told what," I say, watching his face for a reaction, but I don't get one.

"I'm not asking you to lie. I just didn't want you to think I was trying to push you off the swings or anything." There's a gleam in his eye, as though we're sharing a joke, but I'm not in the mood.

"Fine, what's the feature they're asking for?" I say, keen to finish this conversation and escape this small, confined space as soon as possible. The air feels charged in here; it's too hot. My shirt feels as though it's clinging to me, and my neck tingles with heat.

"There's this tech-free retreat," Will explains. "It's up in the Mendip Hills, they want a local journalist to write a review. You go off-grid for forty-eight hours in a bid to 'connect with each other more deeply.'" He pauses, dropping his gaze to the floor, then lowering his voice. "It's a couples' thing."

"Sorry, what? A romantic retreat? You and me?" I ask, then when he nods, I frown. "Was this your idea?"

Will laughs. "Anna, if I wanted to get you alone, I wouldn't have to pitch some lame dating retreat to the *Times* to do it." *Okay, so that put me in my place.* He shakes his head. "Obviously it wouldn't be a real date if that's what you're worried about. We would just need to write it up that way." He pauses, fixing me with a perplexed look. "Have I done something to upset you? Cinnamon bun too cinnamony for you?"

"No, I'm just stretched as it is, and this is one more thing, one more weekend away. You should have consulted me first."

"I can take someone else," he offers, and I wonder if that's what he wants.

"But it's my column idea they like? They want both of us?" I ask, and he nods. "I'll make it work. Just send me the e-mail."

"It's in your inbox already."

"Fine."

"Fine." We glare at each other, the fizz morphing back into friction. He's right, this is a great opportunity. I'm just annoyed because he's sprung it on me, because he lied about Deedee and it makes me wonder what else he might be lying about. I don't trust him. Or maybe it's that I don't trust myself to spend a whole weekend with him.

Looking into his swirling green eyes, at his dark lashes, I remember his words on the phone, saying he thought I was beautiful. My eyes fall to his lips and my breath catches in my throat. I need to get out of here. Will doesn't make a move to leave, so I reach past him for the door handle, my arm brushing against his hip in my hurry to leave. He turns sideways to move out of my way, but then I appear to have forgotten how door handles work, as I turn it from left to right and nothing seems to happen.

"Let me," he says, putting his hand over mine on the knob, gently twisting it, tugging it, and then finally the door is open. I lurch into the corridor, like a greyhound released from its pen, and don't dare look back as I cradle the hand that feels marked by his.

GOOGLE SEARCHES:

*Reconnect Retreats, Mendip Hills*

*Are epilators worth the investment?*

*Spicy books about workplace romance*

**Orders The Spanish Love Deception by Elena Armas**

# CHAPTER 20

"I THINK YOU SHOULD JUST SLEEP WITH HIM," LOTTIE SAYS AS WE stand on the sidelines watching Ethan play hockey for his school team.

"Shhh," I hiss, nervously looking around to see who might have heard her. Lottie is already drawing attention. She's wearing a *World's Greatest Aunt* T-shirt pulled tight around her pregnancy bump and she keeps whooping loudly whenever anyone on Ethan's team has possession of the ball. The sidelines are buzzing with parents, and my heart sinks as I spot Neil standing alone near the goal line. Even from half a field away, I can see his cheek is still a strange purple color.

"I don't want to be another notch on Will's office bedpost," I tell Lottie.

"Maybe it's not that. Maybe he's in love with you," Lottie says, and this makes me burst out laughing.

"That doesn't make any sense."

"Yes!" Lottie says, warming to this theory. "He's had a crush on you forever, but he's trying to rein it in because he knows he's leaving."

Now that I've filled Lottie in on my moonlit flirtation with Will, his kindness over Katniss, and the secrecy over Deedee, she is full of theories and advice, most of which involve "throwing caution to the wind" and sleeping with him.

"How does Deedee fit into this theory of yours then?" I ask, wincing as Ethan takes a thwack to the ankles by someone on the opposing team.

"A distraction," she says.

"It's more likely he got bored in Hay, and *I* was the distraction until someone better came along."

"Better?" Lottie shakes her head. "What planet are you on?"

"What do you mean?"

"You're hot! You turn heads wherever you go, you always have. I don't know when you stopped seeing it." We watch as Ethan runs for the ball and I take a minute to digest her words. *Is that true, or is she just saying it because she's my sister?* "Woohoo! Go, Ethan!" Lottie yells toward the pitch, then at almost at the same volume says, "Will is exactly what you need, a younger guy who knows what he's doing. Break the seal, get your confidence back. If he's not boyfriend material, who cares, have a kinky weekend, then move on."

"Hi, Anna," comes a voice from behind me. Lottie and I both swivel around to see Neil standing right there. His appearance makes me start, not only because he's crept up on us, but also because his face looks even worse at close range.

"Oh Jesus, Neil, that looks . . . bad. Have you seen a doctor?" I ask.

"It's a secondary infection," Neil tells me. "It looks far worse than it is. I'm told the oozing is a sign of improvement."

"Really?" I ask, wincing. "Um, Neil, this is my sister, Lottie."

"Hi," Lottie says, reaching out to shake his hand. "Is your daughter playing in the match?"

Neil nods. "Tilly scored a goal," he says proudly. Then, with his eyes on the pitch, he says, "I told Sheila that you and I were seeing each other. I hope that's okay."

"Oh, right. Um, why?" I ask, a sinking feeling in my chest.

"I want her to know I've moved on. You don't need to do anything. I'm only telling you in case she asks."

Lottie and I exchange a look.

"I'd rather not lie, Neil," I say gently.

"I already mentioned it to a few people. You can spread the word that we broke up if you like," Neil says, stuffing his hands into his pockets. My gut swirls with indignation, and I clamp my jaw shut. This is why people date online—it's easier to never see people again.

"We're going to go and stand over here now. Lovely to meet you, Neil," says Lottie, steering me away from him. She says it with such a warm smile, Neil doesn't even seem offended, he just waves us off.

"This is what happens when you get involved with people you have to see again," I hiss to Lottie. "I can't just have a kinky weekend with Will, I have to work with the guy. Plus why are we even talking about this, because he's clearly not available."

"Why don't you just ask him what's going on? What have you got to lose?"

"My self-respect. Others' professional respect. This whole thing is proving a massive distraction, and I've got a lot on my plate."

"That's just an excuse."

"An excuse?"

"Yes. I can say this because I'm your sister, but sometimes I think you use work or the kids as an excuse to say no to stuff. Stuff that feels scary because it might not work out." She must see my face fall because now she reaches out to put an arm around me. "All I'm saying is, sometimes it's okay to think with something other than your head," Lottie says, thrusting her pelvis inappropriately, just as Jess appears beside us.

"How's Ethan doing?" she asks, taking off her headphones and peering at the pitch.

"He hasn't touched the ball, but he's having a wonderful time," Lottie tells her.

"Look at me!" shouts Ethan as he runs past us, waving his stick in the air.

"Wouldn't it be great to be Ethan," Jess says, and we both laugh, knowing exactly what she means.

"To go through life with the confidence of a seven-year-old boy? Heaven," I say.

"You okay, Jessie?" Lottie asks, and I turn to see Jess's expression falter.

"What's happened?" I ask, reaching out to squeeze her hand.

"At break, Penny told everyone I was changing my pronouns. Now everyone is calling me they/them," Jess says, rolling her eyes as though she's over it, but I see from the set of her jaw she's not. "Which would be fine if I wanted to identify that way, but I don't."

"That is not acceptable. Have you told your teacher?" I ask.

"No, Mum," she says, pulling her hand away. "What's the teacher going to do? Call a meeting about my pronouns? That's exactly what Penny *wants* me to do." She holds out her hand. "Can I have the car keys? I'm going to put my stuff in the car."

"What am I supposed to do about this Penny girl?" I ask Lottie once Jess is out of earshot.

"Nothing," says Lottie. "Just be supportive. Make sure you give her time and space to talk to you about it. Maybe's there's more to it."

"Like what?" I ask. "Did she say something?"

"No, I just sense it. Jess is like you, she bottles things up."

"I don't bottle things up," I say indignantly.

The whistle goes; the game has finished. Ethan runs over to us waving his stick in the air. "Did you see me? Did you see me?"

"You were brilliant," Lottie says, grabbing his stick and jumping up and down with him. "Such excellent running!"

"Did you see when I nearly got the ball?" Ethan looks at me with huge, excited eyes.

"Yes, you were so fast!" I say, giving him a high five.

As we all pile into the car to drive home, Ethan leans forward from the backseat.

"Mum, what's that on your arm? Is that a tattoo?" he asks in dismay.

"What?" Jess shrieks, leaning over him to see. Looking down, I realize the plaster I've been wearing has come off.

"Oh." I swallow uncomfortably.

"When did you get this?" Jess asks, slack-jawed.

"It was a mistake. I'm getting it removed," I say, putting a protective hand over it.

"How do you get a tattoo by mistake?" asks Lottie.

"It was a work thing," I say evasively.

"I love it, it's so cool. Can I get one?" Jess asks.

"Absolutely not."

"What does it mean? 'And'?" Lottie asks while trying to stifle a laugh.

"It's supposed to be a symbolic ampersand rather than literally the word 'and.'"

"I think you should keep it," Lottie says. "It's got so much attitude, like you're saying 'AND?' to the world. 'Yeah, my name's Anna, AND? You got a problem with that?'" Lottie says in a gruff voice, then starts giggling to herself.

"Speak to the and, 'cause the face ain't listening," says Ethan, holding up his hand, which makes all three of them fall about in hysterics. The sound of their laughter fills the car and it's such a wonderful noise, I find myself laughing too, despite their teasing.

WHEN WE GET home, Johnny the handyman has been, and the kitchen cabinets are now a beautiful dark green. They look perfect. Now all I need is some more houseplants, and every meal will feel like I'm foraging for food in a jungle.

"Green, cool," says Ethan.

"The house smells of paint," says Jess.

Neither of them seems as excited about the change as I am, and they soon disappear upstairs to start homework. I should make a plan for dinner, put a wash on, respond to some work e-mails, but instead I head toward the garage.

"Jess, Ethan, I'll be in the garage if you need me," I call up the stairs. "Takeout for dinner. Your choice."

They yell down their approval of this plan. When I open the door to the garage, a cold gust of air hits me. I grab a cardigan from the hall, then plug in an oil heater. Next, I find a folded picnic table in the corner, dust it off, and lay a piece of tarpaulin over the top. Unwrapping the huge block of clay, I lift it onto the table, and it makes a satisfying "thwack" as I set it down.

I've been putting off starting a sculpture, worried my efforts will be embarrassingly childish, fearing I'd misremembered having any talent for this. But seeing Ethan on the pitch today reminded me you don't have to be good at something to find joy in it. Taking out the box of molding tools, I cut off a large chunk of clay. Maybe Lottie is right: I do overthink things; I say no because it's less scary than failing or being disappointed. Perhaps I should try to be more like her and follow my instincts more.

The last few years have been about keeping everyone else happy—trying to cushion Jess and Ethan from the fallout of the separation, soft-stepping around Dan and Dan's mood. I have shut out the voice asking what else I might want, what I might need. As my hands start to warm the cold material, the infinite possibilities hidden in this lump of brown clay make my fingers dance with anticipation.

GOOGLE SEARCHES:

- *Sculpting with clay, tutorial*
- *Is it really naff to have an ampersand tattoo?*
- *Is Patrick Swayze's Ghost on Netflix?*

# CHAPTER 21

"I'M SO SORRY, I DIDN'T KNOW WE WERE DOING COSTUMES," I SAY with a nervous laugh when I see Michael waiting for me in the tearoom. He is dressed in high-waisted breeches, a high-collared shirt, and a single-breasted green tailcoat. He stands, and bows, and then pulls out a chair for me.

"No, no, not compulsory," Michael says, flicking his tails as he sits back down. "I've just finished my shift. I usually play Bingley, but today I am Edward Ferrars, at your service."

The Jane Austen Centre is a quaint little museum dedicated to Jane Austen's life and how she came to live here in Bath. It boasts a wonderful gift shop, a Regency tearoom, and actors roaming the halls dressed as characters from her novels.

"You work here as a guide, as well as delivering parcels?" I ask in surprise.

"Two afternoons and every other Saturday. Austen is my life." His face lights up. "You've read her, I presume?"

"Some," I admit. "I think I read *Emma* and *Mansfield Park* in school. I've watched the *Pride and Prejudice* TV adaptation and Emma Thompson's *Sense and Sensibility*—I loved that one."

Michael's face goes pale, and his mouth falls open in horror.

"That is not the same, not the same at all. An adaptation is but a shadow of the original text," he says, his tufty eyebrows sinking into a frown. "The books offer such a keen insight into human nature. Austen's turns of phrase are exquisite." Michael fiddles with a cufflink, clearly bothered. "Just think what we might have had from dear Jane if she hadn't died so young. *Sanditon,* of course, but what else might she have gifted us with?" Michael lets out a low sigh.

"Which is your favorite novel?" I ask, suppressing a smile.

"Oh, *P and P,* undoubtedly, though I know that makes me predictable. Some claim that *Persuasion* has more depth, that she was a more experienced writer when she penned it, but I don't think you can top the characterization in *P and P.* I have read it thirty-eight times."

"You're kidding me," I say, letting a laugh slip out.

"I never jest when it comes to Jane," Michael says, sitting up a little straighter and adjusting the fold of his high collar.

Our tea arrives, and I find myself intrigued by Michael. I've never met anyone like him. He tells me he read *Mansfield Park* at school and that Fanny Price was his first literary crush. I confess mine was Jo March from *Little Women,* then we have an animated discussion about which fictional characters we'd like to invite to dinner. Michael doesn't ask me anything about my job, my family, or my divorce, he only wants to talk about Austen and books. It makes a refreshing change.

Once we've finished our tea, he takes me on a tour of the museum and launches into a lengthy explanation of the Austen family tree. Watching him talk, my mind begins to drift. What kind of woman might be attracted to Michael? He's not unattractive, he's passionate and well-read, but for me, there's no spark. What is it that creates that chemistry, that attraction to another human being? Meeting Dan so young, I took it for granted that if it hadn't been him, I would have met someone else. But maybe the perfect confluence of factors that makes for a good relationship is a rarity. To have *real* chemistry, to be at the same stage of life, to want enough of the same things and be compatible companions—maybe that doesn't come along very often.

My mind darts to Will. He has stopped flirting with me at work. We're not even playing the chair game anymore, he's let me keep the ergonomic monstrosity all week. When we cross paths in the office, he's professional and courteous, but that's all. He's also been out of the office more than usual. On Wednesday, he took a day's holiday. Who takes a day's holiday midweek? He's also started calling me Anna rather than Appleby, which feels significant. Honestly, I'm relieved. It makes my life simpler. I can get on with my work without being distracted or nervous about the retreat next weekend. I don't have space in my life for a confusing and time-consuming workplace flirtation.

"Let me show you my favorite room," Michael says, pulling me back to the present. He opens a door with a sign saying "Staff only." "The costume cupboard. Do you want to play dress-up?"

I do not want to play dress-up, but when I say as much, Michael looks so disappointed that I am forced to relent. The room has rails full of Regency outfits, and I let Michael pick out a blue Empire-line gown with a matching bonnet that he deems suitable.

"You look sensational," he says, kissing the tips of his fingers, then throwing me the kiss through the air. "Shall we take a turn around the Royal Crescent?" he asks, then whispers, "They let me borrow these, just for a short outing."

"In public?" I ask, horrified. "Won't people stare?" He looks wounded by this, and I hear myself saying, "Maybe just a short walk. Then I really must get back."

The Royal Crescent is arguably Bath's most famous street. An impressive feat of Georgian architecture, a sweeping crescent of historical terraced houses, overlooking Royal Victoria Park. It's not far from the Circus, where Will lives, and I briefly imagine what it must have been like to grow up in a house steeped in so much history. Even when you're not dressed the part, it's hard to walk along this street without feeling as though you're starring in your very own period drama. Michael takes my arm in his, and we amble along the garden side of the crescent. The sun is warm on our faces, and Victoria Park is abloom with yellow tulips. To my surprise, I think I might be enjoying myself.

"Being a Janeite is more than a hobby," Michael tells me. "Some women find this level of commitment challenging." He lifts his hat to greet an elderly man walking toward us, who smiles in bemusement, as though we are lost circus performers.

"My ex Gail was supportive, well versed in the literature. But she also refused to commit to the ball," he tells me. "I'm on the organizing committee, it's important to me, but she booked a trip to Rome the same weekend."

I don't need to ask which ball he's referring to. Each summer, Regency enthusiasts throw a formal, Austen-inspired ball. People travel from all over the world to attend and it's the focal point of Bath's summer calendar. "She also insisted I meet her parents in 'normal clothes.' That's not who I am, Anna. This is normal to me." Michael turns to face me, looking for understanding.

"I'm sorry Gail disappointed you," I say, hugging his arm a little tighter in mine.

Michael squeezes my arm right back. "Do you know what Austen prescribes as the finest balm for the pangs of disappointed love?"

"Wine?" I suggest.

"Friendship," he says. "And I hope you won't mind me saying that whilst I don't see a romantic storyline developing between us, given you have only read two of Jane's novels, I hope that we may become friends?"

"I would like that very much," I say.

As we walk arm in arm, ahead of us one of the doors opens, and a man and a woman step out onto the street. They look familiar, and as we get closer, I realize, with a rising sense of dread, the man is Will. Oh no, oh God, he's going to see me dolled up like a Regency clown. Then I notice the woman he's with, and she is familiar too: she's wearing a bright red top with purple dungarees and has a Liberty-print silk scarf around her head—oh God, it's Loretta, from the theater.

"Anna?" Will says in surprise, looking me over from my bonnet to my feet to fully absorb my ridiculous outfit.

"Will, hi. Um, this is Michael," I say, feeling flustered. Will looks delighted by my lack of composure, then his face starts to look pained, as though it is taking him a huge amount of effort not to burst out laughing. Michael raises his hat in greeting to them both.

"You look very sweet," Will says, regarding me strangely, as though I have sprouted wings. Loretta looks at me, confused. She can't place me. *Please don't let her be able to place me.*

"We're on an Austen-inspired date, hence the getup," I explain, feeling my palms begin to sweat.

"Of course you are. This is a friend of mine, Loretta Fields," Will says. "We're on a fundraising committee together, for a charity choir." Then it happens. Her face shifts into the most enormous smile as she works out where she knows me from.

"Anna, of course! My, my, is that a wig?" She reaches out to stroke my hair. "It looks fabulous—*you* look fabulous."

"Lovely to see you again," I say, desperately thinking of a way to get out of this conversation without appearing rude. "I would love to stay and chat, but we, um, we have to get these costumes back by six—"

"There's no rush to return them," Michael says, oblivious.

"How do you know Will?" Loretta asks me.

"We work together," I explain.

"Anna makes my life a living hell," Will says with a smile, and the glint in his eye, which has been gone all week, is back.

"Well, I hope you aren't working this dear girl too hard. It's important to ease back into work gently. You mustn't overdo it when your body is recovering," Loretta says, reaching out to squeeze my hand. Now Will and Michael are both looking back and forth between us in confusion.

"Um, yes, I think there was a small misunderstanding the last time we met," I start to explain, feeling my face burn. "I'm not ill. I'm not in recovery either. Crossed wires." I hope this will be enough of an explanation, but everyone is still looking at me, so I fear it may not. "I met Loretta at the theater. I was wearing a headscarf as a precaution, against, um, nits, though it turns out I didn't have them. Loretta assumed . . . I should have said straightaway, but I was embarrassed, and you were being so nice. I'm so sorry." This might be the worst conversation I've ever been a part of. Will and Loretta exchange looks, and my heart pounds with mortification; my borrowed finery now feels like a straitjacket.

"You're not in recovery?" Lorretta asks, confused.

"No, and this isn't a wig, it's my real hair."

After a long pause, Loretta starts laughing, and now I can't help laughing too.

"Oh dear, how foolish of me to assume."

"Not at all, it was entirely my fault," I tell her.

"Now you *must* call me for a gin sometime. We can laugh about this some more," Loretta says. "No excuses."

"No excuses," I say, relieved to have the misunderstanding cleared up.

As we say our good-byes, Will looks at me strangely again, then blushes, as though I am walking the streets in lingerie or something equally exposing. I cringe as Michael and I continue our walk along the crescent. Michael gives my arm a comforting squeeze. "You know, I'd wager courting in Austen's day was easier," he says. "Perhaps we have too much choice now, we expect too much."

"I don't agree. I think it's easy to romanticize the past," I say. "But beneath all the beautiful dresses and the formality, marriage was an exchange of property between two men. We wouldn't want to go back to that."

"That is true," says Michael.

Looking up at these stately houses, I wonder how many marriages have played out behind these doors. How many great love stories, how many miserable ones, how many women powerless to leave unhappy marriages. I realize how much I take for granted. I am free to divorce, to date, to earn my own living, to be alone if I want to be, to choose my own happiness. How many women—*people*—throughout history have not had that, *still* do not have that?

"Maybe I don't want to go back in time then," Michael says. "All I want is a woman who appreciates Jane as I do, who's open to a little role play here and there." His cheeks flush. "Who won't be ashamed to go out with me dressed like this. Who will come to the ball having learned the appropriate steps for the cotillion. Is all that really too much to ask?"

"Have you ever tried internet dating, Michael?" I ask him.

"No." Michael makes a face. "I don't think it would be for me."

I explain that while I too had my reservations about finding love online, if he is looking for something quite specific, then the internet might be the perfect place to look. Online, every Janeite cosplay aficionada within a twenty-mile radius would be at his fingertips. "Let me set you up a profile?" I plead, excited about the prospect of focusing on someone else's love life for a change. "Let me find you a date for the Regency ball!"

"This all feels rather Emma Woodhouseish," he says with a hint of a smile. "But okay, I would love you to help me find an appropriate date for the ball."

"Yes!" I clap my hands, inexplicably excited about my new role as Michael's personal Emma.

"On one condition," Michael adds. "You read *Pride and Prejudice,* the book, properly, cover to cover. I don't think we can be friends otherwise."

"Fine. It's a deal," I say, reaching out to shake his hand.

After we get back to the Jane Austen Centre and change back into our normal clothes, I bid Michael a fond good-bye. Then on my walk home, I call Loretta and leave a message on her answerphone, asking when she might be free to meet me for a coffee. Or perhaps a gin.

GOOGLE SEARCHES:

*Dating apps for Janeites*

*West Country Regency enthusiasts*

*Quiz, which Jane Austen character am I?*

*Who was the best Darcy, Colin Firth or Matthew Macfadyen?*

# CHAPTER 22

"WHY CAN'T WE DRIVE AGAIN?" WILL ASKS AS WE WAIT ON A REMOTE country road for our connecting bus.

"Because it's an eco-retreat, they encourage people not to bring their cars," I explain for the third time.

"'Encourage' isn't an outright ban, though, is it?" Will says, stretching out his hamstrings. He really is incredibly tall. I can't imagine what it must be like to take up so much space.

"We've been invited to write about the place, we need to embrace the retreat's ethos." I don't know how I've found myself the champion of this plan. A one-hour journey is taking us two and a half.

"I have better things I could be doing with my time," Will says, checking his watch again.

"And I don't?" I shoot back tetchily. I'm already indebted to Dan for switching another weekend with the kids, and given the confusing vibe between Will and me, I could do without having to spend a whole weekend alone with him, especially on a romantic getaway. My life already feels like one long fake date.

"If only you were wearing that delightful costume from last

weekend. I'm sure a horse-drawn carriage would have rescued us by now."

"Ha ha," I say, ignoring him and turning back to my phone.

"How are you going to cope without your phone for forty-eight hours?" Will asks, watching me tapping away. He walks up beside me and looks over my shoulder. "Why are you on a dating site? Isn't that against the rules?"

"It's for someone else, I'm playing matchmaker," I tell him.

Will's eyes grow playful. "I'll bet you don't last the full forty-eight hours."

"You want to bet? What are you, twelve?"

"Because twelve-year-olds are such notorious gamblers," Will says, raising his eyes to the sky. "First to fold has to . . ." He pauses.

"Has to what?" I ask, keen to see what ridiculous suggestion he's going to come up with.

"Has to cede the chair once and for all." He holds my gaze and I can't help smiling now. He reaches out a hand to shake mine, but I swipe it away, not in the mood for his childish games.

"I like that chair," I say.

"It's my chair."

"Technically it's *Bath Living*'s chair," I tell him, then shake my head. "Fine. Whoever checks their phone first relinquishes the good chair."

Will starts doing a ridiculous victory dance just as the bus arrives. On the bus, I go back to creating Michael's dating profile, and Will gives me a knowing look.

"It doesn't start until we get there," I clarify.

When we finally reach the retreat, the sun is low in the sky, and the gravel track leading off the main road is bathed in beautiful orange sunlight. The location is as stunning as the website promised. Rolling green hills striped with hedgerows, and no sound except the distant hum of the road and chirping of birdlife.

Will is walking in an odd way, hopping around the track. I look down and see he's wearing smart leather shoes and is trying to avoid the mud.

"Ah, poor little town mouse didn't bring his wellies?" I say, feeling smug about my own scruffy pair of trainers, but as I say it, I trip and land my foot right in a deep patch of mud. It splatters all the way up my leg, and I let out an involuntary groan.

"Oh no, did you get muddy, country mouse?" Will says, leaping over a patch of mud to get past me.

We reach a gate and a sign that says "Reconnect Retreats. Off-grid since 2024." On the other side of the gate, a Land Rover is parked in the mud, and when she sees us, a woman jumps out. She's perky and young, with wild brown curls beneath a tweed flat cap. She is Outdoors Barbie in Hunter wellies and a faded Barbour jacket, ready to don a plastic shotgun and shoot some plastic grouse.

"You must be Anna and Will, from the *Times*," she says, and I can't help relishing how good that sounds. "You managed the bus, then?"

"Just about," I say, reaching out to shake her perfectly manicured hand.

"I'm Verity, Reconnect PR," she says, her voice high and light like a tinkling fairy's.

"Great to meet you, Verity," says Will, giving her his most dazzling smile as he leans in to shake her hand. Her eyes widen in delight as she takes Will in. *Yes, yes, he's hot, we all see it.*

As Verity guides us through the woods, she explains a little about the retreat's founding principles. Her jeans are so tight and her bum so perky in them, I'm finding it hard to look at anything else as she walks ahead of us. Did I *ever* have a bum like that?

"Our founder, Malin, met her partner, Brad, when they both bought tickets to a scam festival that didn't exist," Verity tells us. "They found themselves on a remote Caribbean island, left to fend for themselves with no phone-charging facilities and hardly any resources. Maybe it was destiny, but Malin swears that it was not having their phones that caused love to blossom. They were totally present. The principle of Reconnect Retreats is to give couples the space to put the focus back on each other. Whether it's a first date or a relationship check-in, two days here will feel like a month out in the real world."

"How could you scientifically test that?" I ask. "Is that a peer-reviewed statistic? What if you find yourself on a bad date? Isn't that torture, being stuck on a monthlong bad date?"

"Anna is a skeptic," Will explains. "She's also allergic to the outdoors."

"I'm not allergic to the outdoors, I just enjoy the indoors," I clarify.

Verity carries on chatting to Will and ignores my questions about scientific data.

After a fifteen-minute walk through the woods, we come to a wooden shepherd's hut on cast-iron wheels. It's a modern, sleek design, with a large window looking out over the valley beyond. Verity opens the door and shows us both inside. It's stylish and well-appointed, with a double bed, a small desk, and an oil burner, then a separate room with a shower and compost toilet. It's all tastefully decorated with pale wooden beams, pale burgundy bed linens, and elegant throw cushions. But just as I'm warming up to the idea of this "camping without camping" experience, I have a concerning thought.

"There is another cabin, right? You're not expecting us to share this one?" I ask.

"I told them we'd only need one, pookums," Will says. "Was that not right?"

My stomach drops and my throat constricts. He *has* to be joking. I know we're supposed to be writing about this as though it's a date, but having to share a bed would be beyond the call of journalistic duty. Verity lets out a burst of laughter, like a pretty little machine gun.

"Don't worry, there's another cabin just beyond those trees," she says. "This is our 'separate but together' glade, perfect for a first date. We have many combinations."

"I'm offended by how panicked you just looked," says Will, tilting his head to one side.

"You're not together, then?" Verity asks, her eyes flashing back and forth between us.

"First date," says Will, in that voice he uses when he's trying to wind me up. "But there's a lot of unresolved sexual tension."

Verity laughs, as though he's made the most hilarious joke, and I feel my cheeks heat. Is he flirting with her, or me, or both of us? Why am I so bad at reading this stuff?

Outside the cabin, Verity shows us the firepit, which has a large wooden lockbox beside it. "All your food for the weekend is provided, and there's a stocked cool box in each of the cabins. You'll need to cook and heat water on the fire here. Wood, kindling, fire lighters all in the wood store, drinking water from this casket." She taps a large plastic water butt. "You have separate living spaces, but you come together for meals." Verity gives me an expectant look. "We ask that you replenish whatever wood you use from the store; logs to split are over there. And that you leave nothing in the woods but footprints. Finally, phones. There's limited reception in this valley, no Wi-Fi, so it's easy not to cheat. But we provide lockboxes to put your phones in, as it can be hard to break the habit of reaching for them. Did you give family members our emergency landline number?" We both nod, and I feel the first tug of alarm at being completely cut off for two whole days. "If anyone needs to get in touch with you, I'll drive down from the office and let you know. Rarely happens, but it puts people's minds at rest, especially if you have children." Verity smiles at me. *Did I tell her I have kids, or do I just look so tired she assumes I must?*

"This all looks wonderful, thank you, Verity. I feel more relaxed already," says Will, the teacher's pet.

"Each door locks with a code, all the information you need is in this pack." She hands us each a booklet full of "commonly asked questions."

"Your code is written here, five seven zero four," she tells me, pointing to the front page. "It won't lock unless you click the latch like this, so just leave it open until you've remembered the code, or until you're inside at night." Taking in the calm quiet of the woods, I feel my shoulders start to relax. The cabin is gorgeous and the view of the valley beyond the trees idyllic. There are certainly worse places you could be forced to spend a weekend. I've brought *Pride and Prejudice* with me, and without my phone or my laptop to distract me, I'm hoping to get plenty of reading done.

"There are six other reconnectors on site," Verity tells us. "But their cabins are half a mile away at the other side of the woods. They shouldn't disturb you. Our forester, Malcolm, will be leading a guided flora and fauna walk tomorrow. He'll be leaving from the gate at twelve if you want to join in, but nothing is compulsory. There's also a river down the hill with a plunge pool that's safe for swimming, just follow the wooden arrows. If you do go skinny dipping, just be aware that the other residents might also use the pool."

"I'll bear that in mind," Will says, his voice a flirtatious growl. Verity laughs appreciatively. I suppress the urge to groan.

"You are going to have the best time," she tells us. "Two nights here feels like an eternity, in the best way, trust me. We try to leave you to it as much as we can, but if there's anything urgent, there's phone reception on top of that hill and our office is only three miles down the road." Verity points to a hill on the other side of the valley, which looks a long way away. She lingers, shifting her weight from side to side, eyes on Will. "I'll leave you to it then, shall I?" she asks him.

"Yup, we've got it. Thanks, Verity," I say.

Once she's gone, Will says, "She was nice."

"She was," I agree. "Right, I'm going to unpack."

"Don't unpack, let's get the fire going," Will says, clapping his hands, then rubbing them together, his eyes dancing. "Don't you just love camping?"

"This is so your kind of thing, isn't it?" I say, feeling myself smile because it's sweet how excited he is.

"It is," he says, flashing me a grin.

"Were you okay to leave your brother this weekend?" I ask, remembering he, like me, has family commitments.

"Yes, George came down for the weekend to help Dad. Shall we go and look for this plunge pool before it gets dark?"

"I didn't bring a swimsuit," I say, "and before you suggest skinny dipping, it's not happening."

"Suit yourself," Will says. "Shall we keep each other's phones? Otherwise, how do I know you're not going to sneak up that hill to check the *Daily Mail* in the middle of the night?"

"I'm hardly going to do that, am I?" I say, but I turn my phone off and hand it over. He does the same with his, then we head to our respective cabins to get settled.

There's a lockbox in the wall, which I put Will's phone into. Maybe it is better not to have mine within reach. I did secretly download two movies onto it and that's probably not strictly in the spirit of a technology detox. *I wonder if Dan will remember to call the emergency landline number if anything happens with the kids.* I chastise myself for worrying. *They'll be fine. They aren't babies anymore.*

Dumping my bag and the information booklet on the cabin

table, I head back outside, walking carefully down the steep cabin steps. I flinch as a gust of wind bangs the cabin door shut behind me. The sun is low in the sky, and Will has already started to build a fire. Seeing him rearrange kindling in the half-light stirs some primordial feeling within me. This must be an evolutionary trait left over from our cave woman days, to be impressed by a man making fire. It's ridiculous because fire isn't even hard, especially if you have fire lighters. We should be attracted to rarer skills, like the ability to reboot the Sky box without losing all your downloaded programs or being able to shave without leaving the bathroom sink covered in bristles.

Will shoots me a broad smile when he sees me coming, and I notice he's left his glasses behind in his cabin. He's also taken his shirt off and is now wearing a thin cotton T-shirt that clings to his biceps. There's a streak of ash on his cheek and he looks happier than I've ever seen him. He's brought two beers from his cabin cooler and hands one to me.

"Do you think you're going to be able to endure a weekend in the woods with me then, Appleby?" *We're back to Appleby.*

"I'll try," I say, sitting down on a log and raising my beer can toward his. His eyes gleam with playful energy. I can tell he's in a flirty mood, and with Verity gone, there's no one else to flirt with but me. "Stop flirting," I say, narrowing my eyes at him.

"I'm not," he laughs. "This is just my face. What, are you worried you're not going to be able to resist me this time, Appleby?" he says, voice smooth as butter, but his face falls when he sees I'm not smiling. "What's wrong?"

I cross my arms. I hadn't planned on saying anything but now I think I'm going to have to.

"It's all a game to you, isn't it?" I say, taking a large swig of beer. "I don't want to be your plaything when there's no one else around to flirt with."

"Is that what you think? You're not that," he says, leaning his elbows on his knees, brow furrowed in concern. "You're not that to me at all."

"Not that I *want* anything to happen," I say. "Hay was a mistake, I'd had too much to drink. But if you're seeing someone, however casually, I don't think it's appropriate to be so flirty with every woman within a five-mile radius."

"What are you talking about?" he asks, looking genuinely confused.

"Deedee?" I say, watching his face, and I'm gratified to see his eyes shift.

"What about her?" he asks, though his tone is less indignant now.

"I saw you sneaking off with her after Hay." I pause, weighing up how much to say. "And having breakfast with her when you said you were at the dentist."

Will shakes his head, and now I see he's smiling. *Is he enjoying this?*

"It's not funny! You're a real dick, you know that?" I mutter. "I can't believe I ever—"

"Anna Appleby, are you jealous?" he asks, biting his lip, and I feel the urge to throw my beer across the fire at him, to wipe that conceited smirk off his face.

"I am nothing of the sort," I shoot back, standing up now, pacing with restless energy. "I don't care who you're sleeping with, I'd just rather you didn't play these games with me."

"Have you finished?" he asks, and I nod, pulling my elbows into a tight hug. "Deedee is a headhunter. She works for news outlets across Europe. She came to Hay to watch my panel, but then had to fly back to Paris the next morning. She'd put me forward for this job at an international news station, but she didn't think my CV was going cut it against the competition. She persuaded me that I needed to get on a plane and go with her to meet the head of the station, said it might be my only chance to throw my hat in the ring." Will pauses. "She's not someone I'm seeing. In fact, Deedee is married to a friend of mine."

"Oh."

"The guy she introduced me to liked me enough to ask for a screen test. I met Deedee for breakfast the other day because she'd organized one for me in Bath. I didn't tell you, because I don't like telling anyone about interviews. It sucks to have people ask if you got the job when you didn't. I haven't told work I'm looking to leave, so I told a white lie about the dentist's. I'd rather not be pushed out before I have somewhere to go." Will stands up and saunters around the fire toward me.

"A presenting job, wow. That would be incredible," I say, hugging myself even tighter as I process this new information.

"It would," he says, standing just a foot away from me now. The smell of his cologne, his perspiration, and the campfire mingle into a heady combination that puts my senses on high alert. "Anything else you want to say?"

"Sorry," I mumble, eyes on my feet.

"Sorry for what?" he says, his voice teasing.

"Sorry for calling you a dick," I say with a grimace. *How can I have gotten that so wrong?* When I look up, I see he's smiling.

"And for assuming that I'm having moonlit parties with anyone but you, Appleby." His eyes hold mine, and there it is, back like a punch to the gut, the crackle of undeniable energy between us.

"Sorry about that," I say, biting my lip.

"Thank you," he says quietly, tilting his head and then slowly leaning in toward my neck. I can't help inhaling the scent of him now, his skin radiating heat. "I'm sorry you thought Hay was such a mistake. I will try to keep a lid on any such behavior in the future." He's mocking me, but his proximity sends a prickle of anticipation down my spine, a disconcerting throb between my legs. "Now that that's out of the way, can we relax, maybe even enjoy ourselves?" He pauses, watching my expression. "And I would appreciate it if you didn't mention Deedee or my job hunt to anyone at work."

"Of course not," I say, and then move to sit down on a log beside the fire, because I'm feeling giddy. If we're still at war, then Will won that round. Though on this occasion, I don't mind losing, because I'm glad that he's not seeing Deedee, that I wasn't being made a fool of in Hay.

As the sun goes down, we set to work preparing dinner on the fire. Will pulls some baking potatoes from the food box, wraps them in foil, then places them into the firepit. I fill a pot with water and hang it on a pole, suspended across the flames. There's a tub of freshly made soup in the cool box and steaks to fry on the griddle, a laminated menu and instruction sheet. The food smells incredible, there's something so satisfying about cooking outdoors, and Will's relaxed demeanor is contagious. We stick to safe topics of conversation: Jonathan's eccentric wardrobe choices, writers we admire, and the appeal of rural living.

By the time we've eaten, we're both so sated, we lay out rugs either side of the fire so we can stretch out. Lying down, he is all I can see beyond the flames, the trees now hidden by darkness. The firelight turns his skin a warm orange, his eyes flickering with a reflected gold flame. I reach for my phone to take a photo, then remember I don't have it and will have to commit this scene to memory.

"You love all this camping stuff then," I say, watching Will gaze at the fire. "Did you go camping as a child?"

"Yes. Dad hated it, but Mum would take the four of us down to Exmoor every summer when we were kids."

"That must have been hard work for her. I've never taken my kids camping. I've always thought there's so much packing and unpacking involved."

"I'm sure it was hard," he says. "Simon was scared of the dark and the rest of us were not nice brothers. George invented this tale about the Beast of Exmoor, the size of a panther, who dragged boys out of their tent at night. He had us all terrified. Simon ended up having to sleep in the day because he was so frightened of the night. Mum was not happy with us."

"You're making me glad I didn't have brothers," I say, leaning over to pass him another cold beer from the cooler.

"You and your sister didn't wind each other up like that?" he asks.

"Oh, we did, but it was more subtle. I was the mean older sister. Sometimes I used to pretend she didn't exist. She tried doing it back to me, but she'd last ten minutes, then get bored and want me to play with her." I take a sip of my beer, and when I look back across the fire, I catch Will watching me and avert my gaze, suddenly self-conscious.

"She looks up to you?" Will asks.

"I guess so. She's four years younger, so I did everything first. She thought I was the authority on everything."

"You weren't?" he asks, and I shake my head. "I read this article about how your birth order shapes your family experience," he tells me. "How the oldest bears the weight of parental expectation, while the youngest is allowed to be a free spirit. Do you ever think you would have been a different person if you'd been born second?"

"Good question. I don't know." I pause, contemplating for a moment. "Maybe I'd be less afraid of failure. It's a lot of pressure having a little sister who thinks you can do no wrong. How about you?"

"I'm your classic middle child—the diplomat, forever trying to keep everyone happy. Maybe I would have been more ambitious if I'd been the oldest."

"You're ambitious," I tell him, surprised he doesn't see himself that way.

Will blows air through his lips. "I'm hardly running the country or setting up my own hedge fund."

"That's not what ambition is. It's having a clear vision of what you want to achieve and being determined to make it happen. Trust me, Will, you have it in spades."

I shift my gaze back to him now; he smiles and shifts his weight, leaning his head on his hand. "Was that a compliment, Appleby?"

"Ambition isn't always a good thing. Didn't you see *The Wolf of Wall Street*?" I say, and he lets out a deep laugh that resonates around the quiet wood. "Sounds like your mum was ambitious, taking four boys camping solo," I say, keen to hear more about his family.

"She was, she was brave too." He says it so sincerely, my heart aches for the little boy he was when he lost her. "I'll definitely take my own kids camping. I think it's character building." He lies back to look up at the sky.

"You want kids?" I ask, trying to sound casual, but my nose prickles and I feel my chest tighten as I wait for him to reply.

"Sure. Not any time soon, but I've got a lot of good dad jokes I wouldn't want to waste. I love kids." He turns to look at me and now it's my turn to shift onto my back to avoid the intensity of all this eye contact. "Tell me about your parents. Are you close?" he asks.

"Not especially. They live in this old thatched cottage in Frome. When they retired, they worked out they could Airbnb their house and use the money to go on cruises. They've been cruising constantly for years now. I think my mum prefers my dad when there are other people around." I shake my head, imagining my parents and their love of a ship buffet. "When things were at their worst with Dan, Lottie must have called them, told them I needed them to come home. They cut their Caribbean cruise short, and Mum moved in with me for a few weeks. Dan had just left, I wasn't in a great place." I pause. In a quiet wood with no distractions to hide behind, there is nothing to do but talk, and the veil of night is making me honest. "Mum lasted a week. She said it was 'all too depressing' and that she never knew what to do when we were upset, even when we were children. She offered to take the kids on a cruise, to 'get them out of my hair.'"

"Wow. Did they go?" Will asks.

"No. It was term time, the last thing they wanted. 'But the offer's always there, darling,'" I say, doing an impression of my mother's clipped tone. "'I don't want to witness your pain, but I will take your children on a tour of the Norwegian fjords for you.' I don't know why I'm telling you all this. Sorry."

"Rule of the campfire. The fire makes you bare your soul," Will says, reaching a hand toward the flames. "Tell me more about your sister?"

"Why do you want to know about my sister?"

"Because I like hearing you talk," he says, and I notice how kind his eyes are, how deep and complex their color. Never quite the same green from one moment to the next.

"I am basically Elinor, and Lottie is Marianne," I say, Austen fresh in my mind.

"*Sense and Sensibility*?" Will asks, and I nod.

"She's always been the romantic, whimsical one. Her twenties were a succession of intense relationships with various Willoughby types, while I was sensible Elinor who married a sensible man and had a family and a mortgage before any of her friends. Lottie thought I had it all worked out; she'd always call me for advice. Now she's happily married to her Colonel Brandon, killing it at work, about to have a baby—she doesn't need me so much anymore. The whole dynamic between us has changed." I pause, not having articulated any of this before; it surprises me to hear myself say it out loud. "Now she wants to fix me, and I'm not used to feeling needy rather than needed."

"I'm sure she still needs you," Will says. "Even if not in the way she used to. Maybe it's not healthy to be stuck in roles you've outgrown." He leans over to grab another log, and when he throws it on the fire it sparks and smokes. "I have the same. In a family you're allocated a role; it's hard to break out. I don't think my older brothers will ever see me as a professional person, I'll always be the kid who cried when the Rice Krispies stopped crackling in my bowl."

"You didn't!" I say, laughing.

"I was a sensitive child," Will says with a lopsided smile, and my heart thrums at his ability to make fun of himself.

We talk late into the night, jumping from family, to books, to philosophy and travel. He tells me all the places he wants to visit, all the lives he plans to live abroad. I tell him about my travels before children and my bucket list of places still to see. Will is so easy to talk to when he drops the flirty, arrogant façade. It's obvious why so many people are drawn to him. With friends and family I sometimes find myself playing a role, being the person I think they want me to be, a person they don't need to worry about. With Will, I realize I can just be myself, I can be honest, because he doesn't want or need me to be anything. Once or twice I catch him looking at me when I turn away, but it's hard not to feel connected to someone when you're lying beneath the stars sharing your life story. Only when I start to shiver do I realize the fire has burned down to glowing embers.

"We'd better go to bed," Will says, "or put more logs on?"

"Bed, I think," I say, standing up, feeling dizzy from all the smoke and beers. "You know, I haven't missed my phone once this evening."

"Nor have I. Must be the sparkling company."

"Must be." I pause. "Night then. See you in the morning."

Will grins at me, and that look is back, the toying, teasing, flirty look. He raises one eyebrow. "Unless you come knocking on my cabin door. What happens in the woods stays in the woods."

I laugh as I shake out the rug I was lying on. "See you in the morning, Havers."

Will turns on his torch and heads off through the bracken toward his cabin, just visible through the shadowy trees. I turn back to mine, the embers and the moonlight just enough to light my way up the cabin steps. Pulling the door, I find it locked. *Did I click the latch by mistake? No, I know I didn't. Oh shit, what was the code? It was on the information pack, which is . . . sitting on the table inside.* I tap in a few combinations—I know there was a five and a seven involved—but when I twist the handle, it won't budge. I rack my brain trying to conjure the combination but it's gone, and I rattle the handle in frustration. This is not good. If I can't get into my cabin, where am I going to sleep? A churn of nausea whirls in my stomach as I realize what I'm going to have to do.

# CHAPTER 23

THERE'S A LIGHT ON IN WILL'S CABIN, WHICH IS ENOUGH TO GUIDE me. Brambles scratch at my legs as I veer off the narrow path. Taking two deep breaths, I lift my hand to the door, then knock twice, and Will—tanned, muscular, so perfectly himself—opens the door in his boxers. I immediately feel my cheeks heat.

"Well, well, this is unexpected," he says, eyes sparkling with delight.

"I can't get into my cabin," I say, resting a hand on one hip. "It's locked, and the information pack is inside. Do you remember the code?"

"You don't remember the code?"

"No," I say tightly. "If I remembered the code I wouldn't have had to come knocking on your door, would I?" I pause, this situation sinking in. "Can you break the lock?"

"I'm not breaking the lock, Anna." He pauses, turning to face me. "You'll just have to bunk up with me."

"I'm not bunking up with anyone," I say, fuming now. The friendly dynamic by the fire has morphed into something else, and it feels as though he's relishing this power shift.

"Okay then," Will says, pulling on a sweatshirt and then turning into his cabin.

"Hey, wait, where are you going?" I cry.

"I'm going to get your phone out of my lockbox so you can walk up that hill, call Verity, and ask her for the code."

I hover while Will fetches my phone. When he returns, I look slowly back and forth between Will and the pitch-dark horizon. "I don't want to go out there on my own. I can't even see where the hill is, I might fall in a ditch."

Will looks exasperated. "You'll have to sleep in here with me then."

"Can't you come?" I plead.

"You want me to put my clothes back on and walk up a hill in the dark?"

"Yes. Please."

He lets out a groan. "Fine."

Will is not happy about this outing, which he makes clear with an array of sighs and grunts, but he is more confident in the direction of the hill than I am. The moon and Will's torch afford us little light, and it takes a good fifteen minutes to cross the field in the valley and find an incline. After walking in silence for a few minutes, I pluck up the courage to ask a question I've been wanting to ask all night. "Can I ask you something?"

"I imagine you're going to," he replies.

"What happened with you and your ex, Maeve? Why didn't it work out?"

"Why do you want to know?" he asks, his voice uncharacteristically terse.

"When you mentioned it in Hay, I got the feeling there was a story there." I pause, and he doesn't answer. We walk in silence a few more steps and now I regret bringing it up.

"If you must know, I asked her to marry me in a busy restaurant, with her friends and family waiting in the bar next door to congratulate us," he says with a sardonic laugh.

"Oh no. Will, I'm sorry," I say, my heart tightening in my chest just imagining it.

"She said no, was embarrassed I'd made a scene." He pauses, his voice strained in the dark. "She said I'd fallen too deep too fast, gotten carried away, that it was way too soon."

"Was that it then, was that the end?" I ask, wishing I could see his face.

"She said she didn't want to break up, but it's hard to come back from that." He pauses. "It was my fault, I misjudged it. Once I'm in, I'm all in. I thought she felt the same."

"These things are rarely one person's fault," I tell him. "But yeah, if you ever propose to someone again, a crowded restaurant is never the way to go."

He laughs surprisingly loudly, then reaches out his arm, pulls me into a gentle headlock, and messes up my hair. "Thanks for the advice, Appleby." Laughing, I push him away. We walk a little way in silence, and then Will asks, "How did your husband propose to you?"

"In our flat in Bristol. I was already pregnant with Jess," I tell him.

"I know it's probably not a simple answer, but can I ask what happened with you?" His voice is cautious.

"Everyone has their own version of events, so I can only give you mine," I say, pausing to look up at the night sky. "There was no big fracture, no third party involved, it was more a gradual slipping away. We met when we were twenty-one, we were different people back then." I sigh. "For me, falling in love feels like gazing up at a dark sky. First, there is nothing but blackness, then gradually your eyes adjust, a few stars come into view, then suddenly, you see everything—thousands of stars, an infinite spectrum of light. It's mind-blowing. Falling out of love feels the same but in reverse. One by one the stars recede, gray clouds sweep in. Then one day you realize you are alone in the dark, there's nothing out there."

"That's a poetic answer," Will says.

"The less poetic answer is too depressing," I say with a smile. "Going through a divorce is the hardest thing I've ever done."

Halfway up the slope, my phone gets a bar of life, and I squeal with relief.

"You realize I get the chair now," Will says.

"This doesn't count. This is an emergency."

"Oh, this definitely counts, Appleby," he practically growls. On my phone, there are a few texts from Jess and one from Dan, several e-mail alerts. I scan through them, just to check there's nothing urgent. "Anna, I'm not standing out here freezing my bollocks off while you check your e-mail."

"Sure, sorry. One minute," I tell him, bouncing from foot to foot to keep warm.

I find Reconnect Retreats' number on an e-mail and dial it with numb fingers. It goes straight to answerphone. "This is Reconnect Retreats. The office is open from eight a.m. to eight in the evening. If you're calling outside of those times, please leave a message and we will get back to you. If it's an emergency, please call the emergency services."

"It's an answerphone!" I wail. "Now what? Hey, where are you going?" Will has started walking back down the hill toward the woods, and I'm forced to run to catch up with him.

"I'm going to bed," he says. "I'm cold."

"But she said we could call in an emergency."

"Maybe she meant you could call an ambulance or the fire brigade, if it was a real emergency."

"But this is a real emergency. I don't have anywhere to sleep!" I cry. "How far did she say their office was, three miles away?"

"No one will be there now. You can have my bed. I'll sleep on the floor. *Please* let's just go back. We can't call the emergency services because we only have one bed."

He's right, of course he's right, but I'm still tense with frustration. How would this even work? The cabins are tiny, there's hardly room for him to sleep on the floor. Could I call a cab, drive to a hotel? But we've walked out of mobile reception now, and I suspect Will might kill me if I ask him to escort me back up the hill to make another call.

When we reach Will's cabin, the door is closed, and he pretends he can't remember his code. "Not funny," I say, elbowing him in the ribs.

When we're finally inside, I'm shivering. Will puts a hand on each of my arms and vigorously rubs up and down. It warms me up immediately, and I mutter an awkward thank-you. As I'm wondering whether I should offer to do the same to him, he holds out an arm toward the bed.

"All yours," he says as he picks up a pillow and a blanket, then lies down on the floor.

"You can't sleep like that," I say, looking at the pitiful scene of his six-foot-three frame curled into a floor space barely big enough to stand in. "There's not even a carpet. Come on, it's a double bed. We'll just have to . . ." I can't bring myself to say it.

"Try to resist ripping each other's clothes off?" he asks, finishing my sentence, but his tone sounds matter-of-fact rather than flirtatious.

When he stands up again, his broad, firm, hot body is only inches from mine in the confined space. Then he turns and passes me a T-shirt from his backpack. "Something to sleep in."

Wordlessly, I take it, then slip into the tiny toilet cubicle to change because I don't want to get into his bed in my muddy jeans. I inhale the smell of his T-shirt as I put it on; it's clean but still smells of his aftershave. I curse him for smelling so good. His shirt skims my thighs, and I come out, tugging it down, trying to hide my white legs. Thank God I waxed before I came, and that I happened to wear my nice new underwear.

Will is sitting on the bed. "Do you want this side or the wall?" he offers.

"The edge. That way, if you roll on me in the night, I'll just fall out of bed rather than get crushed beneath you."

"I will try not to crush you," he says. He briefly looks me up and down in his T-shirt before squeezing his eyes closed and turning onto his side to face the wall. I flick out the bedside light and climb into bed beside him. Now that I'm lying in it, I discover how small this double bed is. It's almost impossible not to touch each other, even though Will is pressed right up against the cabin wall.

"I'm sorry about this," I say quietly in the dark.

"It's okay," he says gently, and I can feel the heat radiating from his body. "Would you have offered me your bed if it was me who locked myself out?"

"Of course I would," I say, biting back a smile.

"Liar," he says, gently kicking my leg. "Night, Anna."

"Night, Will."

We lie there in silence, totally still. *Is he really just going to go to sleep?* Of course that's what I want, but I'm surprised. Why isn't he teasing me about the situation? Was the "no strings" proposition just banter? Was he just toying with me to make me blush, while the reality is, he would never follow through?

His breath slows as though he might be about to fall asleep, and now I can't help but feel slightly offended. There's a half-naked woman in his bed, and he's just nodded off within a few minutes. He's not lying there tormented by my proximity. He's not even going to try his luck—Will, who tries his luck with *everyone*. With an unnerving, aching clarity, I realize I am disappointed. Every muscle in my body is tense, every inch of my skin alert with goose bumps. I'm not going to be able to sleep while I can feel the heat of his huge, firm frame right beside me, when my mind is running wild.

I squeeze my eyes closed, tell myself to block it out, to pretend he isn't here, but my body wants to nudge toward him, to have him wrap his arms around me, to do things in the dark that we don't have to talk about in the morning. There's a throbbing pulse between my legs that's getting heavier and more insistent. *No, no.* I pull my legs up and hug my knees; I'm just confused, this is unfamiliar territory for me. Will is undeniably attractive, his body is incredible, I haven't had sex in over two years, it's no wonder I'm feeling . . . *Stop thinking about it.*

"Anna?" Will's voice is quiet in the dark.

"Yup," I say, my voice a squeak.

"Are you okay? You sound like you're hyperventilating."

"Do I? Sorry," I say, but my voice comes out as a whimper, and I put a hand over my mouth. *Get a grip, Anna. Anyone would think you'd never been in a small bed with a ridiculously hot male colleague.* Of course I haven't. Who has?

I'm probably just freaking out because Will joked about us having sex; he put the idea in my head. He wasn't serious, he was just teasing me, but . . . *What if he wasn't?* His body shifts, and his breathing sounds shallower. Is he also too distracted to sleep? Now my mind slips into a new gear. *Would it really be so bad if something did happen?* He's planning to leave Bath, to leave the magazine; my nerve endings fizz when he looks at me a certain way; he doesn't want a relationship with someone like me, it could be delightfully uncomplicated . . . *No. Stop thinking about it.* But I can't stop thinking about it, and after ten minutes of tossing and turning, I find myself casually reaching my hand beneath the covers and resting a hand against his back.

As soon as I touch him, he flips over, grabs my hand, and pushes me back, holding my hand down against my pillow. A small moan of anticipation escapes my lips.

"What are you doing?" he asks, his voice low, serious.

"Um, I don't know," I reply, biting my lip. I don't want to talk, I don't want to think, I just want to kiss him, to break this unbearable tension between us.

"Anna," he says, still holding my arm on the pillow, "I'm not going to touch you or kiss you unless you ask me to." His voice is a low growl, as though he's struggling to keep his composure. "I need to be sure I'm not taking advantage of this situation."

"You can, you're not," I say quietly, my hips gently pushing forward. "I want this."

"What do you want exactly?" His voice is calm and still. I feel like I might die of embarrassment or want, or both. I reach for him with my free hand, but he only clasps it with his other hand and pushes that hand back onto the pillow too. He rolls over so now he's hovering above me, both my hands pinned against the pillow. I let out an unconscious groan. I have never felt so turned on in my entire life.

"Words first, Appleby," he says. "Because you're sending me a lot of confusing signals here."

"What do you need me to say? I want you," I say, exasperated. Every cell in my body is alert, all doubts banished. "I want you to touch me, kiss me, fuck me," I go on, breathless but confident. *Did I just say that? I don't recognize myself.*

"Really?" he asks, his eyes locking on to mine in the darkness, his body suspended above me, rock-still. For a moment, there is no sound except for our breathing, there is nothing except him.

"Yes."

And then it's as though the rigid spell of control he is under breaks, and he lets himself go, twisting us around, pulling me on top of him, finding my lips with his, pulling my lower lip into his mouth, kissing me hungrily, hot and hard, running a hand through my hair. Every cell in my body explodes.

"My God, you're sexy," he whispers into my mouth, and I buck into him, wanting more, wanting everything. A feral sex-starved beast inside me has just been unleashed and my head has relinquished all control. His hand strokes down my thigh, up the T-shirt I'm wearing, finding the edge of my underwear, yanking it aside, and I let out a whimper, burying my face in his shoulder.

"You want me," he says, one finger slowly circling its way up my inner thigh. "Say it."

"I want you, Will," I say, my voice breathy as my whole body throbs with anticipation. And then finally there are no more words, only excruciating bliss.

# CHAPTER 24

I WAKE UP SMILING, STRETCHING SLOWLY, LIKE A CAT AFTER A LONG nap. I feel reborn. My whole body alive, revived, yet also gloriously tender. I don't want to move, I want to melt into this bed and feel it all again, and again and again. Rolling over, I reach out a hand for Will but find an empty bed. Turning over, I see he isn't in the cabin. Where did he go?

Stepping out of bed and opening the cabin door, I see him, hunched over the firepit, building a new fire to heat the kettle.

"Morning," I call, waving to him from the door. I'm dressed in his T-shirt and my underwear, and though it's oversized and comes down to my thighs, this morning I feel sexy wearing it.

"Hey," he says, glancing back at me before adding some more kindling to the fire.

"You want to come and help me over here?" I ask, and he looks back over his shoulder to smile at me but doesn't make a move.

"Just at a crucial part of the fire-building process," he says. "I'm making you tea."

He persists with his fire arranging, so I pull on my jeans and shoes and go out to join him. Twigs crack beneath my feet, and the low morning sun dapples the glade like nature's disco ball. "Isn't this wonderful? Waking up in the wild, being right in the forest, the fresh smell of dew and the morning mist still hanging over the field."

"Someone's full of the joys of spring," Will says. He hangs the kettle over the flame, then stands up and strides across the glade toward me, reaching to brush my hair away from my face.

"I am," I say, tilting my head upward to look at him.

"Shall we go swimming while the water heats up?" he suggests. Then he reaches for my hand, and I laugh as he pulls me along the woodland track, following the sound of the river. Small wooden arrows point along the bank toward the plunge pool. When we get close, Will lets go of my hand, pulls off his shirt and jeans in one seamless motion, then, naked, leaps off the bank straight into the swirling dark water.

"That was dangerous," I call, blushing at the sight of him. "You don't know how deep it is."

"It's deep enough," he says, dunking his head under the water, then bursting through the surface, breathless from the cold. He shakes his head, sending water from his hair in a circle of spray.

Pulling off my T-shirt and jeans, I keep my knickers on, attempting to retain some modicum of modesty, then take a small jump into the shallows, squealing at the viselike grip of the water. Will finds my hand and pulls me toward him, the heat of his body confusing my senses in the biting cold.

"Refreshing," I say, struggling to catch my breath, and he laughs. We're face-to-face now, in daylight. His eyes are full of questions, but I don't know what he's asking, so I lean up to kiss him. Last night felt like a fantasy, like it might not have been real, but now that I feel his firm lips, soft and probing, everything comes back in a rush of delicious molten memory.

His mouth moves down to kiss my shoulders.

"How are we going to write about this?" I ask, my voice tight in my throat.

"Heavily redacted," he says, suddenly picking me up and throwing me across the pool so I go all the way under. When I come up, gasping, Will is already on the bank, pulling on his clothes. I put my hands across my chest as I follow him, self-conscious in unforgiving daylight. He turns toward me, and I shoo his gaze away. "Don't look!"

"I have seen you more naked than that, Appleby, in case you don't remember."

"Not like this, you haven't," I say, scrambling to find my T-shirt on the bank and pulling it over my damp head.

Back at our camp, the kettle is billowing steam, and while Will uses a hook to remove it from the fire, I run back to his cabin to find another T-shirt. As I walk back across the glade, Will calls to me, "I remembered your code, if you want to get dry clothes."

"What?" I ask, tilting my head in confusion.

"Your door code, I remembered it in the middle of the night. Five seven zero four."

"It just suddenly came to you?" I ask, eyeing him suspiciously.

"What? It did," he says, shaking his head. Then his brow furrows, and he laughs. "You think I pretended not to remember it, so you'd be forced to sleep in my cabin?"

"Will Havers, you absolute scoundrel," I say, glaring at him.

"I swear, the way Verity said it, in that singsong voice, it just pinged back into my brain when I woke up. You never get that?" Will seems earnest, while finding my suspicion amusing. "You really think I would go through all that—trekking up that hill in the dark, offering to sleep on the floor—just to trick you into bed?"

"A convenient lapse of memory, was it?" I ask, unable to decide whether I believe him or not.

"If I recall, it was you who initiated things, not me." He walks slowly around the fire toward me, and I feel myself unfurl beneath his gaze. "I was happy to keep this unrequited," he says. "Well, not happy exactly, resigned."

He reaches for me, tucking a finger inside the top of my T-shirt, twisting it, pulling me toward him. I push myself up on tiptoes, tilting my chin upward. "I'm going to get a cricked neck if I'm not careful," he says softly.

"I'm worth it," I say, kissing him.

"I love seeing you in nothing but my T-shirt," he says. His eyes meet mine, his pupils wide and full of heat, but then, rather than kiss me again, he unwinds his finger and lets me go. My feet sink back to the floor, disappointed. "Come on, let's see if I remembered that code right." He strides across the glade toward my cabin, then punches in a code. The door clicks. As he opens it, he turns back to me. I'm still standing by the fire where he left me.

"Did you want to go on that guided walk at noon?" he asks.

"Maybe, why?" I ask. He beckons me with one finger, and I follow, a yo-yo on some invisible string.

When I reach the cabin step, he says, "Because I want to know how long I have," which sends an arc of anticipation through me.

"I do not need to go on the guided walk," I say with an uncharacteristically girlish giggle.

"Good," he says, picking me up in one deft movement, carrying me up the steps, then kicking the cabin door closed behind us.

The rest of the day passes like a dream. I am not myself. I am not Anna the mother, nor Anna the journalist, not even Anna the sister. I am not divorced or thirty-eight or anything you could write on paper. I am simply a woman in the woods, in my own private Eden, returned to a raw, animal state. I'm annoyed and delighted in equal measure to discover why this beautiful, arrogant, swaggering man walks through life with such a cocksure gait. In his hands, my body feels like a Ferrari, long parked in a dusty garage, now being driven by a Formula 1 driver who knows *exactly* how to handle one.

Without our phones, I have no concept of time or the outside world. The day unfurls like one long conversation, with no end or beginning, just moving locations. When we're not in bed, we lie outside in the forest glade, Will reading me a chapter from my book, my head resting on his chest. I learn that his physique is not from the gym but from a daily habit of outdoor calisthenics. He can shift his body into incredible positions and tries teaching me how to do a headstand, but it only ends in a lot of laughing and a head rush for me.

When the sun is high in the sky we take a long walk around the perimeter of the field, then find bread, cheese, and salad in the cool box for lunch. That evening we lie out on a blanket in the field looking up at the stars, and I wonder if we have been here for a year or a day. I feel energized, blissfully content, fun, and attractive. If I was in my hibernation era, I am now well and truly awake.

"I love that I can just look at you now," Will says, rolling onto his side on the blanket, propping a hand beneath his head, eyes moving lazily from my lips to my chest, then back to my eyes. "I always felt guilty when I looked at you in the office."

"Why were you looking at me in the office?" I ask, but he just kisses my hand.

"Because it's impossible not to."

"What would people at work say if they saw us now?" I say, covering my face with my other hand.

"I don't think anyone at work needs to know," he says, trailing his fingertips up my arm.

"What happens in the woods stays in the woods," I say, nodding.

Will reaches to cup my cheek, shoots me a look of such tenderness, then groans and falls back on the blanket. "This is the worst timing, Appleby," he says.

"What do you mean?"

"I've fancied you forever. Since I started at the magazine, but you wouldn't give me the time of day. Now this happens and . . ." He exhales loudly. "Jesus."

I beam at this, his words sending delight thrumming through me. "That's not true, don't lie," I say, my cheeks starting to ache from smiling.

"Anna, did you not notice I was constantly inventing reasons to talk to you? I asked you out to dinner twice; both times you shot me down. I was convinced you hated me."

"I kind of did, until Hay. I don't remember you asking me out twice."

"Well, I did."

"And correcting my grammar and trying to steal my column were your way of flirting, were they?" I ask, turning onto my side so we're now lying face-to-face.

"It worked, didn't it?" He shoots me a devious grin, and I pretend to punch him. He laughs, folding his hand around my fist. "No, the column wasn't about you. Jonathan mentioned he was reviewing content on the back page, and I saw an opportunity. As for giving you edit notes, I genuinely just want the magazine to be as good as it can be. Also . . ."

"Also?"

"I love your indignant face. You get this cute little cleft chin, and your eyes go all wild and fiery. It does something to me, I'm sorry." He falls back on the rug with a guilty laugh, and I climb on top of him.

"So you get off on making me angry?"

"Not as much as I get off on making you smile," he says with a grin.

"You are such a cheeseball," I say, leaning down to kiss him. "Why did you pull back after Hay, if you weren't seeing Deedee?"

"*You* cooled on *me*. You shot me down when I mentioned another full moon party at your place. You said what happened in Hay stayed in Hay. I thought you regretted it."

"I didn't, I don't," I tell him, holding his gaze, daring to be honest. "When you left me in Hay, I felt something had changed."

"I'm sorry. I was distracted. I guess I didn't want to come on too strong. I was worried I'd pushed it too far at the window. I wanted to see you in person to gauge how you felt about it." He rolls me off him and sits up, elbows on his knees, palms pressed against his eye sockets. "Why couldn't you have decided not to hate me six months ago? I'm going to Paris next weekend. I have a meeting with the network head there. It's the final round."

"Wow. So it might really happen then," I say, trying to sound happy for him. "That would be incredible."

"It would be. It's just the kind of job I wanted. I'm down to the final three out of two hundred applicants . . ." He trails off, closing his eyes. "I shouldn't get ahead of myself. There's still a sixty-six percent chance I won't get it."

"You'll get it," I say confidently.

"You're making me want to not get it," he says softly, looking up at me now, his eyes laced with sadness. "You can't move to Paris, I presume?" he asks with a wry smile.

"Pretty tied to Bath for the next decade, I'm afraid," I say, sitting up beside him, clasping his hand in mine.

"I don't want to minimize this," he says, turning to look me in the eye. "This is incredible—*you* are incredible." He pauses. "But I also don't want to feel bad about leaving. My brothers are moving back; it's my time to go, whether it's this job in Paris or another somewhere else."

"I know. Will, this is just . . . it's just a weekend in the woods. I don't expect you to rethink your whole life plan for me."

He pulls back to look at my face, trying to read my expression. "What you do mean, 'just a weekend in the woods'?"

"What happens in the woods stays in the woods," I say in a singsong voice.

"Really? You want it to be just this weekend?" he asks, turning away, and I can't tell if he is disappointed or relieved. I'm about to clarify, to say I only said that because I was parroting our phrase. But what else *could* this be? I'm not looking for a boyfriend, certainly not one I'm going to have to say good-bye to in a few months. Then before I can answer, Will says, "Maybe that would be best. It could get messy otherwise." My chest contracts. What does he mean by "messy"? The mood feels spoiled and serious, so I quickly lean in to kiss him, desperate to reclaim the lightness.

"I blame you for starting this," I say into his mouth. "You pretended to forget my code."

"Really, that's the story you're going with?" he says, rolling me over, clasping both my hands, and pulling them above my head as I laugh beneath him, trying to buck myself free, but he's too strong. "Who forgot the code?" he asks again.

"I did, I did," I say, laughing into his lips as they find mine, and we return to the world where nothing outside the blanket matters and words are not required.

There is something different this time. We undress each other, slowly, deliberately. There is none of the wild urgency of last night, or the eager discovery of each other's bodies we had this morning. This is slower, more conversational. He asks me what I like, what I want. It is tender, gentle. It's as though we know we can't take this home, so we want to savor every detail, seal it into our memories; at least that's how I feel. He looks me in the eye, and I feel something forged between us that will not be undone.

Time dissolves into something unmeasurable again. I don't

know how much later it is when we become aware of someone watching us. We're still lying on the blanket, using a second blanket for warmth. I hear the crack of twigs and then I see her, a woman in her sixties, with a gray bun, holding a camera.

"Don't move," she says, her voice quiet, as though we are deer she's trying not to spook. "You look perfect, right there." She snaps her camera, and I pull the rug up around myself.

"What the hell! Who are you?" I yell as Will scrabbles for our clothes and moves in front to shield me from the photographer.

"Stop taking photos, please," he says, his voice deep and stern.

"Greta Van Prague," says the woman unapologetically. "I'm the photographer, from the *Times*." She pauses, looking back and forth between us. "I'm to take photos for your article. I hope I'm in the right place."

"Oh, right," says Will, turning his back to her as he pulls on his jeans, his face puce. "I'd forgotten you were coming."

"You *knew* she was coming?" I cry, crawling to find a T-shirt, wrapping the blanket tighter around myself. When I dare glance back at Greta, she looks amused, one hand on her hip, mouth curled into a smirk.

"Sorry." Will rubs his face with both hands, then paces back and forth, before finally extending a hand toward her.

"You can't use those photos," I tell her.

"They're your photos, you decide what you use. You looked so perfect together, wrapped in those rugs in the dappled light. Moments like that are always better captured than posed." She looks back and forth between us. "This is a romantic getaway feature, isn't it?"

"Yes, but it's not—we're not going to illustrate it with half-naked pictures of ourselves," Will says, shaking his head. "Please delete those."

"It wasn't a close-up. There's nothing to see." She leans over to show Will the photos on her camera screen. "Even if you don't use them for the article, I'd want to keep these if this was me and my partner."

"Oh no, we're not . . ." I start to say.

"No, no, we're not," says Will, mortified.

Greta looks back and forth between us, and I hide my face in my T-shirt.

"We're colleagues."

"Ah, I see," Greta says slowly, then laughs. "Well, I'll take a ton of pictures, you decide which ones you use to illustrate the article." She pauses, looking across at Will, then winking at me. "Nice work if you can get it, hey?"

Greta gives us space to put our clothes back on. Will and I share a mortified smile. Once our faces have returned to their normal tones, Greta asks if she can pose a few photos of us sitting by the fire, then standing outside the cabin with mugs of tea.

"I'll let you get back to it," she says, which turns Will's face pink again. "There must be something in it, then, this Reconnect retreat."

"Please don't tell anyone at the *Times* about this," I plead.

"Honey, relax," says Greta. "When you get to my age, you'll only wish you had more weekends like this." And then she's gone, marching back the way she came.

"I'm so sorry," Will says to me as soon as she's out of earshot. "They said they would send a photographer, but they didn't follow up with any details. I thought they'd come separately to photograph the location." His face is racked with guilt. "That was so unprofessional."

"I can't believe she thought we might want half-naked photos of ourselves in a national newspaper," I say. Then when I catch Will's eye, we both burst out laughing.

"It was a good photo. I might print it out and put it on my desk at work," Will says.

"That might be a little unprofessional," I say, my cheeks aching from smiling.

Then Will picks me up, in one sweeping motion, and carries me across the glade back to his cabin. "What are you doing," I say, grinning up at him.

"I'm going to show you exactly how unprofessional I can be."

# CHAPTER 25

WE DON'T HAVE ANY MORE CONVERSATIONS ABOUT WHAT WILL HAPpen when we get back to reality. I don't think either of us want to think about it. We swim and walk in the woods and lounge by the fire or in my bed. It is a novelty to be touched so much, Will looking for my hand on a walk, throwing an arm around my shoulder, reaching to stroke dirt off my cheek. He is tactile and familiar and unselfconscious. He pulls me onto his lap by the fire or reaches out to stroke my hair. My body relishes it, like stepping into a warm shower after swimming in a cold sea.

On Sunday morning, I get up before Will and light the fire to make breakfast rolls. The smell of bacon and eggs draws Will out of my cabin and when he sees me by the fire, he shakes his head. "I wanted to make you breakfast in bed," he says, then walks behind me and bends down to kiss the nape of my neck.

"Sorry, I woke up early," I say.

Will leans around me and inhales the smell. "Perfectly crispy bacon."

"I forgot I was cooking for a restaurant critic," I say, gently slapping his hand with a spatula as he reaches for a piece.

"At least give me a job," he says.

"Fine, you can serve."

He grins, delighted, then fills one of the buns with a fried egg and two strips of bacon. In the cooler we find a huge array of condiments: brown sauce, mayonnaise, homemade chutneys, and relishes.

"Look at this, haute cuisine in the woods. What do you want on yours?" he asks me.

"Oh, however it comes," I say with a shrug, but he looks at me questioningly.

"But what would you *like*?" he asks.

"Mayonnaise and chutney then."

"You always say 'however it comes,'" he tells me as he makes up my breakfast bun.

"Do I?"

"Yes. Maybe it's a mum thing, my mum used to say that too. One Mother's Day—I must have been seven—I remember asking if I could make her perfect sandwich for lunch, and she said, 'Sure, I'll have a ham and cheese.' But I wanted to know *exactly* what her perfect ham and cheese sandwich would look like. She said, 'However it comes,' but I insisted I wanted to get it just right. Finally she laid it out: she wanted mayonnaise on a piece of rye, followed by ham, then cheese, lettuce, one more slice of ham, then a small dab of French mustard. I made a total mess of the kitchen, but you know, I think it was the best sandwich I've ever made." He grins, and my heart melts. "She could have been humoring me, who knows." He pauses, then says, "She used to remember all our little food preferences. Like how Simon loved Red Leicester, whereas I preferred Cheddar, or I'd eat the salami with the pepper around it, but Harry wouldn't touch it. Every packed lunch she made was this little act of love and remembering." He hands me my roll. "After she died, Dad made the same packed lunch for everyone. We ate what we were given."

"Oh, that's so sad," I say.

"It wasn't a big deal, we weren't too fussy. I just remember it was one of the things I missed. Feeling like someone knew these little details about me."

"Well, this is the best breakfast sandwich I've ever had," I say, feeling slightly choked up by his story. "What are you having on yours? I'm feeling the pressure now."

"Brown sauce, always brown sauce," he says, taking the other roll from the griddle and talking me through his preparation. "Mayonnaise, but only if it's Hellmann's, and never mixed with the brown sauce; you've got to keep them separate, either side of the bun."

"You know, Will, I think eating at all those five-star restaurants has turned you into a sandwich diva," I say, elbowing him.

"Really? Wait, you've got a little—" He reaches across to wipe something from my nose, but when I reach up, I realize he's wiped brown sauce onto it.

"Hey!" I say indignantly, but then I forgive him when he leans in to kiss it away.

AFTER BREAKFAST WE head out for a walk in the woods on the other side of the river, holding hands like teenagers. This weekend has been so perfect—I've never felt this connected to someone so quickly before—but then I remember it has to end.

"Wouldn't it be great if we could just stay here forever," Will says, as though reading my mind.

"I wish," I say.

"Why don't we? I could learn to forage, catch fish?"

"My children might miss me," I say.

"Right," he says, and now I feel like I ruined the fantasy by mentioning my kids. Thinking about them stirs a nagging guilt. I've never been uncontactable for this long before. What if something's happened? When Jess was two, I had a weekend away with girlfriends. It was the first time I'd left her. I had such a nice time, but then came back to find Dan had trapped her finger in the door and they'd ended up in the emergency room. Some part of me felt the universe was punishing me for daring to enjoy my time away.

"I might just check my messages," I say when we get back to camp.

"Don't. The weekend's not over yet. When we let the outside world back in, the spell will be broken."

But now that I've thought it, I can't not. A dissonance crept in the minute I mentioned the children. "I need to," I say, more firmly than I intend. Will doesn't know what it's like to be a parent, he doesn't understand you can never truly check out. A chill wind blows through the woods and something in my gut tells me I need to check my phone.

"Sure, do what you need to do," he says, walking across to the log pile to start splitting wood. I can't tell if he's annoyed or just being matter-of-fact.

Retrieving my phone from his lockbox, I walk out into the valley and up the hill. I feel a surge of anxiety as messages, e-mails, and alerts start to ping in. I home in on the ones from Jess.

Jess

Mum when are you back? I need you.

Mum, call me. Now.

Then a third message, just a sad-faced emoji.

Nothing from Dan, nothing to give me a clue as to what might have happened. I try calling her, but her phone is off, so I try Dan.

"I thought you were off-grid communing with nature?" he

says, and his voice pulls me right out of Eden, slamming me back into real life.

"I am, just checking in. Is Jess okay? She messaged me."

"She's being tearful and weird. Girl stuff. Sylvie's taken her out for a milkshake. You don't need to worry."

"Has something happened with her friends? Is it Penny?" I ask. I hear clinking on the line, the sound of tools tinkering with a bike chain.

"I don't know, Anna, it's probably a storm in a teacup, you know what she's like," Dan says. But now I am worried. Something happened, she wanted to talk to me, and I wasn't there. Now Sylvie's taken her out for a milkshake. Running back down the hill, I see Will is stacking up logs.

"I have to go. I need to get back," I tell him.

"Why? What's happened?" he asks, his face shifting to concern.

"I don't know, mother's intuition. I want to catch an earlier bus home."

"Okay, I'll come with you," he says, but then we look around at everything that needs doing—the blankets strewn in the grass, the cups and bowls from breakfast lying unwashed.

"There's a bus at two," I say, looking at the clock on my phone, then quickly start picking up the rugs, shaking them out, and folding them. Will strides across the glade and takes the rug from my hand.

"I'll do this. You won't make the two o'clock otherwise," he says.

"You're sure you don't mind?"

"If you need to go, you need to go. I'll sort everything out here."

So I run to the cabin to pack, and Will helps gather up my things. When I'm ready to go, he walks me back to the road and waits with me until the bus comes.

"Sorry to break up the party," I say quietly, suddenly feeling awkward in front of him. We're standing a foot apart, and I want to reach for his hand, but I don't know what the rules are. Is it over now, or only when I step onto that bus?

"I guess it had to end sometime," he says, taking a long exhale, reaching out for my hand. I savor the feel of it, the strong heat of his grip. If this is it, if this is all I get, I want to kiss him again. One more chance to hold him to me.

"Will . . ."

"This weekend, Anna, it's been—"

But then my bus arrives, and he doesn't finish the sentence. The spell is already broken. "See you around, Appleby," he says, squeezing my shoulder.

"See you," I say. As I get on the bus, I give him a wave before turning around to let my face crumple. I take a seat next to a window, and the noise of the engine and other people feels like too much. My ears need time to recalibrate, as though I've been living in a quiet wood for months rather than two days.

As soon as my phone picks up a signal, I text Jess, asking what's wrong, to let her know I'm on my way back.

**Just come get me,** she types back.

WHEN I FINALLY make it to Dan's house, Sylvie answers the door. She's wearing skintight cycling gear. I have never seen anyone look good in cycling gear before. Her face creases in concern when she sees me.

"What happened?" I ask.

"Shall we have a quiet word out here, mum to mum?" Sylvie whispers, stepping out into the street and closing the door behind her. *Mum to mum?* A month of being Dan's live-in girlfriend does not make her my children's stepmother.

"What's wrong?" I ask, swallowing my anger in the hope

she'll spit it out quicker. Sylvie knits her fingers together, then bows her head, like a priest about to deliver a sermon.

"Our little Jess became a woman this weekend," she tells me.

"Oh."

"There was a . . . a situation with our white sofa."

"Oh God."

"It's fine. I sorted it out before Dan noticed. The poor thing was mortified. She had some cramping, she didn't have any of the products you bought her. It's been a bit of a morning. But you don't need to worry, we went for a girls' lunch, talked it all through. I bought her a moonstone. My mother bought one for me when I started my journey into womanhood."

The tightness in my chest releases; I'm relieved it isn't something worse. But now my stomach is a soup of unpleasant feelings: sadness that I wasn't here, anger that Sylvie was, heartache that my daughter was embarrassed and away from home. We've had conversations about it, I have a special box of pads at home, just in case, but she doesn't have anything like that at Dan's. I should have planned for this, I should have known it might happen.

"Thank you for doing that," I say to Sylvie, and I genuinely am grateful to her for being kind.

"How was your holiday?" she asks.

"It was a work trip, and it was fine, thanks." I give her a grudging smile. "Are the kids ready to go?"

"Come in, come in," she says, opening the front door and walking through to the beige hall. I don't want to come in, but I don't want to risk looking rude by saying I'd rather wait in the street. Dan is in the living room, wearing cycling spandex.

"Hon, have you moved the Allen key for this saddle?"

"No," I say, a reflex, before remembering he's not talking to me.

"Oh, hey, Anna," he says.

"I haven't moved it," Sylvie says, and there's a sharp edge to her voice. She noticed my mistake, even if Dan didn't.

Seeing Dan in his spandex after so recently seeing Will in much less, I can't help but compare the two. Do Sylvie and Daniel have the kind of sex I just had with Will, or do they have the kind of sex Dan and I had? My mind jumps back to Friday night, Will's commanding voice: "*You want me. Say it.*"

"You okay? You look flushed," Dan asks me, then frowns. "Don't come in if you're sick, I've got a Tri Club event next weekend. I can't get sick."

"I'm not sick, it's just hot in here." *Why did I come in? It's always a mistake to come in.*

Ethan is in the garden playing with a plastic cricket bat and stumps. When he sees me through the French windows, he throws down the bat, runs to pull open the door, then comes in to hug me.

"Hey, kiddo," I say, pulling him into my arms and kissing his hair, inhaling the glorious, sweaty smell of him.

"Did you see how good I got at cricket?" he asks.

"Ethan, let's finish what we were doing. Stumps away," Sylvie says, slowly circling a finger toward the garden. Ethan obediently shuffles back toward the door. "We like things spick and span here, don't we?"

There's a heavy stomping on the stairs, and Jess comes down and stands in the hall with her bag.

"Hey, Jess," I say, giving her a sympathetic look and holding out my arms for a hug.

"Don't be weird. Let's just go," she says. So I follow her out of the house, trying to be as non-weird as possible.

AT HOME, ETHAN runs straight into the garden to play with the cricket bat and ball we keep in our garden shed. While he's outside, I take the opportunity to talk to Jess.

"Sylvie told me you started your period. I'm sorry I wasn't there when you needed me."

Jess grunts in response, and I reach out for a hug. To my relief, she walks into my arms and lets me hold her.

"It was so embarrassing, Mum. I just wanted to be home with you," she whispers into my shoulder.

"I get it, I'm so sorry I wasn't there. It sounds like Sylvie was nice about it though?"

"She bought me this," Jess says, showing me the moonstone bracelet. "She says it symbolizes feminine energy."

"Uh-huh." It's all I can muster.

Jess fiddles with it as she leans against the kitchen counter. "She made out it was this big moment, but it just feels gross and annoying."

"It is a bit gross and annoying, but it's also completely natural." I pause, watching her, my daughter—still very much a child, yet now something else as well.

A ball of guilt lodges itself in my chest. *What was I thinking?* Living out some sexual fantasy in the woods, forgetting about my responsibilities here. I hardly thought about the kids all weekend; I should have foreseen this, but I was too preoccupied by Will. *I am a terrible mother.*

When Ethan comes in from the garden, we all curl up on the sofa together and watch *Miss Congeniality*, a family favorite. But I can't focus on Sandra Bullock's makeover; my mind is still in the woods. I wonder where Will is now. Is he back yet? I fiddle with my phone, tempted to text him. I should let him know everything's okay. I'm not *not* going to text him just because we slept together.

"So how did you cope without your phone for two days?" Jess asks, seeing me grasping my phone, plagued by indecision.

"It was easier than I thought it would be."

"How was Will?" Jess asks.

"Excuse me?" I say, thrown by the question.

"You went with that guy Will from your work, didn't you?"

"Oh, right, yes, fine. It was fine." Why are they asking me questions about Will? They never ask me questions about work, or anything in my life that doesn't directly relate to them. I get up and go to the loo, lock the door, then start composing a message.

**All fine here, glad I came back when I did. Thanks for a lovely weekend.** Then I erase it and retype. **All fine here. Can't stop thinking about you.** No. I can't say that. That's too much, it's supposed to be over. Should I send him a GIF? Something that conveys I'm thinking about him, without being too needy. What if I just said, *Miss you already*? I tap my phone against my forehead in frustration. What is wrong with me? I feel fifteen again, wondering whether Lance Reynolds will notice me more if my hair is up or down.

"Mum, are you okay? You've been in there for ages," Jess calls from the living room.

"Fine. Just a minute," I call back. Quickly I type, **All fine here. Hope you got home okay**, then send it to Will before I can overthink it.

"Can I get an axolotl, Mum?" Ethan asks.

"Show me what they are," I tell him. We look them up on my phone, and I find photos of a strange, smiling pink amphibian with a crown of feathery gills. "They look high-maintenance."

"They're not. They can regenerate their own limbs." Ethan looks at me hopefully.

"Let me do more research, I promise I'll think about it," I tell him, leaning over to kiss his head. "Also, I need another date suggestion, if either of you have any ideas."

"Why can't you date Will?" Jess asks, and the question makes me tense. *Does she know something?*

"No, I can't date Will," I say as casually as possible. "He's a colleague."

"Kenny at school says his grandad keeps a goat as a pet and it lives in his house. It chews all his shoes," Ethan says.

"That makes him eligible, does it? How old is he?"

"The goat?" Ethan asks.

"No! Kenny's grandad. You know what, no, veto. No one from school or connected to school, and no one's grandad." Ethan's face falls, as though I've quashed his dream of meeting that goat. "Why not ask Kenny if you can go meet his grandad's goat one day after school?" Ethan looks thrilled by this suggestion.

"Are you going to see Michael again?" Jess asks.

"Michael was lovely, we're going to stay in touch, he was a great suggestion. But I need a fresh lead."

"Why do you keep checking your phone?" Jess asks me.

"I'm not," I say, pushing it down the side of the sofa.

"Wouldn't it be great if you could have a playdate with loads of people at the same time and then work out who you wanted to be friends with?" Ethan says.

"I think that's called speed dating," I tell him.

"What's speed dating?" Jess asks, and once I've explained the concept, Ethan and Jess agree this sounds like an excellent plan and I open my laptop to do some research.

"Look, there's an over-thirty-fives event. Mum, that's you," says Jess, pointing at the screen.

"I don't know if this strictly meets the column's criteria," I say with a frown. "You really can't think of anyone else?"

The doorbell rings, and I go to open the door. On the doorstep is Noah, holding a mangled milk carton.

"Foxes got into your bin again," he says gruffly, pointing at our wheelie bin. "I've just cleaned it up. You need to put a sturdy brick on the top if you're going to put rubbish out *before* the morning of collection."

"Thank you, but I did put a brick on it," I say, irritated by this admonishment.

"It can't have been big enough," says Noah.

"Maybe the foxes are getting stronger. Maybe they're evolving, working together to get the bricks off the bins," I suggest, my eyes falling to Noah's feet, where I see he's wearing odd socks. One is a smart red tartan, the other gray and woolen.

"Just try to be more vigilant," he grumbles, turning to stomp down the steps, then calling back, "And fill in the form for the hedge arbitration."

I close the door, muttering to myself, "I'll show you more vigilant." Then when I turn around, Ethan and Jess are looking at me with identical looks on their face.

"Oh no, no, no, no. Not him. Veto, huge veto," I say, raising both palms in the air.

"I don't think you have any vetoes left, Mum," Jess says with a sly grin.

GOOGLE SEARCHES:

Can foxes move bricks off bins?

Videos of foxes moving bricks off bins

If there are no blue ticks on a WhatsApp message, does that mean they haven't read it?

How do you know if they have disabled read receipts?

Will Havers, LinkedIn

# CHAPTER 26

THAT NIGHT, LYING IN MY NEWLY ARRANGED BED, I CHECK MY PHONE for the fiftieth time that evening. Will must have switched his phone back on by now, but still he hasn't replied to my WhatsApp. Not that I *need* him to text me, but it would be polite. The ticks have not gone blue, but when I scroll back to previous messages I see none of the ticks have gone blue, so maybe he has disabled read receipts. Is that something people do? Should I be doing that in order to retain an air of mystery? I close my eyes and groan in frustration.

Dating anyone is fraught with risk—the risk they might be a psycho like Neil, a fraud like Parma ham Richard, or a creep like Ryan Stirling. But getting involved with someone like Will, who I *know* is leaving, who I know doesn't want anything serious, that is a different kind of dangerous. I don't know how to do this. I don't know how to have a weekend like we just had and then be fine about his not texting me back. I distract myself by sending Michael two Janeites I have found on dating apps: Olivia from the Cotswolds and Jane (I know) from Bradford-on-Avon. They both seem keen to meet Michael, and I have high hopes for Jane, whose bio contains a quote from *Persuasion*.

*Beep.* What is that? A high-pitched beep, just one sharp sound, then roughly five minutes later another one, *beep.* Now I can't sleep until I find out where that's coming from. *Beep.* How are Jess and Ethan sleeping through that? It's so loud and so annoying. Shuffling along the corridor, I locate the source of the noise—it's coming from the smoke alarm. A red "battery" light is flashing. It's plugged into the mains, but maybe the backup battery is running low. Whatever it is, I can't reach to turn it off.

Maybe I can ignore it until morning. It hasn't woken the children. But once I'm back in bed, all the earplugs in the world won't block out the high-pitched "yip" sound. I'm going to have to try to reach it.

Taking a chair from my room, I head back out to the landing, but stretching up on tiptoes while standing on the chair, I'm still a foot away. Just as I'm about to climb down, Jess opens her bedroom door, then screams when she sees me. The shock of seeing her sets me off too, and both of us screaming wakes Ethan, who comes out of his room armed with a giant Squishmallow.

"Why are you standing right outside my room like that?" Jess asks, trying to catch her breath.

"The smoke alarm is beeping. It's driving me nuts," I explain, pointing up at the box, which beeps again as though to illustrate my point. "I can't reach to turn it off."

"So ignore it," Jess says with a shrug, slipping past me to use the bathroom.

"I can't *ignore* it. I have tried to ignore it. These things are designed to be unignorable."

"Can we use a ladder?" Ethan asks, sensibly.

Yes, a ladder. Dan bought a ladder to clean the gutters. I run down to the garage to see if I can find it. But as I open the garage door I remember; Dan took the ladder in the spoils of divorce.

"No ladder," I tell the children as I come back upstairs. *Beep.*

"Why don't we call Dad?" Jess suggests.

"It's one a.m. I'm not calling your dad," I tell her. I would rather check us all into a hotel than call Dan. I briefly consider calling Will, but that would be even more pathetic. Ethan goes into his room, then comes out again holding one finger in the air, his way of communicating he's had an idea.

"What?" I ask.

"Noah's light is on," he says.

"Oh no, no, no. We're not asking Noah."

"Ask Noah or I'm calling Dad," Jess threatens. "I have a math test tomorrow." *Beep.* "Mum, please!"

Why? Why did I give up the ladder when we were dividing up our possessions?

Throwing on my coat, I trudge over to Noah's front door, simultaneously hoping both that he answers and that he doesn't. I knock quietly, tentatively, then hear footsteps in the hall. Noah opens the door, glowering at me. He's wearing plaid pajamas and moth-eaten snow boots. It doesn't look like he's been asleep. "Yes?"

"Hi, I'm so sorry to knock on your door in the middle of the night, but it's an emergency." I expect his face to soften, for him to ask what nature of emergency I am having, but he doesn't. "Do you have a ladder I could borrow? My smoke alarm is beeping, and I can't reach to turn it off. It's driving us all mad."

There's a long pause before he reacts. I can see from his expression that he doesn't consider this to be the kind of emergency that requires a swift reaction.

"Backup battery's probably gone," he says.

"I had guessed as much," I say, reining in the urge to say

something sarcastic as it might jeopardize my chances of procuring a ladder. "My kids can't sleep through it," I add, feeling he'd be more likely to help for the children's sake rather than mine.

"I have one in the basement," he says, making no move to fetch it.

"Great," I say. "Could I borrow it?"

He opens the door wider. I have never been in Noah's house. It's a similar layout to mine, only mustier, more utilitarian. There are no plants, no art on the wall, and cardboard boxes line the hall. I give an involuntary shiver. I really don't want anything to do with this man. The way he's acted over the hedge tells me he's unhinged.

"This way," he says, leading me through the house. I notice a framed photo of Noah with a woman. I assume she must be his wife. In the picture they are both in a field, wearing wellie boots and binoculars. She has long dark hair, a freckled face, and a wide smile. She looks lovely, and Noah looks significantly younger and less cranky. Noah pauses in the hall, then opens the creaky door to his cellar as though he wants *me* to go down there. "I need you to hold the torch. Cellar light's broken."

*No way.* I am not going into a dark cellar with Noah. Then an unpleasant thought takes root in my mind: What if Noah's wife didn't die? What if he killed her and she's buried in the cellar? Why does Noah even have a cellar? My house doesn't.

"I'd rather not go down there," I say, my hands balled into fists at my sides, ready to punch him if he tries to push me down the stairs.

"I can't carry the ladder and hold the torch," Noah says, holding the torch toward me.

"Maybe I don't need a ladder. Maybe I can live with the beeping," I say weakly, and he glowers at me. "Or I could just move house, then we'd both be happy." I laugh at this, but my laugh comes out like I'm hyperventilating.

"What's the problem here?" he asks.

"I've got a thing about cellars," I explain.

Shaking his head, Noah makes a "humph" sound, then heads down the steps alone. I hear some bashing and crashing, then a couple of expletives from Noah, then eventually him coming back up the stairs with a ladder in his arms and the torch in his mouth.

"Thank you, sorry," I say, feeling bad because clearly, he did need someone to hold the torch for him, and it would have been a lot easier if we'd both gone down there. As I reach for the ladder, he shrugs me off. "I've got it now." He's cross, rightly so. I've disturbed him in the middle of the night, asked for a ladder, then refused to help him get the ladder. I'm the worst neighbor imaginable.

When we eventually get back to my house, Ethan opens the front door holding a bag of crisps.

"Ethan! Why are you eating? It's the middle of the night," I cry, grabbing the bag from him. Salt before bed is not good for his bladder regulation. But I don't have time to get into it because Noah is marching up the stairs, banging the ladder into my lovely wooden banisters.

"Ooh, mind the banisters, you just—" I start to say, and Noah turns to give me another of his trademark glowers. "Never mind. It's fine. Just a scratch."

Once the ladder is up and Noah has reached the smoke alarm, it takes him several attempts and two screwdrivers to pry it open. Finally, blessed silence reigns.

"Noah, thank you so much. You're a lifesaver, I'll relinquish all hedge-cutting privileges as a gesture of my gratitude." I say it with a smile, but his steely gaze tells me it's too soon to be making hedge jokes.

"Mum wants to ask you something," says Jess, now wide awake.

"Not now, Jess," I say, shooting her warning daggers. I'm not asking Noah out, not after tonight. It will have to be Kenny's grandad.

"Mum wants to ask you out," Ethan says, with the subtlety of a chain saw.

"Ha," I laugh, as though this is 100 percent not what I wanted to ask him.

Noah's glower softens. "What?"

"Well, no—well, yes. Not like that. It's for work, for my column." I stumble over the words, my face aflame, wishing I had the sweet refrain of beeping to block out any need for this conversation.

Jess jumps in to rescue me. "Mum's dating men we choose for her. People from real life, not online. It's for her magazine," Jess explains.

Noah looks to me, to confirm this is true, and I nod.

"She hasn't liked anyone we've picked so far, so it doesn't matter if you don't like each other," Ethan adds.

"Thanks, Ethan," I say, clearing my throat.

"And you can't go to the pub. You have to do something interesting," Ethan explains.

"And she doesn't want a boyfriend. She's happy on her own," Jess adds.

How am I in this situation, where my children are pimping me out? And how did no one think it was weird when the boy in *Sleepless in Seattle* did it?

"Fine, sure, if you like," Noah says, nodding wearily, then picks up his ladder. "Night, all."

Ethan and Jess high-five each other as soon as his back is turned. Noah scrapes the banister with his ladder on his way down the stairs.

"Just please mind the—" I start to say, but the angry hunch

of his back tells me to leave it. "It's fine. It looks better that way, more lived in."

And then he is gone, without a backward wave or a word of good-bye. "Thanks again!" I call to the closed front door.

Sitting down on the top stair, I take a moment to check my phone. Still no reply from Will. It's the middle of the night, so it's hardly surprising. I hate this. I don't want to be the person who obsesses over a reply. I also don't want to be the person who has to ask a neighbor for help in the middle of the night. I promise myself that tomorrow I will buy myself a ladder and all the DIY tools I might need, because if I'm going to keep telling people that I am fine on my own, then I want it to actually be true.

GOOGLE SEARCHES:

*Ladders*

*Cheap ladders*

*Why are there so many different types of ladders?*

# CHAPTER 27

**JONATHAN LEANS OUT OF HIS DOORWAY AND CALLS ACROSS THE** office.

"Anna, in here, please!"

When I walk through his office door, I see Will is already there. He *still* hasn't replied to my message and I'm starting to suspect I might have invented the whole weekend. He's wearing a blue suit, a white shirt, and his thick, dark-rimmed glasses. His face is so familiar to me now: the small patch of missing hair follicles on his chin, which you only notice when you're an inch away; the fleck of gray in his green eyes. My belly hums at the sight of him. Was he always this handsome?

"Will tells me the weekend was a great success," Jonathan says gleefully, and now I feel as though I have hot coals pressed against my cheeks.

"It was," I say, my voice coming out at a higher pitch than usual.

"Moonlighting for the *Times*, who would have thought it? I can't wait to read the piece," says Jonathan, offering us each a brandy snap biscuit. Will declines but I take one. Jonathan orders his sweet treats from an expensive patisserie, and they are always mouthwateringly good. Sensing Will looking across at me, I can't bring myself to look at him yet. "Crispin wanted the three of us to jump on a call this morning," Jonathan tells us, picking up his mouse and tapping it up and down on his desk. "Will, can you?" He nods toward his computer. "I can never get video calls working."

Will goes to assist. As he's shifting the screen, Jonathan picks up his newspaper and says, "'Delight,' eight letters, fifth letter S?"

"'Pleasure,'" I say at the exact same time as Will. Our eyes meet across the desk, and I have to look away.

"Excellent," says Jonathan, filling in the clue. Will clears his throat, then turns the screen so we can all see. He's pushed up his shirtsleeves, and my eyes are drawn to his forearms, the light smattering of hair on his arms, his strong broad hands, which effortlessly hold both of mine in one—

"Didn't love your latest column, Anna," Crispin says, and I realize the call has started and my mind is elsewhere. I clear my throat and nod, trying to focus on what's being said. "I liked the ones you wrote about flirting with a twenty-two-year-old and getting stoned at a house party, or nearly giving nits to your celebrity crush; they were funny. Going for a walk in Regency clothes feels rather staid. Where's the romance? Where's the danger?"

I cross my legs, then clasp my hands tightly around my knee. "I think readers will relate to the fact that you won't have chemistry with most people." Now I can't stop my eyes from darting back to Will. He's looking right at me, and his eyes unmoor me from the meeting. I'm back in the woods, lying on the rug, his hand running up my—

"Anna, Anna." Crispin's tsk jolts me back to reality. He frowns through the computer screen. "I need more, Anna. *More.* Were you disappointed not to feel attracted to this man or were you relieved? Do you think he was attracted to you? Do you *want* to meet someone or has your divorce made you cautious? Do you have trust issues? What's your relationship like with your ex? Real questions, real feelings. This column might as well be written in the third person. I don't get any sense of what you were feeling."

"I can edit it," I say, feeling wounded.

"I liked it," Will says, jumping in. "Anna raises an interesting point about the online/offline debate. If you're looking for something niche, that's where the internet really shines."

I know he's trying to help, but I'm annoyed Will feels the need to try to rescue me.

"What I was trying to get at in the column is that dating can forge connections, even if they aren't romantic ones," I explain. "There's an Austen-themed ball next month, and I've promised to help Michael find a suitable date—"

Crispin holds up his finger to silence me, then taps a closed fist against his lips. "Tell me more about this ball."

"It takes place every summer, people get dressed up in Regency clothes and throw an Austen-inspired soiree. It's a big event in Bath."

"This is what your column is lacking, an end point, a goal, a grand finale," says Crispin, smacking one fist into his other hand. "You should go to the ball, choose a date from one of the men you've written about. It will give the column a narrative throughline, bring readers back week after week to see who you'll pick."

"Me, go to the Regency ball?" I laugh, but quickly look back and forth between Crispin and Jonathan and realize no one else is laughing. "I don't even know how to dance."

"You'd better learn, then," Jonathan says. "Oh, what a marvelous lark. Two of the most useful things I ever learned at school, how to rewire a fencing foil and how to dance an eightsome reel." I get the impression Jonathan and I went to very different schools.

"Will's column needs an end point too, something more modern, but also classically romantic," Crispin says.

"I've never seen the Eiffel Tower," Will suggests.

"Perfect!" cries Crispin, pointing down his camera lens at Will. "A weekend in Paris—every girl's dream."

I know what Will's doing. He's future-proofing his column in case he's not in the country to finish it. I shift uncomfortably in my chair. Crispin slaps his desk again, delighted. "Anna goes to the ball, Will goes up the Eiffel Tower—our readers get two happy endings."

"Isn't it a little contrived?" I ask. "What if neither of us find anyone suitable? Dating is as much about discovering yourself as it is about finding a partner, isn't it?"

"You don't have to marry the guy, Anna. People like a resolution," Crispin says, leaning back in his chair, then shifting his eyes to the ceiling. "Look, if you're not comfortable writing a column like this—"

"I'll go. It's fine," I say hurriedly, before I talk myself out of a job.

"So who have you got lined up this week?" Crispin asks, and I sit forward in my chair, feeling ever more uncomfortable, trying not to look at Will, trying not to feel jealous that it won't be me whom he takes up the Eiffel Tower.

"Our neighbor. He's a widower. We don't get on."

Jonathan lets out a sigh of pleasure. "Ah, enemies to lovers, my favorite trope."

WHEN WE FINALLY escape the meeting, I hurry back to my desk, trying to ignore the fact that my whole body feels like a charged magnet, drawn to wherever Will is. I put my headphones in and try to focus on my screen, but then, ping. An e-mail from him.

Will: I thought Crispin was too harsh back there.

Anna: I'm a big girl, I can handle it.

Is this how it's going to be now? We go back to being colleagues and pretend nothing happened? Maybe it's not a big deal for him. Maybe he has weekends like that all the time, whereas I feel bereft, because it's like he's woken me up but now expects me to go back to sleep. Another e-mail.

Will: BTW I broke my phone if you were trying to get in touch.

So he wasn't ignoring me. That's a relief. I reply with an ambiguous thumbs-up emoji. He doesn't reply, and when I turn around, I see he's left his desk. I'm starting to see why workplace relationships might be a bad idea—I've never felt more distracted or less productive. Twenty minutes later, finally, he gets back to his desk and I get another message.

Will: This isn't going to work.

My heart starts to pound before I've even finished reading the sentence.

Anna: What's not going to work?

Will: What happened in the woods. I don't think it can stay in the woods.

I keep my eyes trained on my screen so he won't see me smiling.

Anna: ??

Will: I think it's going to happen again. Upstairs in the archive room in four minutes' time.

And when I turn around, I see he's left his desk and is walking off toward the stairs without a backward glance. *Oh my. What do I do?*

I quickly run through the pros and cons of following Will up the stairs. Cons: I didn't wear my nice underwear today; this is our workplace, it's unprofessional; we could get caught, fired; this is not what we agreed at the retreat. Pros: there's no time to list the pros because I'm already following him up the stairs.

My legs tremble as I climb the narrow stairwell. No one works on the second floor of the building; it's used for storing archive copies of the magazine going back to the first edition in 1954. My pace quickens. I undo the top button on my blouse and pull my hair out of a ponytail so it falls around my shoulders.

Opening the door to the archive, before I can whisper, "Will?" I feel a hand reach for mine and pull me inside. He closes the door behind me. The main strip lights are off, but there's a dim desk lamp on in one corner.

"What are we doing?" I ask, full of nervous energy, my whole body alert with anticipation.

"Shh," he says, raising a finger to his lips. "What happens in the archive stays in the archive." Then he leans down to kiss my neck and every nerve ending burns with pleasure.

"What happened to not letting things get messy?" I say, trying to sound stern, but my voice comes out a whispered moan.

"I was thinking about that," he says, his voice slow as he punctuates each word with a kiss down my collarbone while gently unbuttoning the rest of my blouse with one hand. "I think if it's just this, then it won't get messy."

"Just sex?" I ask, reaching for his belt, pulling his work shirt from his trousers, running a hand up his chest. The smell of him, the feel of him against my palm, makes me heady with need. He leans into my ear, and the sensation of his breath on my neck is intoxicating.

"Right," he says. "No one gets attached, no one gets hurt." He flicks open the last button on my blouse, then kneels on the floor in front of me, laying both his hands across my bare stomach, hugging my hips as he reaches around to find the zipper on my skirt. "If you think that would work?" he says, and his voice catches now, betraying the effort it's taking for him to keep talking.

"That could work," I say, clasping a handful of his hair, biting back a whimper.

"Are you sure? I don't want to hurt you," he says, pausing to look up at me, and our eyes lock in the low light. There's something in his eyes I can't read.

"Don't flatter yourself, Havers," I say, pressing a thumb under his chin and forcing it up. "You're not my type, remember? And I don't think you're boyfriend material."

"Oh, I remember," he says, and there's a flash in his eyes, a smile on his lips. This is all the permission he needs. With two deft tugs he relieves me of my skirt and then my knickers. The smallest groan escapes my lips, and I need to bite down on my fist to keep quiet as his hot mouth makes contact.

GOOGLE SEARCHES:

*Is it illegal to have sex at work or simply frowned upon?*

# CHAPTER 28

ON MY LUNCH BREAK, I RUSH TO MEET LORETTA AT THE HOLBURNE Museum. I suggested we meet for a coffee or a drink, but she proposed art instead. "Much more restorative." She doesn't have a mobile phone, so I can't text her to say I'm running late. As I rush down Great Pulteney Street, I reply to some work e-mails, like a few reels I've been sent on Instagram, and repost the latest *Bath Living* stories.

"Darling, I'm ecstatic that you called," Loretta says as she sees me hurrying through the main entrance. She is dressed in a bright yellow silk dress, neon orange tights, and a headscarf to match. It's a bold look, but Loretta pulls it off.

"Me too, I'm so sorry I'm late," I say.

"Not another word about it," she says with a wave of her hand. "Look at you, you're positively glowing. Now, what are you in the mood for? You don't have long. Paintings? Porcelain? Antique spoons? We can't do it all. Art is like Marmite, a little goes a long way."

"How about the forgeries?" I suggest.

"Excellent idea." Loretta is a patron of the museum, so signs me in as her guest, and we start to climb the grand staircase.

William Holburne was a wealthy collector in the 1800s who traveled Europe collecting art, treasure, and curiosities. Some of the pieces he bought turned out to be fakes or replicas, but the museum has kept some on display beside the genuine artifacts.

"I do like being around art, don't you?" Loretta says as we reach the second floor. "People harp on about the benefits of standing near trees, soaking up their oxygen, but honestly, I find standing next to a Gainsborough far more revitalizing." She pauses, taking a moment to examine my face. "I must say, you are looking most invigorated since I last saw you. Who's responsible? That Regency fellow?"

"No, not him," I say, feeling my cheeks burn. "But I think I might have just started my rock era, Loretta."

"Oh, wonderful." She claps her hands. "Tell me everything."

"I don't know . . ." I smile and shake my head, embarrassed to even think about it. I didn't plan on telling Loretta anything about Will, but I feel so at ease in her company, and I am on such a high from our illicit tryst in the archive, I find myself unable to keep it in.

"I've started something casual with someone I never would have imagined. But I've been out of the game for so long, I can't tell if it's something or if it's not."

"You don't always want *something*. My last marriage was too much of *something*." She grins. We reach the second floor, the gallery of treasures. Loretta leads me to a cabinet of miniature curiosities, tiny cameos the size of thumbprints, portraits carved out of gems and stone. The detail is incredible. Next to it is a display of precious antiques, spoons carved from bone, ornate gilded butter knives. Some are genuine collector's items, others forgeries or replicas. Wooden panels slide to reveal the fakes.

"How do you know if something is real?" I ask Loretta.

"Does it feel real?" she asks, and I nod. "Is it putting a smile on your face?" I grin. "There you are then."

"Which of these do you think is real?" I ask her, pointing to two spoons in the cabinet in front of us.

"That one," she says, nodding toward the higher spoon. We check the answer behind a sliding panel. It's the lower spoon that's real. Loretta shrugs.

"There are forgeries on people's walls all over the world. If they like the art, it hurts no one. If they bought it for the value it holds to others, then maybe they're valuing the wrong things."

As we walk around the exhibition, using magnifying glasses to inspect the smallest cameos, Loretta tells me about her passion for fashion and chemistry. She asks me questions I struggle to answer, like what my most treasured possession is, what I covet most, what I would take from the exhibition if I were allowed to keep one thing. She is a whirlwind of opinions and questions. I struggle to keep up, but I am utterly enthralled.

Back on the stairs we watch a couple standing side by side in front of an oil painting, a portrait of a girl. They are both looking at their phones as they walk down the stairs. "Our greatest invention, a gadget that spawns uninventiveness," Loretta says, giving me a wry smile.

"You really don't have a phone, Loretta?" I ask her.

"Goodness no. If people need me, here I am." She pauses. "You should come to one of my Luddite Lunches, darling. Technology-free, not gluten-free, ha."

"What's a Luddite Lunch?" I ask, intrigued.

"Bring your appetite, not your phone. You'll fit right in."

"I would love to come, thank you. Now, I must run," I say, checking the time. "Thank you for this, it's been wonderful."

"Enjoy your merry nothing," she says with a wink.

"My merry nothing?"

"Your something casual that you're not sure about. I think you're looking for permission to enjoy yourself."

"Are you giving me permission, Loretta?" I tease her.

"No, I am not," she says, giving me a stern look. "You need to give yourself that."

For the walk back to the office, I leave my phone in my bag. Looking up, rather than down, I notice how perfect the clouds are, like white cotton candy strewn across the blue canvas of sky. Taking a deep breath, I put a hand over my heart and feel it beating in rhythm to my steps on the pavement.

FOR THE REST of the week, I take Loretta's advice. I give myself permission to enjoy myself. I am also taking Lottie's advice to think with something other than my brain. My trips to the archive have become a daily occurrence. I don't want to claim to be having a sexual awakening because it sounds pretentious, but that is what I'm having. Maybe the fact it's illicit, that we go back to work and act like nothing happened, is what makes it so intoxicating. Every day we play this game, who will break, who will be the one to e-mail first, just a single word: "Archive?"

We don't flirt over e-mail. We don't text outside of work. We don't mention it when we're e-mailing about the column. It's as though we've put an unwritten rule in place that this can only happen if it's entirely separate, cordoned off from our budding friendship. There is none of the lingering, soulful eye contact we had in the woods, no conversation, no playful teasing. In the dark of the archive, we hardly speak, except to whisper what we want.

I haven't told anyone that I'm sleeping with Will, not even Lottie. I was going to tell her about the weekend in the woods, but when I had the chance, I didn't. I found I liked having something that was just mine, that was nothing to do with my family.

If Will asked to meet up outside of work, I would, in a heartbeat, but I don't want to be the one to propose it. I don't want him to think I'm getting attached, that I need this to be more than it is. I don't. He's like a drug I am getting high on, and as long as I don't get addicted, as long as I keep it recreational, then I will be fine.

ON WEDNESDAY I'M talking to Malik in accounts. My paycheck hasn't cleared yet this month and I need him to check there's not a problem.

"Let me just log in to the online banking system," Malik says. Standing behind him as he taps away, I notice Will is back at his desk after a meeting. My eyes dart across to my computer. From here, I can see my screen—I have a new e-mail. It could be from anyone. It might not even be from him. It's probably just a mailing list I subscribed to. It could be 10 percent off at Boden. It's always 10 percent off at Boden. My fingers dance with the urge to go back and check. My computer screen blinks onto the screensaver, so I can't see the e-mail page anymore.

"Here it is," says Malik. "Right, let me see—"

"Sorry, we'll have to do this later," I say, already striding away. "Something urgent just came up."

GOOGLE SEARCHES:

*How do you stop obsessing over someone?*

*Best bum tightening cream*

*Discount code for Brazilian Bum Bum Cream*

*Can people ever find your search history even if you erase it?*

# CHAPTER 29

ON THURSDAY MORNING, ON MY WAY INTO WORK, I SEE WILL PACING in the street. He's talking on the phone, gesticulating wildly. He looks annoyed. All I hear is him saying, "No, I need to do it, they're counting on me." I don't linger as I don't want him to think I am eavesdropping. Was that about the job? Maybe he didn't get it. Part of me hopes he didn't, but then I feel guilty, for putting my desire over his ambition.

When he finally comes in and sits at his desk, he doesn't e-mail about the archive all morning. I'm busy working on a story so I'm happy to wait him out. Then, at midday, while I'm making coffee in the shared kitchen, I turn to find him standing in the doorway. He rarely comes in here, equipped as he is with his own thermos of gourmet coffee.

"Hey," he says, shifting his weight awkwardly, clearing his throat. Today, I see none of the confidence or command he conveys upstairs.

"Hey," I reply, self-conscious. I stir milk into my coffee just to give my hands something to do. Will hovers by the door. I hear him tap his foot against the sideboard.

"The *Times* is pushing our piece back to later in the summer, so we don't need to submit a draft until next month now," he says.

"Good, it might take me that long to work out what to write," I say, giving him a lopsided smile. He shoots me one right back.

"I also have a favor I need to ask," he says.

"Oh?"

"I'm involved with this inclusive choir. It's a charity, I'm on the board with Loretta." I nod, remembering he mentioned it when we ran into them. "It's a huge part of Simon's life. They're having funding issues, they might lose access to the space where they rehearse. If he lost the choir . . ."

"How can I help?" I ask, taking a sip of my coffee and realizing this is the first non-work-related, fully clothed conversation we've had since the bus stop.

"The choir is singing at the abbey tonight. I said I would film it, shoot some interviews, edit it together to make a fundraising video. It's a simple job, but my cameraman is now stuck in Birmingham." He pauses, looking at me guiltily. "I've rented a decent camera, I just need someone who knows how to use it. I was remembering . . . you did a news journalism degree, so maybe you do?"

"Yes, but I'm rusty, I haven't shot anything for years," I say, but pivot as his face falls. "But I'm sure it's just like riding a bike. If you need me, I'll be there."

"I wouldn't ask, sorry. I know you're busy, I just can't let Simon down, not right now."

"It's fine. Just tell me where to be and when." I turn my back on him to put the milk back in the fridge, and when I turn around, he's taken a few steps toward me.

"Anna." His eyes hold mine. I stand still, watching his face, trying to read his mind while he tries to read mine. He closes the space between us and tentatively reaches for my face. The tip of his finger grazes my chin before a voice behind him fractures the moment. Karl and Steph have come into the kitchen, chatting noisily, and Will moves his hand away, gives me a curt nod, and leaves the room. Turning around to face the fridge, I press my tingling palms against the door.

Back at my desk, I find I have two missed calls from Dan. I call him back, worried something might be wrong.

"Hey," he says, "I'm near your office. Free for a coffee? I need to talk to you about something."

"Sure, I can nip out. Is everything okay?" I ask.

"Yes. I'll be there in five minutos."

He hangs up before I can ask him to wait in the street. I don't need him being a source of speculation among my colleagues. But as I'm gathering my things to intercept him, I see Dan already loitering in the hallway.

"Is everything okay?" I ask, hurrying over to meet him.

"Fine. I already said. Don't stress," he says, and now I'm annoyed that I've agreed to spend my lunch break with him when I have work piling up.

"I wanted to tell you in person," he says as we turn a corner to walk up toward the Circus. "I never see you on your own now, so I was passing your work and—"

"Tell me what?" I ask.

"Sylvie is pregnant."

*Sylvie is pregnant?* "Oh, wow," I say. "That was quick." I'm surprised, but no wave of emotion follows. I feel strangely neutral about the news.

"She didn't want me to be an old git in the dads' race at school. She said if we were going to do it, she wanted to get on with it."

"You've only been together a few months."

"It's been a bit longer than that. We're happy, Anna." There's a warning note in his tone. "I'm not asking for your permission. I'm telling you first, as a courtesy."

"Great. Good. I'm pleased for you," I say, feeling a jolt of injustice. I was only pointing out the facts, not making a judgment.

"It's early days, but Sylvie wants to tell the kids now, I don't what them to feel . . ." Dan trails off.

"Replaced?" I offer.

"Right." He frowns, then shakes his head. "No, not replaced, left out." We walk past a sign for a pub and Dan nods toward it. "I might need something stronger than a coffee."

"I thought you didn't drink anymore," I say, but Dan is already halfway down the steps. The pub is empty, having only just opened. After ordering a pint for Dan and an orange juice for me, we find a table in a dark corner. He takes the chair that faces out toward the room, then sits down and gazes into his pint. His face is pinched with tension, and I wonder if this might be about more than just the baby.

"It's a big deal, me having another child. I didn't want you to feel weird about it," he says, fingers swiping at the condensation on his pint glass.

"I don't feel weird about it," I reassure him, and as I say it, I realize it's true. A month ago, Dan moving in with Sylvie felt like a massive deal, but now, with this much bigger news, I feel surprisingly unaffected. It will be significant for the children, of course. Jess will be delighted; she always wanted another sibling. Ethan might struggle, especially if it's a boy. But it doesn't feel like it affects me that much. I don't feel sad that it is not me having Dan's third child. If anything, I feel relieved. I don't think I realized it until now, but I don't want any more children; that part of my life is well and truly done.

"Congratulations," I say, raising my glass to Dan's with a wide smile. "Sylvie must be thrilled."

"She is. She's had me glugging this fertility juice, full of spirulina or some bullshit, so at least that can stop." He looks across at me and smiles, and it's the first joke we've shared in a while, certainly the first at Sylvie's expense. Dan shakes his head. I notice his hunched body language, his fingers tapping against the table.

"You're allowed to be a bit scared, you know," I say gently.

"I am happy about it, I am," he says, shifting in his seat. "It's what we both want, it's just . . ." I leave the silence, waiting for him to speak. "The baby stage is tough."

"It is."

"They're so much easier now, the kids. Maybe it's bad for me to say this, but I get on with them so much better now, since the divorce. When we were married, they always preferred you. Now, when they're at mine, they ask me to do stuff with them, they talk to me. I like how things are, I don't want to jeopardize that."

"You won't," I say, and reach across the table to squeeze his arm.

"I don't miss the sleepless nights, the nappies, the lack of . . . well, I like it just being me and Sylvie."

As he's talking, I realize that he's here because he wanted to confide in someone. Dan has a lot of friends but not many he would be able to admit these vulnerabilities to.

"That's understandable. You haven't been together long. You want to enjoy the honeymoon period a little longer," I say.

Dan looks sheepish. "Is it weird that I'm talking to you about this?"

"Maybe, but I'm glad you feel you can."

Dan leans back against the pub bench and runs a hand across his scalp. His shaved hair is growing back, making it more obvious how far his hairline has receded. There are new lines around his jaw and forehead. Despite all the new muscles and dental work, he is still not aging backward. No one can.

"What's going on with you?" Dan asks. "Anything worthwhile come out of this dating column? What happened with Ryan Stirling?"

"Turns out, he's not as nice as his character on screen. The column's a bit of a gimmick, I'm not really looking to meet someone."

Dan nods, and for the first time I think he understands—I'm not single because I'm still heartbroken, I am alone because there's also joy in being single.

"It's a good column, you're always funny when you write about yourself. I liked the one about the twenty-two-year-old," Dan says, shooting me a genuine smile that I haven't seen in a while. I blush, embarrassed that he's read it. "Who'd have thought you'd be the one off dating twenty-somethings, partying till all hours, and I'd be signing up for another eighteen years of parenting," he laughs, but there's a flicker of remorse about it.

"The grass is always greener," I say, resorting to cliché. Dan takes another swig of beer, his forehead creasing into a frown as he thumps down his empty pint glass.

"I love Sylvie, I do. She's great, it's all great . . ." He trails off again, and I watch him struggling to find the right words. "But, well. You look like you're having a lot of fun. What if I missed my chance to mess about a bit more?"

A glow of satisfaction seeps in, and I gently kick him beneath the table.

"Sorry, but no, you don't get to say that. Your doting girlfriend is pregnant. Come on, Dan, don't be an arsehole."

"Sorry, I know." He shrinks down, shoulders slumping, like an admonished child. "I don't mean that. I don't know why I said that. Stuff in that department with Sylvie, it's—"

"Whoa there! Let's have *some* boundaries." I put my hands over my ears, which makes him laugh.

"Sorry." He covers his face with his hands, embarrassed. "Remember that first night we came back from the hospital with Jess?" Dan says, looking more relaxed. "We were so tired, we couldn't even make it up the stairs, we just slept in the living room in this nest of duvets, next to her cot. I remember walking up and down all night when she had reflux. We listened to *The Great Gatsby* on audiobook, do you remember? It was hell, but also, it wasn't. You and me in the trenches together."

"They were the best of times and the worst of times," I say, reaching out to put a hand over his.

"They were the best," he says firmly, pausing, looking me in the eye now. "Thank you, for being cool about this. Sylvie thought you might be weird about it."

*Of course she did.* "Why would I be weird about it?" I ask, jaw clenched beneath my smile.

"She thinks . . ." He clears his throat. "And this isn't me saying this, this is her. She thinks subconsciously, you thought we might get back together one day."

"Ha," I say, blowing air through my lips, but now that I look at Dan properly I see he's watching me with curiosity. *Did he think that too?* "I don't think that. I don't want that," I tell him. "But we've shared half our lives, Dan, we're responsible for two humans, that's not something that ever goes away."

"I know. She'll get her head around it." He cracks a smile. "Sylvie's made all these 'parenting mood boards.' I don't think she realizes it's mainly changing nappies, being knackered, wearing tracksuits with milk stains down them. I can't see her being good at all that—she has a seven-step cleansing routine."

"I heard. But she'll figure it out," I reassure him. Watching Dan's face, I realize he looks different. His expression open, the tension gone. "While we're being so honest, can I say something?"

"Sure."

"I need you to help more with the boring stuff, the kids' washing, their homework, remembering to pack Ethan's shin pads and gum guard for hockey. I can't have them come back to my house with black bin liners full of washing."

Dan's body language grows defensive as I'm talking. "It's

hardly worth me washing their clothes when they're only with me two days. Plus when I'm at work all day, how am I supposed to—"

"Dan," I cut him off. "I know it's not always going to be possible, but I need you to try. I work full time now too, remember."

He pinches his lips closed, then nods once. "Can I say something too? I know the lawyers agreed on all this, so it would be up to you . . ."

"What?" I ask nervously.

"I don't love that they come for a night midweek and then only two nights every other weekend. They hardly have time to settle in, and it always feels like they're living out of an overnight bag. I'd rather see them after school on a Wednesday, then have them stay for three or four nights together every other week." He pauses. "I think they might prefer that too."

"Have they said that?" I ask.

"Not in so many words."

"I don't know, that's a big change."

"It wouldn't be any extra nights, just more nights together. Think about it? If you don't want to do it, that's fine. I'm just putting it out there."

I nod; I'll think about it. "Since we're being so open, can I say something else that bothers me—" I pause. "Sylvie said something about the kids having two mums now."

"I know, it's too much. I'll talk to her—" Dan says.

"I don't want to be precious, it's just—"

"You're their mother, Anna," Dan says, reaching out to squeeze my shoulder. "You're a great mum, you always have been." He lifts his glass to take another drink before realizing it is already empty. "I'm sorry, for how things were at the end. I know I must have been hard to live with. You were right about me being depressed. It wasn't your job to fix me, I see that now."

Dan has never apologized, never acknowledged that his mental health impacted our relationship. I'm so genuinely surprised I don't know how to respond. Eventually, I say, "Thank you. I don't think either of us were good at communicating." I smile across the table at him, and his mouth smiles back, but his eyes look sad.

"I know you blame me for ending us, but when I started getting depressed, it wasn't just about work or whatever. I could see something had gone for you, as far back as when Ethan was a toddler."

"That's not true," I say, shaking my head.

"Yes, it is. You stopped loving me before I stopped loving you, though you'd never admit that, not even to yourself." His words burn, and I swallow a lump in my throat as he squeezes a hand over mine. "Sometimes I wonder, if we hadn't met so young . . . you know."

"It was still worth having, wasn't it?" I say.

"It was."

Then he reaches for my hand and lifts it to his mouth to give me a friendly peck. His eyes look glassy as he quickly wipes at them with his other hand. We exchange a meaningful look, a bridge built over something that was broken.

Stepping out of the pub into daylight, I take a moment to enjoy the feeling of sun on my face. Dan walks me back to my office and we say good-bye in the hall. He leans in to hug me, a real hug. "Thank you," he whispers in my ear before turning to go. I don't know if I've fully digested this news about the baby, but that's the most honest, constructive conversation we've had since the divorce. If that's what our relationship can look like going forward, then it's a cause for celebration.

Walking back to my desk, I realize my long hug with Dan was visible to the whole office. Glancing across at Will, I see he's watching me. There's a flash of something—jealousy? Something he wants to hide, because he swiftly pulls his gaze away. That afternoon, neither of us e-mails about the archive.

GOOGLE SEARCHES:

*Tutorial, basic DSLR camera setup*

*Statistical likelihood of being pregnant if I have an IUD and used a condom?*

*Do multiple orgasms make it more likely you could get pregnant?*

# CHAPTER 30

WILL THROWS THE RENTAL CAMERA BAG OVER HIS SHOULDER AS WE walk out of the office.

"Thank you so much for helping," he says as we walk down Milsom Street. "I really appreciate it."

"No problem," I say, feeling strange about how formal we're being with each other. I tug at my shirt; it suddenly feels too tight. Have my boobs grown? Since my conversation with Dan, I've spent the afternoon being paranoid that I could be pregnant. No preventative measures are 100 percent effective. What would I do if I was? I *really* don't want a baby, least of all the baby of a man who's leaving town. Casual sex might have its downsides.

"Do you mind if I grab a sandwich on the way? I didn't have a chance to get lunch," Will asks as we pass a popular new bagel place.

"Sure, of course," I say, and we walk in together. There's a line, and just as we get to the front of the queue, Will's phone rings. He looks at the screen, and I can see him deliberate about whether he has time to take it.

"I can order for you if you need to get that?" I offer, and he looks relieved. "What do you want?"

"Anything," he says, then steps out of the line to take the call.

"Next," calls the flustered deli owner. "What can I get you?"

"Can I get a bacon, lettuce, and tomato on rye, please, the bacon extra crispy, and do you have brown sauce? Great, thank you."

"Mayo?" he asks.

"Yes, if it's Hellmann's, no, if it's not." He nods. "Just a little of that too." I watch him start to make the bagel in front of me. "Can you put the mayo on that side of the bagel, and the brown sauce on the other? Great, sorry, thank you."

When I finish ordering I turn around and see Will watching me. He's finished his call and is giving me a strange look.

"Are you okay? What's wrong?" I ask. "I ordered you a BLT, I hope that's okay?"

"Nothing. Thanks," he says, but he's still looking at me as though I've rescued a puppy from a storm drain rather than just ordered him a sandwich.

"What?" I ask, laughing now, but he just shakes his head, his cheek creasing into a dimpled smile.

Outside the abbey, we sit down on a bench so Will can eat his bagel while I take a look at the camera he's hired.

"Is it the right kind of camera?" he asks as I open the case. It looks completely different from the models I've used in the past, but after a brief pause, I nod confidently.

"Sure," I say.

"You know, this is a really great bagel," he says with an unnervingly sincere expression.

Once I've worked out how to turn the camera on and found the screw for the tripod base plate, we head over to the abbey. I've been inside Bath Abbey many times over the years, but the building never ceases to amaze me. The huge, high, fan-vaulted ceilings and the enormous stained-glass window at the end of the nave, an intricate tapestry of color, towering up like a rainbow skyscraper. It's impossible not to feel awed by the grandeur of such beautiful, ambitious architecture.

The choir pews are abuzz with activity. Everyone is wearing matching Raise Your Voice yellow T-shirts. There is a small orchestra of musicians warming up, and as soon as he sees people singing, Will's shoulders relax.

"Will you come and meet my family?" Will asks, his eyes lighting up, as he leads me through the bustle of people. We reach a man who must be his father, because he has Will's tall stature and the same expressive face. His posture is more stooped, and his hair is entirely white, but he's clearly a Havers. Simon, on the other hand, looks nothing like his brother. He's got red hair and a smattering of freckles. He sits in a lightweight wheelchair, which he shifts around to face me.

"Dad, Simon, this is my friend and colleague Anna, she's helping me out today," Will says. I reach to shake their hands, feeling disproportionately pleased to be introduced as his friend. "Anna, my dad, Rory, and my annoying little brother, Simon."

"I'm very sorry," says Simon somberly, and I notice his voice has a slight slur. He takes my hand in both of his and squeezes it.

"What for?" I ask, confused.

"That you have to work with my brother," Simon says, which makes me laugh.

"Thank you. It is challenging at times, but I do my best to endure."

"Does he give everyone advice they didn't ask for?" Simon asks.

"He does," I say. "Hunting out my grammatical errors is his favorite pastime."

Will shakes his head at us both, but the smile lines around his eyes crease. "You're ganging up on me already?"

"It's not Will's fault," says Rory, slapping Will on the back. "When you have four boys, they all take a role, a way of asserting their identity in the pack. George was the bookish one, Harry was sporty, Simon's always been the joker, and Will—" He pauses.

"What was Will?" I ask, taking an unexpected pleasure in hearing about him from his family.

"Will is the sensitive one, takes everything to heart," Rory says. "That's why he likes things to be just so. Disorder upsets him. You know he irons his boxer shorts?"

"That's more than enough," Will says, shoulders hunched in discomfort. "Anna doesn't want to hear this."

"Oh, I do," I say, grinning as I turn back to Simon. "Come on, dish the dirt."

"He had a soft toy he took to bed until he was thirteen," Simon tells me conspiratorially. "Dodge the dog."

"That is not true. I was ten." Will looks genuinely irritated now.

"Thirteen," Rory mouths to me.

"And you wonder why I never bring any friends home?" Will says. Simon has a monogrammed *SH* embroidered on his yellow T-shirt, I notice, then I see Rory's T-shirt has an *RH* on his.

"I like your shirt," I tell Simon. He glows with pride and claps his hands.

"Simon likes to sew," Will explains. "I bought him a monogram kit for Christmas. Now if you leave anything around the house, you'll find it monogrammed the next morning." *So that's why Will has so many things monogrammed!* My heart leaps at this precious detail.

"Do you want anything monogrammed, Anna?" Simon asks, his voice hopeful.

"I will let you know," I promise him.

"We're going to interview a few choir members before you start. Si, who should I start with?" Will asks.

Simon suggests the choir director, a woman called Janet;

then Carly, a woman in her twenties with Down syndrome who has been with the choir since the beginning; then Todd, who at thirteen is the youngest member. Will tells me Todd has cerebral palsy, that he lives in foster care, and that he has been with the choir longer than he's been with any one family.

Setting up the camera in a quiet corner of the abbey, Will leads the interviews. Janet tells us that she set up the choir for those with physical and neurological challenges, to help foster a sense of community and raise awareness, but also just to celebrate the power and joy of music. It's clear she volunteers a huge amount of her time and expertise to the project. Hearing her talk makes me feel bad for spending so much time worrying about myself.

Will is a skilled interviewer. He knows just which questions to ask. When Todd tells us that the choir is his closest family, I feel myself on the verge of tears. Once we've interviewed five of the choir members, Will tells me, "We still have twenty minutes before they let the audience in. Is there anything else you think we should get?"

"How about we interview some of the carers, about the impact the choir has had on them," I suggest. "What about your dad?"

Will pauses; I'm not sure if it's because he doesn't want to interview his father or because he hasn't thought of it, but then he says, "Sure, good idea."

Rory is happy to oblige, and I mic him up.

"So, as Simon's dad, tell us what the choir means to you," Will says.

"It means everything to us. When Simon had his accident, it was tough, on everyone. Once we got over the shock of it, it was Simon's mental, rather than physical, health I found most challenging to deal with. He couldn't see much to be positive about. He lashed out at the people who loved him." He shares a look with Will, and I can only imagine what they've experienced together. "But over time he learned to adapt. He got movement back in his arms, which doctors never thought he would. He found things to be positive about, made new friends. This choir was a huge part of that. We plan our week around it. I honestly don't know what we would do if we lost the rehearsal space."

Will looks to me, wanting my input.

"Maybe just rephrase that end part into a more concise sound bite? Like 'It's played a huge part in my son's recovery. I honestly don't know what we would do without it.' Something like that." I look to Will, worried I'm overstepping, putting words in his father's mouth, but he gives a nod of appreciation. "Let's do one more take."

As the audience starts to arrive and fill the pews, I move the camera to the back of the abbey and get some wide shots of the choir's first song, Bill Withers's "Lean on Me." The sound is haunting as it fills the enormous space. The choir are all so expressive, I know it would help to get some close-ups, so I take the camera off the tripod and creep to the front with it, trying to be as unobtrusive as possible. As I slip back to stand beside Will, I see Loretta a few pews away and we wave to each other.

"Did you get what you need?" Will asks, and I nod. He is swaying to the music, fully engaged with the performance. "I can take the camera if you want to go?"

"I'd like to stay."

"Don't feel you have to," he says, his eyes wide and hopeful.

"Will. I want to stay."

And then the choir starts to sing "Build Me Up Buttercup" and Will starts quietly singing along. "Now I know why you're always singing that song," I whisper.

"I've been practicing with Simon over breakfast," he tells me, and the image of them singing together over their cereal cracks something open inside of me. As we listen to the rest of the concert, Will reaches for my hand and squeezes it. Heart full, I squeeze back, reluctant to let go. But my pleasure is tempered by an uneasy feeling. Our boundaries are blurring. I had Colleague Will and Archive Will clear in my head as separate entities. But here is Will from the woods. This is the person he is around his family; here in this room is what matters to him.

"How was lunch with your ex?" he says, and I sense he's trying to sound casual. "It looks like you're on better terms now."

"Yes, good," I tell him. "He's having another baby."

Will turns to face me, while the choir belts out "This Is Me."

"I'm sorry," he says, trying to read from my expression how I feel about it.

"No, it's fine," I say, dropping his hand. "I'm happy for him. It's made me realize I don't want that. I don't want any more children."

"Really?" he asks, and there's so much in that "really." My heart swells with hope, because it makes me think perhaps it's not just the archive for him either, but it also makes me want to cry because we are on such completely different paths.

"No, that part of my life is done," I say, then look back toward the singers.

I stay through the encore, but Will doesn't reach for my hand again. At the end, when Will goes to make an announcement about donations, I slip quietly away.

When I get home, I run straight to the bathroom to do a pregnancy test. I am being paranoid, I know I can't be pregnant, but my heart pounds in my chest as I wait for the result, and when only one line appears, I let out a breath I didn't know I was holding.

GOOGLE SEARCHES:

*Raise Your Voice, inclusive choir, how to donate*

*Where to go on a date with someone you hate*

*Is there going to be a movie version of The Spanish Love Deception?*

# CHAPTER 31

OF ALL THE DATES I'VE HAD, THIS ONE, WITH NOAH, HAS TO BE MY least anticipated. I am not relishing an evening of being lectured about my "responsibilities as a bin owner."

Lottie arrives to babysit and makes me change twice, telling me I have to look like I "made an effort." When Noah knocks on the door, I am glad I changed, because he *has* made an effort. He's freshly shaved in a clean checked shirt and well-fitted jeans. There's not a sock-and-sandal combo in sight.

"Oh wow, hi," I say, remembering how attractive Noah is when he's not wearing weird clothes and being a grump.

"Ready to go?" he asks, still terse even in a button-down.

"So, I thought we'd get the bus into town, there's one in eight minutes."

"I am aware of the bus timetable," Noah says. *Oh boy, this is going to be challenging.*

As we walk along the pavement and turn toward the bus stop, a car pulls up on the other side of the road. I pause because I recognize the driver. *Will. What is he doing here?* I stop and watch as he gets out of the car with a huge bunch of giant pink peonies.

"Hi?" I call across to him in confusion.

"Oh. Hi." He crosses the road toward us, looking back and forth between me and Noah.

"This is my neighbor Noah," I explain. I already told him about my next date, so it shouldn't come as a surprise. "Noah, this is my colleague Will."

"Hi." Will nods toward Noah, but there's a coolness in his gaze as he sizes him up. "Sorry to interrupt. Bad timing. You disappeared yesterday. I, um—" Will holds out the flowers, and it's adorable how awkward he looks. "A thank-you for yesterday, for helping me out."

Noah looks between us, perhaps curious about what I did to deserve such a decadent bunch of flowers.

"Thank you. You didn't have to do that, I was happy to help," I tell him.

"Simon insisted," Will says, his eyes now focused on me. "I've watched the footage you shot, it's perfect."

"Sorry, perfect?" I ask with a smile, my finger to my ear. "No feedback, no notes?"

"No notes," he says with a grin, our eyes drinking each other in.

Noah clears his throat. "Our bus is in four minutes," he says.

I don't want to take a bunch of flowers into town with me, but I also don't want to leave Noah and Will alone together while I rush back to put them inside. As if sensing my indecision, Will nods toward my house. "Is anyone home? I can drop them in for you."

"My sister is there, that would be great. Thank you."

He holds my gaze a moment longer, as though he wants to say more but can't with Noah here. Noah makes another impatient "humph" noise, so I quickly pass Will the flowers.

"Well, have fun," Will says, then turns slowly back toward my house, letting the flowers drop down to his side.

"Sorry about that," I say to Noah as we walk on toward the bus stop.

"Who was that?" Noah asks. "The man who sent you the clay?"

"Yes."

"He's in love with you," Noah says, as though pointing out that it's raining.

"No, he isn't. We work together." I know that's not strictly true, but I'm not going to tell Noah about my relationship with Will. "It's complicated."

"Those are not thank-you flowers," Noah says, and there's a knowing warmth in his voice now. "Thank-you flowers are lilies or carnations, roses of a moderate size. I know flowers, and those flowers say a lot more than thank you."

"Let's not talk about Will," I say, picking up my pace.

"Did you fill in the form from the council?"

"Let's not talk about the hedge or the bins either, please, Noah," I ask, clapping my hands together in prayer, then raising my eyes to the heavens.

"Fine, we'll bin the bin talk," Noah says, putting a bounce in his step.

The bus is late, so we needn't have rushed. We've only been in each other's company for twenty minutes, and already I'm finding Noah intensely annoying. He is slow and deliberate in everything he does. As we board the bus, he pulls out his wallet, takes out his card to pay, then slowly and methodically puts the card away before walking on to sit down. Why wouldn't he just put the card away *while* he's walking, like a normal person? I can't help thinking how much I'd rather be on this bus with Will, watching him put a smile on the face of every stranger he interacts with.

Jonathan suggested I take my dates to some of the tourist attractions in Bath, "a great way to promote everything this city has to offer." So, we're going to a late opening at the Roman Baths. I've been to the baths several times before, and given how uptight Noah is, now I'm wishing I'd chosen somewhere that serves alcohol.

"Fascinating to think the Romans built all this two thousand years ago, isn't it?" Noah says as we swipe our tickets through the turnstiles.

"The Celts were using the natural spring long before the Romans arrived," I tell him.

"Sure. But the Roman baths, the engineering," Noah says. "The network of channels and sluices harnessing heat from the underground spring. Remarkably sophisticated, even by today's standards."

We walk through to the first room of the museum, where there's a model of what the baths looked like when they were first built, along with some of the original walls, pillars, and engravings paying tribute to the goddess of the thermal springs, Sulis. Noah stops to read every information board silently, then scans every QR code with his phone to download "extra information."

"It's nearly impossible to read everything in one visit," I say tactfully. "Have you been before?"

"Yes. You always learn something new, though, don't you?"

The museum is quiet, and my mind starts to wander. *What did Lottie think about Will delivering that enormous bunch of flowers? She's going to read into it, she reads into everything. Did Will remember that peonies are my favorite flowers, or was that a coincidence?*

"Come and look at this," Noah says, pointing to a glass display cabinet. "People would scratch curses and wishes onto bits of pewter, then throw them into the springs, asking the goddess for help in punishing those who had wronged them."

"'Docimedis has lost two gloves and asks that the thief responsible should lose their mind and eyes in the goddess's temple,'" I read from one of the translated inscriptions. "That feels harsh. Losing your mind *and* your eyes over a stolen pair of gloves." I look across at Noah, who is still busy reading.

"Look at this one. 'Please protect my hedge from unsanctioned pruning,'" he says, not cracking a smile or turning his head. "What would you write?"

"I would ask the goddess to remove the giant stick from my neighbor's arse," I say, and Noah lets out a hard, sharp laugh. "And to stop him from reading every sign in the museum, or we'll be here until three in the morning."

"Fine," he says, shaking his head, but he's smiling, and I notice how warm his eyes look. We walk out onto a walkway in the open air, where a series of stone pillars surrounds a green pool of water.

"Funny to think how different their lives were but how similar some of their day-to-day concerns," I muse. "Meeting at the baths to curse those who've wronged them. It's like ancient Rome's version of online trolling." Noah laughs. "It's sad, isn't it? All that's left in the world of this Docimedis guy is his complaint about a lost glove."

"Two lost gloves," Noah corrects me.

"Right."

"Gemma used to think about this, when she was sick," Noah says, his expression pensive. "Because we didn't have children, she wondered who would remember her when she was gone. She was working on a PhD in plant biology, but she never got to finish it. It bothered her, that lack of a legacy."

"I'm sorry I didn't know her," I say softly. "What was she like?"

Noah's face lights up. "She loved nature. She was constantly foraging, bringing bits and bobs into the house—plants and twigs, abandoned bird nests, unique shells and stones. She was always befriending animals in our garden, had endless bird feeders and squirrel feeders. She planted lavender for the bees."

"She sounds magical," I say, enchanted by how animated he has become.

"When we moved in, the hedge was scrawny and diseased," Noah tells me. "She made it her project to revive it. She pulled out bits that were dead, replanted, treated the leaves, nurtured it back to life."

"Oh, Noah, I'm so sorry," I say, reaching out to touch his arm. "You should have said."

Noah drops his head. "I know she's not the hedge," he says, quietly now, "but when I see how big it's grown, I feel like there's a part of her inside it. I look out of the kitchen window and it's like she's telling me, 'I'm still here.'" His voice cracks, and he swipes at his eye with a palm.

"I'm so sorry you lost her. She sounds like an incredible woman."

Noah tells me how they met at a wildlife preserve, how they'd planned to move to Scotland and set up a bird sanctuary, but he didn't want to do it alone, didn't want to leave the house they'd shared.

"It's been what, eight years?" I ask as we walk past a projected hologram of people dressed as Romans having massages on stone tables. Noah nods. "And have you met anyone since?" He shakes his head. "Because you haven't wanted to, or . . . ?" I trail off.

"I could never love anyone as much as I loved Gemma," he says firmly.

"I don't want to compare what you've been through to my situation, but I never imagined being thirty-eight and starting all over again. I do understand."

"I'm sorry if I haven't been a good neighbor," he says slowly.

"I'm not good with people. Gemma used to say I had the social skills of a garden gnome."

"What do you mean? You're a great neighbor. You take in my packages, you lend me ladders, you let me know when I've put the recycling bins out at the wrong time. What more could I ask for?" Noah rubs his chin, and his eyes crease into a smile. "Come on, let's go drink this 'healing' spring water."

At the end of the exhibition, there's a water fountain where you can drink the water coming up from the geothermal spring. Some people believe it has healing properties, a cure for whatever ails you. Noah passes me a small paper cup and asks, "What are we drinking to?"

"A truce?" I suggest.

"A truce," he says, raising his cup and taking a gulp of water.

"Oh, that's disgusting," I say, swallowing it with a grimace.

BY THE TIME we get home, Noah and I are laughing as we get off the bus. He is still awkward and quiet, sometimes curt, but I feel as though I understand him a little better now.

"Thank you for this evening," he says. "I enjoyed myself."

"Me too," I tell him as we stand on the street at the bottom of my steps. "Why don't you come around for dinner sometime? I can't claim to be a great cook, but we'd love to have you."

"I would like that. Thank you." He nods to the bins. "Remember, blue recycling bin goes out tonight."

"Got it," I say, raising my hand in a salute.

Noah heads to his front door and I walk up to mine smiling. As I turn the key in the lock, I hear voices inside. *Surely the kids can't still be awake?* Then I look at my watch and see it's only nine, we didn't stay out that late. Walking into the living room, I pause at the door, surveying the scene. Ethan and Jess are in their pajamas sitting on the floor, Lottie is on the couch with a mug of tea, and Will is standing in the middle of my living room, acting out a charade.

"*The Lion, the Witch and the Wardrobe*!" shouts Ethan, and Will shakes his head, miming opening and closing a door.

"Open-and-shut case!" shouts Lottie.

Will frowns, throwing up his arms in frustration.

"Do the second bit again," Jess suggests. None of them have even noticed me come in, they are all too absorbed. Will pulls his earlobe to denote "sounds like," then starts miming climbing some stairs.

"Open climber?" Ethan suggests, and Will points at him, nodding enthusiastically, then pulls on his ear again.

"Open slimer?" Ethan tries.

"Oppenheimer," I say from the doorway, and now they all turn to look at me.

"Yes!" Will says, clapping his hands together once. Then he collects himself and rubs a palm along the back of his neck. "Hi."

"You're back," says Lottie, a huge grin on her face.

"What's going on here then?" I ask, trying to sound casual.

"Will brought you flowers," Jess says, turning around to look at me with wide eyes.

"They're bigger than my head and Jess's head put together," says Ethan. "We measured."

"How was Noah? Did you kill each other?" Lottie asks.

"No. It was fine," I say, still confused as to why Will is here.

"They forced me to stay and eat dinner with them, then play charades," he explains, shifting his weight from side to side, eyes scanning my face. "I'm sorry, I should go."

"Don't go," says Lottie. "Anna is great at charades."

"Yeah, it's your go, Mum," says Ethan.

"Aren't you both supposed to be in bed?" I ask him, reaching across the sofa to tickle Ethan.

"That's probably my fault," says Will.

"No, it's definitely mine," says Lottie, grinning at me. "Come on, Anna, just do one."

The children look up at me with pleading faces, so I agree to do one final charade. I opt for *10 Things I Hate About You*, because it's Jess's favorite movie, so I know she'll get it quickly. She gets it on the first clue, so I clap my hands and insist it really is bedtime.

"I told Will about wanting an axolotl for my birthday," says Ethan. "He says he'll help us build the tank." I look back and forth between Will and Ethan.

"Only if that would be helpful," says Will, eyes shifting to the floor.

"Will's brother has a pet tortoise that's sixty years old. Sixty! Can we meet him? Can we? I'm great with animals," Ethan says excitedly as I cajole him toward the stairs.

"I've got this," says Lottie, putting her hands on Ethan's shoulders to steer him upstairs. Turning to me and nodding her head toward Will, she silently mouths, "He's great."

"Let me see you out," I tell Will, grabbing his coat from the hook and following him out onto the front doorstep.

"Sorry, I didn't mean to stay so long," he says once we're alone on the doorstep. "Your sister is highly persuasive."

"She is," I say, then we smile at each other, politely.

"How was your date with the good-looking neighbor?" Will asks, eyes shifting from me to the doorframe.

"It was eye-opening. What's wrong?"

"I hate the idea of you out with a man who isn't me."

"Is that why you're here?" I ask, crossing my arms, lifting my chin to look up at him.

He steps forward, slipping his hands around my waist. "Can I do this?" he says, tugging me to him. I feel that magnetic pull, as though every cell in my body is supercharged, drawing toward him.

"I don't know, you made the rules," I tell him, allowing myself to sink into his embrace. His hands run up my back, holding me close.

"*You* made the rules," he says.

"You said it should stay in the woods," I remind him. "You said it should stay in the archive."

"You said I wasn't boyfriend material, that I wasn't your type," he counters, looking down into my face, jaw set, his eyes hopeful.

"Because you're leaving," I say, breaking away from him, dropping my gaze to his chest. "Now you're here making my family like you."

"I like them," he says.

"Well, don't promise them fish tanks, then disappoint them when you disappear."

"Is it your kids you're worried I'll disappoint, or is it you?" he asks, his voice low, eyes trained on me like laser beams. "What do you want, Anna? Just tell me what you want this to be."

"I don't know, I don't want you to go—" I say, feeling my eyes well up, and then, before I can anticipate it, he lifts his hands to my face and leans forward to kiss me. His hot, firm lips on mine, possessive, transport me straight back to the woods, to the archive, to the only place I want to be. As he opens to me, I feel myself melt, the flutter of a thousand wings beating in my belly, all my senses overwhelmed. When he pulls back to look at me, I step away, trying to put space between us so I can think straight.

"You didn't let me finish." I reach backward for the door to steady myself. "I don't want you to go, but I wouldn't want you to stay either, not for me. I can't see how this works—we want such different things."

His face falls. "Are you serious?"

Someone calls, "Mum!" from inside. "Let's not have this conversation right now," I plead. I don't want to say something I might regret when I don't even know what it is that I want. "Thank you again for the beautiful flowers."

He reaches for my hand as I turn away and says quietly, "This is real. You know that, right?"

I nod but then pull away and go inside. Leaning my back against the door, I fight the urge to go back out, to call after him, but I don't know what I could say that would make our lives line up.

GOOGLE SEARCHES:

*What is the difference between lust and love?*

*How much work is an axolotl?*

*Direct flights between Bristol and Paris?*

# CHAPTER 32

IF I HAD TO IMAGINE A LOCATION WHERE I MIGHT FIND LOVE AGAIN, a setting that inspired hope, romance, and magic, it would not be the Drunk Prophet on Westgate Street. Doing something like speed dating with a friend could be a funny story; alone, it would feel mildly tragic. Having concluded that all my friends are married or live too far away, I then remembered Loretta's offer to be my wingwoman. I left a message on her machine, and she called me back a few hours later saying, "Sign me up, chickie!"

Loretta meets me outside the Drunk Prophet. As soon as I see her, I'm so glad I invited her. She's wearing a red dress, a sequined leather jacket, and a bright blue headscarf.

"So what are we doing exactly?" she asks as we walk down the dingy steps of the basement venue. "You know, don't tell me. I like surprises."

We are given name badges and clipboards by a woman wearing a purple beret, corduroy dungarees, smudged lipstick, and a badge that reads, "Betty." She's attractive, in that kooky way more admired by women than men.

"Hi, Betty," says Loretta.

"First-timers?" she asks us.

"Yes," I say, furnishing her with the most enthusiastic smile I can muster.

"You get a drinks voucher included," she tells me. "Dutch courage."

"Can I just say, I don't know many people who can pull off a beret," Loretta tells Betty. "Especially outside of France. But you, darling, you pull it off with aplomb."

"Thank you!" Betty glows with pleasure, then hands us both two extra drinks tokens. "Here you go, have a great night."

"Can I? You have a smudge," Loretta asks, pulling a tissue from her bag. Betty nods in bemusement, and Loretta fixes her lips. Inside, there are a few people milling about, but we're some of the first arrivals.

"Don't be offended, Anna, but I think you've undercooked it outfit-wise," Loretta says, looking down at my jeans, sweatshirt, and scraped-back hair. All the other women here are wearing dresses or sparkly tops with big earrings. "Come on, let me do a zhuzh."

"A zhuzh?"

"A zhuzh!"

She guides me to the ladies' and opens her enormous handbag, pulling out a selection of hair ties, clips, and scarves. "Can I?" she asks, eyes gleaming with excitement at the prospect of a makeover.

"Sure, why not." I shrug. She gets me to take off my sweatshirt and fashions a halter top with a paisley blue silk headscarf. It looks pretty, but it reveals far more cleavage than I'm used to.

"I can't go out there like this!" I protest, putting a hand over my chest and reaching to get my sweater back.

"When you've got the goods, you might as well flaunt them," she says, then adds with a sigh, "I used to have fantastic breasts." I let go of the sweatshirt, resigned. It's impossible to argue with that.

She takes down my hair, brushes it into a side parting and adds a few clips, then gets out a red lipstick. I know I can't pull off red lips, but I let her apply it. She's enjoying herself, and I'm never going to see any of these people again.

When we emerge from the ladies', the room has filled, and Betty is tapping her glass to make an announcement. "Welcome, everyone! Welcome to our thirteenth microdating event. So lovely to see so many of our regulars here and some new faces too."

Taking in the gathering, I realize I'm on the younger end of the spectrum. The age range was thirty-five to fifty-five, but most people here look to be in their fifties. "Each microdate will last three minutes," Betty continues. "Please don't tell your date whether you rate them or not, just fill in your ticks afterward. When you hand in your card at the end, if you've ticked one another, we'll e-mail you each other's contact details. If you tick someone who doesn't tick you, they'll never know. Oh, and if you tick no one, then you get a free ticket to next month's session. The bar is open. Any questions?" No one has any questions. "Fab. Then ready, steady, date!"

The back room has been arranged into twelve small tables, each with two chairs. I sit down at one and pull out my score chart. A balding man in his fifties sits down opposite and holds out a hand to introduce himself.

"Hello, I'm Roger," he says. As I shake his hand, I feel calluses on his palm.

"Hi, Roger, I'm Anna," I reply.

"You look too young to be at this session," he says, and his toothy grin reminds me of my late grandfather. He glances at my ridiculous cleavage and then blushes, purposely raising his eyeline to a few inches above my head.

"I'm actually fifty-eight," I tell him. "I just look good for my age." He laughs. "What brings you to microdating then?" I ask. I know immediately Roger is not someone I'm going to be attracted to, but that doesn't mean we can't have an enjoyable conversation for two and a half minutes.

"My daughter put me up to it," he says, his eyeline cautiously returning to my face.

"My son suggested it to me," I say, giving Roger an encouraging smile because he looks nervous. "How old is your daughter?"

"Twenty-two. She thinks I don't have enough hobbies. I've been to this event twice before, and it's always a friendly bunch. Plus, you're home in time for the nine o'clock news and a mug of Horlicks. I met an accordion player last time; she persuaded me to sign up for classes. Did you know the accordion is made from a hundred different parts? Fascinating."

"I did not know that," I say, with a genuine smile now.

Watching Roger's warm, open face, I feel guilty for my lack of enthusiasm. This isn't all desperate loners looking for love, it's also people trying to connect, daring to try something new. I look across to the next table and see Loretta roaring with laughter. I promise myself I will try to be more open-minded, to be more like Loretta.

The bell rings and I say good-bye to Roger. I don't tick him, because I don't want to date someone who reminds me of my late grandfather, but I wish there was another way of communicating that I enjoyed our conversation and to wish him luck with the accordion playing. As I'm deliberating, a gaunt, olive-skinned man in his forties takes the seat Roger has vacated.

"Fabian," he says with a heavy accent. He quickly tells me he is Italian, has recently moved to Bath, and doesn't know many people. He mutters "*bellissime sfere*" while looking at my chest, which reminds me that I really do need to retrieve my sweatshirt. After Fabian I meet Greg, an electrician with a phobia of mice. He has distractingly hairy nostrils and tells me how difficult it is to find trousers to fit his body shape. "Most men don't have hips, you see." Next is Levi, a musician. He's forty-two, still lives with his parents, but is at pains to explain that he has his own front door, so can come and go as he pleases. He tells me I'm "well fit," and I end up ticking him because he's vaguely attractive, he has no visible nostril hair, and I feel obliged to tick someone.

Next up is Ben, who must be in his seventies and is certainly at the wrong event because he is expecting us to be playing checkers. Mitch, a boxer with cauliflower ears, wants to know what my resting heart rate is. When I tell him I don't know, he reaches for my wrist to find my pulse, then starts heavy breathing in a way that makes me uncomfortable. When the bell goes, I brace myself for who's coming next, hoping for elderly and harmless rather than young and pervy. But when I look up, I see Will.

"What are you doing here?" I ask, shaking my head as he sits down, trying to hide my pleasure in seeing him.

"Research. I needed to see how this works," he says. "Jesus, you're going to give half the men in here a heart attack with that top." He eyes me boldly, sitting back languorously in the chair.

"This is the wrong age category for you. Twenty-five to thirty-four is another night," I say, moving both elbows onto the table to cover my chest.

"I lied about my age," he says in a whisper, raising a finger to his lips. "Let's see who you've ticked so far then." He whisks the clipboard out of my hand before I can stop him, reading down the list. "Levi? You ticked Levi, which one is he?" He looks around the room, and I snatch back the clipboard.

"Shhh," I say, embarrassed that someone might hear him.

"That guy? Really?" He grimaces. "Are you going to tick me?"

"I'm not ticking you." Watching him in the low-lit bar, something seems different about him.

"Why not? I'm ticking you," he says, putting a large tick next to my number. Then I realize what's different—he's drunk.

"Will, stop it, this isn't a joke. I'm here for work," I hiss across the table.

"Have you told people you're an undercover journalist?" He says it playfully, but his words plant a seed of disquiet. *Am I being disingenuous?*

"No," I say, looking from side to side to check no one is listening to our conversation, "and keep your voice down." Now his face shifts, the playful mask dropping. His eyes are full of torment as he holds my gaze.

He reaches across the table to take my hand. "I need you." He looks down at my hands now, clasping my fingers through his. "Come to mine after this, I want it to be like it was in the woods."

I start to nod; I want that too, more than anything. But reason holds me back. That look in his eyes; there's something he isn't telling me.

"You got the job, didn't you?" I ask on a hunch.

He nods, then looks away guiltily. "I did," he says, then after a pause adds, "I don't have to take it, though."

"Yes, you do," I say firmly. "You have to take it. This is exactly what we were trying to avoid." Then the bell goes and we're out of time; other people start getting to their feet.

"Last night you said you didn't want me to go," he says.

"I also said I didn't want you to stay on my account."

A man hovers in my peripheral vision, waiting to sit down. I nod toward him and Will reluctantly stands. "I'll wait for you at the bar."

My next date is blond and bearded; I don't even catch his name. I try to focus on what he's saying, but I can't help glancing across at Will, my mind raking over his words. I can't let him stay for me. He wants this job. He deserves it. Could we keep something going if he left? My mind runs through all the possibilities, doing the same calculations I did last night, trying to produce a different outcome. It would be unfair to keep him tied to Bath. It would be selfish; he would come to resent me. I can't have another man resent me for holding him back.

When the last date finally ends, the host invites us to mingle and stay for drinks at the bar. Loretta is arm in arm with Roger and pulls him toward me, waving her bonus drink vouchers. "This place smells like a giant's armpit," she cries. "Did you meet Roger? Isn't he a darling? We're going to down these, then go for a tipple at Circo Cellar. Are you coming?"

"I'm afraid she has plans with me," says Will, sweeping in beside me, his eyes now slightly bloodshot. *How much has he had to drink?*

"Hello, Will darling, I didn't think this was your kind of thing," Loretta says, leaning in to kiss him on the cheek. I forgot they know each other.

"It isn't," he says. "I'm only here for Anna."

"I'll get queuing at the bar," says Roger, while Loretta looks back and forth between Will and me with undisguised delight.

"Will you excuse us a minute?" I say to Loretta, taking Will's hand and pulling him toward a fire exit. "We'll be right back."

"I thought that would never end," he says with a sigh, bending down to nuzzle into my neck, then reaching a hand around my waist. Once we're in the quiet of the corridor I spin around and step back, creating space between us. "I've missed you."

"When did you find out about the job?" I ask him.

"Today. It wasn't until they offered it to me that I realized I don't want to go anymore," he says, reaching out to stroke my cheek with the back of his hand.

"Because of me?" I ask, feeling a wave of nausea.

"What other reason would there be?" he says archly.

"That's a lot of pressure," I say, drawing back from his hand, trying to put space between us, because his touch makes it so much harder to think straight.

"I know it's crazy, and the worst timing, and maybe I'll ruin my life and never escape this town," he says, his lips loose with alcohol. "But when you've fallen in love with someone, you don't have a choice. You choose them."

*He's in love with me?* That's the booze talking. With curdling clarity, I realize I'm not going to be able to talk him out of this by being rational.

"That's not what this is, Will," I say, my voice firm and measured. "We've been caught up in the thrill of sneaking around. I'm flattered, but honestly, it's just good sex, it isn't something you change your life plans for."

He flinches, drawing back, but after a brief pause, he says, "It isn't 'just' anything, and don't tell me how I feel." His eyes flash with anger. "I know you feel it too. You felt it in the woods."

I stare up at him, trying to hide the truth. My throat burns as I force out more words. "I'm sorry, but this was just a fun distraction for me. I'm not looking to be in a relationship, I was clear about that from the start."

That does it. His face falls, and his eyes well with tears. "That's not true, you just feel bad about me giving up the job, but that's my decision to make," he says, his voice a whisper. He presses a palm against the wall beside my head, leaning toward me, searching my face for the truth, and I try to drink him in, every inch of his face, knowing this will be the last time I see him like this.

"It's too deep, too fast, Will." I want to die saying it, playing on his biggest insecurity, on a confidence he shared. It feels unnecessarily cruel. But it works.

He drops my arm as though I've burned him. All the light in his eyes disappears. He backs away from me, then turns to leave, striding out through the half-empty bar.

Walking home, numb to the evening chill, I can't help doubting myself. Can something that feels so awful have been the right thing to do? I could call him now, take it all back. But by the time I have walked home, I have convinced myself that it was my only option. Not just for Will's sake, but for mine too.

I've been in a relationship where I've been loved reluctantly, stayed with reluctantly, and it doesn't feel good; it doesn't end well. I was a broken shell when Dan left. Piece by piece I've put myself back together, I've regained control of my life, of my heart. This last month with Will, I've felt that control slipping away. I refuse to make myself vulnerable to that kind of pain again.

GOOGLE SEARCHES:

*What's more painful, heartache or gangrene?*

*Pictures of gangrene*

*Uplifting books about being alone and being fine*

**Orders Braving the Wilderness by Brené Brown**

# CHAPTER 33

CRISPIN HAS CALLED EVERYONE IN FOR A MEETING. I HAVE TO GO IN. I can't invent any more reasons to work from home. He's going to announce his plans for the restructuring, and we'll find out who's being made redundant. I've been so distracted, I've hardly had time to worry about the prospect of losing my job. Jonathan sits with the rest of us, while Crispin has taken the large armchair in the middle of the living room. It denotes an unnerving power shift—Jonathan is no longer in charge.

As I walk in, Crispin beckons me over. "Anna, I loved the column about the widower," he says. "The stuff where you compare divorce to the death of a future, lovely stuff, very moving."

I feel myself swell with pride. I have been trying to put more of myself into the column, and I'm pleased he noticed. Then he waves for me to sit down with the others and addresses the whole room.

"When I came on board just a few months ago, *Bath Living* felt like a publication from a different era. It was stale, out of touch, sales were dwindling," Crispin tells us, pressing his fingers into a spire. "With our shift toward online and a change in focus, we've already seen a marked upswing." *Phew! The business is saved.* "Unfortunately, it's just not going to be enough to make the magazine profitable in its current format. The only way to keep the publication going is to scrap the print magazine entirely, close the Bath office, and run the online edition from our digital hub in London."

There's a collective intake of breath. I glance around the room. Jonathan looks devastated, but everyone else looks as though they knew this was coming. Was I the only one caught off-guard?

"We'll still employ a small team of freelance journalists to create local content. There will be work for many of you, though in a slightly different capacity." Crispin looks to Jonathan, who wrings his hands, then addresses us.

"I can only apologize to you all. I do hope you won't blame Crispin here. We were already up a gum tree without a paddle when he came on board. We would have had to close entirely if it weren't for him. This way, the publication will continue, the name will live on."

"I don't want anyone to panic," Crispin says. "There'll be a transition period, generous redundancy packages, new opportunities. This is an evolution, not an ending."

But from the looks on everyone's faces, it feels like an ending.

As the meeting disperses, I listen to people chatting. It sounds like Kelly already has another job lined up; others have been interviewing, putting out feelers. Am I the only one who doesn't have a backup plan? I've been so preoccupied with the dating column, competing with Will, sleeping with Will, I've failed to see the writing on the wall. In the open-plan office, people discuss their options, while along the corridor Jonathan sits in the living room drinking scotch, staring out of the window. He looks like an emperor overseeing the fall of Rome, his life's work crumbling around him.

Crispin has scheduled meetings with departments and individuals to discuss how their role will be "transitioned." Will and I are called in together. I avoid his eyes as we make our way to Jonathan's office, which Crispin has requisitioned.

"It's good news for you two," Crispin says, slapping a hand on the desk. "The dating column has been a hit. It gets a high volume of click-through and has been the most shared link these last three weeks. You're recognizable faces for the brand now. We'd like to keep you both on, though in a freelance capacity." He pauses, waiting for us to look delighted, which neither of us is. "Though there might be less job security, there will still be plenty of work."

"I won't be staying," says Will. "I've taken another job."

"Oh, that's a shame," Crispin says, his face falling. "Where are you off to?"

Will fiddles with his glasses. I glance across at him, but he won't look at me.

"An international news station in Paris," Will says. "I'll be presenting their arts and culture segment."

While my heart feels like it's imploding, I am also thrilled for him. He will be so good at that job and I know it's what he wanted. What he *really* wanted.

"Congratulations," I tell him.

"I was holding off accepting," he says, finally looking across at me. "But since the situation here is now clear, I have no reason not to go."

"Damn shame. Can we tempt you to keep writing a column from Paris?" Crispin offers. "An Englishman dating abroad?"

"I won't be able to in my new role, I'm afraid," Will says. His manner is so stiff and professional, I can't believe this is the same man who kissed me so passionately. "I'll be sure to deliver the last few columns before I go."

"You'll have time to fit in that final date up the Eiffel Tower,

I hope?" Crispin asks. "We've already trailed it as the column finale alongside Anna's Regency ball."

"Yes, of course," Will says, eyes now firmly on Crispin.

"Well, I can't say I'm not disappointed to be losing you. You've been attuned to my vision from the start." Crispin turns his gaze to me. "I hope you aren't going anywhere, Anna?"

"Nope," I say with a pang of regret. My opportunity to move to Paris and go on exciting adventures has long passed. My chance with Will, gone too. My life is here.

"And you'll be happy to stay on the same day rate? You won't have the same holiday or pension entitlement, but that's a standard way of contracting journalists these days." Crispin shoots me a tight smile. "The amount of people Jonathan had on staff payroll was totally untenable, I'm afraid." He turns to start tapping away at his computer, as though my agreement is merely a formality. He shifts his eyes from his screen, straight to Will. "Put a lunch in my diary before you go, Will. I'll share my contacts in Paris."

"No," I hear myself say.

"No?" Crispin asks, turning to me, then laughing. "You don't want me and Will to have lunch?"

"No to the question before, about accepting those terms." I look Crispin in the eye.

"What do you mean?" Crispin asks, screwing up his face in confusion.

"If you want me to go freelance, I want a higher day rate." I feel sick saying it, when all this is about the magazine not having enough money, but he just said they need me and I've been underpaid for years.

"A raise?" says Crispin, as though I've asked for the crown jewels. "Anna, do you understand what's happening here?"

"Yes," I say, keeping my cool. "I've been here a long time. I know the magazine inside out. You asked me to step up with this column, to deliver something different; I have done that. I'm writing the most-read page in the online publication. With Jonathan stepping down and Will leaving, you're going to need continuity, my connections and standing within the local community. You're offering less security and you're slashing your overhead; it stands to reason my day rate should increase." *I can't believe I'm saying this.*

"Fine, we can discuss a small raise," Crispin says with a frown. "Just—"

"I think ten," I say, cutting him off, about to suggest a 10 percent raise, but now Will is shaking his head and subtly raising two fingers. "A two percent—" He shakes his head again and mouths "twenty." "A twenty-five percent raise," I blurt out. *What made me say twenty-five? That's a ludicrous amount. He's never going to pay me that.*

"Twenty-five percent?" Crispin asks, balking. "Somewhere closer to four or five might be attainable."

"Twenty percent would take her up to what I'm on," Will says. "Anna has more experience than me. She'll be invaluable for a smooth transition."

"Fifteen," says Crispin, his jaw tensing. He tugs at his collar, then pulls his shirtsleeves down beneath his jacket.

"Twenty. If that's what Jonathan was paying Will, that's what I'm worth." I hold firm, my hands clasped in my lap, my gaze unwavering.

"That's a little ambitious, Anna," Crispin says, looking ruffled.

"And when was ambition ever a bad thing?" I say, and now I see Will smile from the corner of my eye.

"Fine," Crispin says. He shakes his head, but there is admiration in his eye. "Welcome to Arch Media, Ms. Appleby."

I leave his office feeling exhilarated. Did that really happen? Today has been a pinball of emotions.

"Thank you," I say, turning to Will, then hold out my arms to see if he will let me hug him. He does, though his body feels tense.

"I didn't do anything. That was all you," he says, his voice soft.

"You're really moving to Paris then?" I ask, my eyes drawn to his lips.

"I am." He pushes his hair out of his eyes.

"You aren't wearing your glasses."

"Someone told me I didn't need to hide behind them." He gives me a wry smile. "That I didn't need them to look smart."

"Will, I'm so sorry—" I start to say.

"*I'm* sorry," he says, cutting me off. "For reading things so wrong, for turning up in that state on Friday. I was way out of line."

I want to scream that he wasn't, that he didn't. "Will you stay in touch? Let me know how you get on?" I ask hopefully.

"I'm sorry, I don't think I can," he says, and I know I deserve that. "They're not going to make me work my notice. Any loose ends with the column or submitting the *Times* article, you can ping me via e-mail." He pauses. "And I think we've been over everything else." The cold finality in his voice makes me want to cry. He is hurting. I hurt him, despite my best intentions. "I'm having a few leaving drinks on Saturday, inviting everyone from work. I'd appreciate it if . . ."

"If I didn't come." I finish his sentence, and he nods. "I understand. Well, good-bye then. You'll be brilliant, I know you will."

"Good-bye." He gives me one final nod, then turns to go. My shoes feel like lead weights, and I blink back tears. I don't want to follow him into the office while I'm feeling emotional, so I turn and walk the other way, toward the living room, where I find Jonathan still sitting alone.

"How's the end of days?" he asks mournfully when he sees me come in.

"Not too bad," I reassure him.

"My grandfather would be turning in his grave. I have let everyone down," he says, closing his eyes, leaning back in his leather armchair.

"No, you haven't," I say, crossing the room to put an arm around him. "Times change, tastes change. It's happening to a lot of print magazines; you can't blame yourself."

"You're to be kept on? I told Crispin he needs you and Will to stay."

"Will's going, I'm staying."

"Oh, I thought you two . . ." He gives me a long look, but I shake my head. He pats the arm of his chair. "Drink?"

I nod. "What will you do?" I ask him.

"Retire. My house in Italy needs refurbishing. I've been wanting to spend more time out there."

"That sounds lovely," I say, then pause, noting his forlorn expression. "You don't look happy about it."

"I am heartbroken, darling. I love this place as one might love a spouse, and you are all family to me. But no one can say I didn't try. If my family blame me, I will be able to look them in the eye. I will grab them by the lapels with both hands and cry, 'I tried, by God, I tried!'"

"You did," I say, surprised to see Jonathan so animated. He hands me a tumbler of whiskey.

"I shall be sad to leave this spot especially," he says, turning to me with a sly smile. "My father always told me the upstairs floor was haunted. Some poor soul with unfinished business, roaming the halls. I didn't think I believed in such things, but of late, I'll swear I've heard some poltergeist haunting the archive, having a rather lovely time by the sound of things." I must flush scarlet, because he pats me on the hand. "I wouldn't let that slip away if I were you."

"Some things are too difficult," I say, quietly mortified.

"Can you honestly tell me you tried, you tried with everything you had?" He regards me over the lip of his whiskey, then swigs it down. "Don't let life make you hard, Anna. It's the soft, gooey middle that makes it all so delightful."

"I will drink to that," I say, raising my glass again.

"Though you'd better not have gotten any gooey middle all over my archive magazines."

"Jonathan, please, I don't know what you're talking about," I say, suppressing a smile. "Maybe you'll find your gooey middle in Italy?"

"I'm sure I shall. Italian men can't resist me."

AT HOME, ALL I want to do is get into my pajamas, hole up with the children, and forget all about Will Havers. It's done now, he's going. I was infatuated with him, that is all. It was ridiculous of him to use the L word. I might have liked him a lot, but I don't believe in instalove. It was only a few weeks; getting over him will be easy compared to getting over a marriage. I just need to focus on the children, on work. I should put more energy into socializing, try to nurture meaningful friendships rather than looking for romantic love.

When Jess gets home from school, she grunts hello and goes straight up to her room. I hear her bedroom door shut and "Believer" by Imagine Dragons start to play. I know something is up with her, more than just Penny, but she's chosen not to tell me. Then I remember what Lottie said about making time, giving her enough space to unload. So I go upstairs and knock gently on her door, then peer around it.

"Will you come into the garden with me?" I ask.

"Why?" she asks, rolling over on her bed.

"It's a warm evening, the sky is this amazing pink color, I want you to see it."

"Mum," she groans, but I wait, and she sighs, then rolls off her bed.

Outside, the sun is low in the sky, the dying light of the day, red and pink bleeding into dusk—a beautiful, calming scene. It would be even more beautiful if this huge fucking hedge weren't in the way.

"Isn't it pretty?" I say to Jess, handing her a cup of milk, then cradling my own mug of tea.

"Yes, very sky-ey," she says, indulging me, and we grin at each other.

"I'm sorry life is so busy, that we don't get a lot of time to hang out, just the two of us," I say tentatively. Jess shrugs. "I want you to be able to talk to me, about anything."

"Can I get a nose piercing?" she asks hopefully.

"Hmm, no. Ask again when you're sixteen," I say, and she sinks down further in the wicker garden chair. "Are you really ready to say good-bye to your Sylvanian Families?" I ask gently.

"I'm not a little kid anymore, Mum."

"I know, but I thought you loved making those little stop-motion animations." Jess shrugs again, and I force myself to sit in the silence. *Come on, Jess, talk to me.*

"They're lame," she says, rocking her head back. We sit in silence again, for what feels like an eternity, then finally she says, "Penny found one of my videos online. She wrote mean comments underneath." Jess tugs at her hair.

Usually I would react, ask what the hell Penny's problem is, but I don't, I just take a beat. "That sounds really hard, Jess, I'm sorry," I say. I see her soften, then she pulls her phone from her pocket and turns it around in her hand.

"It's not just the video," she says quietly. Then she unlocks her screen and shows me her class WhatsApp group. She covers her face as I scroll through the messages. Among all the unintelligible communications, I find references to Jess, some written by

Penny and a girl called Cleo, some from unknown numbers that aren't saved in Jess's phone.

Jess Humphries is so fugly.

Jess H plays with baby toys.

Then there's a link to one of her YouTube videos.

Who wants to go to Burger King after school? JH, SK, TT NOT INVITED.

Would you rather have Jess H's ugly nose or Tiffany's massive butt?

Then someone has created a poll.

Reams and reams of abuse; the messages go on and on. I cover my mouth in horror. How can twelve-year-olds be so cruel?

"Jess, this is, wow, this is not okay," I say as calmly as I can. "How long has this been going on?" She doesn't answer, but I scroll back and see it started over a month ago.

"It's not that bad at school," she says quietly. "It's mainly Penny and I just avoid her. They take me off the chat sometimes, then add me back. I can't escape it, Mum."

My heart breaks for her. I want to tell her she can leave, we'll find a new school, I'll quit my job and homeschool her, but I bite back all my solutions, pull her into a hug, and let her sob into my shoulder.

"I'm so sorry, I didn't realize this was happening. Why didn't you tell me, honey?" I whisper into her hair, and she shrugs.

"I didn't want you to worry. I didn't want you to be sad again."

That hits me like a truck. "I'm sorry, Jess, but we have to tell the school." She holds on to me, nodding into my neck. "I need to screenshot some of these messages, okay? Then I think you should come off this group. It's important, for your sanity and your safety."

She pulls away from me, and I look down at her tearstained cheek. It feels like only yesterday she was learning how to walk, how to talk, and now she has to deal with all this.

"Whatever Penny's problem is, you know it's not you, right? It's not babyish to have an imagination, it's wonderful."

"Did you give them away, my Sylvanian Families?" she asks.

"No, they're still in the kitchen cupboard."

She gives me a grateful smile, and I wipe the tears from her face with my thumb. When we walk back into the kitchen, I hand Jess the plastic bag. She pulls me into a tight hug. "Thanks, Mum." I know I haven't solved anything, but *something* feels mended.

GOOGLE SEARCHES:

*What do I do if my child is being bullied?*

*Going freelance, what you need to know*

*Axolotl breeders, UK*

*Will Havers*

# CHAPTER 34

DISCOVERING WHAT JESS HAS BEEN GOING THROUGH LIGHTS A FIRE beneath me. I have been sleeping on the job and I need to wake up. I call Dan, fill him in on the situation, and book us an appointment with the head teacher for the next day. To their credit, the school takes the allegations seriously. They promise to carry out a full investigation and to review their antibullying protocol. A week later, three pupils end up being suspended, Penny included, and a new module, "Bullying Awareness and Prevention," is added to the curriculum. It's not a magic wand, but already I can see Jess is less tense, as though a weight has been physically lifted off her. I've also instigated a new house rule: no phones upstairs and they're switched off after eight p.m. It's a bit draconian but Jess seems fine with it, and it's helping me too. I'm reading more books. I've finished decorating my reading nook, and I've even called the rescue center to be put on a list for a new cat.

As for Will, he's been gone two weeks now. It feels like an eternity. The office will stay open for another few weeks, but the huge task of packing up all Jonathan's books and antiques will take months. I have been working from home, keeping myself busy, trying to distract myself from the unpleasant feeling that Will's distance brings. I want to call him, to know if he is happy in his new life, but I know I've given up the chance to be his friend. Luckily, he is not on social media, or my new phone policy would not be going so well. I did find his first news broadcast. He was, unsurprisingly, brilliant.

Crispin has asked for at least one more date for the column, to "make it lucky seven," before I choose a date for the ball. I currently have Noah penciled in as my only realistic option. The children have been proposing people all week, but so far, we've struggled to come up with anyone for date seven. They both kept suggesting Will, and I had to explain that it needs to be someone who lives in Bath, preferably someone available before next Sunday.

On Monday, Ethan persuaded me to ask someone out in the supermarket. I'd just plucked up the courage to ask when the man's wife appeared from the next aisle holding toilet paper and Pepto-Bismol. It was awkward, especially when we had to stand behind them in the checkout queue.

On Thursday, I buy the kids ice creams on the way home from school and we sit in the garden in the sunshine. Ethan suggests Kenny's grandad again, saying he "really isn't that old." Then he suggests we call emergency services and hang up until we get a "man on the phone." I'm forced to have a serious conversation with him how important it is to never call 999 unless it's a life-or-death emergency, and that your mother needing a date does not qualify.

Just as I'm about to admit defeat and text Kenny's mum, Jess holds a finger in the air and cries, "Wait! I've got it. Ethan's swimming teacher!"

"Who? Mr. Bellingham? He's got warts on his face," Ethan says, screwing his nose up in disgust.

"No, the new one. Warty Bellingham left, remember?" Jess says.

"Oh yeah, Andre!" Ethan nods. "He was a stunt double in Hollywood. He knows everything about the Marvel universe, plus he's got massive flip-flops and says I've got amazing froggy legs."

We google the leisure center on my phone and up pops a photo of Andre Johnson, an exceptionally attractive man in his midthirties with dark skin, well-defined pectorals, and a perfect Hollywood smile.

"Holy bejesus," I exclaim, because we might have just hit the jackpot. "You have swimming after school tomorrow, right?" I ask Ethan, and he nods. Before I can drill him on what else he knows about Andre, Noah's head appears over the top of his hedge.

"Sorry, are we being too loud?" I ask, preempting a complaint.

"No, but do you mind if I make some noise?" Noah asks, holding up a chain saw. Then he starts cutting off a huge chunk of branch from the top of the hedge.

"Wait! Stop! Noah, what are you doing?" I call. "I don't care if the hedge blocks out our light, I know what it means to you!"

"You're right, it's gotten out of hand," Noah shouts over the sound of the chain saw. "And she's not in the hedge, she's in here!" He taps a hand against his chest, then almost loses his grip on the chain saw, and I rush my children inside before someone loses a limb.

On Friday I go along to Ethan's swimming lesson and wait at the end to ask Andre Johnson if he'll go out with me. To my surprise, Andre not only seems charming and normal, but he is also gorgeous and single and readily agrees to go on a date. His only caveat is that he's booked up all of Saturday with swimming lessons, but if it needs to be this weekend, I could join him for his

Sunday morning climbing session. It wouldn't be my first choice of activity, upper-body strength not being my strong point, but I've got myself a date, just before deadline.

"Mum, you know what I really really want?" Ethan asks me as we walk home from swimming.

"An axolotl?" I guess, and he nods, eyes hopeful. "Well, lucky for you, I've finally done my research and found a reputable breeder."

"You're kidding!" he squeals, jumping up and down in the street.

"But you'll need to be in charge of feeding it."

"Of course! That's the best bit. Will said he'd help build the tank, we need a whole filtration system." Ethan pauses. "Maybe we could ask Dad or Noah?"

"*I* will construct the tank," I tell him confidently, and he starts skipping in delight. "I might need to watch a few YouTube videos, but I am an intelligent woman, I'm sure I'll work it out."

ON SATURDAY NIGHT, I host a pottery party in my garage. It's the first time I've had people over in a long time. Noah brings wine, Lottie has made tacos, Loretta has invited Roger from speed dating, and Michael has brought Jane, the Janeite I set him up with through the apps. (She's writing her PhD thesis on "fashion in the age of Jane Austen.") I am supplying the clay and giving everyone a tutorial on how to construct a basic pinch pot.

"I hear you've just read *Pride and Prejudice* for the first time," Jane says with a demure smile as I show her how to roll the rim for her pot.

"Yes. I loved it. It really pulled me out of a reading slump," I tell her.

"I'm so glad, and I hear I have you to thank for setting Michael up online. I have never met a man who has such an encyclopedic knowledge of eighteenth-century fashions." When she looks across the room at Michael, I see her visibly swoon, and my inner Emma glows with pride. Maybe there really is someone for everyone.

Moving around the circle to see who else might need my help, I notice that Loretta has abandoned her pot and is molding a phallic object.

"Keep it clean," I say, crushing her clay phallus with my fist and nodding across the room toward Jess, who is busy making a small house for one of her stop-motion videos.

"Hey," Loretta says, cackling, as she elbows me away. "That was a masterpiece!"

Roger leans in to give her a clay flower, which she takes in delight. On the other side of the room, Noah is getting frustrated with an overly ambitious design for a bug house. I try to offer him some pointers, but he won't let me help.

"Anna, I am *loving* tonight," Lottie says, following me into the kitchen to fetch more drinks. "This house feels so alive again, like old times. Loretta is hilarious."

"Isn't she?"

Lottie bends down to put bowls in the dishwasher and when she stands up, she winces and rubs her bump.

"What? Are you okay?" I ask, reaching out to support her arm.

"Fine, she's just kicked me."

"I still can't believe my little sister is going to have a baby."

"I wanted to ask you something actually," she says, biting her lip. "How would you feel about being my birthing partner?"

"Me? What about Seb?" I ask.

"He's squeamish about blood. He can't cope with seeing people in pain, least of all me. I think he might be more hindrance than help. I'd like it to be you, if that's not too weird."

"It's not too weird, but—" I pause.

"What?"

"You know me, I'm not really an 'imagine your cervix opening like a lotus' type of person."

"No, you're not," Lottie laughs. "You're the kind of person who will advocate loudly for me, who will insist on the most experienced anesthetist there is." She grins at me. "I want you to do it *because* you're you. I trust you."

As I pull her into a hug, my eyes start to well up. When she sees my face, she gives me a skeptical look.

"What? Why are you crying?"

"Nothing." I wipe away the tear. "It's just, it's nice to know you still need me."

"What do you mean? Of course I need you. You're my sister."

"I know. It's just . . . this is going to sound silly." I drop my eyes to the floor. "This last year, I worried you'd lost a bit of respect for me, when you realized I didn't have life all figured out."

"Lost respect? Anna, I have *more* respect for you. The way you've handled everything, always putting the kids first—you're incredible. I feel closer to you than ever."

"Really?" I say, surprised to hear her say this. "But we've always been close."

"Sure, but sometimes it felt like you were infallible. Honestly, a little impenetrable. You didn't even tell me you were having marital problems until Dan had moved out."

"So, I'm more relatable now that I'm a screwup?" I say with a smile.

"You're more relatable now that you let me in."

She pulls me in for another hug and then pinches my bum to make me laugh. When she finally lets me go, I say, "There is something I wanted to get *your* help with. The living room. I've got the rest of the house feeling like mine, but in there, I just don't know where to start."

"Yes! I thought you'd never ask," Lottie yells. "What were you thinking?"

So, I talk her through some of the ideas I had: stripping the carpet out, sanding the floorboards, maybe wallpapering a feature wall. She has plenty of great ideas too and says she'll bring Seb and a floor sander around next weekend to get started.

Back in the garage, I look around the room at my eclectic bunch of friends. I wouldn't have gotten to know any of these people if it weren't for the column. Something good has come out of it, even if it wasn't love. This is what I have missed, hosting friends, bringing people together, the sound of laughter filling a room. The house no longer feels haunted.

Now that I'm freelance, I won't be so wedded to an office. I will have time to get out more, to say yes, to try new things. I don't know which hobbies I will choose in the drop-down box of life, but whatever they are, I'm excited to find out. I've already signed up for a weekly sculpture course. I know I want to travel more, to go to galleries, take day trips to London. Who knows, maybe I'll even try cycling again.

ON SUNDAY, I take a bus to the climbing wall and look down at the ampersand on my arm, the symbol of a new chapter. I had meant to book an appointment to have it removed, but now I've decided to keep it. A bit like my divorce, it's not something I would necessarily have chosen, but now that it's here, I've grown to appreciate it.

Andre meets me at the reception holding climbing shoes and a harness. "Have you done any climbing before?" he asks with a flash of his wide Hollywood smile.

"I haven't, but I'll try anything once," I tell him.

"That's the spirit," Andre says, clapping his hands and releasing a cloud of chalk dust.

My new can-do attitude doesn't last long. It turns out you

need an extraordinary amount of upper-body strength to pull yourself up a thirty-foot wall, but as I collapse in a heap at the bottom, Andre refuses to let me give up.

"Don't think of it as 'pulling yourself up'; you need to spread your weight, it's about finding a good position, a good grip with your feet as well as your hands." He takes time to show me. He's a good teacher, patient and generous with his praise. When I get ten feet up the wall, he hollers and cheers in a way that's embarrassing and adorable all at once. Eventually, my hands refuse to try anymore, and I opt to sit the rest of the session out so I can "watch and learn." Andre sprints up the wall like a vertical gazelle, and from the comfort of the floor I enjoy the view of his stuntman physique.

After the climbing session, Andre and I go for coffee, and he is just as lovely to talk to as he is to watch climb a wall. He tells me he worked as a stuntman in the US for eight years but came home after a shoulder injury forced him to retire early.

"What did you love most about being a stuntman?" I ask him.

"I got into it because I was an adrenaline junkie," he tells me. "It never gets old, throwing yourself off a bridge or running from an explosion, but then, I also came to love the problem-solving element, working with directors and stunt coordinators. I guess every job is problem-solving. You've just got to work out what problem you want to solve."

"Children not being able to swim being your current problem," I say with a smile.

"Right, exactly," he laughs. "What's your problem, work-wise?"

"Working out how to say something interesting that resonates with people. Keeping my integrity while also moving with the times." I take a sip of my coffee. "Making sure I back up my laptop."

"Sounds challenging," Andre laughs, then looks up at the menu board. "The waffles here are supposed to be incredible. Can I tempt you?"

"Why not? I burned so many calories sitting on the floor watching you climb."

Andre laughs again, which makes me glow with the delightful feeling of being found funny. "Do you want toppings?"

"Oh, just however it comes," I say, then catch myself, taking a moment to consider what I actually want. "No, wait. Could I have blueberries and strawberries, mascarpone, and maple syrup, but on the side? Thank you."

"Great choice," he says.

I can't fault my morning with Andre. It's been a perfect date. After our waffles, he walks me to the bus stop, tells me he's had a great time, and asks if he can take me out to dinner next week. I say yes, because he's lovely and I've enjoyed his company. But then on the bus home my heart starts to race, my fingertips tingle with nervous energy, and I have to get off the bus because my chest hurts and I'm hyperventilating. Standing on the pavement, bent double trying to catch my breath, I cannot work out what is wrong. I had a lovely morning, with a lovely man, so why does it feel so wrong? Why am I bursting into tears in the middle of the street, then texting Andre to politely decline his invitation to dinner? Why does my heart hurt?

A CUP OF decaf coffee in hand—worried too much caffeine is why my chest felt weird earlier—I sit at my desk and stare at a blank document. I still haven't written my half of the article about Reconnect Retreats. I've been putting it off, staring at a blinking cursor every time I sit down to write it. The deadline is tomorrow, and I still have nothing. Will sent me what he'd written last week, the sight of his name in my inbox giving me a jolt of illogical hope, which quickly evaporated when I read the brief, perfunctory e-mail.

*Copy and photos attached, happy for you to choose whichever ones you think we should use. Once you've written your copy, just submit it along with mine directly to the editor, details enclosed. Thanks, W.*

He doesn't even want to read what I write before it goes out. It's as though he's purposely shutting off any need for further communication between us.

Opening the Word document, I reread his copy now. He describes the concept behind the retreat, the idyllic location, how he rediscovered his love of fire building and wild swimming. He doesn't go into too many specifics about me, but he says it was the perfect way to get to know someone and that two days there felt like two months. There is one sentence that jumps out at me: "If you want to know whether you could fall in love with someone, this is the ideal place to find out."

Opening the photo files from Greta, first I see the posed shots of the cabin, Will and me by the fire, an arty shot of sunlight on the glade, then Will trying to stack wood. Greta is a skilled photographer; you can practically hear the birds in the trees. When I scroll to the end, my breath catches in my throat. Will and I are wrapped in blankets sitting up in the grass; my shoulders are bare and so is his chest, but the rest of us is covered by the rug or shadow. The light hits Will's cheekbone; he looks beautiful. But it is me my eye is drawn to. My hair is disheveled, wavy and wild, like an ethereal woodland nymph's. In the photo, I'm gazing up at him, and there's a lightness in my face; my eyes shine almost gold in the light, we are smiling at each other, and I look so full of joy, so self-assured. I stare at the photo. Is that really me? The photo is a fleeting moment captured perfectly by her lens. Greta was right, it is tasteful, and more beautiful than anything that could be posed.

And now I know why I had that reaction on the bus. It hits me all at once, like the sun emerging from behind a dark cloud, landing with such an urgent clarity I feel the need to say it out loud: "I am in love with Will Havers."

Suddenly, I know exactly what I need to write.

## CAN TURNING TECHNOLOGY OFF BE A TURN-ON?

As a newly single divorcée, I found the prospect of being thrust back onto the dating scene terrifying. Online dating, specifically, seemed about as appealing as the three-day-old cup of tea you find abandoned in the microwave. Having met my husband at university and experienced the slow build of friendship that ignites into something more, I had no concept of dating someone I didn't already know. I couldn't fathom how one could judge someone on a snapshot or a list of their interests. Even if I could get past the concept of "swiping," a few hours in a bar with someone felt too pressured, too much like a job interview. So when I heard about the concept behind Reconnect Retreats, I was curious. How might it feel to get to know someone cut off from day-to-day demands and distractions? And could I survive a whole weekend without access to my phone or Wi-Fi?

While on paper I might be "single" again, my true status is complicated. The fallout from divorce is like the aftermath of a nuclear explosion. There's the initial shock wave, the devastation and upheaval. Beyond the initial blast radius, there's a wasteland: your shared dreams, the job of disentangling your finances, your living situation. Once you've gotten through that, there's another fallout zone full of more nuanced challenges: loss of confidence, confusion, jealousy, anger, being left with a heart that—while it might no longer be broken—has gone into hibernation for its own protection. To put it simply, I wasn't open to a new relationship.

As a self-confessed phone addict, going into this retreat, I was honestly more interested in seeing how I was going to manage without my smartphone than I was in finding a romantic connection. But as soon as I arrived in the woods, what struck me was how fine I was without it. The reflex was still there, reaching for my phone to take a picture, then remembering I must commit such things to memory instead.

With a comfortable bed and a fully catered menu, this retreat was my kind of camping. I soon fell in love with the quiet, the sound of the woods, listening to the gentle crackle of life in the trees. Time feels different when it's marked by the movement of the sun rather than a clock. I did not expect to enjoy it as much as I did. I was even more surprised by how I came to feel about the person I was with.

Will is someone I have worked with for six months. As colleagues we were prone to rubbing each other the wrong way. But in the woods, lying by a campfire, with all life's distractions muted, we were finally honest about miscommunications, misconceptions we had about each other. I discovered the boy who delights in building fires, learned about the people in his life, began to understand where his driving ambition comes from. I uncovered a man who takes delight in small things and is wonderfully unjaded by heartache. Talking late into the night around the fire, my numb heart began to melt. The beam of Will's attention was like the warmth of the sun on your face after a long, dark winter. We connected in a way that excited and terrified me in equal measure, because it made me feel vulnerable again. I don't know if I fell for Will because we were alone in the woods together or if it would have happened anyway, but it felt like the retreat removed all barriers.

On Sunday, turning my phone on, a hundred e-mails pinged into my hand, messages I couldn't ignore, and the bubble of the retreat burst. Back in reality, all I saw were the reasons a relationship with Will wouldn't work. An eight-year age gap, being at different life stages, a job that was going to take him away and a life that would keep me in Bath. There were simply too many obstacles, and the woods were not real life. So, I pushed him away, I wasn't honest about how I felt.

But now I look at this photo and realize the woods were as much a reality as the world outside. The baggage we carry isn't a bad thing; it is our substance, our history, the experiences that make us who we are. All the reasons not to be together might be surmountable, because love is rare, and if you're lucky enough to feel it, you shouldn't let it pass you by.

A few months ago, I wouldn't have dreamed of sharing this photo; it is too personal, unfiltered. But now I know that if I can share a picture of myself in my most vulnerable state, then I am not broken. I have loved and I have lost, but my heart still works. There will be other chapters. I will love again. Because—whatever the fallout—to feel like this about someone, to see and be seen so entirely, it is worth any risk. What I really reconnected with at the retreat was myself—what I need, what I want, and what I am capable of feeling.

PS: Will, I am in love with you. Call me.

My eyes are clouded with tears by the time I finish typing. Before I can talk myself out of it, I send it to the *Times* editor, along with Will's copy and the photos I've selected.

As soon as I press send, I feel a jolt of adrenaline. How will he feel about my sending this to press? But then a wave of calm settles over me. Even if I'm too late, even if he doesn't call, I still needed to say it. Because true love does not cower in the shadows; it roars, loud and proud, until it has given its all.

GOOGLE SEARCHES:

*Do-it-yourself Regency hairstyles*

*What kind of underwear did Jane Austen wear?*

*Video tutorial, Regency dances*

# CHAPTER 35

THE DAY OF THE BALL ARRIVES, AND I AM NOT FEELING AS NEGATIVELY about it as I might. Noah has agreed to come as my date, which Crispin is thrilled about. *Bath Living* is sending a photographer, and he thinks "the hot widower" will look great in the photos. Poor Noah, so objectified.

It's been a week since I submitted the article. The editor, Fiona, sent a gushing reply saying how much she loved it and suggested only a few light edits. It was published in the *Times* supplement this morning and I have been watching my phone, willing it to ring. He must have read it by now. But though I have received hundreds of messages from other people, there is nothing from Will.

Lottie

Wow! You look incredible. This article is EVERYTHING. Has he called??

Loretta

Announcing your rock era in the Times. Wonderful.

Jonathan

I am so proud of you, darling.

Crispin

Yes, Anna. THIS. This is what I wanted from you. I knew you could do it.

Dan

Getting lots of messages about your article. Happy for you, A. (Though not sure nuclear fallout is best analogy for divorce. Radioactive land cannot be reinhabited for hundreds of years.)

Unknown Number

Welcome to the "in love" club. Membership perks—a full heart and a happy soul. Sylvie.

How does Sylvie even have my number? By the afternoon, I decide to mute my notifications because it is too much. I don't need friends from school whom I haven't heard from in years messaging to say they're sorry to hear about my divorce or happy to hear I've "found love" again. I suppose this is what you get for oversharing in a national newspaper. I just need to put the whole thing out of my head or I won't be able to get through today.

Michael has invited Noah and me to get ready for the ball at his flat. He's ordered our costumes and insisted on choosing my gown, claiming, "You'll just pick the first one you see otherwise," which is true. At his flat, Jane is already in full costume, her hair set in perfect ringlets and a ribbon band. Her manner is so sweet, her voice so demure, it feels as though she has stepped out of the pages of *Mansfield Park*. Though she lives two hours away from Bath, I can see from their body language neither of them will mind traveling.

"You really expect me to wear that?" Noah groans as Michael holds up a pair of breeches and riding boots.

"You will look marvelous," Michael tells him. "Just don't eat anything while you're wearing them, we can't risk stains. Anna, are you ready to see what I've got for you?"

"Go on then," I say, and Michael opens his wardrobe and pulls out the most exquisite Empire-line, russet silk gown, with neat puff sleeves. It is embroidered all around the hem with an intricate floral design. "Michael, no, that's too much!"

"It's an exact replica of a dress from the era," Michael says, clapping his hands in glee as though he's pulled off a masterstroke. It requires all three of them to help get me into the gown without ripping anything. Then Jane insists on redoing my poor attempt at a hairstyle, repinning it in a complex arrangement of plaits and curls. When I finally dare look in the mirror, I have to admit, I look sensational. Maybe all my feminist misgivings about the Regency period and the oppression of women could be allayed by looking this fabulous.

"Wow," says Noah, who looks equally dashing in his outfit.

"When it comes to costumes, it's always worth going that extra mile," Michael says. "Now we must make haste, our carriage awaits!"

"You didn't really hire us a carriage, did you?" I ask, and he shakes his head.

"A carriage of the Uber variety. We shall close our eyes and pretend it's a horse-drawn town coach."

The guildhall is already teeming when we arrive. Walking into the imposing building, with its high ceilings and ornate chandeliers, feels like stepping into a costume drama. I want to take a photo, but no one has their phone; Michael insisted we leave them behind.

"There are no phones in the eighteen tens. No chewing gum either, thank you, Noah."

Michael holds out a gloved hand. Noah frowns and then spits it out. Apart from wanting to send Jess and Ethan a selfie, I'm glad to be without my phone tonight; I want to try to enjoy the evening without any distractions.

Inside, the ballroom is thrumming with people. As we walk in, we hand our invitations to the herald, a barrel-shaped man in a dark tailcoat, who announces our names as we enter the main room.

"Master Noah Philips and Miss Anna Appleby," he calls in a booming voice. The formality of it is enchanting. A string quartet plays to one side as the dance master calls for the cotillion. Michael and Jane hurry to take their places, while Noah and I hang back.

"Do you want to dance?" Noah asks, tugging at his collar.

"Maybe not quite yet," I tell him as we find our table at the side of the room. "Shall we get a drink first?"

As we watch the others form into lines, dancing and twirling in their sets as the string quartet plays, I can't stop my mind from wandering back to Will. He had his Eiffel Tower date last night. Jonathan told me he went with a woman called Céline, someone he met online and wrote about in last week's column. Is that why he hasn't called? Maybe he is still with her and hasn't even gotten around to reading our article.

"Are you okay?" Noah asks, and I blink a few times, realizing I was somewhere else.

"Sorry, yes, just taking it all in," I say, mustering a smile.

"I think you're very brave," he says quietly, eyes shifting to the floor. "Writing what you did."

"Thanks, Noah," I say with a smile. "Brave or foolish."

"No, just brave," he says firmly. Then he reaches for my hand. "Come on, we should get into the spirit of things."

When they announce the next dance, Noah leads me onto the dance floor.

"Thank you for coming with me, I know it's not your thing," I say, forcing my focus back to the person I am here with.

"Thank you for getting me to leave the house," says Noah with a wry smile.

As we dance, I glance over at Michael and Jane. She is the most accomplished dancer in the room, showing everyone else the steps, and Michael is gazing at her with undisguised wonder. Then when I look back to my dance partner, he is not where he's supposed to be. He's stepped back out of the line, and someone is tapping him on the shoulder. A long arm, in a black suit, dark hair leaning in to say something in his ear. A man dressed in black tie, asking to cut in.

Will. *Will is here.*

*What? How? Why is he here?* I blink, unable to believe what I'm seeing. Noah bows, steps back, and Will takes his place in the dance. He looks at me, green eyes shining with delight, his mouth a broad smile. I am frozen to the spot, and it is only when my neighbor nudges me that I step forward to meet him in the dance.

"What are you doing here?" I murmur, surprised I can speak at all because my heart is in my throat. "And what are you wearing?"

"There were no Regency costumes to be found between here and the Eurostar," he says, beaming down at me as we both step forward to join the other dancers in a turn. "Appleby, can I just say, you look phenomenal." He spins me around but doesn't know the dance, and now the rest of the set are moving and we're tripping people up. A man with a gray mustache mutters, "Keep up, keep up." I take Will's arm, turning us around and guiding him to the right place.

"You came all the way here, today?" I ask, still unable to compute his presence.

"I got the first train I could—" But now we're being forced to change partners, and we lose each other in the line. Will is swept away by an older woman in a long purple gown. As she takes his arm, she glares at Will's outfit in disapproval. Will's eyes stay on me, and I feel panic as he disappears across the room, lost to me already.

He politely disentangles himself from the woman in purple and tries to dance back to me, but now he's messing up the whole set, so I step out of the line, offering my apologies to the other dancers, before taking his arm and pulling him away, across the room, and slipping out onto the balcony.

"Did you mean what you wrote?" he asks, reaching for my hand, stroking his fingers across my palm. Looking up at him, I don't know how it's possible, but Will looks even more handsome in black tie. He's dazzling.

"Yes, every word," I tell him. "I can't believe you're here."

"Why didn't you call me?" he asks.

"I was so mean to you when I last saw you, I thought it needed more than a phone call. Why didn't you call this morning when you read the article?"

"I thought it needed more than a phone call," he says, grinning. "So, Anna Appleby, you don't hate me, you love me."

"I love you," I say, grinning back, but then I shake my head. "But it's impossible—"

"It's not, because I love you too." He gazes down at me, his cheeks creased into smile lines, his green eyes swirling with adoration.

"You look really good in black tie," I tell him, breaking eye contact to fully absorb his whole outfit. "Really, really good."

"I know I do," he says with a cocksure grin. "And you look incredible in whatever this is." He tugs gently on one of my curls.

As he leans down to kiss me, I shake my head, suddenly feeling as though we're missing a step. "Wait, how is this going to work? You live in Paris. I live here."

"We'll work it out," he says.

"We'll work it out?"

"We'll work it out," he says with a shrug. "There's a direct flight from Bristol to Paris, you can be at my apartment in three hours. I'm excellent on the phone, I don't know if you know that." I pretend to glower at him. "Can I kiss you now?"

"Please do," I say, putting my hands around his broad back, but as he leans down, I remember the other reason this wasn't going to work. "Wait, what about children? You want them, I don't want more."

"Anna. I've been traveling for seven hours. I bought a tux at King's Cross station. I haven't thought beyond getting here and making sure you know that I'm in love with you. Whatever the future has in store, I know I want you in mine. As for the rest, well, as the saying goes, *que será, será*."

I bite my lip, looking up at him. "Okay. So, are you going to kiss me, Havers, or what?"

"Not if you kiss me first," he says, standing tall, teasing me because he knows I can't reach his lips unless he bends down.

There's a bench on the balcony, so I hitch up my gown, climb up onto it, and then throw myself off the bench and into his arms. He catches me, laughing, and now our faces are level, and I kiss him with everything I've got. Behind us there's a flurry of applause and we turn to see Michael, Jane, and Noah all cheering us on, but then the master of ceremonies, a man in his seventies with bushy muttonchops, pushes himself forward.

"Sir, I am sorry, but you can't attend the ball unless you're wearing the appropriate attire," he says.

"He's here to make a grand declaration of love," Michael

says, squaring up to the man. "I can assure you, Austen would have approved."

"I'm afraid I can't make exceptions, it's not fair on the other guests." We all look back and forth between each other, reluctant to break up the party so soon.

"I'll go, it's fine. I'll just meet you afterward," says Will, squeezing my hand.

"No," says Noah loudly, and everyone turns to look at him. "Will, meet me in the toilets." Will looks confused. "So we can swap outfits."

"You don't have to do that," I say, touched by Noah's offer.

"He's come all the way from Paris, he can't leave so soon."

"Oh, Noah, that's so sweet of you," I say, running forward to hug him.

"What are neighbors for?" he says with a shrug, his cheeks glowing pink.

So Noah and Will disappear to swap clothes. When they return, we all laugh because Noah's breeches look like lederhosen on Will, and Will's tux is far too long on Noah.

"Good enough for an eightsome reel?" Will asks the master of ceremonies, and the man gives a sharp nod of grudging approval.

"I'll wait for you all in the bar downstairs," says Noah, pulling his book on rare bird species out of his satchel.

So, Will and I get to dance, a proper old-fashioned reel. I haven't learned this one yet, so neither of us know what we are doing. But as the music starts and we gaze at each other across the dance floor, I'm confident we'll work out what we're supposed to do.

# NINE MONTHS LATER

THE WEDDING IS A QUIET AFFAIR. THOUGH WHEN I SAY "QUIET," I mean sixty people all dressed in the loudest colors imaginable. The dress code on the invitation was "Loud and proud." Loretta looks ravishing in a purple gown and her hair has grown back enough for a short updo. Roger is wearing a yellow tuxedo and looks, quite frankly, ridiculous, but Loretta appears delighted with him.

Will puts his arm around me during the service. He's wearing a Hawaiian shirt with a red trilby, which looks ludicrous for a February wedding, while I am in a bright pink cocktail dress I bought especially for the occasion. "Third time lucky, hey," he says, nodding toward Loretta.

"I think she makes her own luck in life," I say, leaning my head on his shoulder.

The reception is at the Pump Room. The ceiling has been decked out in a riot of streamers and rainbow bunting, and they've hired an accordion band. Will pulls me onto the empty dance floor while everyone else mingles and eats canapés.

"We can't dance before the bride and groom," I say, grinning into his shoulder, but the bride and groom are still outside having photos taken. Will has flown in from Paris for a long weekend. We've been taking turns to travel back and forth. We usually manage to be together at least once a fortnight. Though he prefers to get the Eurostar so he can work on the train, while I like the speed of the flight. I thought doing a long-distance relationship would be impossible, and sometimes it is hard, but other times I think it suits us perfectly. We speak every day, we work hard when we're apart, I have time to dedicate to my children. And nine months on, every time we're together it still feels like our first date.

Dan and I have adapted our childcare arrangement, so the children now spend long weekends with him. Regardless of my needs, I think we all prefer it that way. Though it's taken work, I'm grateful that Dan and I have remained civil, perhaps even friends. It makes the logistics so much easier. Though on the flip side, Sylvie invited me to her baby shower and that was a special kind of hell I don't need to go through ever again.

On top of getting to spend time with the man I love, our unique arrangement has allowed me to scratch a long-suppressed itch—to travel more. I've been working on my laptop from cafés on the Champs-Élysées, learning French via an app and some haphazard practice. In the spring we're taking two weeks off to backpack around Italy together.

"Mum, you're so embarrassing," Jess hisses from the edge of the dance floor. Ethan runs around and around making strange firing noises and using his blazer as a cape, then pulls on Will's arm until Will throws him up in the air in a move they call "flying cannonball."

"Dance with us," I call to Jess, but she resolutely shakes her head. Jess has stuck to her uniform of black and white, and I can tell she feels uncomfortable because today, rather than blending in, her monochrome look is making her stand out. She was reluctant to come to the wedding; her group of friends are going paintballing and insisted it wouldn't be the same without her. Though she still struggles in social situations sometimes, Jess is so much happier at school. She set up an afternoon animation club, where she's found a wonderful group of like-minded people.

"You want to wear my hat?" Will asks her, as though sensing her discomfort. She nods and he places his red trilby on her head, then pulls her into a spin. She does that face where she pretends to be mad but really, she's delighted. I think she gets that face from me.

This is the only real tension in our new setup. The kids love Will and Will loves the kids. They want to come with me to France so they can see him, and when he's here, he wants to spend time with them. They'll play a Jenga marathon at ours, or we'll be invited to Will's dad's house to have Sunday lunch with all his brothers. Much as I love these big family occasions, selfishly, I long to have Will to myself. I love the mornings where we wake up alone in his Paris apartment, sun streaming through the window, long lazy breakfasts in bed. But in Bath, if Ethan's playing a hockey match or Jess wants dropping off at a friend's house, Will is always the first to volunteer. In truth, the time and energy he dedicates to my children only makes me love him more.

The only other slight issue, from my point of view, is that now that he's a TV news journalist, Will has a small, though dedicated and obsessive, fan base. There's an Instagram account called @IWantWillHaversBabies and a website dedicated to screenshots of his forearms, which makes me a little uncomfortable. I am no longer on Instagram, which has helped with both my screen time and my feelings of irrational jealousy.

As Loretta and Roger make an entrance, we clear the dance floor for them and cheer as they start a dance routine that looks like they cobbled it together this morning. Knowing Loretta, they did. At the door, Lottie and Seb arrive late. They were invited to the service, but Lottie was worried that baby Josie might cause a disruption. I wave across to them as she bounces up and down, holding Josie in the carrier. When Jess sees them, she sprints across the room to ask if she can hold her little cousin. Jess is obsessed. Will's arm tightens around my waist as we watch Lottie hand Jess her baby.

"Do you feel like you're missing out?" I ask him quietly, because even though our relationship is still quite new, it is something I worry about.

"No," he says. "Not at all. I have all the family I need right here." Then he looks at me suspiciously. "Why? Do you?"

"Absolutely not," I tell him.

"I don't know where you got this idea from, that I was so set on having children," he says.

"From you! In the woods, you told me you wanted to take your kids camping. You were very specific."

"I was probably trying to impress you, reassure you I'd be good with children." He pauses. ". . . Your children." He leans in to kiss me and his hot, firm lips send me giddy. I love that he still has the power to make me lightheaded.

"So you're happy?" I ask.

"So happy. You?"

"Yes. Happy on my own, but even happier with you."

I lean my head on Will's shoulder and when we turn back to look at Jess, we see she's dancing in the corner, singing to Josie. She never sings in public. It's lucky Jess likes babies so much, because she now has two in her life. Sylvie gave birth last month, to a little boy, Will. Yes, they called their baby Will. Sylvie swears it was top of her baby name list for years, and she was hardly going to change it on account of her partner's ex-wife's new boyfriend. It makes life confusing for everyone, except, I imagine, her.

As I wave across the room to my sister, Loretta reaches out and pulls me onto the dance floor with her.

"All's well that ends well," I tell her, my hands around her shoulders.

"No. It's only the end when you're dead, darling," she says, and then she pulls up her sleeve to show me the ampersand tattoo she got to match mine.

**THE END**

# ACKNOWLEDGMENTS

FIRSTLY, I MUST THANK A DEAR FRIEND WHO LET ME PILLAGE SOME anecdotes from her life for this novel. It's always dangerous being friends with a writer, because you might just find little bits of your life in their book, so thank you for continuing to tell me stuff.

A little shout-out to Bath, the city where I was born. I had a lovely weekend revisiting your cobbled streets, dressing up at the Jane Austen Centre, pootling around the Roman Baths, and generally being inspired to set a book here. In the words of Catherine Morland, "Oh! Who can ever be tired of Bath?"

Thank you, as ever, to my brilliant agent, Clare Wallace; my editors, Kate Dresser and Phoebe Morgan; and the wonderful teams at Putnam and Hodder. To my friends and family who continue to show up to my book launches and support me, even though the novelty of knowing someone who writes books has probably worn off by now. To my support network: Tim, JANSS, Rids, Haz, my Jersey girls, and my fellow rom-com writers.

A thank you to the librarians who put my books on their shelves. To writers who are kind. To bloggers and bookstagrammers who make time to support the books they love. Most importantly, thank you to you, lovely reader. Thank you for choosing *this* book when there are so many out there to choose from. Thank you for being a reader when there are so many other things vying for your time. I hope you have enjoyed this story, and if you have, I hope you will share it with others or write a review online (writers love reviews!). Until next time.

# DISCUSSION GUIDE

1. The title of this novel is inspired by the song "Is She Really Going Out with Him?" by Joe Jackson. How does this song symbolically speak to Anna's experience with dating? Without knowledge of the song, how did the title set your expectations of Anna and her view on love?
2. The story opens with Anna reading a fairytale to her son Ethan's class. How does this scene illustrate Anna's grapple with love and societal expectations?
3. As Lottie pushes Anna to get herself back out there—whether for dates or hobbies—Anna recalls the many divorced women she's seen on Instagram who have "risen from the ashes" and embraced their next chapter. Discuss whether this narrative around the postbreakup glow is one that is more helpful or harmful.
4. More in the pursuit of financial security than true love, Anna allows her children to pick her dates. How do you think her children's criteria for choosing potential partners might differ from an adult's?
5. *Is She Really Going Out with Him?* showcases how motherhood and professional and personal obligations compete with

romance. How does Anna's role as a mother—and wanting to protect her children—complicate her journey toward love?

6. Through Anna and Dan's relationship, author Sophie Cousens paints divorce and singledom in an inspiring light. What do you think we're supposed to learn from Dan's character and Anna's relationship with him?
7. Anna goes on numerous dates. To what extent do you believe dating is a numbers game? In the modern world, do you think it is possible to date entirely offline?
8. Anna and Will have a complicated dynamic. At what point could you discern Will's more-than-friendly affection for Anna, even if she couldn't? Which of his gestures gave him away?
9. Cousens is known for her well-drawn romance tropes, from friends-to-lovers to fated love. Discuss the tropes in this novel. Which trope would you want to experience if your life were a rom-com?

PHOTOGRAPH OF THE AUTHOR © MAX BURNETT 2020

**Sophie Cousens** worked as a TV producer in London for more than twelve years and now lives with her family on the island of Jersey, one of the Channel Islands, located off the north coast of France. She balances her writing career with taking care of her two small children and longs for the day when she might have a dachshund and a writing shed of her own. She is the author of *This Time Next Year, Just Haven't Met You Yet, Before I Do,* and *The Good Part.*

VISIT SOPHIE COUSENS ONLINE

sophiecousens.com

X SophieCous

Sophie_Cousens

SophieCousensAuthor